Emilie Richards is the autho... ...ve been published in more t... ...een languages.

...milie is a multiple finalist for the ...nce Writers ...merica, and a RITA® winner. ...mantic Times magazine has ...her multiple awards, including one for career achievement. ...regularly appears on bestseller lists including the USA Today list ...d many of her books have been made into television movies ...rmany.

...ie divides her year between Chautauqua, NY and Sarasota, ...is an avid gardener, kayaker and quilter and the mother ...children and three grandchildren, whom she regards as ...test creative endeavours.

EMILIE RICHARDS

When We
Were Sisters

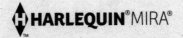
HARLEQUIN®MIRA®

First Published in Great Britain 2016
By Harlequin Mira, an imprint of HarperCollins*Publishers*
1 London Bridge Street, London, SE1 9GF

When We Were Sisters © 2016 Emilie Richards

ISBN: 978-1-848-45663-1

1016

Our policy is to use papers that are natural, renewable and recyclable products and made from wood grown in sustainable forests. The logging and manufacturing processes conform to the legal environmental regulations of the country of origin.

Printed and bound by
CPI Group (UK) Ltd, Croydon, CR0 4YY

To parents everywhere, birth, adopted and foster,
who make the welfare of everybody's
children their highest priority.

When We Were Sisters

1

Robin

The stories of our lives can be told in so many ways, but no one account, no matter how carefully rendered, is completely true. Words are, at best, only an outline, something I discovered years ago whenever I was asked about my childhood. In the same way, I'm sure I'll tell the story of last night's accident differently every time I'm forced to recount it.

I hope that won't be often.

Right up until the minute I slid into the backseat of Gretchen Wainwright's Camry, I remember everything that happened yesterday. For better or worse I remember little that happened afterward. The neurologist on call at the hospital promised that wisps of amnesia are not unusual, that after even a minor brain injury, patients often recount "islands of memory," when past events are viewed through fog. Sometimes the fog lifts, and, blessedly, sometimes it does not.

Here's what I do recall.

Meadow Branch, a housing development just outside Leesburg, Virginia, is more than my home. This little patch of earth is my refuge and my center. The friends I've made here are more important to me than I am to them, which is not to say they don't care. They do. But I treasure each of them in a way they'll never understand. To my knowledge I am the only woman in our neighborhood who grew up without a real home or family. And before Meadow Branch I never had a friend who didn't blow away on the winds of fortune. No friend except Cecilia, of course. Cecilia, my sister, and—of no real importance to me—a superstar singer-songwriter, is my anchor in a way that even Kris, my husband, will never be.

In the past year, as my neighbors have begun to drift into new chapters of their lives, I've been discouraged. Our house is strangely quiet. The small group of women on our street no longer see each other regularly, no longer huddle together at soccer games, passing communal white wine in GoCups up and down bleacher rows. These days, our sons and daughters travel to matches all over the state in jewel-tone polyester jerseys, like flocks of migrating parrots. At home they're busy preparing for ever-increasing batteries of tests or studying karate, piano or ballet.

Most of my friends have jobs now, and we no longer sweat together in the Meadow Branch exercise room. Some work part-time so they can continue being the family chauffeur. Others send their children to after-school care or to a stranger who's paid by the hour to make certain they arrive at scheduled activities on time. So many rituals have ended.

I miss the rituals *and* the women, so I'm particularly grateful that our monthly dinners have continued. Each time I get an email announcing time and place, I close my eyes for a quick prayer of thanksgiving. Every month I wait to learn that this, too, has quietly died away.

Last night as I put my children's dinner on the kitchen table, I tried to remember when I'd last seen all my friends in the same place. When the telephone rang I was still going over the past month in my head. The moment I realized Kris was the caller, I considered not answering, but I knew nothing would prevent him from leaving a message.

I took the telephone into the living room and asked him to wait as I yelled up the stairs to tell Nik and Pet to come down and eat. At twelve Nik likes to ignore my summons, but ten-year-old Pet managed an "okay." Then I took the phone out to the front porch and closed the door behind me.

"Are you calling from the car?" I asked.

A pause. I pictured a bleary-eyed Kris checking his surroundings to see if he was on the road home.

"I'm still at the office."

I lowered myself to our porch swing, which was swaying in a breeze growing colder as the sun dropped toward the horizon. "Kris, I have to leave in a little while. I'm riding to the restaurant with Gretchen, and she'll be picking me up right on time. She's nothing if not punctual."

"You need to find somebody else to watch the kids tonight. I'm sorry, but a potential client just showed up, and this is important."

I watched a heavier gust of wind ruffle the chrysanthemums I'd planted in brass pots flanking our steps. I fill the pots according to season. This fall they're particularly beautiful, the chrysanthemums in hues of bronze and deepest purple interlaced with silvery dusty miller and trailing sedum.

At one time in my life I didn't speak at all. No matter how badly I wanted to, I couldn't push words out of my throat. Even now I sometimes fall mute when I feel strong emotion, but this time I managed a sentence.

"Kris, *my* plans are important, too."

His sigh carried the necessary miles, and I pictured him sitting in his expansive Tysons Corner office with its coveted view of a nondescript street below. Without facial clues I couldn't tell if Kris was upset that I hadn't just snapped my heels and saluted, or if he was upset with himself for disappointing me. I didn't want to guess.

He was speaking softly now, as if someone might overhear. "Listen, Robin, I know going out with your friends is important. I really do. But this guy flew in unexpectedly—"

"And Buff assumes you'll drop everything and take him to dinner because you always do." Buff is a senior partner at Kris's law firm and the one with whom he most often works.

He fell silent.

I filled the gap, unusual in itself. "Pet and Nik will be fine alone for the time it takes you to drive home. Leave right now and tell Buff you'll bring the client with you. Pick up pizza or Chinese. You can return him to his hotel once I'm back."

"You always seem to be able to find a babysitter. Just call somebody. Promise you'll pay them extra."

"I'm supposed to leave in…" I looked at my watch. "Twenty-five minutes now. I can't find a babysitter in twenty-five minutes."

"Look, I don't know what to tell you about *that*. But I *am* telling you I can't come home. I'm sorry. If you can't go out tonight, maybe you can arrange another dinner with your friends sometime soon."

I closed my eyes. "Do what you have to, but please come home."

"You should have arranged something ahead of time. Just in case."

And there it was. *I* should have arranged for a babysitter, because I should have known Kris would disappoint me.

"I'm hanging up now." I ended the call.

When the telephone rang again, I wondered foolishly if Kris was about to apologize. With the client, without the client, I didn't care, but surely he wanted me to know he was on his way home to be a father to the children who rarely saw him.

Of course the person on the other end wasn't Kris.

"Robin! Were you sitting on the telephone?"

I stared at the darkening sky and pictured Cecilia, auburn hair waving down her back, expressive, exquisitely pampered face scrunched up in question. I couldn't picture the spot from which she was calling. She might be in a dressing room, getting ready to go onstage, or at her home in Pacific Palisades looking over the ocean.

"No," I said, "I just hung up with Kris."

When I didn't go on she lowered her voice. "Is everything okay?"

"Not so much." I blew out one breath before I gulped another. "In the scheme of things it's nothing."

"Tell me what it *is*."

So I did. Cecilia doesn't give up, and I had to leave time to call Talya and tell her that Gretchen wouldn't need to stop at my house on the way to dinner. I wouldn't be going.

After I finished, Cecilia was silent a moment. She doesn't like Kris and never has, but she knows that criticizing him will drive a wedge between us. Cecilia would hate that worse than anything, even more than she hates the occasional scathing review of a concert or album.

"Call your next-door neighbor," she said.

"Talya's going to the dinner, too."

"Her husband isn't going, is he?"

"Michael?" Michael Weinberg is an anesthesiologist and never on call at night. "Ask Michael to *babysit*?"

"Why not? He'll be babysitting their daughter anyway. What's her name?"

"Channa. But Michael bores Nik to death. He's always

trying to get him interested in chemistry or astronomy, and Nik hides when the Weinbergs come over, just to avoid him."

"Too bad for Nik, but who's more important, you, a grown woman who needs to see her friends, or a twelve-year-old boy? Besides, Nik's probably really hiding from Channa. The last time I saw her she was growing up and out, and I bet he doesn't know what to say around her anymore."

I carefully weigh advice from Cecilia, at least advice of a personal nature. Her life is larger than mine, larger than almost anybody's. There's not much room for simple matters, and other people, like Donny, her personal manager, handle those.

Still, she's often surprisingly insightful, and this time she was right about Michael, and about Channa, who one day in the not so distant future would be as pretty and well-endowed as her mother. Cecilia has been behind me pushing hard since the day we met. And this time I needed the shove.

"You nailed it again. I'm going to hang up and call him." I glanced at my watch. "Can we talk another time?"

"Okay, but don't put me off. Something important's come up, and we need to talk. So call when you're free and I'll drop everything." She hung up.

I could probably put my children through college on what a tabloid would pay me for Cecilia's private cell number.

Twenty-five minutes later, Talya and I climbed into Gretchen's car, me in the front, Talya in the back next to another neighbor, Margaret. Our neighborhood is made up of young to middle-aged professionals, but the similarities stop there. We represent every religion and political outlook. Gretchen, a Reese Witherspoon look-alike, is a professional fund-raiser for the Republican Party. Brown-haired ordinary me assembled campaign literature during both Obama campaigns. Black-haired Talya is a Conservative Jew; red-haired

Margaret planned to shut herself away with the Carmelites until she fell madly in love in her senior year of college. The other four women we were meeting at the restaurant are just as diverse, one from China, another who grew up on a farm in South Africa.

I wasn't looking forward to a confrontation with Kris when we both got home, but I *was* looking forward to conversation and a meal with my friends in the meantime.

Two hours later, as we stood up to leave the restaurant, I was sorry I had come.

On the way out the door Talya and Gretchen were still locked in the conversation that had consumed them through-out dinner. I had been sitting beside Talya, but we had hardly exchanged a sentence. She and Gretchen had discussed their jobs, volleying questions and responses back and forth across the table. Talya, who is now managing a small local theater, wanted Gretchen to give her tips for their next fund-raising drive.

On my other side Lynn, who had once been my favorite tennis partner, had chatted with another woman about camps their children might attend next summer. Margaret, across from me, spent a large portion of the evening texting a col-league, apologizing for texting and then texting some more.

Our lives are now separate. My neighbors are moving for-ward without looking back. The common ground we once shared is giving way under our feet.

Halfway through the meal I'd finally admitted to myself that I was the only one at the table with nothing new to say.

In the parking lot Gretchen unlocked the car, but instead of sitting in the front passenger seat, as I had on the trip there, I opened the rear door.

"Robin, I'll be happy to sit there again," Talya said.

"No, you sit up front with Gretchen. You two haven't finished your conversation."

Talya looked puzzled, as if she heard the undertone to my words. I felt her hand on my shoulder. "Why don't you and I *both* sit back here so we can catch up? We hardly had a chance tonight, and I never see you anymore."

How differently the evening would have ended if I'd said yes. But I didn't. I remember smiling. I remember that the smile felt like aerobic exercise. I remember the seconds the exchange took, seconds that later might have made all the difference. Then I remember shaking my head and gesturing to the front. "We can talk another time. You go ahead."

Talya and I had been friends for so long that she knew I was hurt. Recognition flashed across her face, but she smiled, too, as if to say, "We have a date," and climbed into the passenger seat beside Gretchen.

Ten minutes later Talya took the brunt of the impact when a driver streaked through a stop sign and plowed into the right side of Gretchen's car. I think I remember seeing the small SUV inexplicably heading for us. I do remember terror rising in my chest, like the bitterest bile.

I don't remember the crash itself. When I came to in the hospital a doctor told me Talya was gone.

Talya died instantly, and I'll spend the rest of *my* life wondering what might have changed if she and I hadn't traded seats.

2

—

Kris

After my conversation with Robin I turned off my cell phone. Turning it off was stupid, spiteful and weirdly satisfying, but after she hung up I figured we had nothing else to say to each other. And if I was wrong about that, I didn't want to know.

Even though our call had ended, I know Robin well enough to imagine how she must look at that moment. Her round blue eyes would be shuttered, as if somebody had extinguished the light. Her lips wouldn't be pursed, since that's too obvious a signal, but tension would pull at the corners.

Robin hides emotion well, which only makes sense. If you know you'll be challenged or punished for everything you feel, you soon learn to make sure those feelings are private. After thirteen years of marriage, most of the time I still have to guess what's going on inside her.

This time, though, there would be no guessing. My wife asks for very little. Tonight I'd made certain even that was too much. But knowing this, I'm still powerless to fix the situation. I'm at a critical stage in my career, and nobody will benefit more than my family if things go well for me at work.

Lately Robin has seemed preoccupied, even distant. If I sometimes feel I'm on a treadmill that's speeding up with every step, Robin seems to feel her own treadmill has slowed to a standstill. She has too much time to look at the view, and I don't think she likes what she sees.

I worry. She may not think I notice, but her happiness is important to me. Still we planned our future *together*, and now we just have to weather this storm.

In the next hours I sat through a dinner I didn't want to eat with a man I didn't want to talk to. But increasingly that's what my job at Singer, Jessup and Barnard has come down to.

I'm not one of those people surrounded by admirers at every party, and I can't tell a joke or a funny story without mutilating the punch line. I'm not a glad-hander or a hand holder, but I do seem to inspire trust in potential clients. I make them feel our firm will do everything possible for them, and better than any other firm. I also seem to know how to get the best outcome from the time I spend marketing, and my contacts pay off. Consequently I'm getting a reputation for bringing in high-value clients, a rainmaker. Senior partners have noticed.

Singer, Jessup and Barnard is a large firm, with multiple offices in multiple countries. I specialize in complex civil litigation, and I work closely with our product liability practice group, one of those attorneys who makes sure defective or dangerous products are discontinued, or conversely, and much more often, makes sure they stay on the market and the makers escape liability for any resulting harm. It all depends on who's paying us and how much.

Last night's client falls into the latter category and will have to pay the firm big-time to win his case. Mervin Pedersen is the CEO of Pedersen Pharmacies, a small chain of compounding pharmacies that allegedly produced an injectable antibiotic that was so contaminated, six patients were hospitalized and one, as he put it, "succumbed." When Pedersen

Pharmacies refused to admit blame and recall their other so-called sterile products for FDA testing, the FDA warned doctors and hospitals to avoid everything they make.

Now Pedersen wants to sue the FDA.

According to good old Merv, the young woman died from complications of her original illness. And the contamination? That occurred after the drug was manufactured, thus placing all blame on the distributor. The problem is that the contaminant was also found in product samples at the company's labs. Merv made sure I understood that those few bad samples had been set aside for destruction after undergoing stricter testing than they're required to do by law. And hey, the contaminant was discovered in only that one small batch.

In Merv's unbiased opinion no other product or sample was ever contaminated. The Pedersen facilities are pristine, sterile, unsullied.

Uh-huh.

I did my job. If Pedersen decides to go ahead with the lawsuit, I'm almost certain my firm will be chosen to represent his company. I just hope someone else is assigned to the case, because in my heart I know Merv Pedersen is scum. He's the kind of guy who would piss on his factory floor if he could get away with it. I'll do my best to convey my opinion when I report what was said at dinner, but how can I justify rejecting a lucrative client just because talking to him spoiled my appetite?

I dropped Merv off at his hotel downtown, and only then, still at curbside, did I remember to check my phone. I flicked it on and saw I had a call from, of all people, Cecilia, the diva with no last name—because, let's be honest, a last name would make her an ordinary human being like the rest of us.

Cecilia never calls me. We only agree on three things. We

are both Democrats. We both love Robin and my kids. We dislike each other.

Cecilia is the only human being who can reduce me to muttering under my breath, and tonight was no exception. "To what do I owe this honor?" The sentence emerged as one long word.

I scrolled through my recent calls, but there were none from my wife. I thought maybe Robin had called to provide clarification or warn me what was coming. I did see an unfamiliar number with a Virginia area code, and hoped Pedersen hadn't gotten up to his room and remembered something else he wanted to discuss.

I considered ignoring Cecilia, but I know her too well. She'll continue to call until we finally speak. Cloudy skies had just turned to rain, and I didn't want a conversation on the road during a storm. For the most part I don't think phones and cars belong together anyway. That makes me hopelessly old-fashioned, but I can live with it.

Cecilia answered immediately. "How is she?"

For a moment I wasn't sure who she was talking about. "How is *who*?"

The pause was pregnant. "You don't know, do you? What, Kris? You haven't checked your phone all evening?"

I turned off the engine. "How is *who*?"

"Robin was in an accident tonight."

For a split second the world went white. I wondered if I tossed my cell phone out the window, would everything immediately return to normal? I would drive home. Robin and I would probably argue, and I would go to sleep with her fuming safely beside me.

I pulled myself back into the moment. "What happened? Is she okay?"

"She's at the Inova Loudon Hospital. Where *you* should be.

I'll be on my way there as soon as I make arrangements. But the doctor says she's going to be all right. Moderate to severe concussion, dislocated shoulder, maybe mild whiplash. They want to keep her a night or maybe two to do more tests. As a precaution."

I'm no expert but that didn't sound too bad. My heart began to slow. "Do you know what happened?"

"She was in a car with three other women. She had that dinner—"

I wondered how Cecilia knew about Robin's dinner. "Go on."

"The police think the driver of the car that struck hers might have had a heart attack at the wheel. He ran a stop sign and hit the passenger side of Robin's car. He died."

"Robin was driving?"

"No, the car she was riding in. Somebody named Gretchen was driving, and she was injured, too, but not badly. So was a woman named Margaret. She was taken by helicopter to a trauma center."

I knew these women, had known them for years. My heart began to speed again. "You said four?"

"Talya was in the car, too." She paused. "I'm sorry, Kris, but Talya was killed. She was sitting in the death seat."

"Death seat?"

"Passenger seat. That's what Donny calls it."

I don't remember exactly what I thought next. Maybe that tonight Michael Weinberg was trying to deal with the worst news of his life. That the unidentified call on my phone was probably from the Loudon County Sheriff's Office or the hospital where Robin had been taken. That my children were now at home with somebody—who?—and I needed to get to them immediately. That my telephone had been turned off while all this was happening because I'd had an argument with Robin.

And finally that my wife, who I have loved since the first time I saw her taking photographs across a crowded room, was in a hospital grieving the loss of our next-door neighbor. Talya, the young woman who had shared so many good times with our family, the young woman who Robin was closer to than any other woman in the world except Cecilia.

Cecilia had remained silent so I could absorb this. I made my way back to our call. "Why did they call *you*? How did they know who to call?"

"They checked Robin's cell phone. I'm listed under her contacts as her sister."

And then I said something supremely stupid. "You were *foster* sisters."

She snorted. "I have a flight to arrange."

"You don't have to—" But Cecilia had already disconnected.

She didn't have to fly in. Who knows what she was leaving and who would suffer, but Cecilia would come anyway. Because in her heart, and in my wife's heart, too, even though they don't share a single gene, they are honest-to-God sisters, right down to their bone marrow.

3

Cecilia

I've never liked hospitals. Three months ago I spent two weeks incarcerated in one, and now I like them even less. Sure, I still realize the occasional necessity, but I also realize how important it is to be freed as soon as possible. On that one point alone I agree with insurance companies.

For the majority of my childhood I escaped the notice of doctors. On the rare occasion when Maribeth—the woman who gave birth to me—focused long enough to realize I was sick, we sat in emergency rooms and waited. Once she left me alone for hours after telling me she was going to the bathroom. When it was my turn to be seen, the staff refused because Maribeth wasn't present. Just as they were about to contact the police she showed up again with a good enough story to explain her absence.

Growing up, I heard so many of Maribeth's good enough stories that I don't remember the juicier details. I only know our wait began all over again. It was nearly morning before they diagnosed pneumonia and gave her a prescription and instructions for taking care of me. The only surprising thing? I think she actually filled the prescription. *That* was unusual enough to be memorable.

The smallish hospital where the paramedics took Robin two nights ago looks like hospitals in well-to-do suburbs everywhere. Tan facade of mixed materials, clever use of glass and soaring ceilings. Fresh, clean lobby to promote confidence. By the time I arrived in Leesburg, almost forty hours after the accident, visiting hours had already begun for the day. Traveling to Phoenix, then scheduling a flight to Dulles was surprisingly difficult, but I didn't have enough time to wheedle anybody's private jet.

Donny accompanied me, all personal manager and bodyguard, and now he was the liar who was taking care of the business of getting me to the right floor. "My wife Jennifer and I," he said in introduction before he asked where we could find Robin. The receptionist didn't even glance at me.

Donny has been my manager for close to five years, and he has a genius for handling difficult situations or spotting them before they erupt. Today I wasn't dressed as a big star. One of Donny's shirts streamed over my tank top and baggy jeans, and my hair was pinned underneath one of his ball caps. No makeup hid my infestation of freckles, but tinted Harry Potter spectacles shaded my eyes. If anyone had caught me on camera this would have been a "before" shot. "Your Favorite Celebrities and What They Really Look Like."

Luckily no one had realized I was in Arizona, and apparently no airline or airport employees had reported us, either, so nobody had followed us to the airport or sent photographers to greet us when we landed.

When we were alone in the elevator on the way to Robin's floor he asked how I was feeling.

I'm not sure how a genuine nice guy makes it in this business. Donny looks like a high school history teacher—a little too preoccupied to remember to get his hair cut regularly or clean his glasses. He's easy to look at, brown hair and eyes, even features, but he never makes an effort to be more. He has some kind of advanced belt in karate, and he's been known to sail a twenty-four-foot sloop through Pacific Ocean squalls on his own. So he's muscular enough to keep fans at a distance, but by no means a bodybuilder. Unless he's in high-level negotiations or in danger of being photographed with me, his uniform is a faded concert T-shirt and discount store jeans.

The casual facade fades when he's concentrating on contract concessions or higher royalties. He's focused, determined and unfailingly polite. Nobody tries to take advantage of him a second time. Despite that, everyone likes Donny. And me? I would trust him with my life, and do.

"I feel fine," I told him. "I'm not fragile. I'm not falling apart."

"Nothing I said implied you were."

"Thanks to you." I glanced at him. "You kept that whole mess in Sydney under wraps. Not a single headline about my suicide attempt, or my bipolar diagnosis, or the way I shaved my head to get attention in the hospital."

"If that's a wig, I think you should keep it."

I sent him a tight smile. Unlike Britney Spears I've never been bald, nor have I ever tried to commit suicide. And I'm not bipolar, although quite possibly my mother was—but how would I know since she abandoned me when I was nine?

Still, three months ago I *had* spent two difficult weeks in an Australian hospital crying my eyes out, and somehow Donny had kept that a secret.

"I'm sorry I jumped down your throat," I said.

"Robin's going to be fine."

"As fine as somebody can be after she nearly dies and her next-door neighbor actually does."

"You think her husband will be here?"

I didn't. Today is Wednesday, and since Robin isn't terminal, cynical me is pretty sure Kris will be at work. Talya's funeral is probably sometime this afternoon. Her family is Jewish, and by custom the service should take place immediately. How can Kris get away from his office without weeks of preparation?

"I'm hoping he's somewhere getting ready to attend the funeral," I said.

"You're not thinking of going, are you?"

I understood Donny's subtext. If I were recognized, the service would be all about me.

"I hardly knew her. I'll stay with Robin."

We got off the elevator and found the right hallway. I bypassed the nurses' station and headed right for my sister's room. At the door I paused to listen for voices, but the room was silent. I pushed the door wider and walked in. Donny leaned against the wall outside, arms folded over his chest.

Robin was alone lying in the bed with her face turned toward the window. Her shoulders were hunched, and I doubted she was asleep.

"Robin?"

She turned, and I saw she'd been crying. "CeCe! I told you not to come."

"Yeah, yeah." I crossed the room and perched on the bed beside her. "Since when have I listened to you? I'm just sorry I couldn't get here sooner."

She sniffed, then she held out her arms for a hug. "How did you get here at all? Where were you?"

I hugged her gingerly, remembering the shoulder. "Arizona. Out in the middle of God knows where on a ranch. You saved me from having to get on a horse. You're my hero."

"You used to ride. You could have been a rodeo queen."

"It's been a long time since I made friends with a horse."

Robin's hair is a rich chocolaty brown, longish and straight, with bangs brushing her forehead. I touched a strand, swiping it off her cheek. I was thirteen when Robin and I became sisters, and I thought right away that her heart-shaped face needed bangs. She's worn them ever since, and they highlight eyes as blue as her namesake's eggs. Today she was pale, but normally she has the clear, rosy complexion of a milkmaid. The first word people use when they describe her is *wholesome*.

"I'm kind of surprised to find you here," I said. "Donny checked this morning, but I thought maybe they sent you home after lunch."

"The hospital has a special concussion program." She made a face. "I have my own nurse navigator. She wants me to stay another night."

"Why?"

"Just a precaution. I can't seem to remember everything that happened when…" Her eyes filled.

"Thank God."

"My thought, too."

"So you'll get out tomorrow?"

"Unless something else turns up." The tears pooled, and she sniffed. "But I wanted to get out today. I want to be at Talya's funeral."

"When is it?"

"In an hour and a half. They'll do it at the graveside." Finally the tears spilled onto her cheeks, and she dabbed at them with her fingertips. "Kris said he would go and represent both of us, but just now when I called his office he was still in a meeting. He won't make it in time."

I swallowed everything I wanted to say. That took a while.

"He was here most of yesterday morning," Robin said as I gulped. "But we didn't talk much. I was in and out for tests. I'm not sure he realizes…"

I had to change the subject. "How's the other woman…
Margaret?"

"Holding her own. They think she'll pull through."

"That's good."

"It should have been me."

I stared at her a long moment before I spoke. "Please don't
ever say something like that again, okay? You think you deserved to die more than she did?"

Words spilled out the way tears had a moment before. "I
was the one sitting in the passenger seat on the way to the restaurant. When we were ready to leave Talya said I should sit
there again, that she was happy in the backseat, but all through
dinner I'd been feeling left out. I didn't want to sit up front
and listen to her and Gretchen talking over me. I wanted to
sit in the back with Margaret, who was busy texting. I wanted
to feel sorry for myself, like a sullen seventh grader."

"And you feel *guilty*?"

"It should have been *me* in that seat. I should have been
sitting next to Gretchen. Or maybe if I hadn't debated seat
arrangements with Talya, maybe those few seconds would
have made all the difference. Maybe Gretchen wouldn't have
caught the red light on the way out of the parking lot, and
we would have been well beyond the spot where that car ran
the stop sign."

"You know how self-defeating that kind of thinking is,
don't you? You didn't look into the future and trade seats
with Talya so you could stay safe. Reality is random. It was
chance. And if it wasn't, then God decided who would live
and who wouldn't."

"You don't believe that and neither do I."

"Not the part about God, no. The part about random?
Absolutely."

Robin didn't argue, but I could tell she wasn't buying it. "I can't even be at the funeral to say goodbye."

I make decisions quickly. I've always had to. "Do you feel well enough to go?"

"I feel as well as I'm going to for a while."

"Can you get up and wash your face? Comb your hair?"

"I had a shower earlier. I was fine."

"Then do both. I have a dark skirt and blouse that will probably fit well enough in my suitcase. Or has Kris brought clothes for you to wear home?"

She shook her head, and the movement made her wince. For a moment I reconsidered. Maybe she really did need to stay here another night, more tests, more observation. Then I remembered the tears.

Robin so rarely cries.

"Donny's here. He'll go down and get my clothes for you. Meantime I'll talk to the— What did you call her…?"

"Navigator. Nurse navigator."

"That's the one. If I can find her I'll tell her we're navigating you right out the door, and she can set up an appointment or whatever she's supposed to do. But she'll have to do it without you lying here."

She bit her lip, considering. "Okay."

That's when I knew Robin really needed to go to the funeral. Because defying authority isn't part of her emotional makeup. Or possibly whatever defiance she was born with was bled out of her one drop at a time by her sadistic grandmother. But this time? This time she was ready to do exactly what she needed to.

"Wash, brush. I'll be back. Do you know where the cemetery is?"

"I think so."

"I'll have Donny find that out, too. We have a car and a driver. We'll get you there in time."

She was already swinging her legs over the side of the bed. "The hospital won't be happy. They'll try to stop me."

I stood and leaned down to kiss her hair. "You're kidding, right? I'll make sure they're thrilled beyond belief. You wait and see."

4

Robin

Talya loved autumn, the changing colors, the smell of wood smoke and pumpkins piled high at farmer's markets. So many October afternoons we sat in my garden sipping tea or home-brewed lattes, and admired borders of nodding sunflowers and the heavy perfume of sweet autumn clematis. I had a trunk of garden hats, and Talya always picked through them to find just the right one to match whatever she was wearing. Whenever I saw colorful or whimsical hats I bought them, just to delight her.

I loved Talya. We were just neighbors until she became pregnant with Channa and a month later I became pregnant with Nik. We used to joke there must have been something in the water at Meadow Branch, and our pregnancies brought us together. We shared morning sickness, traded maternity clothes, took bets on who would deliver first, since Nik was a big baby and showed signs of arriving early.

As our children grew so did our friendship, until recently when changes swept her in other directions. Now death had removed her from my life forever.

Cecilia reached over and covered my hand as the Town Car driver came around to open my door. Her long, perfectly shaped nails were painted the palest aqua. My nails were at best clean, my hand trembling.

"Channa will need you, Robin. Now and when she grows older. You'll be able to tell her who her mother really was, what kind of woman and friend you knew her to be. Girls need to learn how to have and be a friend. It will help."

I'm sure all over the world people think my sister is just an empty-headed publicity hound with big boobs and a bigger voice, but Cecilia hasn't gotten where she is by chance. She understands the big picture. How else would she have gotten to the top?

"Michael will move away," I said. The Weinbergs' house would be filled with memories, and he and Channa would see Talya everywhere. They had never, as hoped, filled the house with children, and the stone and frame Colonial had always seemed too large for just the three of them. For two it would be impossible.

"If he does move, you'll stay in touch. Talya would want you to."

I squeezed her hand and dropped it. "You're going to wait here?"

"We'll park down the road to leave room for mourners. We'll pull back around when it's over."

I didn't ask her to come with me. Cecilia's presence would be a distraction. When the door opened I stepped out into bright sunlight wearing her blouse and a skirt I had rolled three times at the waist. The glare gave me an immediate headache, and I fished in my purse for the sunglasses Cecilia had given me, nodded to the driver and started down a grassy slope to the graveside.

Channa and Michael, as well as his family and Talya's, hadn't yet arrived, but someone had set up a lectern with a guest book, and I signed my name and scribbled a quick condolence before I moved forward. Until I saw Gretchen sitting under a canopy in a row of chairs at the very back, I didn't recognize anyone in the gathering of about sixty. Her black clothes didn't suit her pale blond coloring, nor did the red-rimmed eyes or the narrow bandage across her forehead. I made my way around the crowd to sit beside her.

"This is my fault," she said when I kissed her cheek in silent greeting.

"Of course it isn't."

"I should have seen him coming. I should have—"

I had an unwelcome glimpse of the SUV streaking toward us, a rocket about to launch. "There was absolutely nothing you could have done. He came out of nowhere."

"Did you know there have been other accidents at that intersection? Other people have run that stop sign. Other people have died!"

It was like Gretchen, political to the bone, to focus on the civic problem instead of what was about to happen. But I nodded, because I understood. I wished I could be angry today instead of frightened and lonely.

Except, of course, I *was* angry. Angry at God, and angry at my husband who was supposed to be here to let the Weinbergs know how much Talya had meant to us.

"I didn't expect you to come," she said. "Not after… You're…okay?"

"Okay enough. And you?"

"Just cuts and bruises. They let me out bright and early yesterday."

"Thank God. And Margaret?"

"She's out of the woods, but she'll need rehabilitation. Lots of it."

Her eyes had filled again. I looked away. "I repeat—this was not your fault."

"You'll tell me that for a while, won't you? Because it's not getting through."

Nobody understood that better than I did.

A fleet of black limos pulled slowly into view. My heart beat faster, and I glanced at Gretchen. She had seen them, too, and she reached for my hand. We remained that way until the prayers were said, the eulogy given and it was time to line up to scoop dirt onto Talya's coffin.

Afterward we didn't approach Michael or any of Talya's family, although almost a dozen neighbors I hadn't noticed when I arrived joined us to flank the path as the family went back to their cars.

As she walked past, Channa saw the tears rolling down my cheeks and broke ranks. She darted over for a hug before she continued on with her father. Michael nodded to me, and I could see he was barely holding himself together. We would speak when we went to the house to sit shivah. If we could find words.

Only then, after I'd said goodbye to Gretchen and was walking up the road where I saw the Town Car in the distance, did I catch a glimpse of Kris alone in our silver Acura cruising slowly past, as if he were trying to find a parking space.

I kept walking.

Nik and Pet weren't home when Cecilia and I arrived. Ideally Kris should have taken them out of class for the afternoon and let them accompany him to the funeral. I don't believe in protecting children from death or from the necessity of goodbyes, and I would have brought them with me if I'd been in charge.

I don't know if Kris chose not to include them because of

conviction or logistics. And since he didn't get to the service in time anyway, what did it matter?

"Get a drink and make yourself at home," I told Cecilia. "I'm going to change. Then I'll join you."

She would pour herself a diet Dr Pepper, one of her few food vices. I always keep them for her, even if she hasn't visited for months. It's one of our little secrets. She never drinks any kind of soft drink in public. My sister is a vegan food crusader. Talya, who grew up in a kosher home, was less concerned about what she ate at my table than Cecilia is.

Upstairs I noted our bed wasn't made, but the room was otherwise neat. I knew if I went into his closet Kris's dirty clothes would be in his hamper and his shirts would be hanging according to sleeve length and color. He's not obsessive, he's just busy, and anything that saves him time in the morning is a bonus. I might find hair in the sink, or the toilet seat up, but his toiletries would be sitting in single file in the order he needed them each morning.

I wasn't glad to be home, and I added that to my load of guilt. Views of the Weinbergs' house would be a constant reminder of Talya. When would I stop expecting her to drop in with half a coffee cake her mother-in-law had baked or a handful of exotic herbs she wanted me to try?

I removed Cecilia's skirt and blouse, dark brown designer pieces that had hung on my thinner frame like sackcloth, and folded them neatly. I pulled on leggings and an oversize T-shirt before I went downstairs again. I could see Cecilia outside on the deck. Blessedly it's on the garden side of our property, and the Weinbergs' home is barely visible through the trees.

There are no words to express how much I love this house and our garden, which I created myself and tend with only minimal help from a local landscaper. Meadow Branch is a newish development on what was formerly a horse farm. Our home was the original farmhouse, burgundy brick with a high peaked center gable and a ground level front porch that was probably tacked on as an afterthought.

The house was built in the late 1800s, when bathrooms weren't recreational and bedrooms were mostly for sleeping, but it was so filled with character, so settled, that after one look, Kris and I knew it belonged to us. We didn't allow the developer to tear it down to build two houses on our one-acre lot, as he could have. We bought it exactly the way it was, multiple flaws and all, and slowly renovated it without destroying its character. Eventually we added a master suite upstairs, and a combination family room and sunroom below, along with a compact studio for me and a dark room, which gets very little use since digital photography came to stay.

I'm not sure why the neighborhood children always found our house so appealing. But as Nik and Pet grew, we were usually the center of activity. We had no basement rec room, as all of them did, with built-in bars and home theaters. But the sunroom was open to our kitchen, and snacks and drinks were always in easy reach, along with games, both board and video, and pillows and blankets to make tunnels. And outside? Outside we'd splurged on climbing equipment and a wooden playhouse that could be a fort or a palace.

I miss the comings and goings, the slamming of doors, the chatter, but today I was glad for the silence.

I poured myself a glass of ice water, took two ibuprofen and went to join Cecilia outside. My head was pounding, but the nurse had warned me I might have headaches for the next few weeks. She had also warned me not to miss the appointments she would schedule for me, but she had agreed to let me leave the hospital. I don't know what Cecilia said to her, but I won't be shocked if my sister makes a surprise appearance at their next benefit.

"It's so pretty out here." Cecilia was staring at our glimpse of the distant Catoctin Mountain ridge. "And your garden is spectacular, as always."

As a young teenager I had helped our sunken-cheeked foster mother grow vegetables on a Florida ranch. Those memories include insects, snakes, hot sun beating on the back of my neck and bare arms, so I never expected to like gardening. But when I arrived at this house, I knew immediately that Kris and I would create garden rooms, defined by shrubs and perennial borders. I've made this garden happen, and yes, now it surrounds the house and often stops traffic.

I lowered myself to the glider beside her. "I'm always a little relieved when winter heads this way. Then the only real gardening chore is leafing through seed catalogs." I pointed to her glass. "Aren't you hungry?"

"You don't have to take care of me."

"Good, I'm not sure what's in the fridge. I've only been gone two days, but Kris and the kids might have filled it with doughnuts and lunch meat." Although, of course, that would mean that my husband had gathered himself to visit the grocery store, and I'm not sure he even remembers how to find it.

"Do you know where the kids went after school?" Cecilia asked.

"Kris was hoping to find a neighbor who would watch them when they got home today. I gave him a couple of names."

"They'll be glad to see you're out of the hospital."

I hoped it was true, but it seemed like a long time since my children had been glad to see me. "They're growing up, CeCe. Mom is no longer the center of their lives. They're breaking away big-time."

"That's natural."

"I'm not sure." I sipped my water and considered. Cecilia knows I talk in spurts and it's never easy.

"The thing is," I said, putting the glass on the table in front of us, "it seems to be more about anger than breaking away. I have to be good guy and bad guy, helper and tormentor. I'm the one who tells them how great an A is and the one who has to let them know it's not all right when they don't do homework or study. It's always something, and I'm always right here taking care of it. Nobody else is around to deliver bad news."

It was as close to an indictment of Kris as I'd ever made in Cecilia's presence. I was immediately sorry. She didn't need more ammunition against him.

"Maybe they aren't angry at *you*."

"Angry at the world?" I shrugged.

"Angry at their father for not being around while they're growing up."

I started to protest but didn't get far. Because I know that Nik, in particular, needs more time with Kris. He's twelve, tall and gangly and, according to his pediatrician, already into puberty. We started the "birds and the bees" discussion years ago in this garden, where the birds and the bees are actual residents, but the last thing my son wants now is to talk about sexual feelings or his changing body with his mother. And when can he talk to his father? Not on the fly during the rare times when Kris drops him at school on his way into work. Not late at night when Kris stumbles home so exhausted he can hardly remember his own name.

"It's a problem," I said. "Kris is a hot commodity. We don't see a lot of him."

She wisely didn't follow up on that, at least not exactly.

"Remember the night of the accident, when we chatted and I told you I needed to talk to you about something?"

I thought back and was glad I could remember. "You told me not to put you off."

"Do you remember when I was in Australia on tour?"

"You got the flu and laryngitis and had to cancel the last week or so of concerts, right? Every time I called, Donny said you were fine but resting your voice."

"I had a..." She angled her body toward me so she could see my face. "I had what they used to call a nervous breakdown. Now whatever they call it comes down to long paragraphs of psychobabble. But in essence, I had about a month when I couldn't function. I was in a hospital for two of those weeks."

"CeCe..." I covered her hand with mine. "Why didn't you tell me?"

"What would you have done? Flown to Australia? Worried? Besides, I had to deal with my problems on my own. I needed time to cry and think. I did a lot of both."

I didn't know what to say. Cecilia is the strongest person I know, but even strong people can snap under the right pressure.

"A lot of it was exhaustion," she said. "I chopped the old candle into a thousand pieces and burned every one of them at both ends. There was a doctor there I liked, a woman, Dr. Joan. She said that anybody who works as hard as I do is always avoiding something."

"What were you avoiding?"

"You know better than anybody. Where I come from. Who I was. Who I am now. What I never had. The whole nine yards."

"Most people would find even one of those topics intimidating."

She laughed a little. "Devoted to making everything as momentous as possible. That's me."

Even without makeup, even wearing a man's loose dress shirt, Cecilia is beautiful. She hasn't always been. She grew slowly into her quirky, oversize features, but by the time she turned eighteen her carroty hair had darkened to a spectacular auburn and her figure had ripened into something astonishing. She's lovely up close, but onstage? Onstage she's a goddess.

"How are you now?" I asked, because to look at her, no one would know she'd ever experienced turmoil, much less recently.

"Determined."

"You're *always* determined. You've been determined since the day we met. You always have a plan."

"This is a little different. *Before* I was determined to remake myself, to pretend I was somebody else. *Now* I'm determined to let the world know who I really am."

I was puzzled. Mystique is a part of celebrity, and Cecilia already shares so much with her audiences. She's loved for her energy and her ability to make her fans feel as if they know her. But, of course, they don't know her at all.

She stood and went to the railing, turning to face me. "Almost two years ago a film producer named Mick Bollard contacted me. Do you know the name?"

"The same Mick Bollard who makes the award-winning documentaries?"

"I figured you would know."

Once upon a time I was a professional photojournalist. But even if the path of my life veered away from the profession I once loved so well, I do keep up with my colleagues.

"I may not have seen everything, but I've seen most of his work," I said.

"He told me he was doing a documentary on the foster care system, and he was looking for someone to narrate, someone famous to feature. He wanted a celebrity who had been a foster child, somebody to convey what the experience is like from a child's point of view. He thought that would be a draw for the audience, but also a testament to how foster children can triumph."

Cecilia has never flaunted her past, but neither has she hidden the basics, partly because it's not easy to hide anything when hungry journalists are looking for a story. I'm always impressed by how well she feeds information to the press without whetting their appetites or lying outright.

"What did you tell him?" I asked.

"I said no."

That didn't surprise me, and it probably hadn't surprised Mick Bollard. "Did he refuse to take no for an answer?"

"Actually he was understanding. That was the end of it until I got home from my Australian adventure. I started thinking about confronting my demons, and I got back in touch with Mick. We got together. I told him my entire history."

I whistled softly. That alone had to be a first.

"Yes, I know," she said. "He was fascinated. He went back to his hotel, and the next time I saw him he had moved well beyond what he'd first asked for. Now he wants to focus a large portion of the documentary on my childhood. Since you know his films, you know how that will work. We'll go back to the places that were important in my personal story. I'll be on camera, telling the audience what I remember. He'll intersperse those segments with footage he already has, historical photographs and videos, interviews with social workers and the directors of innovative programs, and then he'll shoot more footage, closer looks at the child welfare system I grew up with and where it is now."

I could picture it. And having Cecilia sharing her own life on camera? What it had been like to be an actual foster child, maybe even what her life had been like before the state took over? Done well, this could win awards. And nobody would do it as well as Mick Bollard.

"Will this help or hurt your career?" It was the next logical question.

"I don't know."

"What does Donny say?"

"Donny says what matters is whether I think it will help or hurt *me*."

I've always liked Cecilia's manager, who isn't quite the shark his colleagues are. I liked him more now. "And what do *you* think?"

"I think I need to do this." She leaned forward. "And Robin, I really think you need to do it with me."

5

Kris

I'm the younger of two children; my sister, Lucie, is six years older, and we rarely fought. Lucie doted on me and thought it was hilarious when I tried to argue. I was the crash-test dummy for the parenting skills she would need later in life with her own four children. Consequently, when my children fight, I have no clue how to respond. My usual reaction is to respond badly.

"Cut it out," I said when the shrieking in my car reached a painful pitch. "What's wrong with you two? Can't you just let go of this and move on?"

Pet, who looks enough like Robin to confirm that the hospital sent us home with the right baby, was close to sobbing. "But that's *my* notebook, Daddy. Nik stole it from my desk."

"I didn't steal it. You took it out of the supply cupboard and hid it, and I had to go into your desk to find it. But it's not really yours, because you aren't even using it. I need it."

"Put the damn notebook on the dashboard. Now!" I took a breath and lowered my voice. "Really? A spiral notebook is so important you're screaming at each other? Put it on the dashboard right now, Nik." *Or else* was clear.

"Whatever."

My son's voice is deepening. I hadn't noticed this until yesterday, but he is moving from childhood to adolescence, and not gracefully if today is any example. He and Pet both realize they nearly lost their mother two nights ago, but neither has said a word about it to me. Instead their fighting has gotten worse, as if their mother's brush with death was a hiccup.

The coveted notebook thumped against the dashboard, and Nik, in the seat beside me—the death seat, according to Cecilia—folded his arms. I glanced at the notebook and understood the fight. *Rock Star* was emblazoned across the front.

Cecilia again.

I sighed and glanced at my son. While Pet resembles her mother, Nik has my dark blond hair and greenish eyes. I'm not sure where his features come from, but even at twelve, they work together nicely.

"When we get home, we'll flip a coin," I said, adding when they began to protest, "Or I will dump the notebook in our recycling bin. Got it? You two decide."

Stony silence ensued until we were just a couple of miles from home. I broke it. "What kind of pizza do you want tonight?"

"We had pizza last night." These days Nik has turned sullen into an art form.

"We had pizza last night because your mother is in the hospital. Remember your mother? The woman who normally cooks for you? We had pizza because she wasn't there to cook for you yesterday, nor is she there to cook for you today. And since we live too far out of town for any other kind of delivery, we will happily eat pizza again so we can leave early enough to visit her at the hospital. Since I couldn't get you there last night."

Now *I* was close to screeching. I let seconds pass before

I spoke again. "Look, I'm sorry. It's been a tough couple of days."

"Sure. All that work and kids to take care of, too. Who could stand the pressure?"

"You're such a turd, Nik," Pet said from the backseat. "Leave everybody else alone, okay? Can't you be miserable on your own?"

"Stop it, both of you." I tried again. "Whether either of you has said a word about it or not, I'm sure you're both worried about your mom."

"She's going to be fine. You said so," Nik said, as if this was the most boring information in the universe.

"She is, but the whole thing is a shock. The accident. Mrs. Weinberg." I didn't know what else to say. Feelings are not my strong suit.

"Yeah, well, it's all over and done with. Can't we just move on?" he said in imitation of me.

I had an inkling, just an inkling, of why parents snap and hit their children. I tried again. "I know you were there when the police called Michael—Mr. Weinberg. It must have been hard."

"Yeah, that's what you said the night it happened. It was harder for Mr. Weinberg, don't you think? And for Channa?"

"Hard for everyone, Nik, of course, but especially them."

"Channa didn't even cry," Pet said.

"She was in shock, stupid," Nick snapped back.

"Well, I was in shock and I cried anyway."

I let the name-calling pass this once. "In a crisis everybody reacts in different ways. There's no good or bad way."

"What's your way?" Nik said in a tone that made it clear he really didn't care. "Staying away from funerals? Working harder?"

"You're about one second away from a week without television."

"Who cares?" Nik turned his head toward the window to watch the passing scenery.

Nik has never been an easy kid. As a baby he had colic, and by the time he grew out of it Robin swore she would never give birth again. We skated on smooth ice through age two, which is why Pet was conceived, but three was a nightmare. That's been Nik's pattern, a good year or two, followed by a dark period when nothing feels right to him. He's a sensitive kid and notices everything. And he lives for justice. Robin says *he'll* be a lawyer, too.

If he is, I hope he loves the work more than I do.

"We'll go to shivah tomorrow." I had already explained that Talya's family would stay at home for seven days to receive guests and we would be expected to be among them. "I wish I hadn't missed the funeral, but we'll let Mr. Weinberg and the family know how sorry we are tomorrow night."

"I don't want to go," Nik said.

"Me, either," I said. "But this isn't about us—it's about them."

For once he didn't argue.

The rest of the trip was blessedly silent. I parked in the garage that Robin and I added when we extended the house. Those days, far behind us now, were golden. Redesigning with our architect, watching the future come together one expanse of cedar at a time, imagining the years in front of us. Robin was right on-site through the noise and confusion, but she made friends with our crew and insisted she didn't mind. Sometimes when I came home in the evening I found the men still sitting around our temporarily relocated dining table, going over plans for the next day while they drank a well-deserved beer.

Robin seems shy at first, but she loves anybody who loves her back. That's not hard to do.

"We can do wings with the pizza if you'd like," I said as we got out of the car. Concessions can work wonders at home as well as the negotiating table.

"Maybe we should get a salad?" Pet asked.

Nik whistled. "Wow, Mom's little helper. And she's not even home to know how good you are."

Only she *was* home. We opened the door, and Robin was right there, waiting for us. For a moment I didn't know what to say.

"They let me out for the funeral," she said, holding out her arms. "And here I am."

Pet leaped forward for a hug. If I'd had any doubts my daughter cared what had happened, they were allayed immediately. She was sniffing back tears.

"Hey, I'm okay," Robin said. "Really. How are you?"

Pet pulled away. "Mad at you!"

"I'm sure. And, Nik, you're okay?"

"Why wouldn't I be?"

I stopped staring at my wife to glance at my son. His voice had cracked, just a little, and his expression wasn't as steely as he probably hoped.

"Indeed," Robin said lightly. She finally looked at me. "Cecilia's here. She baked a file in a cake and sprung me."

I really should have expected that, but I had been so busy absorbing everything else I hadn't gotten around to processing details.

Cecilia. Of course.

I made what passed for a protest. "You were supposed to stay in the hospital until tomorrow."

"Yes, and isn't it nice I'm home instead?"

"If you're actually well enough to be."

"I'm standing here smiling at you, aren't I?"

She was expecting something, and I realized it wasn't an apology for missing the funeral. At least not yet. I moved forward to hug her, too. She felt like a bird in my arms, her robin namesake, fragile and ready to take flight.

"I'm just worried about you, that's all," I said, stroking her hair. "And who did Cecilia pay to get you out ahead of time?"

"I don't even care. I'll do the rest of the tests as an outpatient this week, but there's no reason to worry. Everything looks fine."

"We're having pizza for dinner again," Nik said. "And we even get to pick what kind."

I was still holding Robin, but I could almost hear my son rolling his eyes.

"Actually we aren't," she said. "Donny's been set loose to find and retrieve dinner. And he'll pick up food to take to the Weinbergs' while he's at it." She pushed away. "Were you planning to go next door tonight or tomorrow?"

Only then did I finally note the anger simmering behind her smile.

"I got held up in traffic, Robin. I tried to get to the funeral in time."

"You got held up in a meeting first."

"You were checking on me?"

"Oddly enough I needed reassurance that one of us would be there for the Weinbergs."

"One of us *was*. Even though she shouldn't have been."

"One of us felt strongly enough to make it happen." She closed her eyes a moment, as if to wipe out the anger. "Come say hello to Cecilia. She's flying out tonight, so she'll only be here for dinner."

The kids had already galloped off to find her. They love my sister, Lucie, but Cecilia's their favorite aunt and Pet's godmother to boot. And why not? She never arrives without posters signed by the pop group of the month, CDs not yet released to the public, swag from her Grammy gift bag. One year she gave Nik glasses with a frame of blinking lights that she swore Elton John had worn on tour.

"I'm sorry," I said, now that we were alone. "I'm dancing as fast as I can, but I should have walked out of my meeting sooner."

"You're going to have to learn how to, Kris. Because you're going to be needed at home for the next few months."

"I do my best."

"Well, you'll have to do even better. Because it's possible I won't be around for a while to take up your slack."

Before I could ask what she meant, *she* disappeared, too.

6

Robin

I'm not sorry I can't remember details of the crash that killed Talya, but I would be devastated if I couldn't remember the day I met Cecilia.

I was nine, and Cecilia was thirteen. My grandmother had just died, and while therapists tell you that children mourn the loss of even the worst caretakers, *I* can tell you it's not always true. Yes, I was frightened my new life might be even harder. I was so frightened, in fact, that once again I lost the power of speech. But I wasn't sorry that Olive Swanson was gone from my life. I can't remember my mother, who vanished before I was two, but I'll never forget my grandmother.

Years after Olive's death, when my case manager decided I needed to know about my past, I learned why my mother hadn't wanted me. Details are sketchy, but it seems likely I was the child of date rape, not that the term was often used in 1978, when I was born. But from information a social worker gleaned as my grandmother lay dying, at fifteen my mother, Alice, sneaked out of the house to meet a boy, who reportedly refused to take no for an answer.

My mother was almost five months pregnant before my grandmother figured out why she was gaining weight. By then it was too late for an abortion, but Olive wouldn't have allowed one anyway. Clearly Alice needed to suffer the full consequences of her disobedience, and Olive demanded she continue to attend school until I was born, even though the other kids probably made that hell.

Afterward, when Alice wanted to place me for adoption, Olive took custody instead, most likely so I would be a constant and visible reminder of her daughter's sin.

I don't think Olive believed my mother would have the courage to leave home, but immediately after graduation Alice disappeared for good. Olive transferred her disdain from her daughter to me.

The foster home where I was taken the day Cecilia and I met wasn't the first I'd lived in. Olive was ill for almost two years before she died, and at the first sign of cancer she had surgery. Since there was no family to take care of me, I was placed in care until my grandmother was able to resume custody. Each subsequent time she was hospitalized I became a foster child again until she was well enough to claim me once more.

Prior to Olive's illness, I slowly became mute. Normal speech, which my medical records claim I developed as quickly and normally as any child, almost disappeared. To combat this, my grandmother did her best to scare words out of me. I was sent to doctors and speech therapists, but any progress I made disappeared at home.

Of course the explanation is simple. Nothing I had to say was welcome or correct. Why speak when I would be instantly challenged or shamed? Selective mutism was a simpler solution.

To make matters worse I was painfully shy and terrified of new situations, even though I badly wanted to escape my daily life. I was frightened that everyone would treat me the way Olive did, so I rarely made eye contact and preferred escaping to places where nobody could judge me, often inside my head.

Olive was a great believer in diagnoses but not in therapy. She simply wanted an excuse for the way I behaved. One psychiatrist labeled me autistic, but once I began first grade I excelled at written work and scrupulously followed the most complicated directions, disproving that diagnosis, which was then traded in for the more generic "depression." This one, with its finger pointed straight at my grandmother, surely pleased her less.

Rather than being traumatized during Olive's hospitalization, I began to interact with other foster children and to slowly speak again. Not often or fluently, but well enough to get by. Each time my grandmother underwent more treatment, my speech temporarily improved. Each time I went home again I regressed.

My grandmother died when I was nine. I had been placed in emergency care two weeks earlier when she was rushed to the hospital. Just before she passed away I was taken there to say goodbye. I brought flowers the sympathetic foster mother and I had picked from her garden. Olive took one look at them and me, then turned toward the wall to block out the sight of such a common gift and useless child. My foster mother explained that my grandmother was too sick to know what she was doing. But I knew better.

None of the homes I had stayed in previously were available after Olive's death. The county looked for mature, experienced parents committed to helping me and thought a therapeutic foster home with one other child would be helpful.

The right parents were Dick and Lillian Davis, and the other child was Cecilia Ceglinski, nearly thirteen. Within moments of our meeting Cecilia demanded that the speechless me call her CeCe. By then she had already decided that someday she would be famous enough to jettison her last name.

On the day I was taken to the two-bedroom concrete tract house in an older neighborhood of Tampa, Florida, social workers were still attempting to find my mother, whose rights hadn't been formally terminated. I knew from conversations I overheard that my chances for adoption were slim to none. I was too shy, too withdrawn, and while authorities no longer believed I was autistic, that diagnosis remained as a question in my records and was guaranteed to give even the most enthusiastic adoptive parents pause.

I was all of nine, but the people in control believed it was enough at that moment that I was safe and well fed. After their own children left, Mr. and Mrs. Davis had welcomed more than a dozen children into their home. They were strict but fair, affectionate but not demanding, and they were happy to work with other professionals to provide the best for their kids.

Cecilia had already lived with the Davises for four months before I arrived to take the place of an eleven-year-old girl who had wreaked havoc. Cecilia claims that no matter what was wrong with me—and in her estimation there was plenty—she saw right away that she could finally sleep with both eyes shut. If I was too scared to get up and use the bathroom at night, I was unlikely to murder her in her sleep.

Cecilia isn't prone to downplay anything in her life. In the retelling a casual date becomes a marriage proposal. Polite applause becomes a standing ovation. I'm one of the parts she doesn't have to exaggerate. She saw something in me that convinced her I needed her. No one but Maribeth, her drugged-out mother, had ever needed her for anything.

Cecilia looked at me and saw a project that might have a happy ending. That was enough.

My grandmother had named me Roberta Ingrid after two maiden aunts who had raised and molded her into the woman

I feared. Cecilia was the first to call me Robin. The day we met I was wearing a red sweater. With my pale brown hair and red breast she thought I looked exactly like one.

When I turned eighteen I petitioned the court to make Robin official. By then Cecilia had been there first to remove Ceglinski.

Kris claims I've always allowed Cecilia to make the important decisions in my life. If he knew how hard she lobbied me not to marry him, he might feel differently.

I thought about that now as the house grew quiet and I heard Kris turning out the lights downstairs before he came to bed. Earlier Donny came back from town with enough takeout to last for several days and casseroles to carry next door tomorrow. My children devoured rotisserie chicken and sides. Kris finished a beer and picked at whatever was in reach, and the rest of us enjoyed vegan dishes from an Indian restaurant. Then, after sisterly advice on how to take care of myself for the next few days, Cecilia and Donny left to fly back to Arizona.

I'm sure my husband is delighted they're gone. Kris is always polite to Cecilia. Cecilia is always polite to Kris. Their pseudotolerance comes down to insecurity. Neither of them is sure who will win if I'm forced to choose.

I was carefully smoothing a nightgown over my hips when Kris came into our bedroom. His wheat-colored hair was standing on end, as if he'd run his fingers through it repeatedly, and he looked exhausted, which was no surprise.

"Did you tell Nik he could stay up and read?"

I had expected something a little warmer, but I wasn't surprised by his question. Even when Kris arrives home early enough to see his kids, he's usually on his computer or the phone and they're already asleep by the time he comes upstairs.

"He's always allowed to read if it's a real book and he's in bed."

"I asked him what he was reading, and he said, and I quote, 'A book. Can't you tell?'"

"He jumped on the one Cecilia gave him tonight. He started reading the moment he got into bed."

"Let me guess. A rock star biography."

"Boy band. It's a Horatio Alger story updated for the twenty-first century. Kids from a tough neighborhood who find their way out through talent and drive."

"Well, he needs sleep more than he needs fairy tales."

I didn't remind him how close the book was to Cecilia's life story. "I'm sure you made a hit if you called it a fairy tale."

"I've already had more conversations with our son today than I needed."

I tried to sound pleasant, although it was getting harder. "Is that how it works? We get to choose a number? Because some days one is too many."

"He's hostile and rude. Oh, and let's not forget sarcastic. What's come over him? Or do you even know?"

"I have some good ideas."

"He seems to think he can get away with it."

My head was starting to throb again. "I hear an indictment of my parenting skills."

He didn't answer directly. "What are you doing to change things?"

I swallowed a reminder that the decision to have these children had been mutual. "Truthfully, nothing seems to work. He's never made transitions well, and becoming an adolescent's a big one."

"We need to set rules and stick to them."

"*We*, Kris?" I sat on the edge of the bed and reached for the jasmine-scented hand cream I use at night.

"We can figure them out together."

"And I can enforce them."

"Well, according to your little zinger earlier, you're not going to be around. What was that about, anyway?"

"Do you really want to get into this now?"

"I have to leave early in the morning, and I won't be home until it's time for shivah. So now makes sense."

He sounded angry, or rather, controlled, as if he were afraid the anger would erupt in unpleasant ways and he was working to contain it.

I capped the hand cream and lay down facing his side of the bed, propping myself up so I could see him better. I waited until he changed and got in beside me. All these years of marriage, and I still find my husband attractive. Kris has strong Slavic features that accent wide-set hazel eyes. Despite hours at a desk he usually finds time midday to go to the gym, and he watches his diet.

I would have preferred a more romantic homecoming, but the only fairy tale in our house tonight was the one Nik was reading down the hall.

"Cecilia is coproducing a documentary about foster care with a well-known filmmaker named Mick Bollard. We watched one he did on Ronald Reagan, remember?"

"No."

In truth *I* had watched it, and Kris had walked in and out of the room with his BlackBerry. I wasn't surprised he didn't remember.

"Well, he's amazing. For this one he wants a celebrity who actually *was* a foster child to be part of it. Cecilia's…" I tried to figure out how best to explain this. "She's come to realize she needs to tell her story. For herself as much as her audience. So they'll be filming in places where she lived, and she'll talk about what her life was like there. Of course it'll all be interspersed with history and facts about child welfare. You know how that works. But she may do a lot of the narration, and her life will be the thread that's woven all the way through."

"Why does that have anything to do with *you*?"

"Cecilia wants me to be the production stills photographer. They'll need photos for publicity, and Donny's already spoken to publishers about a book on the making of the documentary. The right photograph can convey the point of an entire film. It's an exciting challenge. She showed my work to Mick Bollard, and he's enthusiastic."

"There are a thousand photographers who could do that. A million."

I tried not to let him see his words had hurt. "Of course. There may be that many, and, who knows, all of them may even be better than I am. Although if somebody like Mick Bollard thinks my work's good enough, that's a pretty good sign I have talent, wouldn't you say?"

"You know I didn't mean it that way."

"How *did* you mean it?"

"There are other photographers who have the credentials besides you. And a lot of them would probably kill for this opportunity."

"So why me?"

"Listen, it was rhetorical, okay? I know why *you*. Cecilia's been trying to get you to work for her as long as I've known you. Longer, even."

"And I have carefully not done so. Not because I'm not good enough, but because my life has gone in other directions."

"And..."

I knew what else Kris was referring to. Years ago, during my college internship with famous celebrity photographer Max Filstein—an internship Cecilia had arranged for me—Max had given me some sage advice. In between critical tirades he'd admitted I had talent, yes, but he had insisted

I should never focus it on my sister. Because even though I had a gift for exposing souls, when it came to Cecilia, I was clueless.

Max still calls regularly and rants about the way I'm wasting the skills he taught me. These days I take photos of my flowers and shrubs for gardening magazines, and sometimes I do photo shoots for local families or school fund-raisers. Once I opened an envelope to find magazine photos of my old roses torn to shreds with Max's business card nestled among them.

"I think enough time has passed that I can do this and do it well," I said, hoping it was true.

"How long is she talking about? A week? Two?"

"Live filming begins in a little more than three weeks and goes through January. Maybe a bit into February."

He made a noise low in his throat, as if to say, *you're kidding*.

"There will be times when I can fly home to visit. Thanksgiving for sure, and I told Cecilia we're going to the Czech Republic to be with your parents for Christmas. I told her those ten days are nonnegotiable."

I hoped Kris would see I was already thinking of him. His father, Gus, was teaching for a year at the Academy of Fine Arts in Prague, a triumphant return after years of exile. It would be the family trip of a lifetime.

"Don't you think that whether you'll go to Prague is kind of beside the point, Robin?" Now he was unable to hide the anger in his voice. "In the meantime you're talking about leaving the kids and me at home taking care of things for months while you trail your sister all over the country or wherever the hell you'll be going."

I was sorry Cecilia's offer had come up now. I should have presented the whole thing with more tact, and I should have considered it carefully for more reasons than I was willing to go into with Kris. But I'd lashed out at him earlier, and this is what I got. Of course no matter how I phrased it, I was dropping a bombshell.

"I haven't decided yet." I hoped that would delay the discussion, but it was not to be.

"Then please decide not to go, okay? It was hard enough handling things while you were in the hospital."

Suddenly he wasn't the only angry person in our bed. "Really? I'm so sorry I inconvenienced you. Maybe I should have stopped the car that plowed into us with my superpowers. Or maybe I shouldn't have gone to dinner at all, considering that I had to beg poor Michael to babysit because you had something more important to do."

He stared at me, and I stared right back.

"Let's face it," I went on. "*Everything* is more important than spending time with your kids, Kris. Everything except me and what I need. You wonder why Nik is surly? Maybe it's because he's beginning to realize he won't have a father to guide him through the difficult waters ahead. While you're at it, take a look at your daughter. Girls develop so much faster these days, and when it comes to men, Pet will need help figuring out how to separate the wheat from the chaff. She'll need a role model. And what kind of role model is a man who's too busy to spend time with her?"

"Is that what this is about? You're trying to force me to be a hands-on father? You couldn't just ask?"

"I *have* asked until I'm blue in the face. But believe it or not, this decision is mostly about *me*. I willingly gave up my career when we had Nik. But I never said that would be permanent. Now I have an amazing opportunity—"

"To photograph *Cecilia's* life—"

"It was *my* life, too! Cecilia's life and mine intersected for years, remember? She says she needs to go back and confront her demons. I'm not sure I don't, as well. This life with you and the kids isn't the only one I've had. And even if I can't remember the accident, I bet *that* life was flashing in front of my eyes as the SUV got closer."

Regret transformed his face. For a moment he looked more like the man I married, the one who wasn't too busy for conversations like this. "I'm sorry for everything that happened. More than you apparently believe. I'm so grateful we didn't lose you. But my childhood wasn't all milk and cookies, either. We didn't know what a leftover was. Some months my family had to choose between electricity or heat. So you know why I work as hard as I do. I want us to be secure, not to worry about whether the kids will get scholarships to a good school, not to worry whether Pet can afford a nice wedding if she wants one."

"Right now Pet needs a father, not a husband."

"You're determined not to understand, aren't you?"

"I *do* understand. But *you* can't see what your determination not to be like your father is doing to us. Gus is an idealist, an artist, a dreamer, and when you were growing up he didn't always worry about paying your gas bill. But he was there for you, Kris. He adores you. Cecilia was there for *me*, and not only don't I want our children to grow up with an empty space where their father ought to be, I want to do this for my sister. I want to be there for *her*."

If he was moved, this time he didn't show it. "You said you haven't decided."

"That's what I said." I hesitated before I shook my head. "But I want to do this. I need to. If I decide to go ahead I won't simply walk out on you. I'll find help, and I'll come home whenever I can. I'll call and text and email, and the kids will always know I'm there when they need me."

"What good will that do if you're a thousand miles away? They're too young to be here alone."

"I can hire somebody to be here when the kids come home from school. I'll make sure she cleans and has dinner on the table by the time you get home to eat with them, too. But I need to do this. The night of the accident? Everybody at dinner had moved on with their lives, and they were all so excited, even if they were feeling overburdened. And me? I had nothing to contribute except the name of Nik's orthodontist."

"You could have dropped Cecilia's name. That always gets attention."

I just stared at him.

"I'm sorry," he said stiffly before he rolled to his back and stared at the ceiling instead of me. "But you just don't have a clue what this will do to my career. The only reason I've been able to get where I am is that I work harder than anybody else."

"At the expense of your family."

"*For* my family!"

"No." I turned away and flipped off the bedside lamp. "I need a good night's sleep. I couldn't get one in the hospital."

"You've pretty well guaranteed that neither of us will get one tonight."

I heard him get up and leave our bedroom. I wondered where he planned to sleep, but I didn't get up to look for him, to try to smooth things over so he would come back to bed. This couldn't be smoothed over. Because even though I hadn't said it in so many words, I had made my decision.

I fell asleep thinking not of Kris or Cecilia, but of Talya. My friend had been so excited about her new job, with so much to talk about. What would I talk about if our monthly neighborhood dinners reconvened?

My trip into the past with Cecilia, or my impending divorce?

7

Cecilia

I have four homes. That's excessive, I know, but I figure I'm making up for all the ones I never had growing up. Real estate and art are the only investments that make sense to me, and I love to watch run-down properties come back to life under my loving care, along with the talent of architects and designers. But I never give any design professional carte blanche. These are homes, and I want them to reflect my taste. I don't care how much time or money that takes.

My home in Manhattan is a neo-Georgian brownstone, and my condo in Nashville is at the top of a high-rise with a sweeping view of the city. I probably spend most of my time in the ecofriendly contemporary I designed and built in Pacific Palisades because I conduct more business in Southern California than anywhere else, not to mention that looking over that stretch of coastline—fondly known as the Queen's Necklace—is a great way to rev my creative juices.

Each house is completely different, and I love them all. But my favorite sits directly on the Gulf of Mexico, on Sanibel Island in Southwest Florida. If I could only have one place to call my own, I would be happy forever at *Casa del Corazón*.

I've been in Sanibel a week, but I never tire of waking here.

If I'm *up* early enough I can look left to watch the sun rise down the beach, and if I'm *home* early enough I can turn right and watch the sun set. When I bought this slice of paradise I knew I wouldn't have to choose between them.

Donny flew in yesterday evening, and a few minutes ago he joined me on the screened porch off my great room to watch the show begin. I was surprised at his interest, since I never think of him as a morning person. But despite years of working closely together there are probably many things we don't know about each other.

One thing I do know? We've kept it that way on purpose. Neither of us wants to ruin a great working relationship with a lousy personal one.

I do have a talent for lousy personal relationships. Married once and quickly divorced from a country singer—which is how I picked up the condo in Nashville—I've known a lot of men and slept with a few of them. The better I know them the less I like them. There's a lesson there.

When the sun proved it could be counted on, I put my arms over my head and stretched. "Sometimes I go down to the beach and walk toward the sunrise and pick up shells along the way. No matter what time of year it is, there are always at least a few other people doing the same thing, and when the sun peeks over the horizon, they almost always applaud. It's like a prayer."

Donny was standing silently at the railing looking out over the water, a cup of cooling coffee in his hands. "My kind of prayer. Heartfelt and doctrine-lite."

"Not a churchgoer?"

"No more than you."

"I sneak in and out when I have the chance and sit in the back. I figure it can't hurt and might help."

"You're nothing if not flexible."

I laughed because that's absolutely true. You can't be rigid in the music business, not if you expect to get anywhere.

He stopped ogling the horizon and turned to me. "I'm heading for New York about noon. Can we carve out some time to talk now? We have a lot to go over."

"Ginny cut up fruit and warmed muffins a while ago. Everything's ready in the kitchen, and if you eat up here with me, that will save her from having to take a plate to the guesthouse." Ginny is a local woman in her fifties, tanned and wiry, who takes perfect care of the house and cooks whenever I'm in residence.

"You ate already?"

I shook my head. "I'll eat with you. We can talk over breakfast."

In the kitchen I poured myself a cup of green tea and grabbed a muffin. Ginny's struggling to become a vegan cook, which isn't easy on an island where two small supermarkets stock limited options. Nevertheless she has learned to make delicious muffins because she knows how much I love them. The muffin today is pumpkin apple spice.

Donny poured a new cup of coffee from the pot Ginny had brewed just for him—I don't drink the stuff. We filled bowls with cut fruit and berries, and took breakfast outside to the table on the porch where we had greeted the sun.

My house, gated and private, is flanked by porches overlooking the beach, and a stone and tile courtyard in the front. The guesthouse, where Donny stayed last night, is on the beach side, with its own shady patio off the pool and a well-stocked kitchen tucked on one end. Choosing a place to eat at *Casa del Corazón* is a joy.

We settled in and chatted about his plans for the rest of the week, and then about negotiations he was conducting with Cyclonic Entertainment for my next album. I love the music of Ma Rainey and Bessie Smith, and I want to do my own adaptations of songs like "See See Rider," and "Down Hearted Blues." Lately I've been branching out from my standard sound, characterized by more than one reviewer as gospel rock. I'm carving personal niches in bluegrass and jazz, but the blues of the 1930s fit perfectly with the songs that made me famous, songs about strong women who don't take shit from anybody and don't need a man to be happy. If the right man arrives? Just something to think about.

Donny cradled a coffee mug in both hands against his chest, as if he needed protection. "If Cyclonic agrees to let you do a blues album, they're talking about another tour to promote it."

Donny and I work on the fly, so we find moments to confer whenever and wherever we can. But this quiet time with only waves and seagulls as accompaniment put a fresh spin on the conversation. I wasn't in the mood to make lists or demands.

"I don't need another tour. I need more of this." I waved my hand in the direction of the gulf to make my point. "More sun and sand. More breathing."

"Then you'll need to think about what you can offer as a compromise. Limited cities. Smaller venues if that feels more comfortable."

"How does limited and smaller equate with what I just said? I'll repeat. I don't need another tour."

"Any tour at all? Or just the exhausting variety, like the last one?"

"Right now I need to get through the next few months. This documentary's not going to be a piece of cake. I don't know how I'll feel when it's over. I might need a straitjacket by the time I've spilled my guts and revisited all my nightmares."

"You can pull back." He reached over and rested his hand on mine, an unusual gesture from a guy who's 90 percent business. "Mick told you that. He's not expecting you to reveal anything you don't want to. The minute things start to get tough you can stop. Mick can turn a conversation about your favorite shampoo into a masterpiece."

I decided to keep things light. "Shampoo? Perfect, because I'm still a foster kid at heart. Most of the time I use whatever's on sale or dip into my storehouse of hotel amenities. Try Rose 31, courtesy of the Fairmont. I think there's some in the guesthouse."

He lifted his hand to grip his mug again. "That's the kind of thing Mick will relish. I guess I'm just saying that if you don't want to reveal the worst moments, you don't have to."

"And to think you got your start as a promoter."

"I'll tell Cyclonic the tour is off the table for now, and we'll see what they come back with."

"I wonder if I'll know when to stop touring or recording or even singing in the shower. Don't you wonder if *you'll* know when to let go for good?"

"Sometimes." He sounded like he was trying to be agreeable.

"I'm serious, Donny. When will you have another chance to watch the sun rise with a cup of coffee in your hands and nowhere you have to be right away?"

"Could you be happy without performing? Because it jacks you up. Every time. You fly high for hours afterward."

"But I don't want this to become an addiction, you know? I already have a recurring nightmare. I'm in the audience at a stadium in some city or another, and I'm sitting in a wheelchair down at the front because I'm so old I've forgotten how to walk. But that doesn't seem to matter because I'm still trying to find a way to get up on the stage and perform."

"You're making that up."

"I wish." I smiled a little. "Well, okay, maybe. But the scenario's in my thoughts a lot. I'm forty-two, on my way to a facelift, and sure, lots of people older than me continue to do extravagant world tours. The Stones and the Beach Boys are going to die onstage, and maybe Cher. But I paid close attention last time, when we set out on that tour from hell. It took at least two days to set up for each concert. We had four container trucks loaded to the ceiling, six buses and seventy-two staff, if you include my cook and Andy. Remember Andy? The personal trainer who quit halfway through because the schedule was too grueling? And let's not forget the musicians, dancers, backup singers, the stagehands and construction engineers."

"So? You gave a lot of people jobs and made a lot of fans deliriously happy."

"I made myself sick. I made myself crazy. And I can't know for sure that if I don't stop pushing so hard it won't happen again. I've been warned."

"I think about a different life, too. It's almost impossible to imagine one when every second isn't a competition or a negotiation or a pep talk."

"I've had my share of your pep talks."

"Here's another in that long line. You already know the documentary can both help or hurt your career. You'll seem more human—that's the good part. On the other hand, you'll seem more human and—"

"That's also the bad part," I finished for him.

"I know this is incredibly personal for you, that you want to share the realities of foster care with the world. That you want to change lives…"

I nodded, waiting, because I heard a "but" coming.

He hesitated, then he smiled. Donny doesn't smile a lot, but the room warms when he does. This one was gentle, the way one good friend smiles at another when bad news is on the way.

"Whose life do you want to change, Cecilia?"

"Mine, of course, and the people who watch the film."

"How about Robin's?"

I pondered that. "Everything we do changes us, doesn't it?" I asked at last.

"Nice save. So let me rephrase. Have you invited her to be part of this for herself or for you."

"Are you questioning Robin's credentials?"

"I could. She's a talented photographer, but she's never done anything quite like this."

"Max Filstein says she can do anything she wants. She's that good. I asked him specifically if she could handle this project, and he said of course."

"Don't forget I was at the party where you and Max had that conversation. What he *said* was that she would be perfect for the project if she can achieve the distance she needs."

"Robin knows me better than anyone. She took off the rose-colored glasses a long time ago."

"Last week I sensed tension between her and Kristoff."

"I like the way you use his full name. So old-world."

"You're changing the subject."

Changing the subject is something I'm particularly good at. This, too, I attribute to foster care. Deflecting unpleasant realities is a foster child specialty.

"There *is* tension," I said. "She's starting to realize what a shabby deal she's getting. He earns the money. She does everything else. She can't count on *Kristoff* for help or even for making good on his promises. He was supposed to come home the night of the accident and take care of their kids. He didn't. He was supposed to go to the neighbor's funeral to represent their family. He didn't get there in time. When I first met her, all those years ago, Robin was so traumatized she couldn't speak. These days she just has trouble speaking up."

"Are you trying to pave the path to divorce?"

Apparently Donny had given up on the soft approach. "You've really picked up big-time on this little drama, haven't you?"

"You and I have worked together for five years. I know what makes you tick. And I hear ticking."

"If you really knew what made me tick you would have said goodbye a long time ago."

"I may not know every detail, but I do know you. Nobody's as hard on you as you are on yourself."

I finished the last of my muffin. I wanted another, but they're vegan, not low cal, so I sadly dusted my hands over the plate. "I don't like Kris all that well. He sucks the joy out of every room. But I don't want Robin to be unhappy, either. I just want her to have the time to figure out her life. And I want her to remember she's more than a wife and mother."

"You've decided that's not enough? Because those are fighting words for a lot of women."

"No! I'm a big fan of mothers, never having had one who did anything more domestic than open a vial of crack. Robin's done the domestic thing and loved it. I don't begrudge her that. But she's also immensely talented, and she deserves more from life than to continue being Kris's house elf."

"For what it's worth I don't think Kris sucks the joy out of a room, and I don't think he sees her that way. He's not one of those guys who launches himself into every conversation or regales everyone with stories about how important he is. He's thoughtful and serious, but I think he was shaken by the accident. He couldn't take his eyes off Robin at the table the other night. And I think he's the kind of guy who closes in on himself when he's in turmoil. For that matter, she does the same thing."

"When did you become a psychologist?"

"When I came on board as your manager." He winked. "It's a job requirement. A necessity for survival."

Unwillingly I smiled. "What else do we need to talk about?"

"I've got a list, but let's take a walk on the beach first. You game?"

I tried to remember if Donny and I had ever taken a walk together just for fun. Fun was intriguing and a good delaying tactic. "I have sand pails for shells if you find anything to collect. This is the best shelling beach in North America."

"I might. I have a niece who loves pretty shells."

"You have a niece?" I wondered why he had never mentioned her before.

"I'll tell you all about Jenny, unless you think it will destroy my mystique."

I got to my feet. "You have no mystique, and it's a deal. Besides if we take a walk, I can have another muffin."

"Let's walk far enough for two."

That was almost too much pleasure to imagine. "You've got a deal."

8

Kris

When I was a teenager and wanted to sneak out of the house on a school night to be with my friends, I tiptoed shoeless to our creaky front door. Then I waited for some blast of neighborhood noise, a car passing with its stereo blaring, sirens or a truck rumbling along the main street a block away. The moment I had cover I opened the door just enough to squeeze through and stepped out to the porch, where I pulled on my shoes before I headed down the street.

I was seventeen the first and last time I was caught. I returned from a night out to find my father in the living room reading a month-old issue of *Lidové Noviny*, "the *People's Newspaper*," sent by a friend from the country that was still called Czechoslovakia, although not for much longer.

My parents came to the United States during the Prague Spring, when the Soviets marched into Czechoslovakia and stamped out budding reforms. My father, Gustav—Gus— was a leader in the artists' community, and his paintings were political in nature, which meant he was in danger. He, my mother, Ida, and sister, Lucie, escaped and eventually made their way to Cleveland, Ohio, where I was born.

On this night he looked up from that nostalgic taste of the

country he had been forced to leave and pulled his glasses to the tip of his nose to see me more clearly. "You won't do this again, Kristoff, correct?"

I remember considering. Sneaking out was one thing, but lying to my parents another.

"I would not like to buy a padlock for our door," he said, while the moral implications were still racing through my mind. "In case of fire, that could be troublesome."

I made my case. "I work hard at school, Táta. I'm on the forensics team and the editor of the yearbook. I'll probably get a college scholarship that pays all my expenses." To my credit I didn't add the obvious, that a scholarship was the only way I would get a higher education.

"All this is true," my father said in his lightly accented English. Unlike my mother he had studied the language before fleeing the country of his birth. Her English came after intensive study here, and Maminka still speaks Czech at home and anywhere else it's understood.

"I need to have a little fun," I whined.

"In a car coming home with other boys who have had too much to drink?"

"I walked home."

He nodded. I remember thinking I was gazing into a mirror or a time machine, because someday I would look much the same. Except for straighter hair and darker eyes I strongly resemble Gustav Lenhart.

"Fun is good," he said. "We need fun. I am too serious. I know this. I take life too serious. I take myself too serious. I am afraid sometimes I have passed this on to my children."

"Let tonight be proof you haven't."

He laughed. He continued as he preceded me up the stairs. My father has a deep rumbling laugh, and despite taking the world seriously, he still laughs frequently.

He wasn't laughing a few minutes ago when I hung up from our transatlantic telephone call.

This afternoon as I prepared to leave our suite of offices I didn't have my shoes in my hand, but I might as well have. I was making a concerted effort not to alert anybody I was leaving before six. Robin had scheduled two housekeeper applicants to interview before dinner. She'd asked me to try to get home to meet them so I could tell her my preference. She's already done all the footwork, checked references, conducted initial interviews.

Frankly I couldn't care less whom she chooses. I don't want *any* stranger in my house. At the same time I want her to see I'm involved in decisions about our family. Robin has exaggerated my lack of involvement, built it up until it's now an insurmountable wall between us. Not that she doesn't have anything to go on. I work long hours, and the nature of my job means I'm at the mercy of our senior partners and clients. Nobody gets ahead at a law firm by saying no, so I can't always be counted on to arrive home when she wants me to.

The flip side is that in the long run, all this work will be worth it. I made partner at thirty-three, and my star is rising due to hard work and good decisions, but being a partner doesn't mean my job's secure. Until I move up to the next level, I'm really just a glorified associate, only I'm paid more. The minute the firm believes I'm letting them down, my rising star becomes a meteor crashing to earth.

I had almost made it down the plushly carpeted hallway to the door leading outside to the elevator when Larry Buffman saw me.

I waited as he approached. He spoke when he was still a few yards away. "I was just on my way to your office, Kris."

Buff is a nice guy, the senior partner I most often work with. He's pushing sixty but still filled with energy and savvy.

He's also on his third wife, but not of the trophy variety. Lee was his high school sweetheart, and they found each other again at their thirtieth college reunion. His first wife died too young. His next marriage was short-lived and pure rebound. This one seems solid and happy.

Buff understands about marriage, but he's never let that stop him from staying late. And he's never let *my* marriage influence him to give me a pass, either.

He glanced at his watch. "Mervin Pedersen wants a conference call in fifteen minutes. For the record, he says he likes you and wants you in court, so he wants you on the call. I told him that was our plan all along."

Hearts don't sink. It's physically impossible. On the other hand, they sometimes feel as if they do. Witness mine.

I nodded as if I was happy at this news. "So he's determined to go ahead with suing the FDA?"

"He's decided to let us handle whatever we decide together. This could be worth a lot of money to the firm, and I plan to let you bill for a majority of the hours. That should provide the boost you need."

I knew what boost Buff was talking about. The next step in my career is a promotion to equity partner, where I'll share in the firm's profits, resulting in a significant increase in compensation, as well as attain a new level of job security. I'm young for this, and to get there I have to prove once and for all that I can bring major income into the firm and have every intention of continuing to do so until I drop dead at my desk.

Buff tilted his balding head. "Were you heading somewhere?"

"Robin wanted me to come home and help pick a new housekeeper, but we both know she'll pick the one she likes best anyway."

"Wise man. She'll understand if you stay later?"

I nodded. She would understand. She wouldn't agree, but she would understand what was behind my choice. I'd told her often enough, especially lately.

Buff was nodding along with me, and we probably looked like a couple of bobblehead dolls. "When I had to work late as a young man I had a system. I added up the hours when I should have been home with Nan, my first wife, multiplied by ten and sent flowers worth that much. Or sometimes I took her to 1789 in Georgetown when the figure got high enough. If I tried that with Lee she would divorce me. She can't be bribed or cajoled."

Lee Buffman has a lot in common with my wife.

"Robin's going out of town to work for the next few months," I said, since letting Buff know right now might cushion the blow when I started leaving work earlier. "She has an opportunity she can't afford to miss."

"Tell me again what she does? Something to do with flowers, right?"

I managed not to wince. "The garden's more of a hobby. She's a photographer, a photojournalist." I realized he needed a little more, and I'm not ashamed to brag about my wife. "That's how we met back in 2000, during the Gore-Bush election recount. She was there as a freelancer taking photos. One of them made its way to *U.S. News & World Report*. She's had others in *Time, People*." That last, of course, was a photo spread of Cecilia.

"You have young children." It wasn't a question.

"Not that young. Ten and twelve. I may be working from home a bit more than usual in the next few months, but we're hiring the housekeeper to take up the slack."

"Slack doesn't begin to cover it, Kris. If I was lucky I saw my children on weekends. Then, by the time they hit puberty, *they* weren't around on weekends anymore. Now I have grandchildren I rarely see." He paused, looked wistful just long enough, and then grinned. "Truth is, I never did like little kids all that much."

I laughed, because whether he liked kids or not, the story, like all Buff's stories, was purely for effect, one of his friendly little object lessons. They worked especially well in a courtroom.

"I need you for that call," he said, getting back to business. "And you need to be there for your own reasons."

"I'll call Robin and let her know."

He clapped me on the back. "Good man."

In my office I loosened my tie, a Father's Day gift last summer from Pet and Nik. If you look closely you see that the pattern is actually hands clasped, dozens in each row, but from a distance it looks like just another geometric exercise. Last week Robin told me the tie is like life. You have to examine both carefully to see how closely woven we humans are, but the truth is always right there if we look for it.

Robin isn't particularly philosophical, or at least she wasn't. Nothing is quite the way it used to be before she began the slow crawl toward her fortieth birthday. How much of that was a factor in her decision to follow Cecilia around the country? How much was Talya's death or her own brush with it? I guess it hardly matters.

I dialed our home phone and let it ring repeatedly. If she was in the garden it might take her a few moments to get to her feet and inside, find where she'd left it and answer. I was about to try her cell, even though she rarely remembers to carry it, when she picked up.

"Kris? Are you in the car?"

That was becoming as common a salutation as "hello."

"I wish. I got caught just as I was walking out. I doubt I'll get out of here in the next hour. Can you go ahead without me? I'll just have to trust your judgment on who to hire."

She ignored that. "I just hung up with your mother."

I put the phone on speaker and my head in my hands. "I was going to tell you about that tonight."

"You canceled the trip to Prague? Without talking to me first?"

"I wanted to make sure I could actually get most of our money back before I told you. By the time I talked to somebody at the airlines it didn't make sense to do anything but cancel. The rep was willing to bend a few rules and help us, and I wasn't sure the next one would be so accomodating."

"Ida says you have to prepare for a trial? She's very unhappy. She called me to see if there was anything I could do." Robin gave a humorless laugh. "That was the only funny part of the call."

I let that pass. "If everything goes well maybe we can get over there in the spring for a few days."

"But Lucie's whole family will be there at *Christmas*. Last week your mother emailed a list of places she and your father want to take us while we're all together, places your family came from, elderly relatives we'll only meet this once. This means *everything* to them, especially Gus. He's seventy-two, and he needs you to see him as a success, Kris. He left everything behind when he fled, including his best chance to be an artist people will remember. Now he's getting a little of the recognition he deserves at last. He needs you to see that before he dies."

For a woman who had once refused to express herself, Robin had come a long way. "Do we have to do this over the phone?"

"Please reconsider."

"It's not just the trial. With you leaving I'm going to be

out of the office more. I can't afford ten days away, even over the holidays."

"You're blaming this on me?" She sounded incredulous.

"No, it's just a fact. If you go, even if we hire Mary Poppins, I'll still be away from my desk more than usual." I thought about the conversation I'd just had. "And now it's more crucial than ever for me to perform at top speed."

"*If* I go?"

"The timing couldn't be worse for me."

The line was silent a moment. "Let me ask, then. Are you saying that if I stay, you'll take the time at Christmas, and we'll fly to the Czech Republic to be with your family the way we planned?"

I've had to make a lot of decisions I don't like lately, and I'm not always happy with the man I've become. But one thing I'm not is a blackmailer.

"I'm not saying that. I can't go away no matter what. It's true your leaving would have made going harder, but it's the trial that makes it impossible."

"Glad to hear it. For the record, I wasn't going to accept the blame and stay home."

"Are we done?"

"Not quite. I've been waffling. I got the tentative filming schedule today. No matter how much I don't want to, I'll have to miss Pet's big piano recital. And neither of the housekeepers I'm interviewing is interested in attending Nik's soccer games."

"Welcome to the too-busy-at-work club."

"But the difference between *us*? I would never, under any circumstances, miss an occasion as important as the Christmas trip. This is one of the most memorable moments in the life of your family, and you're not going to be there to share it."

"You know what? You're blowing the whole thing out of

proportion because you never had a real family of your own *or* memorable moments." The moment the words emerged, I wished I could crawl under the desk and bang my head. "Look, that sounds a lot worse than I meant it to. I just mean I had lots of memorable moments when I was growing up, and this is just one more."

"Oh, I heard you. I was waffling a little, but now, you know what? I'm not. I have your permission to hire the housekeeper I like best?"

"Do what you want."

"I'd suggest eating dinner before you come home because I'm not cooking tonight. I'm going to let the kids sit in on the interviews, and we can make our choice over dinner. See, I actually do have a family, and I'm going to make a memorable moment with them on my own. Without you. You have a nice evening."

She hung up and I stared out the window that had been my reward when I made partner the first time. How much bigger would the next one be?

Would it be worth everything I would have to do to earn it?

9

Robin

Of the two women I interviewed for the second time, Elena Martinez was my favorite, and the hands-down favorite of Nik and Pet. I offered her the job, and she accepted.

Elena is young and attractive, with curly dark hair that bounces over her cheeks and eyes the color of cocoa. She's also the single mother of a four-year-old son, which might be a complicating factor, but Elena's own mother lives near her apartment, and Elena says her mother will take Raoul if he's too sick for day care.

Her references are excellent, too excellent for a temporary job. It turns out that when this position ends, her plan is to move to California to be near Raoul's father. She doesn't want her son growing up without a role model.

I can certainly relate to that.

Elena arrived about an hour ago to go over everything one more time and meet Kris. While we waited for him we went over schedules and food preferences. I showed her where to find every cooking and cleaning utensil, as well as my extensive lists of the children's friends and the professionals we use for everything from steam cleaning carpets to filling cavities. I'll carry my cell phone, but I want as few questions as possible.

Tomorrow the airport shuttle picks me up at the crack of dawn. I could have asked Kris to drive me, but starting tomorrow he has new responsibilities. Somebody will have to get the children to school every morning. Most days Elena won't come in until noon.

Now Elena and I were strolling through the yard, and she was admiring the last gasp of my roses. "Your garden is so pretty."

"The landscaping crew will come and do whatever's needed. If you look out the window and see men in bright blue shirts mowing and trimming, pay no mind."

"That's good, because I don't know a thing about plants."

"And I know way too much, as you can see."

I would miss my garden. Late October was definitely not a peak, but I still had the roses in bloom and clouds of windflowers, along with bright Peruvian lilies and late-blooming daisies.

"Can we ever have too much to love?" she asked.

"I used to have garden parties out here with my friends. Little tables with sandwiches and cakes, everyone in skirts and floppy hats. Silly but fun."

"No more?"

"Our children grew—we got too busy." I thought of Talya, who had always helped me pour tea. "Some of us are gone now."

"New friends will take their place."

In this case I knew better. As I had predicted, the Weinberg house was already on the market, and no matter who moved in, things in the neighborhood would never be the same. Michael had already closed on a new town house in our school district, and he would probably be moved in by the time I returned. When I had gently questioned his haste, he'd claimed Channa was looking forward to the change, as well, but I wondered. At the conversation's end he had offered me Talya's dressing table. I hope he hasn't banished everything that's a reminder of the woman he and his daughter have lost. I'll cherish the table and keep it for Channa, just in case.

"Do you have any questions?" I asked. "About anything we went over?"

"Mr. Lenhart knows I must pick up Raoul from day care at six-thirty? They will charge for every minute I'm late."

"If something does happen, you'll bill him for those minutes, right?"

"I will, but my time with Raoul is precious. I don't want to miss any of it."

"Don't forget, in an emergency you can call the women I've highlighted on my list."

She shook her head. "That will be Mr. Lenhart's job."

I realized how far ahead of me she was. "You're right. If *he* has an emergency, he can fix it. The list is just in case he doesn't."

She smiled, showing pretty, even teeth, but I thought the smile said, *he'd better.*

As if in emphasis, Elena glanced at her watch. "I'm sorry, but I need to leave in a few minutes."

Luckily Kris took that moment to walk out to the back deck, then down the steps toward us.

I smiled at him when he reached us, but his was only for show. He's still angry with me, and I try not to be reminded of my grandmother, whose anger destroyed my childhood. Luckily I'm an adult, and this time I haven't lost the power of speech.

I made the introduction, and Elena offered her hand. Kris's smile was warmer when he focused it on her, as if he realized *she* wasn't the culprit.

"I hope you'll enjoy working for us," he said.

"Miss Robin made a list of all your expectations, Mr. Lenhart."

"Call me Kris."

She smiled, but I knew that he would be *Mr.* Kris no matter what he told her. When I asked Elena to call me Robin, she'd told me that in Colombia, where she had lived for the first part of her life, there was a useful line between domestic help and employers, and she planned to observe it here. In turn I had told Nik and Pet to call her Miss Elena.

"Do you have any questions for me?" he asked, as I had earlier.

"I explained to Miss Robin I have to leave here at six, not a moment later."

"Pet and Nik should be fine for a little while if I'm not home right on time."

She was still smiling politely. "I can't leave them without supervision. If there was a problem, I would blame myself."

Kris looked taken aback. "Could you just leave them for a few minutes while you fetch your son and bring him here?"

"His day care is half an hour away."

He recovered. "I'll do my best."

She examined him much the way I remember examining algae under my ninth grade microscope. "I'm sure your best is perfect." She said goodbye and left to pick up her son. Kris watched her go.

"You couldn't find somebody more flexible?" he asked after she disappeared from sight.

"Kris, if you really can't get home on time, feel free to hire someone to come in when Elena leaves. But the other woman I interviewed refused to stay beyond five-thirty. I bought you an extra half hour to make it back from work."

"We're paying her enough to make some exceptions."

"She has a life and a son." I couldn't help adding, "Sometimes there's not enough money in the world to convince a parent anything in life is more important than their child."

"And apparently sometimes there *is*. You know, like a job you can't say no to?" He let that rest a moment before he added. "So what about *your* life?"

He had turned my salvo around and aimed it right at me. "Me? I've been busy setting everything up to make our transition as easy as possible. So I'd appreciate a moratorium on criticism. See how Elena does. If you're not happy, feel free to make arrangements that suit you better."

"Are you packed and ready?"

"I guess I was saying goodbye to the garden."

"It's on its way out, isn't it?"

I wanted to stand here with Kris's arms around me and start our goodbyes. I wanted us to forgive each other and move on. Distance in miles doesn't have to mean emotional distance. I'm not leaving forever. But he was a yard away, arms folded against his chest. The signs were clear he didn't want to move closer.

"It's on the way out. I'm glad I'll be back in time to get it in shape for the spring."

"I wonder—would you have been as willing to go off with Cecilia if the garden was in full bloom?"

I watched my windflowers dance in the breeze. "Please don't make this opportunity sound like an extended vacation and shopping trip with my sister, okay? I'm jump-starting my career."

"You could do that right here."

"Which part of 'this is important to me' eludes you, Kris?"

"How much of 'you need to spend more time with your kids' factors into your decision, Robin?"

"You *do* need to. While they're still around."

"Wouldn't it have been simpler to just plan a family vacation?"

I watched as he realized what he'd said. Without thinking he'd just thrown himself on a bomb that was about to scatter body parts to the four winds.

"We did," I said. "Just ask your parents how well that turned out."

Pet's room is painted a color our painter calls kimono purple, as luscious as a Concord grape. She has a fluffy white area rug and billowy curtains, and she collects metallic gold accessories. Picture frames, a spray-painted bamboo tray on top of her white dresser, a beige bedspread covered with gold and silver flowers pulled neatly over her trundle bed. She's ten. I look forward to seeing her talent for design blossom, because the room is beautiful, and all the ideas were hers.

Ida believes Pet's artistic gift comes from Gus, who is far too modest to say so. Pet likes art classes, but right now her first love is set design. The theater camp she's attended for several years recognized her talents this past summer and put her to work designing the Emerald City.

When I went to say good-night—we no longer call this tucking in—my daughter was on her knees saying bedtime prayers. Kris's mother is Catholic, and Kris attended Catholic school as a boy, Notre Dame as an undergraduate and finally Georgetown Law School. We were married in his family's church and I converted afterward. I wanted us to attend church as a family, and we do. On Easter and Christmas Eve.

At the moment Nik has no interest in religion, but Pet, whose given name, Petra, is a feminine version of Peter, takes religion seriously. She's already talking about attending a Catholic high school in nearby Fairfax when the time comes.

I waited until she crossed herself and got into bed before

I went to perch on the edge beside her. I ask the same question every night. "Homework all done and everything ready for the morning?"

"Who's going to ask that when you're not here?"

"Well, Daddy, for one. And I'll call most nights to ask you myself."

"That won't be the same."

"Change isn't bad—it's just different."

"Different isn't always good."

I reminded her of a promise I had already made. "Don't forget, I'll come home whenever I can, but the moment the timing works out, I'm going to whisk you to wherever we're filming so you can watch. That'll be fun, don't you think?"

"Nik won't come? You promise?"

"Nik will come at a different time."

"Daddy doesn't want you to leave."

Children pick up on everything. "Daddy's going to miss me, too," I said.

"He doesn't want to do the things you do for us."

"I think he's a little afraid he won't do them well enough, don't you?"

She considered. Then she shook her head, her long brown hair fanning over the pillow. "He's probably right."

"You have to help him, Pet. Let Daddy know if he forgets something, and don't expect him to be perfect right off the bat, okay?"

I didn't want to drag this out. The longer I stayed, the more my own ambivalence would infect the room. I love my children, and spending this much time away suddenly seemed impossible. Still, my childhood was one long series of good-byes, and I know how to make them.

I stood and bent over. "I know you're ten, but may I kiss you good-night anyway?"

She sat up and hugged me hard as I kissed her cheek and stroked her hair.

"I love you, and I'll be home for Thanksgiving if not before. We'll do all our favorites. If you want, you can make the pumpkin pie all by yourself."

She sniffed, and I kissed her again. Then I left the room without looking back. I learned that in foster care, too.

Nik's room was across the hall from Pet's. About three months ago he push-pinned a sign to his door, a skull and crossbones and the words *Stay Out On Pain of Death*. Kris wanted to remove the sign, but we aren't raising a serial killer. We're raising a normal twelve-year-old boy who values a little privacy in a life filled with family demands and social interactions. I compromised and let him have the skull and crossbones but not the threat.

I knocked. Almost a minute passed, but after my second attempt he mumbled something close to "come in."

"Just saying good-night," I said after I opened the door. While Pet keeps her room so neat it looks as if she's planning a photo shoot for *Architectural Digest*, Nik's is always strewn with projects and clothing. My son's childhood has been spent flitting from one great idea to another. He takes up and abandons hobbies at an awesome rate. He collected coins, built entire villages out of Popsicle sticks, created sculptures from clay, raised gerbils and kept a garter snake named Walt, who happily moved back to my garden after a month in captivity.

The one hobby that seems to have ridden the wave is music. My son's gray walls are covered with rock-star posters, most signed to Nikola Lenhart from friends of Cecilia's. He has an electronic keyboard on a stand in the corner and a guitar in the opposite corner. So far, unlike Pet, who is making steady progress on the piano, Nik has shown not an ounce of talent. But Cecilia has pointed out how many music industry jobs only require a love of music and an assortment of other abilities. When Donny was here after the accident, he and Nik chatted about the skills needed to manage an artist or an act. Nik looked a little interested, which, these days, means he was totally captivated.

I saw he was sitting at his desk wearing an old T-shirt and pajama bottoms with tattered cuffs, and I joined him, peeking over his shoulder. "Homework all done?"

"Everything but this stupid essay."

Nik's a good student and likes his classes. When he momentarily forgets he doesn't like *me* anymore, we actually enjoy discussing what he's learning.

"The one about talking to people whose political ideas are different from yours?"

"Yeah, how lame is that. Like I care."

I messed up his hair. "You'd better care."

He swatted my hand away. "Miss Greene wants me to say I should listen with respect and talk about my *feelings*."

"But you don't want to do that?"

"I'd rather tell an idiot to stop spouting garbage and then go talk to somebody who has a brain."

"That'll get you an F on the essay and no friends, because eventually you'll run out of people who agree with you."

He shrugged, but I'm not worried. Nik will find a way to complete the assignment that works for him. And what twelve-year-old boy wants to politely agree with anybody? Especially his mother?

I changed the subject. "I'm leaving early tomorrow. You know I'll miss you, right?"

He shrugged again. "Miss Elena says she'll make tacos."

"I bet they'll be amazing."

"Maybe she won't try to sneak in vegetables, like you do."

"That's me, sneak extraordinaire."

"You don't have to call all the time."

"I'll remember that. Maybe I'll just call once a day."

"Aunt Cecilia told me she couldn't do this without you, and she hoped I didn't mind loaning you to her."

I was touched Cecilia had managed to get Nik aside and tell him that on the one afternoon she was with us. "Do you? Mind, I mean?"

"Why should I?"

"Such an excellent question." I straightened, and then before he could escape I launched myself at him for a hug and a kiss on the cheek. "I love you more than roses in spring and sunsets in summer."

He pushed me away. "Stop that!"

"Your turn."

"We haven't done that since forever."

"Your turn."

He groaned. "I love you more than pizza and orange juice, okay? Jeez!"

"That'll do. Pepperoni pizza?"

"Leave me alone."

I did, but reluctantly. A firstborn child holds a special place in any mother's heart. Except apparently *my* mother's. And Cecilia's.

When I got to our room Kris was nowhere in sight, and I hoped he was on his way upstairs to say good-night to our children. I took a shower and washed my hair since there would be no time in the morning.

Sometimes showers are the only time I can think without interruption. Now as I lathered and rinsed it seemed to me that this entire trip had moved forward without me. From the beginning I'd been pushed and pulled between Cecilia and Kris, with very little time to face my own feelings. I had been so busy responding to everyone else that I had pushed down the fear that had built steadily inside me. Finally it was erupting into panic. Logic dictated I should be sure I was doing the right thing before I got on that plane tomorrow, even if backing down at this late date created myriad problems for everyone.

How could I leave my family? How could I expose my marriage to greater stress? Did I really believe I still had the talent to pull this off?

Did I really want to face Cecilia's past and the role I had played in it?

The water had grown cold when I finally stepped out. No matter how frightened I was, I was on a path now, and I saw no way to turn around. But this was not the way a journey should begin.

As I dressed for bed I forced myself to concentrate on the mundane. My suitcase and camera bag were already downstairs. I had been told to pack light, that our hotels would do our laundry and cleaning, but I had the added burden of my equipment to drag along with me. When photography was my full-time job I developed a tried-and-true system for travel. A knit dress, tights and black flats, two pairs of lightweight pants, three shirts ranging from semidressy to casual and a vest with multiple pockets. Quick-dry underwear I can wash out and hang up at night is a given, and two plain T-shirts I can sleep in or wear if necessary. For this trip I added a fleece cardigan and a heavier waterproof jacket I would carry on the airplane.

My photography bag contains cameras—including a new Canon I bought for this occasion—an assortment of lenses, filters, cables, memory cards, batteries and more. My second carry-on is a backpack with my computer, tablet and personal items, but it's large enough to hold camera equipment if necessary later on.

Our first stop will be western Pennsylvania, the town where Cecilia was born. We probably won't be there long, but the temperature will be in the forties at night. At this point the next destination is still under discussion.

I was about to give up on Kris and try to get some sleep when he finally came in and closed the door behind him.

I sat up. "Is Nik still working on his essay?"

"I don't know. He was in bed."

"You'll need to check with him tomorrow. It's due at the end of the week."

"I'll put that on my *list*."

His tone didn't bode well. "He'll be glad to talk about the essay. *We* talked a little tonight. He's trying to figure out what he should say, that's all. Maybe you can help."

"I'm going to take a shower."

He made a wide berth around the bed, as if he was afraid I might leap out and grab him.

"You could wait," I said.

"I'll be busy in the morning."

"I mean wait a little while." I patted the bed beside me, willing to take a risk because Kris's arms around me tonight would go a long way to quieting my fears. "Wouldn't you rather snuggle and maybe say goodbye properly?"

He finally looked at me. "You're getting up early. You ought to go to sleep."

"I can sleep on the plane."

"I'm not in the mood, Robin. Do you know that in order to get home on time to meet Elena I had to blow off a meeting? I've been on the telephone all evening catching up with what I missed."

"Okay." I turned away from him. I knew better than to say more because at moments like these words are dangerous weapons.

He spoke to my back. "I don't want to be this angry. For the record."

"Does that mean you think you're overreacting or that it's my fault?"

"I wish I knew."

I rolled over again and faced him. "I'll be gone for a while on this first leg. Do you really want to say goodbye this way?"

"Remember me? The guy who doesn't want to say goodbye at all?"

"*For the record*, in case you're still mulling over your choices? You're overreacting."

"Maybe so, but how much worse could your timing be?"

"For which of us? The one who's trying to figure out her life by doing something other than wait on her family hand and foot? Or the one who can't figure out how to incorporate that same family into his world?"

"Look, I know the accident has a lot to do with this."

"Not as much as you think. It just sped up the process."

"Maybe I'll get used to seeing you walk out the door, Robin. Maybe I'll even start to look forward to it. Who knows?"

My voice remained steady, but only with great effort. "Could be. Maybe you'll find having a paid housekeeper is every bit as good as having me. And maybe I'll find that having no husband isn't all that different from having you."

We stared at each other. The weapons had been launched. Maybe both of us were torn and wishing we could take back our words.

Or maybe that was just me.

I turned away again, and moments later I heard the bathroom door close behind him.

10

—

Kris

Robin's gone. I had counted on waking up to say goodbye before her airport shuttle arrived. I wanted to wish her well and restore at least a fraction of goodwill, but apparently I lay awake for too much of the night thinking of exactly what I would say and how I would absolve us both. Midnight problem solving takes a toll. I didn't hear her get up, much less go downstairs. Now she's gone, and frankly I wouldn't even be awake right now if Channa Weinberg wasn't standing in the driveway next door sobbing.

Channa, who lost her mother less than a month ago, a woman I admired and whose friendship I enjoyed. The same woman who took the place of *my* wife on the night of the accident.

My wife? While Talya left this earth without a goodbye, this morning Robin left our home without learning how much she would be missed, how glad I am that she survived the accident, how sorry I am that I've been acting like an asshole ever since.

Now I heard Michael comforting his daughter, although at this distance the words weren't clear. But as I slid out of bed and started down the hall to wake my children, I wondered what *I* would say in the same circumstances.

Michael probably understands what Channa needs, and acts accordingly, despite his own grief. Then there's me. The man who fully intended to be a hands-on father and found that eking out the time was a lot harder than he expected. Of course I had the perfect stand-in. Robin is a wonderful mother who has always been right here so I can be a wonderful wage earner. And now she's changed the rules and taken off to leave me in charge of both.

The first glimmer of anger reappeared, and I welcomed it. I didn't have enough time to be angry at myself *and* Robin this morning. I made the obvious choice. Suddenly I missed my wife less.

Pet was already up, which I should have expected. Fully dressed for school, she opened her door and stared at me standing bleary-eyed in her doorway in my pajamas.

"Doesn't your bus come soon?" I wasn't quite sure what time it was because I hadn't checked the clock. And strike two? The bus schedule was posted downstairs.

Clearly, from Pet's expression, my IQ had dropped a few points this morning. "I have to eat, don't I?"

"Exactly what are you wearing?"

My daughter isn't sophisticated enough to hide guilt. She has fair skin like her mother, and now I watched the color in her cheeks deepen before she looked down. "Everybody wears skirts like this."

The skirt barely covered my daughter's tush. Maybe everybody wore them, but I was pretty sure that unless they were auditioning for a reality show called *Preteen Hookers*, they wore them with something else.

I pointed toward her closet. "Wear something under it or change."

"Daddy!"

"It's fall. You'll freeze, and besides you'll spend the whole day pulling your skirt down. If they even let you stay in school."

"But I told you, everybody wears skirts this short."

"Does your mom let you wear that skirt to school without something under it?" The "something," whatever it was called, wasn't in my vocabulary. I would Google this mystery later so our next conversation could be more precise.

She didn't answer.

"Go." I pointed again.

"Fine, but I'm going to be late!"

That was already clear. I headed down the hall to pull Nik out of bed. As expected, he was still sleeping. The one thing I remembered about the bus schedule was that Nik's bus came later, because middle school started later. If I was lucky at least one of my children would board a school bus today and not require a personal chauffeur.

Except that, of course, that would mean Nik would be here alone after I left with Pet. Could I trust my increasingly rebellious son to get to his bus stop on time. Or at all? I really didn't know.

"What do you want for breakfast?" I asked on my way out of his room.

"What I always have."

"And that would be?"

"What Mom fixes."

"Then I'll fix whatever I feel like fixing unless you give me a better clue."

"Waffles."

Robin had pointed out the frozen waffles in our freezer. "You want sausage or bacon?"

"I don't eat pork. Do you know what pig farms do to the environment?"

"You can tell me all about it some other time."

Downstairs I found the waffles, read the directions and slid them into the toaster. I took out cereal and milk, bananas and berries, juice. I located the syrup and butter, and had everything on the counter by the time Pet arrived wearing something that stretched to her ankles under the skirt. I hoped she didn't strip off whatever it was as soon as she was out of sight.

As I got bowls and plates my cell phone buzzed. Pet had already informed me she liked toast and strawberry jam with her cereal, so I had popped out Nik's waffles to replace them with bread.

"Can you pencil in a breakfast meeting first thing?" Buff said without the usual pleasantries. He named three other attorneys on our floor and a local coffee shop. "Everybody else can be there."

I did calculations in my head. I had to dress and drive Pet to school. I had to figure out what to do about Nik and whether I could safely leave him here to do what he was supposed to. Then I had to drive into work. Since that would be later than usual, I would be hampered by rush hour.

Trying to do the impossible wouldn't win me points with Buff, because clearly I would fail. And in any law office, it's all about results.

I told him the truth, then I finished with, "But I'll try to get there by the end of the meeting and someone can catch me up."

"Robin left this morning?"

"It may take a day or two to get into the swing of our new schedule."

"We'll do what we can without you today."

I didn't miss the slight emphasis on "today."

I called upstairs to Nik, who didn't answer.

"He's always slow," Pet said through a mouthful of toast. "Sometimes Mommy has to go up and shoo him downstairs."

"Does your mother leave him here to catch his bus if she has to take you to school?"

"I don't know. She always makes sure I'm on time for my bus."

"You're old enough to take on that responsibility, Pet. You can set your alarm."

"Like you set yours this morning?" She cocked her head in question.

"Let's just pretend that once upon a time you missed the bus. Let's say you fell and skinned your knee, and by the time it was all washed and bandaged and you had changed your clothes, the bus had left without you."

She waited.

"Now your mom has to take you to school, right?"

She shrugged.

"So, would she leave Nik here to finish getting breakfast and out to the bus on time?"

"Are you kidding?"

I had been afraid of that. I tried to sound sure of myself, responsible, in control. "Everybody's going to have to pull their own weight from now on."

"You mean like deciding what we can wear to school and stuff?"

Pet had always been so much easier to parent than Nik that I don't think I'd ever noticed that under that sweet smile a demon was lurking.

Nik slouched down the stairs just as Pet finished her cereal and went to brush her teeth.

"I'm going to drive your sister to school. Then I'll come back and make sure you're all set," I told him.

He put his hand over his heart and widened his eyes. "Gee, you'll trust me for the what, twenty minutes it takes to get there and back?"

Since I didn't trust *myself* to answer, I left him to eat alone, and went upstairs to shave and dress for what was clearly going to be a very long day.

11

—

Robin

Late to work. Sorry you didn't get me up before you left. I assume Pet's not allowed to wear a short skirt over bare legs. K

As love notes go, Kris's email sucked. I slipped my cell phone in the pocket of my jeans in case more recriminations were on the way. There was no telling what Kris was really sorry about on this first morning of our new life. That we hadn't said a fond goodbye? That he had overslept and wanted me to take responsibility for that as well as everything else?

And Pet? The handwriting was already on *that* wall. Our daughter was testing her father. I doubted this morning would be the last time.

Switching gears from loyal wife to career photographer, I felt disoriented, and I stopped to regroup. I think I've forgotten how overwhelming an airport can be. I should remember. In college I chased internships and visited Cecilia wherever she happened to be. After graduation I took a job with a charitable foundation that required me to travel internationally to photograph good works and horrifying tragedies.

These days I rarely fly without family. A few times I've visited Cecilia on my own, but mostly when I leave town my children are with me and we're heading off on vacation. Kris joins us when and if he can, but I can't remember the last time the two of us went somewhere by ourselves.

Newark Liberty International Airport reminds me of a science fiction space station or Tomorrowland at Disney World. Glass and lights, sky-high ceilings floating overhead and shining terrazzo floors underfoot. As I walked toward the gate where I was to meet Cecilia and everyone flying with us, I pretended I was on my way to accept a new command: six earth years exploring outer space with the crew of the Starship Enterprise. When we were growing up Cecilia and I watched *Star Trek: The Next Generation* whenever we were allowed to. Space catastrophes are often more palatable than real life.

I had been surprised to find I would be flying to Newark to meet the others before continuing on to Pittsburgh, and then to Uniontown for the night. Tomorrow we drive from there to Randolph Furnace in Fayette County, south of the city, which is Cecilia's birthplace. I'm not sure why I wasn't booked directly to Pittsburgh, but I'm sure this trip will be filled with surprises.

The usual number of people were milling at the gate when I arrived, camera bag hanging from my shoulder and backpack carefully balanced. I'm an out-of-practice sherpa, so I was happy to take a seat and set everything on the floor in front of me.

I was adjusting my load when a man took the seat beside me. I was so glad to be temporarily free of paraphernalia that I didn't pay attention until he spoke.

"Cecilia sent me your bio. You're Robin Lenhart, aren't you?"

I realized Mick Bollard himself was sitting beside me. I smiled and offered my hand. "I'm such a groupie—I know who *you* are."

His hand was broad and warm. "It looks like we're the first ones here."

"I had no idea you'd be on this flight, too."

"I thought we might get some footage of the trip. Just in case it makes sense later, which it probably won't."

I was starstruck. I was sitting next to one of the best documentary filmmakers in the business. While I've never considered a similar career, I appreciate everything about the genre. Working next to Mick Bollard was as much of a draw as helping Cecilia face our past.

He was somewhere in his early fifties, with a mop of graying brown hair that curled over his nape and the tops of his ears, along with raisin-dark eyes and a warm smile. He was dressed as casually as I was—faded jeans, buttoned shirt, a light windbreaker.

He seemed to like what *he* saw, because his smile broadened. "I'm glad you're coming along. I'm hoping you'll answer some questions about Cecilia's childhood."

"On or off camera?"

"Up to you. It's just that you seem to have lived through a lot of her foster-care experiences, too."

We were interrupted by a teenager who took the seat next to Mick. "I found the trail mix you like. The one with the cashews and apricots." She turned to me, leaned over and extended her hand. "I'm Fiona Bollard."

"Fifi," Mick said. "My lovely daughter. She'll be traveling with us."

Fiona was about fifteen, but already self-possessed enough to have extended her hand and held my gaze. She was a pretty girl, with hair the dark brown her father's must have been and the same lively eyes. Her face was longer, though, and her lips were a small, perfect bow.

As if she was used to the next part, she explained her presence without being asked. "I'm homeschooled. Mick figures

I'll learn more on the road than I will in even the best private school."

I noted the use of her father's first name and that Fiona had attributed that sentiment to him, not to herself. I wondered how she felt about missing the chance for social interplay with her contemporaries.

Mick answered my unspoken question. "Fifi spends summers with her mom, and Glo gets her involved in all kinds of activities to make up for her gypsy life with me."

"He just needs somebody to carry equipment."

Mick slung his arm over his daughter's shoulders. "Cheaper than another production assistant. You have children, don't you, Robin?"

As I nodded I thought about my two and wondered how they would like to have Fiona's life. If a dose of it would give them her relaxed confidence, I would be happy to yank them out of school for a few months.

We chatted a moment before another man approached. He was in his thirties, bearded and thin as a drinking straw. His hips were so narrow he had to be wearing suspenders under his sweatshirt, because I couldn't imagine a belt that would hold up his jeans. Mick introduced him as Jerry, director of photography.

"Which means that on this leg he'll be doing everything that involves a video camera. Jerry's one of the best in the business, and we're honored to have him."

Jerry, who had a surprisingly deep voice, nodded to a group heading in our direction. "Looks like we're about to start work." As he spoke he flipped the locks on a wheeled case and pulled out a camera.

I know how much technology has changed my own field and was prepared for the changes in cinema cameras, but this one was so much smaller than I'd expected. Thumbelina had replaced King Kong.

There was no time to consider that further. The small group was attracting attention, and I saw that my sister was right in the middle of it.

Cecilia was flanked by Donny and another larger man in a sport coat who hadn't been with her at my house. A pale blonde pixie in her twenties followed behind with a wheeled suitcase, but Cecilia herself was toting a faux-leather bag large enough for a weekend of travel. She wore faded jeans ripped at the knee, like the ones we had scored at church rummage sales back in the day. In contrast, the sparkly four-inch heels and boho-chic embroidered cape hanging casually over her shoulders would never have graced a table at First Baptist.

I started to move forward to greet her, but Mick was standing now, and he rested his hand on my arm.

"You're the photographer today, right? Not the foster sister?"

"Sister," I said automatically, and then chagrin filled me. "And of course you're right. I need to get busy. This is going to take some getting used to."

"No doubt. And for my part? *Sister*. I hear you." Mick left to greet Cecilia.

As I grabbed my case and lifted out the best camera and lens to document this scene, more people recognized Cecilia and crowded in. I thought about Max Filstein and what he would say. Max is nearly always right, and this was turning out to be no exception. I probably wasn't the best person for this job. Not only had I momentarily forgotten why I was here, but I hadn't prepared my equipment. And even when I was organized and working on cue, could I be trusted to take the shots that were really needed? The ones that portrayed Cecilia in an unfavorable light? The ones where she was clearly tired, where she looked her full forty-two and then some? The ones where she exploded in anger or sobbed in despair?

Right now, after too many years away from the career I

had loved so well, I felt like a mute eight-year-old again, an unloved and unwanted child who had been given a camera by a compassionate therapist and asked to take photos of the most important moments and people in her life.

Thirty years ago that camera, one of the first generation of disposables, had changed everything. Today I would take whatever photos were required. Because Cecilia and everything this trip represented were suddenly as important to me as almost anything I had ever done.

And once again, I wanted to make myself heard.

Having a superstar on board doesn't work magic with the airlines. We sat on the tarmac for more than an hour while rain pelted our plane and ground crews unloaded and reloaded cargo. We were never told why.

Cecilia saw the delay as a public relations opportunity, and with the flight crew's permission she went back into coach and shook hands with starstruck passengers, signed whatever they had handy, gave tips to three teens who had-rock star aspirations and serenaded an old man who swore he had every album she had ever made, including the vinyl of her debut album, *Saint Cecilia*.

Jerry took footage of the visit to coach, and when I was granted permission I took photos and had subjects sign a model release app on my phone in case one was necessary later. I planned to make extensive notes about what was happening in today's photos and those I took later, so I could pass them on to the writer if a book really materialized.

None of it was easy for me. None of it seemed natural. I hoped that would change, because hesitation and second-guessing would affect my work.

By the time the plane took off, Cecilia had made two hundred friends who would recount this meeting for weeks to come.

"There are two kinds of performers," she told me when she finally plopped back into her seat next to mine. I was sitting in first class, too, which I was pretty sure had more to do with being her sister than her photographer.

"What kind are you?" I asked.

"The kind who honestly likes her audience and wants to give them a thrill. The kind who hugs them tight when she can because life's a bitch, and a little fun, a little glitter, makes it a lot easier. I have friends in the business who are so cushioned nobody gets close or feels close. They're the performers who won't let people take photos and Tweet during the show. And my God, video? YouTube scares them shitless. They never go into the audience to shake hands or chat. I drive security crazy, but I'd rather take a risk and be loved for it than be so safe nobody remembers my name."

"Everyone on this plane knows your name, that's for sure."

"And so will their friends and *their* friends."

"That's a pretty big piece of yourself you doled out back there."

Her smile was like a burst of sunshine. "Yes, wasn't it?" She glanced at me. "I love it."

She did, I could tell. She was glowing. Cecilia is never happier than when she's the center of attention. Growing up, she had so rarely been seen that she was making up for it now. On the other hand, I consciously chose to continue watching life from the sidelines so I could put my own editorial spin on it with a camera.

"Will you ever get tired of this, do you think?" I asked.

My question sobered her. I love Cecilia's profile, topped off today with an elaborate braided knot of glistening auburn hair. Even an old-fashioned paper silhouette of my sister would be expressive. She's more than just a singer. She's acted in some good movies and some not so good ones, but at no time on or off film is Cecilia's face ever truly blank. I'm not sure we see what she's really feeling, but we always see *something*.

"I get tired of being mobbed." She turned away and closed her eyes. "I get tired of being grabbed and crowded. When I'm alone at home I really like the quiet and the space. I didn't always. For a long time it gave me too much time to think."

"And remember."

"That, too. We'll be doing a lot of that in the next weeks. I haven't been back to Randolph Furnace since my mother left me at my grandparents' house for almost a year. She came back and got me when I was maybe six, and that was that. I *must* have been six, because I started school in Pennsylvania. Unless they had kindergarten…"

"That's one of the problems with our childhoods. Unless a social worker was around to document whatever was going on, we lost the details. Now it's just vague memories."

"You don't have many of those."

I had made sure of that. "You've never talked much about yours."

"I'm foggy on dates, but I sure have memories."

"Do you have any good ones of Pennsylvania?"

For a moment it seemed as if she didn't want to answer, but then her shoulders lifted under the elaborate cape. "My grandparents. I loved them. Maybe that's why I never went back to Randolph Furnace. They died while I was still a child, and by then the mine had closed and the town was practically deserted. I held dying against them, I guess. You know, dying when they knew I was out there somewhere in the world with crazy Maribeth."

I knew the answer but asked a question to keep her talking. "Your grandfather was a miner?"

"Not the healthiest profession. As it turned out neither was construction, since that's what killed my father."

Cecilia's father had died in his late teens, when she was still just a toddler. A beam fell on him and quickly destroyed their little family and her mother's ability to cope. The irony? He had chosen construction instead of mining because it seemed safer.

I was worried. These weren't good memories. "You'll be okay going back tomorrow? Complete with film crew and me?"

"Tonight."

I wondered what I had missed. "Tonight? Once we settle into the inn in Uniontown there's a crew meeting to go over what we'll be doing." Mick had explained what would happen. Everything we would do each day would be covered at a meeting the night before, from a briefing on the topic to transportation arrangements, our roles, logistics for each location, what shots we would cover and estimated wrap time.

"Yes, I know. I'll be briefed after the meetings on whatever I need to know."

I continued. "So I was told that tonight we'd be going over details for filming in Randolph Furnace *tomorrow* and maybe the next day, depending on weather and whatever else happens."

"That's Mick's plan. But I've made my own. I want to go back without the crew first."

I was sure Mick wasn't going to like that. The point was to document Cecilia's initial reactions on film. Not leftovers or replays. Mick was after the truth, or as much of it as anyone ever knows.

"I won't go to the house," she said, as if she knew what I was thinking. "I just want to drive around town a little, get a feel for what it's like now."

"Why?"

"So I don't turn tail and run."

"Isn't this going to be one of the easier places we visit?"

"The first time you do anything it's never easy. Like sex. Remember? Or the first week of a diet? Or how about that first baby you pushed out? You were in labor for what, ten years?"

"It only felt like ten years."

"Come with me. We'll steal a car." She laughed at the noise I made. "Actually we'll take Wendy's rental. She won't tell because she thinks I'll fire her if she disagrees with me about anything."

Wendy was the blonde pixie from the airport entourage. She was Cecilia's assistant, hairdresser and makeup artist— which meant she did whatever Cecilia asked and then some. Of course there was also Hal, the big guy, who was a combination bodyguard and gofer, and he didn't look easy to fool. Cecilia was insisting on as little security as was absolutely necessary. The crew and Donny would be performing publicity sleight of hand throughout the trip. She wanted to be one of the gang.

"Won't Hal know what you're up to?"

"He'd better. That's what I pay him for. But I'll tell Hal hands off. He answers to me, whether he likes what I'm doing or not. Donny's the only one who might cause a problem. But he'll probably be meeting with people. We'll be able to sneak out."

"Did you have any idea we would so quickly revert to our past? You plan escapades guaranteed to get us both in trouble, and I go along because I love you?"

"Even the worst childhoods have their high points." She rested her head on my shoulder and closed her eyes for the rest of the flight. I leaned against her and made myself comfortable, too.

12

—

Cecilia

Robin didn't look happy when she slipped downstairs to join me after everybody else had gone up to their rooms for the evening. She had planned to call home and check on her family before we made our getaway, but I wasn't sure asking how the call had gone was a good idea. I wasn't sure she would be honest with me anyway. Donny, annoying insightful man that he is, had asked if I was trying to pave the path to divorce for Robin and Kris, and ever since I've wondered.

Do I need my sister's love and attention so much I don't want to share her with her husband? Despite my spectacular Australian collapse I hope I'm psychologically healthier than that. Whatever I am, though, I am absolutely sure I don't want Robin to be unhappy.

"You okay?" I hesitated a second, then added, "Family okay?"

"No one set the house on fire." As we let ourselves out the front door and headed toward the parking area, she dragged a smile into place. "Though Kris might be happier burning it down and moving into a condo next door to his office."

I had to laugh. The smile had been an effort, I could tell, but she was digging for humor. "How's the nanny?"

"Lord, we can't call her *that*. The kids would have a fit. She's the *housekeeper*. I only talked to Nik. Pet had dinner with a friend, and Kris was off picking her up. Nik says nobody misses me, which means he does. Elena made chicken and rice for dinner, and she told him she made enough for tomorrow, too. I guess I forgot to tell her my son doesn't like leftovers."

"Poor, poor Nik."

"Maybe Elena will train him for me."

"Is she going to train Kris, too?"

"Not so far. Nik said he was late coming home from work."

"*His* problem, right?"

"That kind of thinking's going to take a while."

"Will she quit if he keeps it up?"

"Won't Kris have fun if she does?"

I noticed Robin was carrying her purse and a camera case, along with a windbreaker. "You're not planning to take photos, are you?"

"Get used to it."

"I thought we could just hang out, you know, and insult each other, like sisters do."

"I can insult you and take photos, too. I'm good." She hesitated. "Or at least I used to be."

I didn't want to tackle that. It made sense that Robin wouldn't feel fully comfortable yet, and I didn't want to make more of that than necessary.

A platinum moon was beaming at us just beyond a stand of trees. Not everywhere we stayed would be as lovely as this. But for the next few nights Mick had booked us into a historic brick inn on a farm just outside town. We had enough rooms for everybody, divided between two houses, and tonight we had eaten at a farm table scattered with miniature pumpkins, in front of a fire that smelled of apple wood.

Autumn colors might be fading, but the trees are still spectacular, even now when they're well past their peak. A field of drooping sunflowers greeted us as we drove in. I am such a sucker for sunflowers. I'm coming back next year when they're at their peak.

Wendy's rental compact was parked at the end of a short row. She and Fiona had brought us dinner from a local Italian restaurant so I was betting her car smelled like garlic.

When I opened my door I found it also smelled like cigarettes.

"She smokes?" Robin made a face. "*Your* assistant smokes?"

"She probably rented the cheapest car they had so she can pocket the rest of the car allowance. Can't blame her for that. I remember pinching every penny when I started out."

"You must have pinched hard. Moving from the Osburn ranch to Manhattan with nothing but a little money from Betty Osburn to get you started."

Some stories are best left untold. My early months in Manhattan are one of them. How I even got to New York? Nobody knows that but me.

"Generous Betty and Jud," I said. "Foster parents with big hearts." Robin knew I was being sarcastic.

"And for Jud, at least, a big mouth," she said, right on cue. "Plus a big appetite for the waitress at the Blue Heron diner."

"His downfall."

Jud Osburn was the final foster father in a long series for both of us. Near the end of our stay at the Osburn ranch in Cold Creek, Florida, he and the black-haired temptress who had faithfully served him ham and eggs on his trips into town had disappeared on the same day. Thoughtfully Jud had left a note for his wife.

Not coming back. Dont give a rats ass what you do with this hellhole you call a ranch or your wornout useless body. Don't want a thing that blonges to you.

Jud had never been much of a speller.

Neither Robin nor I had been sorry to see him go. I was pretty sure Betty hadn't been sorry, either. She sold the ranch and left Florida forever.

We were due to film at the ranch sometime after Christmas. Since Robin had lived there with me, returning was going to be tough for her, as well. I had asked to make the ranch our final stop, a chance to put memories firmly behind us at the end of this trip before we went back to our lives, and Mick had agreed.

Robin slipped behind the wheel, turned the key and immediately put the windows down. I have cars at most of my houses and use them when absolutely required, but nobody will ever vote me driver of the year. I learned how to brake and steer in the battered pickup Jud used exclusively on the ranch, followed by years in Manhattan when I didn't drive even that much. Donny swears he's going to hide my license because his livelihood depends on me staying in one piece.

I got in, too, tossing a jacket on the seat behind me, and we sat there a moment letting the car air out while she familiarized herself with the dashboard. Then she backed out, following the farm drive to the road and, once there, turning in the direction the innkeeper had told us to go.

"It's lovely country," Robin said.

"Coal country usually is—until the mining companies destroy it. And let's not talk about mountaintop removal."

"How close to Randolph Furnace do you want to get?"

"As close as I can without having a panic attack."

Robin kept her voice casual, but I knew she was worried. "That's something new, isn't it? Panic attacks, I mean."

I'm almost as good an actress as I am a singer, so I sounded casual, too. "I've probably been having them for years. Smaller ones, of course. I thought of them as nerves. Stage fright. Whatever I could call them to make them seem normal."

"You're one of the most courageous people I know. You always keep going, no matter what."

"Not so much anymore."

"What do you call *this*?" Robin glanced at me. "I don't know anybody else who would decide to expose herself to the world as a way to drive out her demons."

"Demons. Perfect. I like that better than nerves."

"I'm serious."

"It's not courage. I just know I have to put things in perspective. My life now. My life then. My life tomorrow."

"What part of your life *now* isn't going to follow you into the future?"

"Trust you to go right to the heart of it."

"Are you thinking about slowing down? Having a different life?"

"I'm thinking about a lot of things." I let the subject rest. Robin doesn't push. If I don't embroider, she knows I'm finished. Sometimes learning the fine art of conversation late in childhood is a plus.

"What about you?" I asked, after a few minutes of silence. "Just coming along with me is a huge change. Is this the start of something new? Or a temporary aberration?"

"I would never call you an aberration. Annoying, sure, but that's as far as it goes."

I *also* know better than to push. We talked about Mick and the crew. They had met before dinner to discuss what tomorrow would bring. Mick seems like a laid-back guy, but

Robin said the meeting was under his tight control every minute. He briefed everyone on the logistics of our location and concerns to watch out for, including a neighbor at the home where my grandparents had lived, who had flatly refused to allow any shots of his home or yard. I zoned out when she recounted information on storyboards, equipment and shot lists. Thankfully she covered most of that quickly.

In addition to Jerry, the DP who had been with us on the plane, a gaffer and sound technician had joined us at the inn. While Mick was both producer and director, a line producer whose job was day-to-day production would join us early tomorrow morning. She was still finalizing details.

Documentaries are often shot with skeletal crews because finding enough money for salaries and expenses is problematic. Since this one had enviable funding, including a grant from a foundation dedicated to improving the future of dependent children, we had our own executive producer in New York. He might visit us at some point, but his job was the business side of making this film, securing more funding and publicity, but not the creation. That was all Mick.

We drove for ten minutes before Robin slowed. "City limits." She nodded to a sign on the right and slowed so we could read it. We could have parked in the middle of the road; we were the only car in sight. Off to the left was what looked like a man-made mountain, maybe of coal that had never been shipped, with what looked like trees and shrubs springing out of it. It seemed familiar.

Randolph Furnace. I licked my lips. If the sign had been here when I was living with my grandparents, I'd been too young to read it. "'Population 803.' The place is booming. Quick, let's buy property before it skyrockets."

"I guess it was a different town back in the day, when the mine was open."

"The mine closed a year or two after my mother swept me back into her hopeless little life. She hated everything about this town, although at that time she probably could have found a job. She had bigger aspirations, though. Places to see, things to do."

Through the years I've learned to tell that story without bitterness in my voice, but Robin knew me well enough to hear the undertone.

"It's really a pretty area, CeCe. Frank Lloyd Wright's Fallingwater isn't far away."

"I don't think Frank was building coal patch houses. You'll see the one I lived in tomorrow. Most of them started life as duplexes sharing a porch. I think my grandparents' kitchen was in the back with the living room in the front. I do remember a big coal heater that stuck out into the room. At least heat must have been cheap. Coal was probably free, and I remember holes in the floor upstairs so when the heat rose, the bedrooms were warm. The holes were covered with grates, and I was told over and over again not to step on them."

"Do you want to drive by?"

I didn't know. I didn't want to spoil tomorrow for Mick. I had made it this far, and that was probably good enough to get me back tomorrow. There was just one other thing I wanted to do.

"Let's get a drink. There has to be a bar, right?" I asked the question like I didn't know the answer right in the center of my gut. "Eight hundred people means bars and churches. Maybe next door to each other."

"You'll be recognized."

"Way ahead of you." From my handbag I pulled out a cap with a Pittsburgh Pirates logo. I rummaged and found oversize aviator glasses with pink-tinted lenses while I explained.

"Wendy got me the hat when she went out to score dinner. Local color. Do you know experts in eyewitness identification claim that eye color and the way the eyes are set are what people remember, plus hair color and style? Head and face shape matter, too. A baseball cap and sunglasses cover just about all those factors, which is why you see us celebrity types wearing them so frequently." I could sense she wasn't sure. "Robin, it's dark, right? It's a bar. It will be dark in there, too, and nobody is expecting me to be in town."

"Pink-tinted lenses? You think that's a trend in Randolph Furnace? Designer glasses aren't going to set you apart just a little?"

"Where's your sense of adventure?"

"You don't drink."

"Not true. I drink on special occasions."

"A case could be made for every day of this trip being special in some way."

"Addiction was my mother's thing, not mine."

"How do we find this bar?"

I scanned both sides of the intersection. "This has to be the main street, or else Main Street intersects with this road. We'll cruise and look for a busy parking lot. I'm thinking there's not much else to do here at night except drink."

We went in search. I wondered if Robin was in a hurry to get back to the inn so she could call Kris, but when I asked, she said no, the telephone worked in both directions.

I didn't look too closely at the town, which didn't seem to have much going for it, although I did note a park and a steepled church. We found a bar, the Evergreen, at the end of what was probably the main drag. So many years had passed, but my stomach tightened as Robin pulled into a small lot inhabited for the most part by pickups and cars manufactured in the US, and turned off the engine.

I wanted to tell her to turn around and head back to the

inn, but this trip was about facing ghosts. And I supposed I could start right here.

Robin, who still didn't look comfortable with our new plan, got out, and after donning my hat and glasses, I followed.

The inside was basic, to say the least. The bar counter was faced with varnished plywood, and I wondered if the owner had gotten tired of customers kicking in more expensive woods like oak or cherry. Plywood could be quickly and cheaply replaced, and the countertop of dark laminate was also a quick fix. Plain stools with backs faced it, and half or more were occupied. An old television with a picture that faded in and out was fastened on the wall high over the bartender's head. In addition to the usual shelves of liquor, there were two refrigerator cases, one stocked with soft drinks and mixers, the other with snacks. The requisite flag completed the decor.

Robin was still worried about hiding me. "You find a corner. I'll get the drinks. What do you want?"

I really didn't want anything except to see if I was okay in this place. But I told her to get a whiskey on the rocks because I knew they would have it. This wasn't a white wine joint.

I found a seat in the corner where I could see most of the room. Madonna's "Like A Prayer" was playing over loudspeakers. I wondered if anyone had updated the playlist here since the '90s or if we were listening to AM radio.

I got a few glances, but nobody seemed particularly interested in making contact. We weren't the only women, and the men who weren't accompanied were riveted to their stools, conversing loudly with their neighbors. Recognition is 90 percent expectation, and nobody here was expecting me.

Robin returned with two identical drinks and sat catty-corner so she could look out on the room, too. "I can't imagine why you wanted to do this."

The song changed and we both fell silent. "No Man's Good Enough for Me," my first entry on Billboard's Hot 100 list was halfway through before Robin spoke again.

"Does this feel even stranger now?"

I took a sip of my whiskey. It was surprisingly mellow with a nice kick. I put the glass down because I never drink if I'm enjoying it. That decision has kept me sober even though my genes are swimming in their polluted little pool clamoring for me to get hooked on something.

"The thing is it's probably not the first time I've sung here."

"I'm sure they play your music a lot, especially if anybody's figured out you were born here."

"No. I mean I think I've sung here in *person*."

Robin sipped her drink, and when I didn't go on, she prompted me. "I'm assuming the Evergreen wasn't on one of your recent tours?"

"Didn't I ever tell you about Maribeth's favorite trick? Other than prostituting herself, I mean? Drugs were her addiction of choice, but drinking wasn't far behind. When she didn't have money for anything else, she'd drag me into places like this one, and she'd get me to sing. People would give me tips, and then she'd have money for beer. As a reward she bought me potato chips and Coke for dinner."

Robin was visibly affected. "I think you skipped that story."

There are plenty of stories I've skipped, and Robin has her own. There's nothing to be gained by recounting every rotten detail of our pasts.

"I guess I just didn't think it was that interesting. The cops were called a few times because kids aren't supposed to be in bars. Bartenders routinely tossed us out, but sometimes they didn't."

"So you did the dog and pony show here?"

"Maribeth came to get me after I'd been with my grand-parents for a year. They tried to persuade her to stay, get a job, raise me where they could keep an eye on things. I re-member hearing a fight about it. I was praying she would lis-ten. They were my father's parents, not hers, so they didn't have a lot of clout, but she did hang around awhile before we left. She'd found herself a boyfriend, I think, one of a long string to follow, and she was sure he was going to be my next daddy. I think the two of them brought me here one night and I started to sing along with the music. Maribeth always had the radio on, and even then I knew a lot of songs. She told me to sing louder. That was the first time I sang in pub-lic." The rest of that night was a blank. Blanks are my friends.

"Is that why you wanted to come here?"

"I wanted to see if I'd recognize the place. I don't, not really. I'm sure pretty much everything has changed. But it seems like the right bar, if that makes any sense."

"That can't be a good memory."

"I wasn't sure I wanted to share this piece of my past with Mick. That's why we're here tonight without him. I wasn't sure I wanted the world to know this is where my career began."

My song ended and Otis Redding took my place. Robin downed the last of her drink. "How about now?"

"I'll tell him when we get to Jamestown. After we'd been there awhile Maribeth got reported after one bar concert too many and I was taken away from her for the first time. Are you done?"

"Yep."

We rose together. Nobody seemed to care we were leaving, which suited me. This may well have been the first place I learned to love the limelight—and potato chips—but I didn't want either one tonight.

Outside I saw we weren't alone in the parking lot. Two young men, probably teenagers, were under the farthest street-light laughing and pushing each other. I hadn't noticed them inside, but from all signs, they'd been drinking somewhere.

I wasn't worried. Wendy's car was on the other side of the lot, and if they bothered us, we could dart back inside and ask the bartender to see us to the car. But as we crossed I heard a high-pitched yelp, followed quickly by another.

Robin stopped. So did I. We turned and I saw one of the teens pick up an animal of some kind, then drop it back to the asphalt.

"Hey!" I didn't think. I started toward them. "What are you doing?"

The other kid stumbled and fell to his knees and began to retch. The one who was still upright whirled. "None of your business!" Profanity followed, quite a colorful selection, too.

"I'm going to make it my business." I was closer and could see what looked like a small dog trying to slink away, but Profanity Kid was between me and the pup.

"Yeah?" He drew himself up, but he still wasn't as tall as my five-eight.

"Honey, I've got more friends in law enforcement than you have in the whole wide world, and any minute I'm going to get one of them on my phone. So if I were you, I'd split for parts unknown."

Instead the kid started toward me, and the closer he got the younger he looked. Robin grabbed my arm, as if she planned to haul me away. I shook her off and stood my ground, and whatever her original plan, she remained beside me.

"Try anything at all," I said, "and you have a world of hurt waiting for you. I am in the mood to knock you into the next dimension for abusing that dog."

He stopped, clearly unsure that continuing forward was a good idea.

"I'm sure this is a misunderstanding," Robin said, as politely as if she was talking to a rational, receptive adult. "We'll just get our puppy now, and I won't even tell my husband who was kicking her." She paused a moment. "Or your mother, either."

He really *had* been drinking, because suddenly his eyes went wild, as if he expected good old mom to jump out of a shadow. "How do you know my mother?"

I glanced at Robin, who was shaking her head sadly. "Son, *everybody* in this town knows your mother."

He turned and took off. I stood there openmouthed, and both teens were halfway down the block before I could speak.

"I had no idea you could lie that well."

She looked pleased. "Someday I'll tell you how I lied my way into the middle of a UAW picket line and got the photos I needed for my senior project in college."

We started to search for the dog. I had no idea how badly hurt it was or what we could do for the poor little thing, but it didn't take long to find out. We found all six pounds of matted fur resting against a tire, panting as if it had run a mile. The poor creature growled when Robin approached, but she crouched in front of it and spoke soothingly.

"Little guy, we aren't going to hurt you."

"He's not wearing a collar," I said.

"He has to be a stray. He's starving. Look how thin he is."

I really didn't want to look. We had done our good deed, and now I wanted somebody else to finish for us, take the dog home, feed him and take him to a vet in the morning.

I didn't want to, but I joined her down on my knees and

extended my hand. "Poor little guy," I crooned. Then I was singing softly, some nonsense syllables at first, sliding into "No Man's Good Enough For Me." Instant replay.

The dog whined, then, trembling, it scooted on its stomach toward my hand.

"Terrier," Robin said. "Some kind of mix. Maybe part Chihuahua. He's hoping you're going to give him something to eat."

"Uniontown will have a shelter, right? He'll be better off there."

"We can try." Robin sounded doubtful.

"Work up a little enthusiasm, okay?"

"Towns that small? Kill shelters, most likely. Bring in a dog this beat-up?" She didn't finish.

"At least we can try."

"I'm sorry to say it, but this isn't going to end well."

"Look in the car. I left my jacket in the back. We can wrap him inside."

The dog inched closer, whimpering. How could anything this tiny, this abused, still have faith I might help? Trust seemed inconceivable, but there it was. The dog let me stroke his muzzle, then his ears. His eyes closed, and for a moment I thought he'd died happy.

Robin came back with my jacket and her camera. I laid the jacket over him, and he lifted his head.

Not dead. Not yet.

"I'm going to wrap this around you," I told the dog softly. "Then I'm going to carry you to the car."

"He might bite," Robin warned. She lifted her camera, as if she hoped to get *that* scene on film.

"I'll bite him back." I wrapped him up gently. The dog let me, staring at me with sad little eyes.

"Find a vet on your phone?" I looked up at Robin. "There's

got to be somebody who's open twenty-four hours, even if we have to drive back to Pittsburgh. We can leave him there. Leave money for his board and treatment. Maybe the vet will know how to find this poor baby a good home."

Robin snapped a photo and shook her head.

I glared at her. "Well, he might!"

She sent me one of those I'm-smarter-than-you-are smiles that only sisters can get away with. "CeCe, don't you think it's clear by now that if this little guy makes it through the night he's already found one?"

13

Robin

Nik tells me you called. Pet got sick last night from something she ate at her friend's house. What do you suggest if she can't go to school? Elena seems inflexible.

I stared at the tiny screen framing Kris's text from late last night.

Good morning to you, too, husband mine.

I debated whether to call home to check on my daughter, call Elena and ask her to do some problem solving with Kris, or throw my cell phone out the window. I turned it off instead, and just like that, the problem disappeared. I would call Pet in the afternoon to see how she was. But usually when her stomach gets upset the culprit is fried food, which doesn't always agree with her. To combat the problem I dole out an antacid, and by morning she's fine.

Pet knows the drill, and Kris knows the top of our closet is a minipharmacy. Maybe I'll get a follow-up later saying the crisis was averted with a chewable pink pill or, more likely, I won't. Kris seems happiest delivering recriminations by text, and I doubt he'll be in the mood anytime soon to change course.

I miss him anyway. I miss my kids, too, but I'm still happy to be here. While my professional photographer's hat isn't firmly in place, I think it might be after today, our first official day of filming. That doesn't mean I'm glad to be away from my family.

At least not too much.

I pictured my husband coping with short skirts, leftovers, upset stomachs and a housekeeper who isn't afraid to stand up to him. None of it is beyond Kris's capabilities. By the time I return, will he feel comfortable being in charge? What kind of changes will he make in our household?

How much will they still need me?

Someone knocked on my door. I got up and pulled on a pair of knit pants on my way to open it.

Cecilia stood in the doorway. No makeup. The same jeans and T-shirt she'd been wearing last night. She still looked amazing. Her hair fell over her shoulders in natural waves. Her skin was luminous.

I opened the door wider to usher her in.

She came in just far enough so I could close it behind her. "The vet called. Roscoe had a good night. She thinks he'll be ready to leave tomorrow afternoon. They're icing his leg, and they're still giving him fluids and meds for pain and everything else, but he's responding well."

Luckily the dog's leg wasn't broken, but he was malnourished and flea infested, for starters, and the vet practically guaranteed parasites. There were vet visits galore in the little guy's future.

I tried to look sad. "'Leave' as in go to a shelter? Or a home the vet found in the middle of the night?"

"You are so smug. I hate it when you're smug."

"Roscoe?"

"He had to have a name, didn't he?"

"You know what happens when you name a dog."

"The receptionist asked *my* name last night and I told her Cecilia. 'Cecilia what?'" It was a perfect imitation of the scowling woman at the desk, who clearly needed a different job with better hours.

"Did you explain that you're world famous and need at most one name to be recognized?"

"I told her I didn't like my last name so I got rid of it. I think she thought I was trying to duck out on the bill."

"Does this mean poor Roscoe won't have a last name, either?"

She ignored that. "Most of the places we'll be staying on this trip probably don't allow dogs."

"A little thing like rules never stopped you."

"I already talked to the innkeeper here. *Her*, not him. She seemed more malleable."

"How much money did you offer with your sob story?"

"Enough, apparently. She gave me a laundry basket with a blanket for Roscoe to sleep in."

"What if he's not housebroken?" I considered. "And once this is over, what house will he be broken for, anyway? Will he be a California dog? A Manhattan dog?"

"Oh, I don't know—he's so small he can fit under the seat on an airplane."

"You've got it bad." I knew why. The dog needed my sister, and right now, Cecilia needed something to hold on to, something that was more scared about the future than she was. Like I had been all those years ago.

She was pretending all this meant nothing, which was a sign it meant everything.

I had to support her. "If you take him out frequently enough he'll get the idea."

She lifted a perfectly threaded eyebrow in question. "How frequently?"

"Kris and I had a dog. You take them out as often as possible and eventually they catch on. Trust me, it gets old."

"Why didn't you get another dog after...Pickles? After Pickles died?"

"Because I did all the work, and for once I put my foot down when Nik and Pet demanded we get another."

If I'd put my foot down more often, would my life be different now? I gave my own children all the love and attention I missed. Maybe I'd taught them to expect the world on a silver platter.

Maybe I'd done the same with my husband.

"I know this is crazy," Cecilia said.

"Who cares?" I gave her a hug and changed the subject. "You ready for today?"

"It should be interesting."

I was glad we were starting with a town I had no connection to. I had time to prepare a little before my past was dissected, although I, at least, wouldn't watch mine fall to pieces on camera.

She left, and I slipped out my laptop to email my husband, since I'm a fan of keyboards not busy thumbs.

I imagine you've already considered all the options if our children are sick. Staying home with them, bringing them to work, paying Elena a bonus if she can come earlier. The good news is they stay surprisingly healthy most of the time. Robin.

At least I had the grace to sign *my* response.

I sent it, then I went in to take my shower and prepare for the day.

During yesterday's meeting Mick had outlined all the different elements that would go into the final version of the documentary, which so far had no title. He planned to use a variety of techniques. Archival photographs of orphanages and other historical solutions for parentless children, like the orphan trains that carried them from cities like New York to new lives on Midwestern farms. He would use newsreels and footage of past interviews with officials, like the real Father Flanagan of Boys Town in Nebraska, excerpts from books, including the rags to riches Horatio Alger novel *Ragged Dick*, that would be read out loud over photographic montages of real news and shoeshine boys in old New York. Mick was still coaxing celebrities to come on board as readers. So far, having Cecilia involved had made recruiting them easier. Her name lent weight.

Many of the historical elements had already been assembled, although that aspect was still very much a work in progress as new photos and films turned up. The present-day section would include interviews with officials and "talking heads," historians and experts, who would explain the way child welfare in America had developed. Some of the most innovative programs in the country would be featured, along with peeks into residential education facilities—the new term for orphanages. Some of those segments had already been filmed. Mick had promised Cecilia, and me along with her, that we could view some of the footage if we were interested.

Interested? Cecilia was interested in everything. My sister never made it to college; she went to New York to become famous, and we all know how that turned out. But she *is* well-read and intelligent. She can hold her own with almost anyone, and the prejudiced who expect a superstar airhead when they corner her at parties or snag an interview discover immediately that her IQ is just as responsible for her success as her talent and drive.

Since she's appeared in films, much of today would feel familiar to her, although those roles had been heavily scripted, and the set and everything around her had been controlled. Talking about herself was familiar, too. But talking honestly and in detail about hardships she'd endured? Not familiar. She's always been great at dodging the most personal questions.

Right now Wendy was putting finishing touches on Cecilia's makeup and hair while I took photos. To get here we had driven past the "gob pile" we'd seen on our visit last night and the remnants of the coke ovens for which the town had been named. Now we were on the street where Cecilia's grandparents' house graced a corner lot. The house still existed, but at this point that was all we knew. We were a block away, waiting for permission to move closer. Starla Pierce, the line producer who had been absent from yesterday's meeting, was briefing Cecilia as Wendy powdered her nose in the van. Starla was short and stocky, with black hair buzzed short at the sides and back, with the top long and wavy. She had two nose rings and diamond studs outlining the curve of one ear. I liked her no-nonsense style and the way she treated Cecilia as a co-conspirator.

"I'll ask questions, and you'll answer them," she told my sister. "Once the film is edited I won't show up or be heard on camera. The questions are just to get you started. We have permission to walk through the house. If you can, would you describe what you see now, as well as the way it used to be? What you remember? That's what we're looking for."

Cecilia looked in a hand mirror and wiped something off her nose. "What would you like me to focus on?"

"What life was like for your grandparents and for you when you were with them. If you feel like talking about the reason you were here, this would be a good place to do it, too. Sunday we'll go to the cemetery where your family is buried, and we have a special guest who'll meet you there. It's nothing for you to worry about. In fact I think it's going to be something you'll like. But I don't want to spoil the surprise."

"Not a long-lost relative?"

"Not exactly. You can wait, right?"

"What happened with the guy next door? The one who refused to let you film?"

"I talked to his preacher. Reverend Teller convinced him it was good publicity for the area and promised we would be careful not to show street names or house numbers. He's an old man, and he was afraid somebody would trample his vegetable garden. I promised one of our assistants will stand guard to be sure it stays safe, even though there's hardly anything in it now. He's not happy, but he's not going to come after us with a shotgun."

"I'll go see him afterward. Is he old enough to remember my grandparents?"

Starla hesitated, and I could almost watch her forming her response. "I'm not sure that's a good idea."

Cecilia met her eyes, then she smiled a little. "He remembers my mother, doesn't he?"

Starla gave a little nod.

"It's more about *that* than the vegetable garden."

"Possibly."

"We ought to get an interview with this guy on camera. In case anybody harbors any doubt that when I was nine she really left me to starve in a condemned apartment house."

"We considered it."

Cecilia glanced at me. "Are we having fun yet?"

"You're okay, CeCe."

"So far."

We got the nod. Cecilia refused to ride in the van for a

block, so we got out and headed toward her grandparents'
house.

"Who lives here now?" I asked Starla, who was walking
with us.

"A young family. He works in Uniontown, but the rent
here is cheaper. She wanted to stay home with their kids."

I wished her well. "They won't be home?"

"They're spending the day away. They've been very co-
operative. They're thrilled Cecilia once lived in their house,
and they've promised not to broadcast what's going on until
we've left."

We reached the house, and Cecilia stopped out front. Most
of the time so far I'd felt confused about what to shoot and
when to do it, but this time I took photos of her gazing up at
the house and thought that one shot, in particular, had merit.
Her expression said she was surprised her memories weren't
completely accurate, but she still remembered enough that
she could have found the spot without help.

The house was small, even though it looked as if the original duplex had now been converted into a single-family
dwelling. I tried to imagine two miners' families living here,
with assorted children and other members.

Because they didn't want to damage anything, and also
didn't want to crowd Cecilia, Mick and Jerry had decided to
shoot the interior with a handheld camera, although Jerry had
been inside since breakfast with a more elaborate setup, filming B-roll—supplementary—footage that they might use later.

Once-green hills, now brown and gold, were visible in the
distance. I'm not sure what I'd expected to find in this former
coal patch, but Randolph Furnace was picturesque, and so far
the houses were well maintained, with trees and hedges and
chrysanthemums still in bloom despite a light frost last week.
The yard stretched back into thick woods. I could imagine

Cecilia as a child playing on that expanse of dandelion-dotted bluegrass, scouting for insects and frogs, learning to do cart-wheels and somersaults, collecting wildflowers.

I wished I could turn back time and convince Maribeth Ceglinski to leave her daughter right here, where Cecilia had collected her few good family memories. But if things had been different for my sister, where would *I* be today?

Mick came over to greet Cecilia. "All set?"

"It used to be bigger."

"You used to be smaller. We'll start with you on the porch. Then Starla's going to take you inside. She's explained how we'll work?"

Cecilia nodded.

"Robin?" He turned to me. "I think we're going to ask you to stay outside while we film. We'll give you time with Ce-cilia inside once we're done. But we don't want to crowd her. Cecilia, we just want you to feel comfortable, like you're talk-ing to an old friend, showing her pieces of your childhood."

"Of course."

"I won't be there, either. Between Starla and Jerry you'll be in the best of hands. When you get tired, take a break. Don't hesitate if you really need one."

Cecilia smiled at me, then she walked up to the porch. Mick and I watched her go, and I felt relieved I wouldn't be there with her trying to figure out what to photograph and what to ignore. Sadly, I knew I should be sorry I was miss-ing the opportunity.

Mick was watching me. "Jerry and I planned this down to the last detail, so I think it's going to go well. She's such a trooper. I don't know why I was blessed to work with her on this, but I'm not unaware how hard this might be emo-tionally."

Mick projected such a comfortable presence, he was easy to

talk to, and now I did. "I've never been sure whether Cecilia likes challenges or if she just feels life is something you have to plow through. You know, neither rain, nor snow? She's not delivering mail, just herself, her life. And she doesn't let anything stop her."

"I get the feeling she'll ignore any rule if it's in the way of progress. Her progress, and maybe yours."

"So you know about Roscoe?"

There was the faintest note of disapproval in his voice. "I heard you left the inn last night. I was hoping viewing the town today would be new for her."

I angled my body so I could better see his expression. "We didn't get anywhere near the house, Mick. I understood what you wanted, and she agreed. But she needed to be sure she could actually come back today to do this."

"Then it was a good move on your part. Is Roscoe the dog?"

Apparently film sets are like gossipy small towns. I wondered how many people in Randolph Furnace had heard about the puppy a stranger had rescued at the Evergreen last night. Maybe by now they even knew who the stranger was, although I suspected a crowd would have gathered here if that piece of the puzzle had fallen into place.

"Roscoe is the dog," I said. "We'll pick him up at the vet tomorrow afternoon. The innkeeper gave permission. Cecilia is a genius at convincing people to do what she wants."

"She's enormously talented, but I imagine her persuasive powers helped get her where she is, too."

Fiona, brown hair braided back from her fresh young face, came up to join us. She had a travel mug for her father, and I could smell coffee. "Would you like some, Robin? We brought a jug from the inn. I can get you a cup."

"Isn't she a love?" Mick put an arm around her shoulders and pulled her to his side.

I tried to remember the last time I'd seen Kris hug Pet that way. He wasn't demonstrative, but he wasn't aloof, either. These days he just wasn't available. Had he put his arm around her last night when she told him she didn't feel well? Had he gotten her tea? Had he gone in to check on her before she fell asleep, tuck covers around her the way I did when she was sick, kiss her forehead or give her a back rub, and tell her he hoped she felt better in the morning?

If he had, he'd probably made a memory.

"No coffee for me, but thanks." I glanced at my watch. "I think I'm going to call home, just to be sure things are all right this morning."

"Hard being away? That's why I bring Fiona along. Best of everything that way."

I tried not to look envious. A short distance away I slid my phone out of my pocket and made the call. Nobody answered, which was a promising sign. At the same time I was a little sorry.

I could call Kris at work. I could interrupt him in the middle of whatever he was doing, whoever he was talking to, to see how Pet felt this morning. I could tell him how I'm starting to get into the swing of taking photographs again, but that it still seems odd and unnatural, like I'm living somebody else's life.

Sadly, not only is he too angry for that conversation, a long time ago I stopped telling Kris when things were going well or badly.

When exactly did all our communications become about the business of our lives and stop being about things that really matter?

14

—

Kris

Except for one early-morning email, I didn't hear from Robin yesterday. In the afternoon she spoke to Pet and Nik, although neither told me about their conversations. I didn't call back because I really don't know what to say. What am I going to tell her? I'm already worn out? Wearing me down wasn't her point. Robin isn't doing this to prove how indispensable she is. Apparently she needs this trip to find herself. I get that. I'm just wondering what both of us will find by the time she's home again.

I was thinking about this while lying in bed staring at the ceiling. It's Saturday morning, so I don't have to get up quite as early, but a dream woke me—more accurately a nightmare. I saw Robin in a car, another car speeding toward her, and I couldn't scream to warn her. I opened my mouth and no sound emerged. I kept trying and trying....

Stow the steno pad, Dr. Freud. I think I've got this.

Robin did a boatload of work setting up everything so she could leave, but by the end it was clear she couldn't wait to go. She was energized in a new way, excited by something other than us. And me? I'm not going to dwell on this, but I guess I'm jealous. I got used to being the center of Robin's world, used to her holding all of us together in a tight little knot we called family. I could count on that even if I couldn't count on anything else. Robin was there to make sure the knot was strong and nobody could untie it.

Not anymore.

Since stewing isn't helpful, I got out of bed and a moment later my alarm went off anyway. I can't remember when I haven't gone into work on a Saturday. Apparently Robin *can*, because she made no plans for Saturday child care. I didn't realize that until yesterday when I asked Elena what time I could expect her. I have a meeting at nine. She looked at me as if I'd asked her to rewrite the Constitution.

"I don't come in on Saturdays."

One thing about Elena? She doesn't waste words. Her English is perfect—on the rare occasions I hear it, and on that occasion I'd already heard quite a bit because I had been ten minutes late coming home.

"I didn't realize," I told her.

"We have a written agreement."

I wasn't going to admit I hadn't read it because I'd been too busy reading other people's written agreements. "Is there any possibility you can come in tomorrow morning until I make other arrangements?"

"Mr. Kris, I have a son I don't see enough of. He needs to be with me on weekends."

Left unspoken was the rest. *Your children need to be with you.* Or maybe those words were in my head only.

I struggled for compromise. "Can you bring your little boy with you? Just for tomorrow? I bet Pet would love to play with him. And you don't have to cook or clean. Just be here to make sure the kids are okay."

Elena's eyes are expressive and at that moment they were filled with as much annoyance as mine. "This one time only

I can come tomorrow. But that will be time and a half, and I can't stay beyond two. Raoul has a birthday party."

"I'll be home by one-thirty."

I watched her flounce out the door. This morning she would flounce back in, probably with her kid.

The solution to this problem is clear. I have to find somebody to watch Nik and Pet before I get home, so that Elena can leave in time. While I'm at it I need to find somebody for Saturday mornings, too.

Dressed and showered, I went downstairs to paw through the lists Robin had left me. I found the one with local babysitters, teenagers she had used in the evenings when we were both out. None of the names were familiar, but Robin had always taken care of finding and paying sitters, and making sure they got to and from our house safely.

I was keying names and numbers into my phone to call from the office when Pet wandered downstairs. Nik would probably sleep until noon if Elena's son didn't wake him. One less child to worry about right now was a gift.

"Good morning, early bird," I said. "Elena should be here before too long. Want me to make you breakfast?"

"I make my own on Saturdays. Mommy just makes it on school days to save us time."

I realized I'd probably seen her getting her breakfast on weekends. I continued trying to sound like I knew what I was doing. "Just make sure you add whatever you need to the grocery list. Elena shops for us on…" I realized I didn't know.

"Tuesdays."

"Right."

"The list's on the pantry door. I already added frozen waffles and blueberries. We need more milk, too, but Miss Elena said she'll check the fridge and get things like bread and milk every week."

"She's probably bringing her little boy with her this morning. She won't usually come on Saturdays."

Her sleepy eyes brightened. "Does that mean you'll be staying home with us?"

"I'm going to try hard to be home in the afternoons."

"Oh." She started toward the sunroom. I figured Saturday-morning television was still on her agenda.

I halted her progress. "I *will* need a babysitter for the times Elena can't be here. Early evenings and Saturday mornings. Do you have somebody you particularly like? Your mother left a list."

Pet is so much like Robin. Ask her a question and she's never flippant. She gives careful thought to everything. Nik, on the other hand, is impulsive. He rarely thinks before he speaks. Robin says that makes him easier to know, since there's no time for him to hide anything.

I would change *anything* to *everything.* I was once a pre-teen boy, too.

"I do know somebody who might really like the job," Pet said. "Remember my friend Jody?"

"If Jody's your *friend*, she's too young."

"Not her. Her sister Grace. She's a senior, and Jody told me she's looking for a job because she's saving for a car to take to college. She has to earn part of it before her parents pay the rest."

I could picture Jody. She was around often enough that even *I* saw her occasionally. I could also picture a teenager picking her up out front. But the teenager in my memory was a boy.

"I think I remember a brother, not a sister," I said.

"Grace and Gil. They're twins."

"Do you know if Grace babysits? Does she have experience?"

"She doesn't exactly have to change diapers, does she? Besides we're old enough to stay here alone if you and Mommy would just let us."

I made a sound in my throat, and she knew what it meant. She sighed. "She watches Jody all the time. And she was *our* babysitter once this summer."

I couldn't help myself. "Having a babysitter is something Jody's parents require, too?"

She lifted her chin and enunciated, as if I needed the help, "I can give you her number if it's not on your list."

The kids probably *are* old enough to be on their own for a few hours, especially in a neighborhood like ours where somebody is always home to help in an emergency—or at least they used to be. The real problem is that Pet and Nik don't always get along. And leaving them to duke it out without us to referee isn't yet an option.

I thought about emailing Robin to see if Grace might be a good choice. But that would be admitting that the babysitters who'd come and gone here had been invisible to me. Besides, I was perfectly capable of asking a teenage girl to come to our house this evening to talk about it.

"Do that," I said. "You'd rather have Grace than anybody else on the list your mother left?"

"She's cool." Pet realized she might have made a mistake. "But not too cool."

I tried not to smile. "I'll take cool into consideration."

"Hey, maybe we can do something when you get home?"

She said it so casually it didn't sound important. But I heard the undertone. She wanted to spend time together.

"Would you like to go out to dinner?" I asked. "Nik, too, if he wants. How about that Thai restaurant you like?"

"I used to like Thai. Not anymore."

I wondered how long ago that change had occurred. Last

year she would have eaten pad thai for every meal. "What would you like, then?"

"Hot dogs at the movie theater."

I envisioned my whole evening going up in smoke. "Sorry, I have to work tonight."

She cocked her head. "So how long *can* you spend with us? There's always McDonald's. We could be done in fifteen minutes, ten if I gulp."

Robin might be gone, but her doppleganger was standing right in front of me. I tried for compromise. "Choose any place that doesn't come with entertainment afterward, okay? And maybe we can do a movie tomorrow."

"Let's wait and see."

When Elena arrived minutes later with a mop-haired preschooler, Pet was already watching a talking sponge on television.

Elena introduced me to Raoul, who was maybe four, and he stuck out his hand. I crouched to look him in the eye as we shook. "Let me introduce you to Pet."

My daughter reluctantly abandoned her undersea world. "Want to watch TV with me?" she asked when the introduction was over.

"He is only allowed to watch a little," Elena warned as her son followed my daughter.

I was on my feet again. "Pet has a million books and puzzles she's outgrown to entertain him. And again, thank you for doing this."

"I'll help Nik and Pet with their laundry today."

Did my children even know how to do laundry? Had Robin done it for them as a matter of course? Was ten old enough to know what should go in hot water, what in cold? At twelve would Nik even care?

Elena correctly read my expression. "I will teach them.

Your wife assured me that was fine. They may find something dirty after I leave one evening and need to run a load."

"Of course. But for the record, I do know how to run a washing machine."

"Do you?" She looked unconvinced. "But why should you ever have needed to?"

Robin had spoiled us, and we had enjoyed it. Suddenly I missed my wife even more. Not because I wanted to be spoiled again, but because she had taken up so much slack through the years and I had so rarely appreciated the extent of it.

After our morning meeting, which stretched past noon, Buff and I had a quick lunch together, but I had to cut that short to take over from Elena. I worked on the Pedersen case all afternoon. For the record, taking the federal government to court isn't as easy as suing a neighbor for putting his new fence on your property. I didn't believe Pedersen Pharmacies was blameless. Most of the time I'm glad when the government steps in for our safety, and if their role here was to keep more tainted products off the market, how could I fault them?

Except, of course, it's not my job to fault anybody. It's my job to interpret and apply the law to advance my client's position to the best of my ability, knowing that no matter what I do, in the end someone else will be the final judge.

I believe in our legal system. If I don't believe it's always fair or just, I also don't believe that as yet, we've found a better alternative.

At five thirty I took a break to call Jody's sister, Grace, and ask if she would be interested in a job. She agreed to stop by tomorrow to discuss it. Then I went to find my daughter, who had disappeared into the neighborhood. Nik was skateboarding at a local park and had promised to be home by five, although so far he hadn't materialized.

I found both of them at the Weinbergs, sitting on the front steps with Channa. What do you say to a twelve-year-old girl who recently lost her mother and is now moving from the only home she's ever known? Robin would know. I was clueless.

I picked out a step just below them and sat. "Channa, how're you doing?"

"Fine." She smiled, and I was reminded of Talya, then, swiftly, of the dream that had awakened me. Talya and Michael had lived my nightmare, although Talya hadn't survived it.

I managed a smile, too. "If you don't have dinner plans, I'm taking Pet and Nik out. We'd love to have you come with us."

"My dad just went to get pizza. He's getting enough for everybody."

"We were hungry. I figured you wouldn't mind since you were working anyway," Pet said.

I wasn't sure why I did mind, but the feeling was unmistakable. I wondered if Michael had invited my children to eat with them because he didn't know what to say to his own daughter when they were alone.

What would I have said to mine tonight? And to my son?

I got up. "No problem. We'll go out tomorrow."

"Not me," Nik said, glancing at Channa as if he hoped he was about to impress her. "I'm spending tomorrow night with Brandon because we have a project for school. It's heavy, and his mom said she'd take us in her car."

"I'll probably eat with Jody," Pet said. "We're going to help each other with our pieces for the piano recital next Saturday, and her mom said I could stay until bedtime."

"Busy kids I've got." I waved goodbye.

The house seemed too quiet, even after Nik and Pet came home about eight. They seemed more subdued then normal, maybe because the reality of what was happening next door was deepening. I never *finish* working, but I made it a point to *stop* working about nine to say good-night to them and make sure all was well.

Nik was on the phone when I poked my head into his room, and he waved me away. Pet's light was off and she was already asleep, which surprised me, but I guess she had a tiring day.

I stood in the doorway and watched her sleep, and I wondered just how many bedtimes I had missed.

It was too late to go back to work, and by the look of things Nik wasn't going to be off the phone for some time to come. I wondered if the caller was a girl. I wondered if he would tell me if it was.

Downstairs I realized I had never eaten dinner, and I made a sandwich. There was nothing on television I wanted to see, but there was someone I wanted to talk to.

I took my sandwich out to the garden, lit by softly glowing floodlights. I sat on a bench Robin and I had installed before there was even a garden to enjoy.

"I see things this way," she said the first time we'd sat here. She swept her hand to indicate our wide expanse of grass. "We'll divide the space with hedges and trees. Then we can work on it a little at a time."

I can't remember exactly, but I probably said something like, "I don't think Singer's going to take kindly to me leaving early to turn over sod so we can plant flowers."

"We'll have weekends together, and evenings. I'll do a lot of it, Kris. But can't you just imagine how beautiful it will be someday?"

The garden *was* beautiful. The innate ability for framing

and visualization that made Robin such a talented photographer had been put to use here, too. She called each section a garden room, and the description was perfect. These *were* little rooms, framed by shrubs or pathways of mulch or white stones that looked iridescent in the moonlight. As I sat there I almost expected to see each room come alive with fairy people sitting down to dinner or putting their children to bed.

I set down my plate and pulled out my phone. I smiled a little because Robin never remembers to carry hers. A phone is not the lifeline for her that mine is for me, but these days it's our best hope of connection, and she promised hers would be on and with her every minute.

The phone rang five times, then a recording of her voice began. She wasn't able to answer the call. Yada, yada, yada.

I clicked End without leaving a message and slipped the phone back in my pocket.

What other promises would fall by the wayside before Robin came home again?

15

—

Robin

I work most Saturdays but no arrangements were made for the children. I've taken care of it. K

Really, once the book about this documentary is complete, should I contract for a book of my own? Something with a catchy title like, say, *Love Notes from Angry Husbands*?

When I opened my eyes Sunday morning and picked up my phone I had hoped for something a little more enlightening— or enlightened—than Kris's latest text. Now I set the phone on the bedside table and got up to stretch. Breakfast at the inn is an hour later on weekends, and the rest of the day promised to be busy, so I had slept in.

I was tied in knots and the text wasn't helping. By not hiring a sitter for Saturdays I'd hoped Kris would find ways to work from home. Of course closing himself in his study isn't as good as interacting with the kids, but it might have been a step in the right direction.

Now he'd taken care of it. Well, applause from Pennsylvania, but I wasn't inclined to do anything else. What could I say to him that he'd want to hear?

Cecilia's suite was right next door, and for the first time

I heard Roscoe yap. Superstar or not, Cecilia was Roscoe's new owner. She even had a door to an outside porch to make house-training jaunts easier.

Fresh out of the shower I was just wrapping myself in a terry-cloth robe when someone knocked. Apparently I had forgotten to lock the door, because Cecilia and Roscoe trooped in before the last sound wave died away.

"I should take a photo of you," I said.

"Isn't he adorable?" Cecilia held up Roscoe as if I hadn't already seen him. "The cutest little guy?"

In truth Roscoe isn't cute. He is, at best, pathetic. Two days with the vet took care of fleas, ticks and parasites. He got his first round of shots and a prescription for anti-inflammatories while his leg heals, but he's missing large patches of wiry gray fur, and his eyes are still inflamed. He needs at least two more pounds on his thin little frame, and even the slightest noise sets him trembling. Beyond that, even 100 percent healthy, Roscoe is never going to star in his own television series.

Cecilia was advised to make sure he rested as much as possible and stayed off the sprained leg. I have a feeling Roscoe is going to spend a lot of his new life cradled in her arms.

I watched her cooing to him. Roscoe won the doggy jackpot.

When she looked up I asked, "How's the house-training going?"

"He's a natural. Not a puddle anywhere."

"How many times did you take him out last night?"

She shrugged.

Brow raised, I waited.

"Maybe five, okay? Maybe more."

"We're filming today. You remember that, right?"

"Of course I remember. We filmed yesterday, too."

Not only had we filmed the town yesterday and a slate

dump where the local children used to have rock wars, we'd partied afterward. The men at the American Legion Post got word Cecilia was visiting, and they threw her a surprise party. Her grandfather was a legionnaire, and our whole crew was invited. Mick's enthusiasm for this chunk of genuine local color meant that clips of the party will almost surely make an appearance in the film.

At some point during the evening, as polka music screeched over a vintage sound system, Kris apparently tried to call me. I didn't hear my phone, and he didn't leave a message. Now I figured I'd caught a lucky break. The missing message would have been about Saturday child care and why I hadn't made arrangements. This morning, by the time I realized I'd missed his call, I had already gotten his text.

"There's supposed to be some kind of surprise at the cemetery today," Cecilia said.

"Bigger than the party last night?"

"The biggest surprise last night was that they didn't ask me to sing." She smiled thinking about it. "They were happy to have me there, not just because I'm famous, because I'm Frankie Ceglinski's daughter, and Stan and Cammie Ceglinski's granddaughter. Although, let's face it, nobody mentioned Maribeth."

"Somebody did, actually. To me."

"Do I want to know?"

"I think so. An old woman—and I'm sorry I didn't get her name—said you look like your mother. She said your mother and father were so much in love they married younger than they should have. She knew them from the high school. She worked in the cafeteria."

"Beginning of their junior years. They both quit school. I do know that much."

"She said if things had been different, if your father had

lived and Maribeth's parents hadn't pulled up stakes and disappeared, then Maribeth might have made something of herself. But she said Maribeth was like…" I tried to remember the old woman's surprisingly poetic words. "Like ashes in the wind. Everything good inside her shriveled and died, and after his death she went wherever the wind blew her."

"And thoughtfully took me with her."

"Mine *didn't* take me, remember? That was no better."

"So many ways to screw up a kid. So much time to do it. Eighteen whole years. Who can't make a success of that if they really try?"

My own children came to mind, and I hoped I was doing more things right than wrong.

Cecilia understood what I was thinking from my expression, as she usually does. "Your kids are great. And considering our long history of crazy, we didn't turn out that badly, did we?"

"Look at us. Amazing."

With a spurt of maternal instinct, she cuddled Roscoe closer. "And speaking of your kids, how are they?"

I checked the clock. "I'm going to call. I have just enough time before breakfast."

"Roscoe and I will see you down there. He tells me he likes bacon."

"CeCe, we have another night here. Don't push it with Roscoe, okay?"

She left laughing.

While I knew Kris might answer, I was guessing Pet would be first to the phone. Kris has an extension in his study—where I could see him in my mind's eye—but he usually lets someone else answer the house phone. Work calls go to his cell.

Nik answered on the fourth ring.

"Hey," I said. "I wasn't sure you'd be up this early. Without me right there to drag you out of bed, I mean."

"The Weinbergs are moving. There are, like, two big trucks and lots of people shouting under my window."

I wasn't sorry my son was awake, but I was sorry we were losing Michael and Channa.

I thought about Talya's vanity. "They'll be bringing over a piece of furniture Michael wanted me to have. Will you make sure the guys carry it up to my bedroom? I made a space for it on the wall by the window. I'm going to save it for Channa. I think she'll want it someday."

"Yeah, I guess."

Apparently there's a twelve-year-old boy code that states no enthusiasm is allowed when asked to do a chore, particularly if a parent makes the request.

"I appreciate it. You'll be around?"

"I'm going over to Brandon's tonight." He told me about a project he and his friend had finished for their science class, something about gravitational potential energy, which I understood not a word of, then he launched into a thorough dissection of the middle school athletic program. When Nik gets started thinking out loud, I just sit back and listen. Even long-distance.

He finally came up for air, and I cheered from the sidelines. "You are so busy!"

"Yeah, well, I'm busy at home, too. Miss Elena made me do my laundry yesterday. Like I don't do anything else around here."

"Really?" I tried to sound surprised. "By the way, what *do* you do around there?"

"Answer the phone, for one thing. Even when I shouldn't, like now."

I thought about what he'd told me. "Elena was there yesterday?"

"Well, she won't be again, which is great. Dad's looking for somebody else for evenings and Saturdays."

If Kris tried hard enough, maybe he wouldn't have to be home at all.

Nik, who never likes being lectured, said he was going downstairs to get Pet, and that was the end of our conversation.

While I waited I wondered how a mother teaches a son empathy. Was he absorbing it now, from the good role models in his life, so he could express kinder thoughts when he was more mature and in control of his tongue? Could I change anything long-distance? Wasn't dealing with Elena's relationship with Nik up to Kris now?

Would he give it a single thought?

"Mommy!" Pet came on, clearly delighted to talk to me.

"Hey, sweetie! It's so good to hear your voice."

We chatted for a while, and she told me everything she had done since our last phone call. "And I'm going over to Jody's later so we can practice our duet for the recital next Saturday."

I made a mental note to remind Kris that no matter what else he had to do on Saturday, he had to hear his daughter perform. Missing the recital was not an option.

"Are you practicing at home, too?" I asked. "You can play your piece over the phone for me on Friday."

"Miss Elena says I play pretty."

Score one for Elena, at least with my daughter.

"I cut roses this morning and brought them inside, just like you always do. I set them on the piano, and I put some in Daddy's study, on his desk."

I pictured my little girl—who was quickly outgrowing that description—trying to take my place and found it disturbing.

"If you like cutting roses, that's wonderful. But if it's a lot of trouble, you don't need to." I struggled to find a graceful way to make my point. "You don't have to take my place. You know that, right? You have so many things of your own to do—you don't have to do mine. Does that make sense?"

She lowered her voice so I had to strain to hear her. "I know, but Daddy seems lost. Or mad, or something. I wanted to cheer him up."

Did Kris need cheering or simply more people carrying his load? I couldn't ask my daughter, but I did reassure her. "Daddy will be fine. You don't have to worry about either of us. Things are just a little different and it takes time to adjust."

"I'm glad you're coming home for Thanksgiving. I wish Táta and Maminka were going to be here, too."

Both children use the Czech words for father and mother for their grandparents, since that's what their father calls them. Kris's parents are wonderful with Nik and Pet, demonstrative and casual in a way their son is not. They always come to Virginia for Thanksgiving and go to Lucie's family in Chicago for Christmas. When possible, we all go to Ohio for Easter. Even without my husband.

"We'll miss them," I said.

"Will Aunt Cecilia come this year?"

I was sure Kris would rather have a convicted felon at the table. "We'll see when the date gets closer."

We chatted a little more. Then she asked if I wanted her to get Kris.

"I can hear him talking to somebody," she said, before I could answer. "He's in his study."

"I'm sure whatever he's doing is important. I'll talk to him another time."

We sent pretend hugs and kisses through the phone lines. I

would email Kris later. Something like: *I suppose I could have hired a live-in nanny. Then you could work all the time.*

Or maybe not.

My son is rude and lazy. My daughter is taking the burdens of our family on her fragile little shoulders. What had Cecilia said? So many ways to screw up a kid?

I have a feeling that might be my new mantra.

16

Robin

By now I've caught on that Mick specializes in surprises. After all, what's more interesting on camera, unrehearsed emotion or lines read from a cue card? Nobody understands a documentary filmmaker's thinking better than a photojournalist who looks for that one perfect moment when everything comes together for the subject, when reality and even truth slip out of the photograph and into the hearts of those viewing it.

Of course a lot of so-called television reality shows are scripted, but Mick's films never are. At last night's party he told me he's never sure what he's looking for when he's filming, so he lets the subject and the players guide him. But he does look for opportunities and ways to ratchet up the tension and emotion.

Today, as I stood not far from Jerry and watched my sister at the Miners Memorial Cemetery, I could testify that Mick knows what he's doing.

"I'm a big fan of yours," a woman named Thea Garland was telling Cecilia. "It's been an honor to research your family."

Locals and perhaps gawkers from farther away were already gathering outside the cemetery gate, but sheriff's department personnel and two security guards hired by Mick were keeping them quiet enough. Most of the crew was standing on a hill surrounded by wind-twisted oaks and gravestones, many in sad disrepair. A breeze twirled fallen leaves in festive clusters, but the sun kept us just warm enough. Roscoe hadn't been forgotten, either. Wendy had the puppy in her arms and was standing far enough away that if he barked, he wouldn't disturb filming.

Instead of the puppy, Cecilia was clasping a slender cloth-bound book that Thea, a professional genealogist from Pittsburgh, had created for her. In front of the whole world—or, more realistically, the tiny percentage that would see Mick's documentary—Cecilia was about to go from a pathetic foster child, whose family tree had toppled to the ground decades ago to a woman with deep roots in the soil of Pennsylvania, Ireland and Poland.

"You actually found information worth putting in here?" Cecilia held out the book in question.

Thea was shaped like an apple with a gray ponytail stem at the top of her head. Before handing Cecilia her family history she had explained that she had trained as a genealogist so she could find out more about her own family. Since her ancestors had lived in southwestern Pennsylvania for centuries, the area was her specialty.

"Your family is as interesting as any I've researched," she said. "What do you know about them?"

Jerry, camera cradled at his waist when he moved, was catching every nuance of this conversation on film. He had come earlier with the gaffer to set up what lights he could, and now he was quietly working with the sound tech, too, often with hand signals.

Mick was standing to our left using a smaller camera, which surprised me but shouldn't have, since directors often get their start shooting film. At one point he handed the camera to Fiona and pointed to a cluster of headstones far to the right that he wanted her to film. Yesterday she'd taken one of the larger cameras on a skateboard ride through town, a unique way to get a moving shot. The documentary was turning out to be a family affair. Cecilia and me. Mick and Fiona.

I had snapped a few shots of Cecilia and Thea as we walked up the hill, but I was waiting for something more. I wanted to capture not just their interchange but the intent expressions on surrounding faces, as well. My job is to document the making of the film as well as the way Cecilia's story unfolds. I'm still working on what I know, rather than what I feel, and sometimes I wonder if I'll ever find my rhythm again. Maybe at some point between my roses and the photo booth at the elementary school fair, rhythm floated off to provide the beat for someone more worthy.

Thea was trying to draw out Cecilia. "I know a little of your background. Since you didn't really grow up with your family, you weren't around to hear the stories your grandparents told, or your aunts and uncles. The kinds of stories people repeat at funerals and holiday dinners."

Cecilia isn't shy; she leaves that to me. But neither does she talk about everything. This much she seemed prepared to handle.

"The last time I was in Randolph Furnace I was five. My father was an only child, but I remember an aunt—probably a great-aunt because she was the age of my grandparents, or at least that's how it seemed to a little girl."

"Do you remember her name?"

Cecilia smiled, which brightened my mood because it was genuine. "Anchor. But that must have been a nickname?"

"You're almost right. Anka. It's Polish, and so was your great-aunt Anka Ceglinski, your grandfather's sister. She was named for a distant ancestor of hers and *yours*, Anka Dubicki, born in German-occupied Poland in 1852. Anka Dubicki was your great-great-great-grandmother, among the first of your father's family to move to Pennsylvania."

"Why? What brought them here?"

"Poverty, plain and simple, with a side helping of oppression. They had no rights, no land, no education, and they knew to get any of those things, they had to leave Poland. Moving goods down the Ohio River was big business in this area, so they worked as boatbuilders. They settled on the south side of Pittsburgh with other Polish immigrants. Without a lot more effort I could probably find distant cousins whose families stayed in the area."

Cecilia was imagining this. I know her well enough to recognize her expression. She was putting herself in the shoes of those long-departed family members. That's exactly what she does onstage when she's singing. She becomes the person in her song, the woman who can't find a lover to suit her or the one who's gunning for the poor guy who disappointed her. She's more than a mimic, she's a shape-shifter.

Now her eyes were shining. "So the name Anka has a real history."

"That first Anka's granddaughter, who was the second Anka from your family in Pennsylvania, was born at the turn of the twentieth century and married your great-grandfather. He was a blast furnace operator in a steel mill."

Cecilia made a face. "Boatbuilding sounds easier."

"Getting a job in a mill would have been a slam dunk. Poles were chosen because they were so willing to work. Twelve hour days, seven days a week. When the jobs rotated between shifts every two weeks, the men had to work eighteen to twenty-four hours in a row on the day the change was made."

Cecilia whistled softly, and instinctively I got that shot. I had a feeling I would be glad when I went back over everything tonight in my room.

"Would you like to see your great-aunt Anka's grave?"

I could tell Cecilia was unsure by her expression. Thea was no longer telling stories; she was about to ground this one in reality. Cecilia remembered her great-aunt, if only vaguely.

"Of course," she said, recovering quickly.

They walked a short distance as Thea told her that this third Anka, Cecilia's grandfather's sister, had never married. She had worked most of her life in the miners' store as a bookkeeper, issuing scrip and credit that tied the miners even closer to the town where they worked.

"There's one interesting story I discovered about her," Thea said when she stopped beside a grave. "When Anka was twenty-two she was attacked with an ax. Luckily she managed to fend off her attacker. But the story made the Pittsburgh paper, which was lucky for *me*. That's how I found it."

"Why was she attacked?"

"Apparently she was single but not exactly unloved. The *woman* with the ax happened to be married to the object of Anka's affections."

Cecilia laughed. I caught that moment, too, but she stopped when she gazed at the headstone. She reached down to rub her fingertips along the inscription. "Are my grandparents buried nearby?"

Thea started farther up the hill. "Most of your grandmother's heritage is Polish, but some of her mother's family came to Pennsylvania from Italy."

"Really?"

"You've never craved lasagna for no good reason?"

That drew another welcome laugh. They chatted about the Ceglinskis and those first Rosas, who had been stonemasons in Abruzzi and helped construct arches for bridges used by the Pennsylvania Railroad.

Cecilia was touched by the sight of her grandparents' graves. She couldn't hide it, and maybe she didn't even want to. But I knew she wasn't acting. Another revealing photo. Maybe I was finally catching fire.

"They were good to me," she said. "My life would have been different if I could have stayed here with them."

Mick was no longer filming, but Jerry hadn't missed a word. No matter what else was cut from the film, that would stay. Cecilia kissed her fingertips and gently tapped both her grandmother and grandfather's headstones, simple granite markers placed side by side.

Thea gave her a little time, then she asked, "Before we move on to your mother's family, Cecilia, do you want to visit your father's grave? It's here, if you're ready."

"Of course."

Mick signaled, and the crew moved away. They had set this scene earlier and would take up filming once Thea and Cecilia were standing at her father's graveside.

Mick stayed behind, and I noticed he was holding his camera again. The compact digital SLR looked like an extension of his body.

"I wonder why he wasn't buried here beside my grandparents." Cecilia gestured to what was either an unmarked grave or an empty plot.

Thea looked torn, as if she knew and wasn't sure how to answer.

"Oh..." Cecilia looked down again. "There wasn't room for Maribeth."

"After your father died, your family bought sites over that hill so your mother could be with him when the time came. And at the time, that's the way she said she wanted it."

Cecilia's voice was tight. "Did they buy one for me, too?"

"Your mother probably knew you wouldn't stay in Randolph Furnace long enough to be buried here."

"Or she didn't think about including me."

Thea's nod was noncommittal. "We can only guess what lurks behind decisions made such a long time ago."

"My mother died in Savannah. I imagine she's buried there."

"It shouldn't be hard to find out. There's still a place for her beside your father."

"Not as long as I live there isn't."

Thea didn't look surprised.

Mick captured the exchange. Still filming intently he moved into my line of sight, and I raised my camera and caught him leaning forward, with Cecilia and Thea just beyond him. Another photo I might be glad to have.

Cecilia and Thea started up and over the hill, and Mick waited to walk with me. He was dressed in jeans and a beat-up denim jacket, and he looked as if he'd sprung from the ground. He was careful never to become part of the story.

"She's amazing," he said. "Thea, of course, but I mean Cecilia."

"I've always thought so."

"You were nine when you met?"

"And she was a month from turning thirteen. It was a therapeutic foster home. We were both a mess."

"I'm guessing the one thing you could hold on to was each other."

He was encouraging me to talk, and I didn't mind. Mick was comfortable to be with, understanding and unafraid of emotion, unlike the man I'm married to. I was struck by how appealing an attractive man who wants to talk about my feelings can be.

"We were lucky," I said. "Siblings, real biological siblings, aren't always able to live in the same foster home because there isn't enough room, or the age difference is a problem. The fact that our caseworker kept us together when we were moved, even without blood ties, is something of a miracle."

"Today's the easy day. You know that, right? Whatever we get here will be shown later in the film. But we wanted to start shooting with something happier, something to help Cecilia feel she does have roots, before we start exposing how much went wrong in her childhood."

There weren't many happy chapters in Cecilia's childhood and adolescence, but she was known here. Not simply because of her superstar status, but because she was a citizen of this town. And maybe it was just a fading coal patch, but a part of her belonged here and with the distant family she would likely never meet.

I stopped walking, and he stopped, too, lifting one brow in question. I decided to be blunt. "You recorded what she said about not allowing her mother's body to lie beside her father's. Was that wise? Won't that make her seem unsympathetic?"

"Her anger is understandable, don't you think?"

"Of course. But will the audience think so, too?"

"Do they need to? Do *you* need them to?"

And there it was. One of the many times my attachment to my sister might color my judgment.

Mick didn't wait for me to acknowledge what was obviously true. "But yes, they *will* understand. Because we'll take them to the place where her mother abandoned her, so they can imagine that scene. And we've already talked to a former social worker who still remembers Maribeth Ceglinski, even tried to help her and couldn't. This isn't a documentary about happy endings, Robin, although we'll try to find bright spots."

"Like this one."

He moved a little closer. "What about you? Were there bright spots?"

I held up my new Canon, encased in a sound blimp that mostly silenced the clicking of my shutter so it wouldn't be heard on film. The camera and the new Sigma lens I'd gotten were quickly becoming old friends.

"Cameras were my bright spot."

"You have no living family?"

"I probably have a mother somewhere, unless she followed in Maribeth's footsteps."

"You've never searched?"

People rarely understand this, but my mother takes up no real estate in my heart. I don't remember *her*, but I do remember that she left me in the care of her own mother, knowing, even as the teenager she was, that Olive would try to destroy me.

I tried to put the story into words Mick would understand. "She gave me to her mother to raise, like a fairy-tale sacrifice to an evil witch. And if that sounds overwrought, believe me, it's not. I do understand why she left, though, so my gift to Alice Swanson, who reluctantly gave birth to me, is to leave her alone. That way I can pretend she misses me and wishes she could make up for what she put me through. Truthfully, all these years later she probably still wakes up every morning delighted that she had the courage to start a different life."

His expression was sympathetic but not pitying. "And you ended up in foster care."

"I hope you report some of the happy foster-care stories, Mick. There are so many selfless, overworked and underpaid foster families who do what they do because they love kids and for no other reason. Not all my placements were good. You'll see the worst up close when we get to Florida, but I was so much better off in care than I ever would have been with my grandmother. This may sound crass and unfeeling, but my future turned brighter the moment she died. Even though I was suddenly at the mercy of strangers."

He was silent. I thought I'd offended him, but when he glanced at me, I saw he looked pleased. "I think you may just have titled the film, Robin. *At the Mercy of Strangers*. I like it."

"Glad to help." Our gazes held.

He spoke after a moment, and he didn't look away. "I'm happy you took this on. I sense it's not easy on a personal level. You have a husband and family, and exploring this subject is going to bring your own share of pain. No matter what, though, you're going to be a huge asset. I like to give the people who work with me as much autonomy as they can handle, but I hope we'll work off each other's talents. I can use your help, and I may be able to help you."

"You did already." He cocked his head in question, and I explained. "That moment in the airport when I had to grad-uate from Cecilia's sister to professional photographer. You nudged me from one to the other."

"I'll continue to nudge, but you nudge, too. We'll be a team."

I was suddenly all too aware I was experiencing the symp-toms of an adolescent crush. My heart was pounding too fast and my hands were unsteady. I was standing just a little too close to a man I had looked up to for years, a man I had never expected to meet, much less work with. On top of that, Mick was so much more than I had imagined. Warmer. Less apt to insist on having things his own way. And definitely more attractive, despite the years between us.

I thought about Kris, who in all our years together had never quite understood why my past turned me into the woman I am. And here was Mick, almost a stranger, who seemed to understand it perfectly.

"We'll be a team," I said, and silently promised myself I could and would keep our relationship professional. I would not let the problems Kris and I were going through affect the way I viewed Mick.

"Let's go see what else Thea has for Cecilia." Mick started back up the path, and a heartbeat later, I followed, determined to listen carefully to my own words.

17

Cecilia

Roscoe and I like this inn, and we'll be sorry to fly back to California tomorrow. So tonight we decided to take a sunset walk to say goodbye. Alone, without the trusty Hal, who likes to shadow me everywhere I go. I wouldn't be too surprised to learn he's following me with binoculars from a window.

Maybe some deeply buried part of me remembers the western Pennsylvania countryside and knows I've come home. At night here the air smells green and new in a way that feels familiar, even when it's tinged with wood smoke from the fireplace in the inn's keeping room.

No place I live smells quite like this. I'm sure, of course, that when the mines were operating nobody came to this part of the state on a pleasure jaunt. But I think I've discovered why Frank Lloyd Wright built Fallingwater to the east. The family that engaged him must have believed this tiny speck on the map deserved more than smoke from steel mills and the destruction that comes from mining. It deserved a masterpiece built over a waterfall.

When Roscoe finally yipped to get down I set him on the ground between the two rows of sunflowers where we were taking our stroll. Twilight was deepening, and a nearly full moon was peeking over rows of tall trees on the horizon. Robin was inside, on the phone with her children, and some of the crew were sitting by the fireplace dissecting everything they had done today. Mick had been on the telephone for most of the evening, insisting we need another camera operator, and Jerry and Fiona were out shooting B roll of Randolph Furnace at night.

I miss Donny, who had an emergency with a country singer he just agreed to represent and flew out of Pittsburgh this morning. There's no reason he needed to hold my hand through the filming today, but I wish he could have been at the cemetery when Thea helped me figure out who I was and am.

Roscoe growled, and what fur he has at the back of his neck rose like the spikes of a stegosaurus. He began to bark, a shrill shuddering screech that's guaranteed to make every bad guy for a hundred miles wince in pain.

I turned to see what had disturbed him and glimpsed a figure ambling through the half-light along the row behind me. I had expected to find Hal was the intruder, but Donny and I have been together so long I recognize even his shadow.

"How'd you do that?" I called. "Pittsburgh to Nashville and back in one day?"

"Got there and the guy was so coked up he threatened to fire me if I didn't fix his nonexistent problem immediately. So I told him to fire away and caught the next plane back."

I despise drugs because of what they did to Maribeth, as well as to my first manager, a brilliant man who died of a heroin overdose just as my career began its rise. Donny despises drugs because at heart he's a solid Midwestern guy who doesn't believe in flushing talent or money down the toilet, and for someone in his profession, he's surprisingly and blessedly intolerant of bad behavior.

Donny doesn't need more clients. I've asked him not to take on anyone else, but he doesn't have to listen, something he lets me know from time to time. He still represents the occasional talented newcomer, although he has an associate who does most of that work. Donny himself only shows up when things fall apart or take off big-time.

Roscoe and I waited as he caught up. "Was this your *American Idol* finalist?"

"The very same. And after today I know for sure why he didn't win. He's not famous enough to be a brat."

"Hey, I'm famous, and I'm not a brat."

"Debatable, but here's the genuine article." He stooped and scooped up Roscoe who had stopped yipping and taken to sniffing the cuff of his trousers. "How's the little guy doing?"

"Settling in. Why don't I let him stay in your room tonight, and you'll see how well and frequently he announces his need to go outside."

"Your dog, darlin'."

I hated to admit it, but I was glad Donny was back.

He rose, Roscoe draped comfortably over one arm. "May I carry your puppy, ma'am, and accompany you back to the inn?"

"Don't tell me Hal sicced you on me?"

"I was told you needed an escort. And I don't think Mick trusts you not to run back to the Evergreen to see what other wildlife you can pick up in the parking lot."

"Walk a little farther. Then I'll turn around. Mick knows you won't let me do anything stupid. I'm too valuable."

"That you are."

We walked side by side, comfortable in silence for a minute until he spoke. "Okay, I'll ask since you haven't volunteered. What happened today? Start at the beginning."

He could easily have met me in California tomorrow or

the next day, when we'll be talking to the executive team at Cyclonic about my new album. Instead he had come back to check on me. Donny thinks I'm fragile, and he may be right.

"As my manager or friend?" I asked.

"Your friendly manager. Emphasis on friendly."

"It was…" I cleared my throat. "No adjectives available." I told him about Thea and what I'd learned about the Ceglinskis. "After that we went to my father's grave. The crew stepped back and let me be there alone with him for a minute or two."

"I hope you told him about your life. I always update my grandmother when I visit her ashes." He didn't sound as if he were teasing.

"No time for that. I just told him I would be back."

"And will you be?"

"This was a good stop, Donny." I cleared my throat again. More silence. I think he knew I was gathering composure.

I finished when I was ready. "My mother's family was interesting. It seems I might be descended from revolutionaries."

"That surprises me not at all."

"Do you know who the Molly Maguires were?"

"Something to do with mines and mine owners and strikes? Are you descended from the ones who fought the good fight and then got out of town before they dangled from a rope?"

"Thea thinks maybe I am. If it's true I'm not sure whether I should be proud or sorry they ran. I do know I'm not as unhappy with my Malone grandparents as I used to be, and not because of the Mollies. After Maribeth dumped me, no official could locate them. It turns out they went west. A former neighbor who Thea tracked down remembers that after my father died, my grandparents heard there were jobs in California, so they went ahead, hoping to settle there and send for Maribeth and me once things stabilized. But they never made it. Their truck ran off a bridge in Missouri. It was years before they were identified. Thea found an old newspaper article online. And, of course, by then there was nobody left in Randolph Furnace to notify."

"Wow." Donny made the word last for several syllables. "Some saga. Very Steinbeck."

"Donny, something else…"

"All ears."

He was, too. I knew he was listening.

"While we were filming today a crowd gathered by the cemetery gate. Or at least a crowd by Randolph Furnace standards. Anyway? Those American Legion guys from the party? They got together again, made calls, twisted arms. And after we were done for the day the sheriff let a few men through. They presented me with a notebook filled with old photos people found in their attics and notes about my family. Personal accounts. You know? Like the time my grandfather Malone beat up a guy in the local bar for talking trash in front of a woman. And the time Grandmother Ceglinski dragged three dogs out of a burning house."

I was still trying to process this. People often do nice things for me because I'm a star. I get gifts whether I want them or not, usually with strings attached. But nobody here gained anything but goodwill by rummaging through their attics. For the first time in my life I had photos of some of my family, including a faded but still discernible photo of my father as a young teen.

"You come from scrappers," he said. "And a nice little town, to boot. Rough around the edges, but lots of heart."

"Roscoe liked the story about the dogs."

"You're okay?"

"I sang for them. The group kept growing, and pretty soon it was a real audience. After I got the notebook I asked the sheriff's men to let everyone come in, although Mick was wary. Somebody had brought a guitar. They came up the hill. I rested my leg against my—" I cleared my throat, hopefully for the last time "—my father's tombstone, and I gave them a concert. When I was finished, the cheers were like nothing I've ever heard."

He put his arm around my shoulders and pulled me against his side. "Your father was listening, too."

My eyes were filling with tears. "You don't believe that, and neither do I."

"Of course I do. And so do you. Stop being a brave girl and just be happy, okay?"

I liked the way he felt against me, and quite honestly I can't often say that about a man. But he wasn't issuing demands. Just a friend indeed for the friend in need.

"I'm not paying you even a dime more, Donny. No matter how nice you are to me."

"But *somebody* has to make up for what I lost with the *American Idol* guy."

"It won't be me."

He kissed my cheek before he stepped away. "Time to turn around?"

"I like it out here. I wonder if the owners would like to sell this place?"

"You won't find home by buying every piece of property that appeals to you, Cecilia."

"I found a little piece today, though, didn't I?"

"That you did."

"I'll come back and visit."

He handed me Roscoe, then he squeezed my hand. "No matter where we come from? That's all any of us can ever do."

18

—

Robin

Sorry I missed your call yesterday. You've been gone four days. Feels longer. Kids were busy for dinner last night when I wasn't. We need an events coordinator. K

Monday afternoon in my new hotel room in Jamestown, New York, I read Kris's latest—and slightly friendlier—text and wondered if he was beginning to see the shape of things to come. We've reached a point where we need to accommodate ourselves to our children's schedules and not vice versa. Not always, of course, but often enough that they realize how much they matter.

Another, less positive, interpretation of the text? I was missed because somebody needed to be there to keep things organized. I needed to go back home and take over.

Not going to happen.

After our early arrival in western New York, the remainder of my morning was spent at an oval table in the parlor while the crew discussed what was next and what responsibilities each person would take to prepare for Cecilia's arrival on Thursday. We've been housed in a 1930s home built of handmade Belgian brick by a local architect. The vintage beauty, now a bed-and-breakfast hotel, has seen several incarnations and renovations, but much of the former glory is intact. I love my little room with its cozy sitting nook.

Now a late-afternoon rain was falling steadily outside my window, a familiar sight in this part of the world until it turns to snow. Luckily for us, snow isn't forecast today but might be later if temperatures continue to drop.

On the drive north Starla told me that Jamestown was once a thriving city, home to furniture manufacturing, textiles and metalworking, but like much of the North it fell on hard times as jobs and workers moved south. Oddly the halt of expansion seems to have spared many of the gracefully historic buildings, and now even the abandoned brick factories have a charm I found compelling as we drove past on our journey from Uniontown.

At the moment I'm torn between a nap and doing more editing of the photos I've already taken. More time with my camera isn't an option. I have hours between now and Cecilia's arrival to prowl the streets of this city where she was a temporary resident, looking for more evocative scenes to photograph. But since I've already deleted most of what I've taken, I'm not at all sure I would know evocative if it stood in my path, rested its head on my shoulder and wept. Mick asked to see what I've done so far and I reluctantly handed him a flash drive with my best photos, but I'm not hopeful he'll see more in them than I did.

Someone knocked on my door and, glad to stretch, I got up to answer. Mick, in faded denim and a heavy waterproof parka, was shifting his weight from foot to foot in my doorway.

"You busy?"

I shook my head.

"Let's take a drive."

I'm no sissy, but at this point the rain was coming down in sheets. "Right now?"

"It's supposed to slack off pretty soon. I've got my camera. You get yours."

I wasn't going to refuse. The great Mick Bollard was asking me to come along on a photo shoot. I would have followed him into the depths of hell.

I dragged a smile into place. "I'll meet you downstairs."

He disappeared down the hall.

Five minutes later I joined him near the hotel entrance with my camera bag. I brought two folding umbrellas, one large enough to shelter me and another for my camera—which also has its own rain jacket. I opened the first and followed Mick outside to one of the vans that had carried us here, climbing into the passenger seat. Apparently no one else was invited.

I buckled up. "Where's Fiona?"

"Writing a paper on the Austro-Hungarian Empire for a professor at Stanford who graciously agreed to oversee her world history education. She's behind." He smiled, as if silently reminiscing. "My fault. She could have stayed in California with her mother and easily finished, but I wanted her with me on this trip."

"You two are very close."

"Fifi keeps me sane."

"Most teenagers drive their parents *in*sane."

Mick pulled out to the street. "Speaking from experience?"

"My two aren't quite there. But I doubt they'll weather the hormone storm as well as Fiona has."

"I stayed with my wife for years longer than I should have because of Fifi. Divorce is hard on children. I didn't want to cause her any pain. When it became clear staying was going to cause even more, both her mother and I decided we would give her as much or more time separately than we could have when we were together."

"Is more time part of the reason she's not in school?"

"A big part."

We started down a side street that almost passed for a creek. I listened to the swish of wipers across the windshield, the sloshing of tires. If the rain was supposed to diminish, it wasn't following orders.

"I looked at your photos," Mick said.

I saved him the search for a polite comment. "I don't like most of them. A couple are acceptable, if surrounded by better ones."

"Good, then. Because I was about to break that piece of news myself."

"I know." And I did. I explained my lack of ego, so he would understand. "I don't need false praise or kid gloves. I really am a pro, although I didn't give you much on that flash drive that proved it."

"So what's the problem? Because I've seen your previous work. Otherwise you wouldn't be here no matter how badly your sister wanted you."

"You would go head-to-head with Cecilia over me? You're a brave, brave man."

"She's not nearly as strong as she pretends. But let's not make this about her. Let's make it about you."

I was so unused to making *anything* about me, this threw me a moment. "If I understood the problem, I could probably do something about it. I keep hoping I just need to find my groove again, that I've been away from this kind of work so long it'll take a week or so to fall back into it."

"Are you coming closer?"

"I think so. But close enough? Not nearly."

"Is your sister the problem?"

"I just don't seem to be able to judge a good shot until it's too late to take advantage of it. And, of course, that makes no sense. Maybe when I was shooting film and every click had to count, it did. But these days I can take a hundred shots and discard every one without anyone questioning my judgment."

"The camera has to become part of you. Right now it's a novelty, something entirely disconnected."

He was right, but that wasn't news. "The time span between 'maybe this will be a good photo' to 'yes, it will, now how will I best shoot it?' and the eventual click of the camera? That's exactly how long it takes to ruin a shot."

"Figuring that out is part of the solution."

"But it's *figuring*. And the head that figured that out *is* part of the problem. I can't figure out a good photograph and still have enough time to take it. Remnants, yes. Leftovers. Not the shot I wanted and missed."

"That's why we're here today. It's a terrible day to be outside with a camera. You aren't going to get any good photos, and I'm not going to get any good footage. So we're going to relax and enjoy the challenge. Nothing we do matters. If we luck into something? A miracle. Not our doing."

I doubted this would help. I would still miss opportunities, too busy framing shots and figuring the best perspective. Above? Below? Dead-on? My brain refused to disconnect.

"This will help," Mick said, as if I'd spoken my concerns out loud. He pulled over and parked. Ahead of us was a multistory building, tumbling to the ground in a cascade of brick. Vines had overtaken parts of it. In high summer the vines, maybe poison ivy or creeper, would soften or hide the decay. Now, with winter fast approaching and leaves gone, they outlined the problem, as if they were holding the bricks together in one final spurt of defiance.

I squinted through the rain for a better view. "How did you know to come here?"

"I asked at the hotel. They're a wealth of knowledge. To-morrow when you go out alone they'll help you find anything you want."

I hope by tomorrow I'll know what to ask.

He turned in his seat to face me. "Here's what you've forgotten. Photography is like sex, Robin. You can think it to death, or you can let your heart and your body guide you and leave your head out of it. It's instinctual, with a flow all its own, and you can't guide it or harness it. You just have to let go and let it be. That's what your sister does when she sings. Music is like sex to Cecilia. She loses herself inside it, which is why she's such a star. You used to lose yourself in photography, but you've forgotten how. So today we're going to help you find that gift again."

"Sex?"

He laughed, and his dark eyes lit and held mine. "I won't go any further with my analogy unless you make me."

"Very little chance of that."

"Zip up. Have you shot in this kind of rain before?"

I was still processing his lecture and incapable of sifting back through my history to previous photo shoots. "Not like this," was the best I could manage.

"Than I'll play teacher. Make use of reflections if you can so the rain is more obvious. If you can adjust your flash for just the slightest burst of light, that may give you some interesting effects. Find light behind the rain but don't let it overpower your shot. You with me?"

These were all things I knew, but now I could feel my excitement building. Knowing and doing are entirely different.

Like sex.

I laughed softly; he smiled in appreciation. Then I bent

down to open my case. "After that lecture I'm going to feel strangely vulnerable if I pull out my biggest lens," I said.

"It's never size, always prowess."

"Spoken like every man in the universe."

This time *he* laughed. A moment later we were out in the storm together, smiling, both of us, still.

19
—

Kris

Pet's fall piano recital is at three this afternoon, and yesterday I made absolutely certain to clear my schedule. Robin warned me I had to deliver our daughter ahead of time for the rehearsal and not waltz in when she was about to perform. To show Pet my support I was to sit through the entire concert, preschoolers punching out two-fingered "Twinkle, Twinkles" and high school prodigies trilling mind-numbing Mozart sonatas. I know this matters to my daughter. The fact that Robin will check to be sure I made the recital in time is immaterial.

Grace was happy to babysit Friday evening, so last night I stayed at work until late, finishing what I could. Pet was asleep by the time I got home, but Grace said the evening went well, and she'd listened as my daughter played her solo, the Bach "Invention in C Major," over the telephone for Robin. Last year Pet told me that she particularly likes Bach for his crisp symmetry and careful construction. Maybe the words are Miss Cartwright's, her piano teacher, but I was impressed enough to remember them.

I'm stupidly proud that I found and hired Grace, even though, let's face it, that's the kind of job any father should be able to do. Still, my choice was good. Grace is never late when I need her, and the house looks just as clean when I return as it did when I left. Even Nik says she's okay, which is as good as saying she may be his first adolescent crush. Grace is easy on a preteen's eyes, and her twin, Gil, a good-looking kid in a broody, Eminem sort of way, ensures Grace's popularity with their female classmates.

Parenting is not a competition, but for once I'm glad I'll be the parent who actually showed up. I'm beginning to think I need to score a few points with my daughter, who never seems to be available when I am. I don't worry as much about Nik. My son is a complete mystery, and for all I know, showing up in his life between now and college graduation might ruin what's left of our relationship.

This morning I spoke at a men's club breakfast, one of those public relations events that might bring our firm more clients. Grace arrived right on time, and I left Pet a note promising I would be home to take her to the assisted-living facility where the recital is to be held. Miss Cartwright is a fan of captive audiences. Between students' families and residents, Pet would be performing for a crowd.

My daughter is not an inspired pianist, but she practices with enthusiasm and carefully follows direction, so she's easy to listen to. Pet probably won't be courted for Juilliard, but her enthusiasm for decorating the world means the Rhode Island School of Design might come calling.

I arrived home just ten minutes after I'd said I would—and in plenty of time to get her to the recital—to find the house empty. Pet had scrawled a few lines under my note on the counter.

I don't want to be late. Grace is taking me to her house so I can go with Jody. Nik is at Brandon's.

I may not spend enough time with my daughter, but I know Pet well enough to understand what she was really saying in those short sentences.

Dear Dad. You're a failure. You can't be counted on, not even on a day like this one that I've practiced and practiced for. Sure, you said you'd come home in time, but when have you actually made it? I didn't see you at all yesterday, so all I have is this stupid note. Anybody can write a note. Anybody can say they're going to do something and then find something more important to do instead. So I've taken matters into my own hands. Miss Cartwright is making a recording of our recital. You can listen to it the next time you drive to work and not even bother coming to see me in person.

Well, okay, that was laying it on a bit thick, but recrimination did ring through every word on the crumpled paper in my hand.

I don't need Robin pointing an accusing finger to know I'm failing at fatherhood. I was glad I had the rest of the day to make this up to Pet. I didn't need to be at the retirement home immediately, since the actual recital didn't begin for another hour. But I did know something I could do to let Pet know the recital was a special event.

I found the list Robin had left and zeroed in on Brandon's number. He's a relatively new friend, and when Brandon's mother answered I couldn't picture mother or son, but I introduced myself before asking to speak to Nik.

"Yeah?" he said when he answered.

"That would be 'Hello, this is Nik,'" I said.

"Hello, this is Nik," he repeated back in a singsong voice.

"Hello, this is your father, and I'll be by to pick you up in fifteen minutes to go to your sister's piano recital. You've had lunch?"

"I'm not going."

"Of course you are. How many soccer games has she sat through for you?"

"I've sat through her games, too."

"Nobody's keeping score. You will do this. What are you wearing?"

"Clothes."

"I am not happy with this conversation."

Maybe there was something in my voice that alerted him I meant it. Whatever the reason, his tone changed. "I look okay," he said after a long pause, as if he'd just glanced down to check.

"I hope that's true. I'll come inside to thank Brandon's mother. Be ready."

"I hate piano recitals."

"You won't be the first or last person to say that. But you do love your sister."

"That sounds like something Mom would say."

I hung up and realized I was smiling. I had channeled my inner Robin. It actually felt good.

My daughter is a star. Before taking her seat on the piano bench Pet walked to the front of the stage and bowed. Then, settled at the piano, she played the "Invention" without significant mistakes and remained composed throughout.

Her flair for decoration extends to fashion. She wore shiny black shoes and carried a matching purse onstage to set beside her on the bench, as if to say no outfit was complete without one. The dress was new to me, but she looked adorable, swathed in royal blue with a frilly hem so short it made me wonder if she was trying to pull one over on me again. Then I noted that every girl in the recital was wearing one equally as short.

I apparently have a lot to learn about not-so-little girls.

As a finale she and Jody performed a Scott Joplin duet that received a standing ovation. Of course it's entirely possible the seniors and families were just tired of sitting and more than ready to leave.

Afterward we celebrated her accomplishment at a nearby restaurant that specialized in gourmet hamburgers and a French fry bar. Who knew there were so many unhealthy options for smothering French fries?

"I hope you're happy," Nik told her as we drove home. "Brandon's mom rented the first two Jurassic Parks for us to watch today."

"You can see movies anytime. You don't always get to see a virtuoso."

He made a gagging noise.

"It's still early," I said. "Why don't we rent a movie on cable and watch it together?"

"Not *Jurassic World*," Pet said.

Nik gagged again. "Like I'd watch that with *you*. You'd squeal through the whole thing."

"Wait until we get home and we'll see what's available." I punctuated that by pulling into the parking lot of our local grocery store and turning off the engine. "Ice-cream sundaes okay with you? Pet chooses the ice cream, Nik chooses the toppings." I paused. "Or you can consult each other and compromise."

By the time we got home we had two cartons of ice cream—I'd added Rocky Road after they chose Bubble Yum. By the time the final Harry Potter movie, which they'd already seen twice, was finished, the sundaes were memories and my children looked the way they had years ago, when I had to carry them upstairs and tuck them into bed because they were too exhausted to make the trip on their own.

"Great night," I said, flicking off the television. "And late.

You guys go on up and I'll come up to say good-night in a few minutes."

Pet, who had moved ever closer to me on the sofa until she had finally cuddled up with my arm around her, roused herself to stand. Nik was already on his feet.

"I don't need to be tucked in," he said, his voice squeaking on the last word.

"Of course you don't."

"Just so you know." He trudged up the steps, and Pet watched him go.

"Thank you for coming and all."

"I wouldn't have missed it. But for the record, I was home in plenty of time to get you there for the rehearsal."

"I just didn't want to take a chance."

"I know." I stood and hugged her. "Now scoot, okay?" I turned her toward the stairs.

"I think my blue nightgown got washed. My other one's dirty now. I need to get it."

I did know that Elena folded their laundry when it came out of the dryer but left it in the laundry room for them to find and put away. Apparently Pet hadn't gotten to hers yesterday. "I'll get it. You brush your teeth. I'll bring it up in a minute."

"Thanks, Daddy." She kissed my cheek and left.

I've won battles in the courtroom, so I recognized my feelings as I watched her trudge up the stairs. Tonight I'd turned the tide with my children, though I didn't know for how long. We'd had fun. I didn't want to think about the last time I'd been able to say that.

It's odd for anyone to look forward to visiting their laundry room, so I won't go that far. But ours is a good place to drop in from time to time. Robin worked her usual magic here. The walls are a serene gray-green with framed photos of our garden on the walls, and the shelves and cabinets are painted the muted pink of her favorite roses. A hand-lettered sign says Laundry Schedule, and the list ends with Iron: Ha, Ha, Ha! Despite that, there's an ironing board above the dryer that flips down from the wall, and Robin has been known to iron my shirts.

Have I ever really appreciated that a talented photographer was spending her days decorating laundry rooms and ironing shirts without complaint? I usually thanked her when she ironed for me, but at what point had I begun to see those things as her job, even her duty? At what point had I assumed that what I wanted was exactly right for everyone in our family?

Some days I wasn't even sure it was right for me.

Pet's short stack of laundry was neatly folded on a dark green table along one wall. I scooped it up, along with a tall pile of Nik's. I wondered what he was wearing to school these days since almost everything he owned was right here.

I turned off the light and started back through the house to the stairs, arms piled high. Nik was on the phone, so I stacked his laundry on the top of his dresser and ran a finger across my throat to tell him to cut the call short.

I could hear Pet brushing her teeth in the bathroom, so I went into her room uninvited. My daughter's room is almost compulsively neat and everything is so perfectly arranged that dropping even a few shirts on her dresser seemed like sacrilege. I lifted her nightgown from the top of the stack and set it on her bed. Then I opened her middle drawer to set the T-shirts inside. The drawer was already crowded, and I moved a few things to one side to make room.

I stared, for just a moment not quite making sense of what I saw. On the bottom of the drawer, where the shirts had first hidden it, was a clear plastic bag cinched with a rubber band,

and unless my daughter has just taken up Italian cooking, I was pretty sure I knew what was inside.

I was sitting on her bed, the bag resting in the palm of my outstretched hand, when Pet came in from the bathroom. She took one look at the expression on my face and the bag in my hand, and began to cry.

20

—

Cecilia

"I Will Survive" could be my theme song, only I didn't write it, never recorded it and I'm not partial to disco. I was only four when the song topped the charts, and while it would have made a peppy choice for my short-lived barroom Shirley Temple act, Maribeth probably figured that lyrics about rotten men and take-charge women weren't going to go over well with my audience. Not even as a joke.

I do think of my mother, though, whenever I hear Gloria Gaynor belting out those lyrics. Because several years after the song skyrocketed to glory, "I Will Survive" became my personal mantra. By then I had decided that surviving my chaotic childhood would be plenty good enough, at least until I was an adult and able to manage my own life. That's what I must have thought on the day the good people from Children and Family Services here in Jamestown, New York, decreed that singing in bars to support my mother's drinking habit wasn't likely to have a happy outcome.

Of course, considering how I turned out and what I do? Who knows?

Mick Bollard really is brilliant. He filmed the scene of me walking into the Chelsea Lounge and sitting down at the bar to tell my story four times before the content, lighting and sound met his standards. But every single time he and Starla used a different lead-in to get me started, so I wouldn't be parroting things I'd said during the last take. Since I mentioned the song and my personal attachment to it every time, I'm certain that when and if this segment appears on the screen, Gloria will be singing away in the background.

"You okay?" As the film crew packed, Donny came up behind me and dropped my favorite hoodie over my shoulders. I hadn't even noticed I was beginning to shiver.

I slipped my arms into the sleeves. Robin gave me this hoodie. It's hand knit of cashmere and mohair in an unusual shade of golden-brown that she knew would look good on me. She realizes I have more money than any person is entitled to, but that's never stopped her from buying me thoughtful gifts at boutiques and craft fairs.

"This hasn't been fun," I admitted.

"I can imagine, but we're done now. In fact Mick just told me we're probably done in Jamestown for good. He'll send Jerry back to get scenes of your foster home when there's snow on the ground, but you won't need to be here."

There *had* been snow on the ground the day I was dragged from my mother's loving arms, or what passed for them, and placed in foster care for the first time. I remember being so cold my skin was turning blue. I had left my coat in some bar or strange man's apartment, and Maribeth had never gone back for it. I remember being taken by a faceless social worker to an old house with a blazing fire in a stone fireplace. Someone settled me in front of it with an afghan tucked around me and brought me hot cocoa. At some point I learned that I would be staying with these strangers because I had no family to take me in. My grandfather had died, and my grandmother was too ill to care for me.

Funny the things you remember.

The couple who served that hot cocoa, and later bought me a coat and boots, are in their sixties now and reside in Canada. They've agreed to be interviewed, but I won't need to be there. I was with them for six months, but I don't remember them, and frankly, I doubt they really remember me. Mick tells me that fifty-three children passed through the doors of that old house, often for the briefest of stays. They sent him a snapshot of a drawing I'd made, preserved all these years in one of their scrapbooks, and the drawing is more enlightening than their foggy memories.

I was in first grade. I drew a table overflowing with food and a little girl gazing at it from the sidelines. More or less. That's what Mick thinks it looks like, anyway.

I never could draw. Still can't.

Donny was searching my face the way he does when he wants to see how I'll react to something he's about to say. "There's a woman here from the *Times*. Mick would like you to talk to her about what you hope to accomplish by helping with this film. Are you willing?"

On the East Coast the *Times* means the *New York Times*, not to be ignored or dissed. "Right now?"

He inclined his head toward a group of people who were sitting along the bar and at the few tables scattered around the floor to make the scene look real. Most of them were friends of the hotel proprietor or connections of Mick's. Apparently Donny had slipped the *Times* reporter into the mix. "She just wants to meet you today and set up an interview for later."

"I can do that."

Robin had been photographing the bar by kneeling on a stool and leaning over it for a fresh perspective. Now she headed my way. Since I returned from California she seems more comfortable with her job and happier doing it. Mick seems more comfortable working with her, too. She told me that one day they went out in the rain together to shoot old factories. Whatever they did, it's working.

"You were great," she said. I could tell she believed it, because Robin is not an accomplished liar. I always know when she's not telling the truth. On the other hand, she's not exactly objective.

I was trying to think of a reply when she cocked her head to examine me. "This is harder than you thought, isn't it?"

I managed a smile-on-wry with an extra slice of ham. I'm good at ham.

Donny reappeared with a middle-aged woman with unnaturally black hair pulled into a low ponytail, and bright red lipstick.

"Zilla Atkins," she said, extending her hand. "Thanks for letting me sit in today."

I didn't explain I hadn't known. I was pretty sure that was old news to her. "Zilla, this is my sister, Robin," I said. They shook hands.

"I didn't know you had a sister. How did I miss that?"

"We're foster sisters," Robin said.

Zilla dropped Robin's hand as if disappointed. "Not real ones."

I took over, an edge to my voice. "As real as it gets."

"I'm sorry." Zilla knew she needed to get on my good side to interview me, even if she did write for the *Times*. "I just meant you're not *biologically* related."

"Joined at the hip and the heart," Robin said. "Best kind of biological."

Zilla scrunched her face like someone doing hand-to-hand combat with boredom and turned back to me. "I'll look forward to hearing more. You'll have time to talk?"

"Donny can set that up. He has what passes for our schedule."

Donny, who had remained silent, touched her arm to lead her away.

"I get tired of that, don't you?" Robin said when they were out of earshot. "Maybe after the film debuts people will realize there are all kinds of sisters."

"I liked that 'joined at the hip and the heart' comeback."

Donny returned without Zilla, who was gathering her things to leave. "I think the two of you need to go somewhere alone tonight. No crew. No conversation you're too tired to have. You can sit and stare at each other if you can't think of anything to say. Starla or I will take the pup."

"I'm not sure we can be alone anywhere," Robin said, "now that Cecilia's been discovered."

My presence in Jamestown hadn't remained secret for long. Anticipating this, Donny and Mick had hired security for the hotel, and Hal was my constant companion. Hal's been with me awhile, and he's good, but sometimes too good. He even checks the bathroom before I use it, although there's not a lot of room behind the toilet for paparazzi.

"I have that part covered." Donny outlined a plan worthy of the CIA. I love a man who can lie and cheat without blinking an eye. I guess I *am* my mother's daughter.

"I'd rather just carry a gun," I said, once he finished. Robin's eyes widened. She thinks I'm kidding, but I know for a fact I could use one if I had to.

"Self-defense only," I promised. "But I once came within inches of smashing a rowdy fan over the head with my guitar." I was immediately sorry I had brought that image to mind.

Donny, unlike my sister, didn't seem surprised. "No guns *or* guitars. But this plan should work without either. I have to take care of my girl."

My smile inched toward something more genuine. I'm not Donny's girl, but it *is* nice to have a man in my life I can trust.

"You up for this?" I asked Robin.

"I can call home from the car."

This meant, I'm sure, that she didn't expect to talk to Kris, because I would be sitting right there. I don't know what's going on with the two of them, but I get the feeling they haven't had a real conversation since Robin left Virginia.

I nodded toward the corner where Wendy and Starla—Roscoe in her arms—were going over notes. "I'll say thanks to all the extras and pet my dog. Then I'll change. Grab Wendy, will you? She'll need to change, too."

Ten minutes later I left through the back door with Robin. Hal met us in the alley driving Donny's rental car, and Robin and I chatted as we slid inside, our arms heavy with equipment, as if we were in no hurry. I saw a couple of men lurking, but I had on baggy sweats, a heavy jacket and a watch cap complete with long dark hair streaming from the bottom edge. I ignored them; they ignored me.

Inside the bar Wendy was now wearing a wavy red wig, and the skirt and top I'd worn during filming today. She had to roll the skirt at the waistband so it didn't drag to her ankles, but a quick glimpse as she slipped into the BMW that had brought me to the lounge would probably convince anybody I was on my way back to the hotel.

Hal is a black belt, a former army sniper and an amateur race-car driver. By the time he finished winding his way through Jamestown's scenic streets, anyone who'd had an inkling they ought to tail our car would have been left behind.

I removed the cap and shook out my real hair. "Fancy or not?" I asked Robin. Donny had given me restaurant options. She didn't hesitate. "Not."

"Hal?"

"Got it," he said.

Robin was scrolling through something on her phone. "You'll be recognized without the cap."

"Donny thinks of everything." One of the bags I'd carried to the car had a different wig, and I held it up now. "I make a fair to middling blonde. He put in granny spectacles, too. Beyond awesome."

She glanced at the straw-colored wig with the bad eighties perm. The style was mullet-on-steroids. "I don't know if I can be seen with you."

"My hair is this frizzy naturally, remember? You've seen me look worse."

We reminisced about past fashion and hair disasters as she held the phone up to her ear. No one answered, and eventually she stopped reminiscing and left a message, all about Pet's recital today. Yesterday I'd had the pleasure of hearing my goddaughter play her piece over the phone when she performed it for her mother.

She dropped the phone back in her purse and stretched her legs to one side. "Maybe Kris took the kids out afterward. That is, if he went, and if he corralled Nik and made him go along."

I can be devious. "Didn't you tell me Kris said he was going?"

"He hasn't told me anything since I left. We've missed each other when I've called home, and I missed him once when he called the night of the Legion party. I didn't return that one. I'm pretty sure he was calling to lecture me."

"I'm sorry."

"We fight. We're normal. It's just that this feels different. I don't think we've gone more than a week without speaking since the day we met."

"He's probably never been this busy before. Job. Kids. House."

"He has Elena and another babysitter doing the home stuff."

"Does he hold grudges?"

She hesitated before she answered. "Kris struggles hard to be fair."

I thought if he was really trying to be fair he would be on his hands and knees begging Robin for forgiveness. But what do I know? I was only married a year, and Sage and I probably spent less than a third of that time in each other's company.

We fell into a comfortable silence. As darkness descended I watched glimpses of Chautauqua Lake, a sapphire gem, move in and out of view as we drove toward a small town just north of the city. Nothing was familiar. I was in foster care here for just six months before I was returned to Maribeth—along with the Social Security survivor's benefit I was entitled to.

Maribeth had fooled everybody in charge. She took parenting classes, was absolutely sober when visiting me or talking to my caseworker. Even my young foster parents thought she was great—temporarily misguided and depressed, but worth a second chance. After I was returned to her, she found another "perfect" boyfriend, who moved us to West Virginia, where he promptly abandoned us.

I was feeling nostalgic. "Do you ever think that if just one thing had changed when we were growing up, we wouldn't be sitting here together? If Maribeth had left me in Randolph Furnace or here in Jamestown instead of coming back for me? Maybe I would never have been so determined to have a better life or worked so hard for one. Maybe nobody in my schools would have encouraged me to sing or act."

"Or if my mother had actually taken me along. Who knows where I would be now?"

In fact, I knew one possible answer to where, although now wasn't the right moment to tell her. "You and I are living proof of silver linings or, at the least, consolation prizes. We each traded a mother for a sister."

"This from the woman who doesn't know a single ballad with a happy ending."

"As much as I love you, I hope *you're* not my happy ending. I'm not ready for an ending of any kind."

"Amen."

The restaurant was definitely informal. There were no lake views, since it was inland, and it looked as if it had been constructed in phases. Someone decided another room was needed, so they cheerfully plopped one here and then there. Judging by the parking lot the place was crowded, which meant we would blend right in.

Hal left us in the car and went to see how long the wait might be. Donny had called ahead to be sure we could get in eventually.

We chatted about the film and where we might go next. Mick's arrangements are still iffy, and our next destination isn't yet clear. Getting permission to film and interview isn't always easy. That's part of the reason he works the way he does. Firm plans could crack wide-open, so it's more productive to remain fluid. If he can't find what he needs in one place, he can go to another while he waits. Sometimes after longer negotiations he might be successful.

"Thanksgiving's just a couple of weeks away," I said. "Are you looking forward to going home?"

"Pet and I are going to make all the family favorites, even though Kris's parents won't be joining us. Nik will help, too, if we can get him in the kitchen. Where are you going to spend the holiday?"

We both know I won't be spending it with her, although

sometimes I have in the past. The year I divorced Sage I was her guest for an entire week, but this year she doesn't need me hovering as her family attempts a normal celebration.

I haven't given the matter much thought, but when she asked I knew the answer. "Sanibel." The moment I said it, my decision was made. "Gizzie loves Sanibel, so he'll come. He's promised to work with me on a song for the film. Mick's beside himself with joy."

Gizzie Wray is my songwriting collaborator, and our work relationship and friendship go back to my early years in New York. He swears he discovered me, and I love him too much to correct him. We were once constant companions, fellow members of Slaughter Street, my first and remarkably unsuccessful band. Only when we accidentally began to write songs together did the magic commence.

"Perfect," Robin said. "A guarantee you'll have fun. What about Donny?"

"What about him?"

"Will you invite him, too?"

"Donny has a life."

"Really? Because I get the feeling his life revolves around you."

"Don't go there. I'm just the cash cow."

"You think?"

"I *know*. I think he's still living with some interior designer who owns a beach house in Malibu. Every time he goes home she's changed the color of the walls. I know he rents a slip for his sailboat not too far up the coast."

"You *think*?"

It's not my job to keep track of Donny's personal life. I do know he hasn't mentioned her in a long time.

Hal came back to tell us our table was ready. I slipped on

my wig. Robin straightened it for me, laughing at the final product. I donned the granny glasses. "Okay?"

"No one will believe that's really your hair."

"For all we know this is a popular style in these parts."

We got out and scurried through a cold drizzle to the entrance, which was a stone's throw from a cheerful bar. I liked the feel of the place. Casual, warm, friendly. A young woman hugging menus showed us to a booth. Hal said he would eat at the counter.

I learned a long time ago not to expect a vegan offering in rural America. But the restaurant did offer portobello mushrooms in place of meat on their salads, and when I asked our server to leave off the cheese she was more than willing. Robin got fish tacos and ordered a beer from the local Southern Tier microbrewery, which the server recommended.

I caught her just as she was about to leave. "I'll take one, too. Same kind, same size."

The young woman tilted her head and stared at me. "You know what? You kind of remind me of somebody."

"Really?" I smiled without showing my teeth, since my natural smile is supposedly a dead giveaway.

She examined me for a long moment. "Did anybody ever tell you you look like Madonna?"

I widened my eyes. "Really?"

"Like when she was younger. Maybe it's the hair." She turned and left.

Robin was laughing softly.

"I don't think Madge would be at all pleased to hear I'm impersonating her," I said. "Of course she'd be even less pleased if someone thought she was impersonating *me*."

"This is unusual," Robin said. "Not the Madonna sighting. You drinking beer, I mean."

"It's been that kind of day. If I turn into my mother right before your eyes, you'll roll me out the door and into the car?"

"Hal and I will get you right to detox."

I make jokes about Maribeth because I'm in no danger of forgetting her. If I have to carry her in my head, at least I can mute my memories with black humor. Robin understands.

"So back to Donny," she said. "I think you should invite him for Thanksgiving."

"Donny needs a break. The whole mess in Australia was awful. Canceling appearances, trying to keep my condition out of the press, holding my hand during therapy sessions."

"He held your hand in therapy?"

"You have to stop this. Donny and I are not a couple. I tried the couple thing, remember?"

"Donny is not Sage Callahan."

"Of course not. Donny has a voice like a buzz saw."

"Gizzie will bring his partner, right?"

Gizzie has been out of the closet since he was twelve years old and was still known as Gunther. For the past ten years he's been the soul of monogamy with a guy named Pat, a top producer in the world of rock music.

"I'm sure Pat will be with him," I said.

"So *you'll* need somebody. Three is awkward."

"This conversation is awkward."

Robin held up her hands in defeat. Our server returned with mugs of beer and we toasted.

"Best beer ever," Robin said.

I had to agree.

"So this is a different conversation," she went on. "But if Donny's not for you, is there a guy who might be?"

"Nobody who's made it past three encounters."

"I don't think I want to know what *encounter* entails."

"We used to call encounters dates. But the men I meet

aren't into movies, a Coke and a good-night kiss. So I call them encounters. It's more like Sumo wrestling. One person trying to knock the other off his feet. Or hers."

"Three times is the charm?"

"Three times is about as long as I ever want to engage."

"Is this because of Sage? Because you never really seem angry when you talk about him."

I liked the way the beer tickled as I swallowed. If you don't drink very often, the buzz is greater. I was already feeling more relaxed, and when our server reappeared, we both ordered a second. "If I tell you a secret, and I do mean a secret, you'll keep it to yourself? Because I've promised this will never get out." I paused. "Until it does. From somebody else."

"Call me one hundred percent reliable."

"Sage…" I managed a graceful shrug. "He just wasn't into me. I knew it. He knew it. But getting married was such darned good publicity."

She stared at me, clearly unsure what to ask next.

"Sage likes men better than he likes women," I said.

"No…"

"Oh yeah."

"You said you knew it. What did you know? When?"

"Early on. I was like a lot of women. I hoped I could convert him."

Our food and second round came, and we waited until the server left and we were eating before Robin spoke again. "I'm sorry, but I don't believe you."

"You don't believe Sage is gay? Or bi, depending on how you look at it? Because we did have sex, and for a little while he seemed to enjoy it. More or less."

"No! I don't believe you were stupid enough to think he'd fall so madly in love with you that he'd lose interest in men."

"Then what *do* you think?"

"I think if you knew, you didn't really care. If you knew ahead of time, then you didn't marry him because you loved him. You married him because you didn't, and you knew you could get out of it once the publicity waned."

"Wow, you're good."

"CeCe! Did *he* know that was your intention?"

I gave up all pretense. "Of course he did. I figured out he was gay just a few weeks into our relationship, but by then the tabloids were filled with speculation. I was a man-eater, and here this hunky country boy with a guitar had finally brought me to my knees. We watched our album sales climb. I made a surprise appearance onstage at one of his concerts, and we sang a duet. The crowd went wild. In my own way I did love him and he loved me, but we loved the publicity best of all. We got even more after we tied the knot."

Robin's mind was obviously whirring. "And afterward, when you broke up, if his sexuality had ever been in doubt it wasn't anymore, because he'd conquered and married a sexy superstar, which had to prove something."

"For my part I played up the men-are-two-timing-bastards card, which worked for me, too. You know how many great songs there are about divorce and breakups?"

"You took everybody for a ride."

"A harmless Sunday drive in the country, Robin. I wish we lived in a world where Sage didn't have to hide who he really is. But he's not ready to come out of the closet. I'm not sure he ever will be."

"Who else knows?"

I shook my head.

"You mean you didn't tell *anybody* else? Not Donny? Not your therapist."

"Only my sister. Just now."

"This is some weird kind of honor, isn't it?"

"There are some things only sisters understand."

"Even if they're just foster sisters joined at the hip and the heart."

Clearly she hadn't forgotten the reporter's throwaway remark at the Chelsea, and I knew the "real sister" thing had bothered her in the same way it had bothered me, although we had heard it many times before.

And that's when I got one of my best ideas ever. I waited until she was halfway through her tacos before I proposed it.

"I know a great way to end this evening."

"They don't have vegan ice cream here."

"I was thinking about something that lasts longer."

"When you get that gleam in your eye, we're in trouble."

This time I did show my teeth. "You're going to love this, Robin, trust me."

Hal came over to see how we were doing, and I asked him to pay our check. "And while you're at it," I added as he started to turn away, "will you find the name of the best tattoo parlor in the area."

"Oh, no," Robin said. "Count me out. Not happening. No way, CeCe."

I smiled radiantly and finished my beer.

21

Robin

Even as a child desperate for affection I never did everything Cecilia told me to. I am certainly mature enough these days to say no with real force. The thing is, the more I considered it, the more matching tattoos appealed to me.

Or maybe it was that second beer, the one that tasted so good with my tacos?

Whatever the reason, Cecilia and I now have matching tattoos on our hips. They are tasteful and delicate, sweet little hearts with an infinity sign bisecting them. Written into the infinity sign is the word *sisters*.

Even though Cecilia is taller than I am, the artist made certain that anytime we stand side by side and our hips touch, our tattoos will touch, as well.

Joined at the hip.

Cecilia wanted the tattoos inked on our breasts, over our hearts. I had a feeling Kris might not want to be reminded of Cecilia every time we make love. Hips are less intimate, and hopefully soon enough he'll forget the tattoo is there.

If Kris and I ever again have occasion to get naked together.

Kris is the master of bad timing. He called from his cell phone while I was getting my tattoo, so I knew it wasn't one of our children. Since I'm not a fan of pain I was in no position to answer, and when Cecilia volunteered to answer for me I told her not to. But now I'm back in my room with my phone. I just set the alarm so I'll know when to remove my bandage and begin aftercare. Nothing sounds complicated; keeping the tattoo clean, dry and lightly lubricated is all I need to know.

Cecilia is no tattooed Lady Gaga, but the whole process was old hat for her. In addition to permanent eyeliner, she has a cascade of stars on the back of her neck and a Celtic tree of life tattoo above her right ankle to symbolize her connection to the earth and harmony with all living things. On a completely different note she has a viper tattooed on her left-hand ring finger, inked there the day her divorce from Sage was final. Now as I tapped Kris's number and waited, I wondered if Sage helped her come up with the snake to enhance publicity.

When exactly did she learn to be so casually devious?

The phone rang so long that I thought I might need to leave a message, but just as I prepared to, Kris answered.

It seems like forever since I've heard his voice. I didn't even check voice mail. Whatever he needed to say I wanted to hear in person.

"Hey," I said. "I couldn't answer when you called." I decided explaining *why* was not a great conversation starter. "But I'm back in my room now. How are you?"

"I guess you didn't listen to my message, did you?"

I was ready for something a little more intimate, a softer, warmer tone. Not staccato bursts that sounded as if he was biting off each word and spitting it across the miles.

"No…o…o… I wanted to listen to *you*. In person. Apparently I made a mistake?"

"This is anything but a catch-up call."

I sat up. Then this was not a call to recline in bed for. "Are the children all right?"

"That depends on how you look at it, Robin. One of them—our daughter, in fact—had a stash of marijuana in her dresser drawer."

For a moment I couldn't process what he'd said. I was silent.

"Did you hear me?"

"I heard you. I'm trying to make sense of it. Can you start at the beginning?"

"I more or less did. I took her laundry upstairs tonight and decided to put it away while she finished brushing her teeth. When I moved things around to make room, I found a plastic bag with marijuana. I opened it and found some suspicious-looking pills, too."

"Does Pet know?"

"What do you think?"

I was moving quickly from distress to anger. "What I think is that I'm in New York, you're in Virginia and I need some answers that don't come with a side helping of self-righteousness."

He followed an audibly frustrated sigh with, "Pet says she doesn't know where it came from."

"Do you believe her?"

"Would you?"

"It's always better to follow a question with an answer, not another *question*. They may not have taught you that in law school."

Sigh two. "I did not believe her."

"I'm sure you told her."

"I did. And she continues to insist she doesn't know how it got there, even though she burst into tears the moment she saw I found it. Not the reaction you expect from a child who has no idea what Daddy found under her favorite Minion T-shirt."

I knew that shirt. A bright yellow one, with a goofy Minion smile. Pet had loved *Despicable Me*, and still did. Pet was a child. Pet was not a drug abuser. "Had you gone into that drawer lately?"

"Right. I have all the time in the world to straighten my children's clothing, Robin."

I took a deep breath. When he didn't apologize I said, "Look, when you're willing to have a civil discussion and problem solve with me, we'll talk again. But I'm not going to be your whipping girl." I clicked End and put the phone on my nightstand.

I wasn't sure which family member to be most upset with. My daughter, who was lying to protect somebody—I was sure of that. Or my husband.

I'd had the idea that Kris and I were adjusting to the change in our relationship, and I had told myself that as adults who loved each other we would find ways to compromise. Now I seriously doubted I was right. Kris was so angry he wasn't going to simply adjust. He was going to drag me down until I gave up hope of going back to my career. By the time this gig finished I wouldn't dare find another.

Or one of us would find a divorce lawyer.

The phone buzzed. I considered not answering, but in the end I took a chance.

"I'm sorry," he said. "You're right."

I was so stunned I took the high road. "Let's start over, okay?"

"The last time I opened that particular drawer was last summer. I got out a change of clothes for her because you asked me to. You were driving her to a pool party."

"I've put things inside her drawers since then. I usually leave the laundry on her bed, but I think I went ahead and put away clothes right before I left." I thought about it. "I'm sure I did. I would have noticed a stash of drugs."

"You probably would have. It wasn't well hidden."

"So we don't really know where the drugs came from. But they weren't there before I left. Can we figure out who's been in the house in the past week and a half?"

"The kids. Elena. Me. Those are the obvious ones."

I let him continue thinking, because like any good lawyer, he's thorough to a fault.

"Nik hasn't had a friend over since you left," he continued after a moment. "He's gone to Brandon's, though. Maybe Brandon has been here while I've been gone. I can check with Elena and Grace."

"If the owner was one of Nik's friends wouldn't the drugs be in his room?" I paused as something else he'd said hit me. "Grace?"

"Jody's sister. She's babysitting evenings and Saturday mornings now when I need her."

"*Grace* is your babysitter?" Kris and I hadn't spoken since he hired extra help. Pet had said something in passing about a babysitter, but I hadn't followed up. Maybe I hadn't wanted to because I was in no position to critique Kris's choice, and I just assumed he would use someone from my list.

"When I realized I was going to need someone in addition to Elena I asked Pet who she wanted, and she said Grace. She said Grace was—" I could hear him struggling for the precise word "—cool, but not too cool. I interviewed her, and she's had lots of experience with her own sister and some kids in her neighborhood. She's always on time, available when I need her and she's saving for a car, so she needs the money. The house is still standing when I get home."

I knew better than to criticize him for not consulting me. I wanted Kris to take charge. And look how thoroughly he'd done so.

Instead I inched my way in. "She babysat for us a couple of times last summer."

"I think Pet told me that."

"Kris, the second time, her twin came over and apparently called Taiwan or Hong Kong on our phone, I don't remember which one now. Some place our calling plan doesn't exactly cover. When I got home that day Grace didn't tell me he'd been there. I only found out about the call when the bill came. I saw it took place on the day Grace babysat, so I cornered her the next time I picked up Pet at their house. She finally admitted it was Gil."

"Did you tell me this?"

I tried to remember. "I think you were out of town or in the middle of a case and didn't want to be disturbed. But that's why Grace wasn't one of the sitters on my list."

"Pet never told you Grace was helping out?"

"I didn't ask for a name. I didn't want to sound like I was checking up on you, and I bet Pet didn't want me to know. She knew about that phone call. So when I didn't ask, she didn't volunteer."

"Illegal drugs and a telephone call are two different things." His voice said something else, because in the end he really was a father first, but lawyer was a close second.

"Like two different-sized peas in the same pod?"

"Pet won't talk to me. She probably would talk to you."

"I'll be happy to try. Is she still up?"

"I don't mean on the phone."

And here it was again. We had a crisis on our hands, and only I could solve it. In person.

If I actually believed my daughter was using drugs, then I would already be on my way to the nearest airport, or to a rental agency to find a car for the drive home tonight. But I didn't believe it. I was almost sure I knew what had happened.

"The problem with talking to Pet at the moment is that we're forcing her to take sides," I said. "She has to learn to take the right side, but at her age going against a friend's sister and brother? Her best friend at that? It's so hard. And she probably worships Grace. After all, she asked you to hire her."

"So, Robin? You have a solution here?"

"I'd like us to come up with one together."

"I'm so exhausted my brain isn't even processing this call."

Kris never complains. Or he never used to. But I heard what amounted to a cry for help. Maybe it was time to throw him a life preserver. I had been out for a fun dinner and a stop at the tattoo parlor, and Kris had been dealing with a ten-year-old's drug stash. Maybe in years past *he'd* gotten the dinners out and I'd gotten the crises. But that didn't mean I had to let him suffer.

"Let me do what I can from this end. We'll talk in the morning and figure out the rest of it. Will that work for you?"

"What are you going to do from there?"

"Have a heart-to-heart with Lynette. Jody and the twins' mom," I added, in case he didn't remember her name.

"You know her well enough?"

"She's reasonable. I should have told her about the phone call, but Grace promised Gil would pay me back, and she showed up the next day with the cash, so I let it go because I didn't want the whole thing to blow back on Pet."

"This time we can't sit back."

He was right. "Gil's been in trouble with the law. Nothing so bad that I worry about Pet being at their house. Lynette keeps an eye on things there. But he got in with a tough crowd in high school, and some of those kids are still his friends. She's told me she worries about him."

"You're pretty sure he had something to do with this?"

"With a little help from Grace and Pet."

"How am I going to talk to Pet about this? What in the hell should I do about her lying to me?"

In the midst of our mutual anxiety I heard "I." Twice. I had extended a hand to help, and as a result he was no longer expecting me to take care of everything. Exhausted or not, Kris was stepping up to the plate.

If it weren't so late at night I would dig for the lesson there.

"I'll call Lynette," I said. "You go to bed. We'll talk in the morning and figure out what to do next."

He didn't answer right away. When he did, he surprised me.

"I miss you."

I wanted to ask what he missed. Having me take charge of all family problems, the way I had for years? Having me talk to our children face-to-face so he wouldn't have to?

Or maybe, just maybe, he missed *me*. The woman he married. The one he swore to love and honor.

I knew which Kris I missed. The one who used to be truly present in my life. The one who rubbed my feet when I was pregnant, and watered his newborn son's and daughter's bare skin with sentimental tears. The one who hadn't been busy every minute working his way up the career ladder.

"I miss you, too."

"How did all this happen?"

He wasn't talking about Pet. Now tears filled *my* eyes. I cleared my throat. "A little at a time. While we weren't paying attention."

"Do you ever wish you could start all over?"

"Only if I could start with you."

"We'll talk tomorrow."

I put the phone on my nightstand. The tattoo was throbbing, but not as much as my heart. There was no bandage for that, no ointment to soothe it. I would just have to live with this pain until Kris and I figured out who we were to each other again.

22

Kris

I was dreaming about Robin early this morning when the telephone rang. This was not the dream in which I lose her in that awful wreck, but one with a different outcome. I see her as a stranger, a pretty woman standing across a room crowded with angry men and women. She lifts a camera to photograph one of the men, who is waving his arms as if to threaten someone in front of him. Although I can't see his face, I know I'm supposed to protect him, but suddenly she's the one I'm worried about.

I try to get closer, to ask the pretty young woman not to record the argument, but someone blocks every step. By now I'm frantic. Robin is no longer a stranger with a camera, she's the woman I love, and there are too many angry people between us.

I begin to push and shove, too, and at last I make headway. I'll do anything to get near her. And when I finally reach her side she turns and asks, "Are you angry, too?"

I grab her, and all I want to do is kiss her.

When I answered the phone Robin was on the other end of the line.

"I bet I woke you. I'm sorry to call so early, but we're getting on the road in a few minutes and I don't want to talk about this in a crowded van."

"I was dreaming about you. About the night we met."

The angry room had been in Palm Beach. I was a newly minted attorney, chosen to be there with one of the most prestigious partners in our firm, who was assisting Al Gore's legal team. Faceless in the dream, the partner is probably the man I was supposed to protect.

Even though the election had nothing to do with her job Robin found her way inside with several other photographers. She was in Florida that week, and she had decided to see what was happening. She got photos of what nearly turned into a fistfight, and I really did try to stop her. Obviously she ignored me.

I guess even then I really wanted to kiss her, too. Of course we were strangers, so that came later. Although not that much.

"That all seems so long ago, doesn't it?" she said.

"A lot can happen in fifteen years."

"Two children. A mortgage. Differences of opinion."

I was sitting up now. I combed my fingers through my hair as if she could see how tousled it was. "Did you talk to Lynette?"

"Lynette's going to talk to Gil today, but she broke down on the telephone."

"She believed you?"

"A couple of weeks ago she found marijuana and worse in his backpack, so she and her husband confronted him. Gil told them the drugs belonged to a friend who had to go out of town, and he was keeping them because the kid's parents were suspicious."

"They believed that?"

"I'm not sure they believed everything. For one thing he refused to name the friend. They did warn him they were going to be watching closely, and if they ever had another reason to suspect he was using or selling drugs, they were putting him right into a drug treatment facility. He promised to see a counselor to help figure out why he lets friends take advantage of him, and Lynette made an appointment. In the meantime she's been searching the house every day to be sure he isn't hiding anything else."

I was growing skeptical. "So whatever else he had, he hid *here*?"

"I'll tell you what she told *me*. Lynette says Grace always tries to protect her brother. She thinks maybe he convinced Grace that he had to protect this second stash so he could pass it back to his friend when he returned. Maybe she was on her way to our house and he asked her to hide it here."

"In our daughter's drawer, instead of, say, our attic? Do you believe this?"

Robin didn't hesitate. "Are you kidding?"

I gave a short laugh, because neither did I. Gil was the bad kid, Grace the good, and their parents didn't want to see the family any other way. Grace was our babysitter. The drugs were in our house. Yet the parents wanted to place the blame squarely on their son. The same way Grace had blamed him for the phone call.

I guessed out loud. "The drugs could belong to Grace, or maybe even to Grace and Gil together. Could be a family enterprise. She *is* trying to buy a car. But why hide them in Pet's drawer?"

"I've been thinking about it all night, and there's only one thing that makes sense. *Jody* must have been the one who found the second stash, maybe hidden somewhere in her own bedroom. She asked Pet to hide it because she didn't want whichever twin is the problem to get in trouble."

"Pet rode to the recital yesterday with Jody. Maybe it all

happened then." I remembered the way my daughter set her purse beside her on the piano bench when she played. I'd thought it was so cute.

Before I went on I told Robin about the purse. "Pet must have put the bag in her purse. Her drawer was the first place she could think of to store it when we got home, but the purse took up too much room, so she removed the bag. The girls aren't old enough to figure out a better solution on the spur of the moment. Grace is their heroine. They thought they were doing the right thing."

We basked silently in our ability to get to the bottom of the problem.

I came down to earth. "We'll know more after I confront our daughter today, but no matter how this happened, one thing is certain."

Robin knew. "You can't trust Grace."

No matter how I looked at it, she was right. Because even if Jody had given the drugs to Pet to hide, why hadn't she just told Grace, so her big sister would deal with the problem? Unfortunately the answer was clear. Jody must have suspected Grace was involved.

"No, I can't," I said, and thought just how difficult my life had suddenly become again.

"I'm sorry."

"Yeah, me, too."

"After you talk to Pet, I'll call Lynette and tell her whatever you learn."

"Easier if I do it myself so nothing gets left out."

"I did leave a list of sitters. Maybe someone else will be able to fill in."

I didn't want to discuss this any longer. "You have to get going. Where are you headed? I don't know a thing about what you're doing." This was my fault. I hadn't wanted to know.

"For the next few weeks we'll be visiting some residential facilities and foster-care programs. We're heading to Tennessee today. Mick's working out the rest of the schedule, but we'll be ready for a break by Thanksgiving. I'll let you know where I am."

I held out an olive branch, or at least a twig. "Let's catch up for real when this latest crisis is resolved."

"I would like that."

"I'll let you know what happens next."

We both hung up. I tried to think how my wife might handle the upcoming conversation with Pet. I certainly didn't want to let my daughter off the hook, even if she was only trying to help a friend. I should have asked Robin what the consequences should be and how I should get to the truth. I didn't, though, because the moment I admit how confusing I find parenting, I'm admitting that Robin is right. I do need more practice.

There is so much I don't know about being a father. Probably not just because I'm away so often, but because the whole damned process is shrouded in mystery. For everybody.

I knew better than to make my conversation with Pet an event. No meals or snacks. Nothing pleasant, like a walk through the neighborhood or a bench by the pond in the center of our development. But also no time or place where Nik would overhear and add his own take on things.

I was considering my choices over morning coffee when the doorbell rang. I half expected to find Jody's mom on the doorstep with a plea that I not call the police. I was surprised to find Larry Buffman instead.

He smiled apologetically. "I just dropped Lee at a friend's house down the road. Bad time for a social call?"

I opened the door wider. "I just made a pot of coffee."

"I won't stay long. I know this is your day with the kids."

At the moment I wasn't looking forward to anything about being with my kids.

In the kitchen I poured coffee. Then we took our mugs to the sunroom. No matter what he'd called it, this was not a social call. Except for the occasional family picnic, social events within the firm are formal. Buff and I never perch on bar stools shooting the breeze, and while the Buffmans live less than five miles away, our families never flip burgers together in the backyard.

"Not bad," he said after his first sip. "You've been domesticated. You cook, too?"

I tried to remember the last time I'd actually made a meal other than toaster waffles. "I couldn't afford not to in law school."

"Yeah, I remember being poor. I like being wealthy a lot better. You will, too."

Robin and I are already so much better off than we were as kids that I didn't know how to respond. Do I care if I'm *wealthy*? Is some mysterious number consisting of cash and investments what I'm shooting for? The whole exchange bothered me.

"And speaking of wealthy..." Buff set his mug on a side table. "I spent an hour on the telephone with Mervin Pedersen last night."

"He likes to work outside office hours, doesn't he?" An hour of Buff's time any day of the week costs a fortune, which is why the man can use words like *wealthy* without flinching.

"He's flying in tomorrow afternoon. He wants to meet us after work and go out to dinner." He didn't stop there. "He also wants us to fly to Norfolk and tour his facilities. Actually not us, *you*. You're cheaper."

I saw no point in beating around the bush. "I'm also the only parent on-site these days."

"You found child care, didn't you?"

"Not for a trip away from home." I hesitated, then went the whole nine yards. "And it looks like I won't be at the office as late until Robin's back for good. I'll be working here. My extended babysitting just fell through."

"Then you won't be at dinner tomorrow?"

"I can probably find a sitter today since I have advance notice."

"Well, I'm not unsympathetic to problems with an out-of-town trip, but when does your wife come back for Thanksgiving?"

Robin and I hadn't talked about a date, but I suspected she would be home at least by that Tuesday. Most likely everyone on the film would want to be with family or friends for the holiday. I told him, and he nodded.

"That's what I guessed, more or less. So let's see if you can fly out on Tuesday evening and back home on Thursday. He wants to take you to a couple of different locations."

"Come home on Thanksgiving Day?"

"I bet we can find a flight that will get you home that evening so you can have dinner with your family. Or you can always postpone dinner until Friday. I can't tell you the number of times we did that at my house. My first two wives hated it." He looked satisfied with himself, as if he'd solved the problem. "I told Pedersen we might need to do it that way, and he was agreeable. He said he usually works through the holiday. Besides, that will give him time to put his best foot forward, clean up mouse droppings, that kind of thing." He winked.

By then weeks would have passed without seeing my wife. How would I explain to Robin that I was leaving for a business trip just as she got home? On the other hand, if she could leave me in charge for weeks, even months, why not take advantage of her brief trip here? After all, we would have the rest of the weekend.

"We can probably arrange something," I said.

"Good man." Buff took another sip of coffee. Then he got to his feet. "So you're on the lookout for another babysitter? I can see if Lee has any ideas."

I had gone over and over this in my head. If I'd used Robin's list. If I'd done a better interview. If I'd tried to find an adult instead of a teen. If…if…if… I realized Buff was waiting for an answer.

"Thanks, but I don't think so. The kids are pretty self-sufficient, so I get plenty of work finished here on evenings and weekends. I just need to be the one keeping an eye on things after the housekeeper leaves. Too much can go wrong."

"That might cause some problems."

"I have a telephone and a computer, and I can almost always find a sitter if I have some notice."

"Well, your decision."

"Pet and Nik need to know they have a father."

He gave his trademark hearty laugh. "I was never sure if my kids passed me on the street whether they would recognize me."

I didn't stop to think. "That's not a good thing, Buff."

"Maybe not, but it was the way things were. The way they had to be."

"Luckily it's a different world now. Video conferencing, internet, texting. More and more professionals work from home."

"We'll see, Kris. But don't say I didn't warn you."

The day was made for encounters. In the middle of catching up with my email and settling my calendar for the upcoming week, a law school buddy invited me to lunch. Howie teaches at the George Washington University Law School, and I usually do guest lectures for his classes. It's fun being the working lawyer giving students the down and dirty about the job. I like teaching, too. Talking and writing about the law are more fun than practicing it. I've published a couple of scholarly articles, which hasn't hurt my reputation at Singer. Howie said he had some new dates and ideas in mind for the upcoming term.

I was just glad he didn't want to do this over dinner. Lunch I could manage.

My daughter couldn't stay in bed all day. I waited, and just before noon she finally came downstairs and found me in the kitchen. Fortunately Nik was outside raking. I had told him to save two-thirds of the leaves for Pet, and the last time I'd looked outside he was sectioning off our yard with string. I wondered if he was counting as each leaf fell.

When she didn't speak, I did. "I'm not sure whether to ask whether you want breakfast or lunch." I held up a loaf of bread. "Toast?"

"I'm not hungry."

"You won't mind if I eat a sandwich while we talk?"

"What are we going to talk about?"

I almost said "guess," but Robin had made an impression on me. No sarcasm today.

"We are going to talk about your decision to help Jody yesterday by storing drugs in your drawer," I said, trying a favorite courtroom technique. I like to pretend I know things that I don't.

"Is that what her mother said?"

I also know how *not* to answer a question. "Jody's mom and your mom had a long conversation last night."

She slumped, as if that was enough to deflate her. "She just wanted to protect her brother."

"I don't think Gil is the one she was trying to protect."

She sniffed back tears. "He's always in trouble."

"And Grace isn't."

"Gil's the bad one."

"One of the things I know, Pet? Good people don't try to get other people in trouble. Another? There is no such thing as good people and bad people. Everybody's some of both. But the best people don't blame other people when they make mistakes. I know you like Grace, but we both know if she could be trusted, Jody would have given *her* the drugs to deal with instead of you."

"Jody doesn't know who they belong to!"

"Which means they could belong to Grace. And that's what I'll tell her mother when we talk today."

She hung her head, tears spilling down her cheeks. Robin might have comforted her, but I'm not Robin.

I let her know how large a mistake she had made. "I'm an attorney. Do you have any idea how serious this could be for you, not to mention *me?* Depending on what kind of pills were in that bag, possession could be a felony." I listed all the possible charges both of us could have faced, laying it on a bit thick to make my point. "In some states, I would be duty bound as an officer of the court to turn you in."

"You would turn in your own kid?"

"It's always good to know what can happen when you break the law. None of us are above it."

"I wasn't going to keep them! Jody and I were trying to figure out what to do."

"Try telling that to a judge. Do you think he would believe you?"

"I'm sorry, Daddy." She gazed up at me with an expression that would have melted the sternest heart.

I knew this wasn't the right moment to soften. She was ten. We had years ahead when drugs would be readily available, and I wanted her to remember the way she felt right now.

"You gave me lots of time to consider what to do. You know, by not coming down earlier to face the music. So here's what will happen. Today you'll go outside, and Nik will show you which portion of the yard is yours for raking. It won't be hard to spot. I suspect you'll be busy raking today and every day after school this week. Maybe longer if you screw around. You'll have time to do it all, though, because you aren't going *anywhere* until after Thanksgiving. And none of your friends will be welcome here in the meantime. For the record, I'll be around to supervise in the evenings after Elena leaves, and Grace won't be coming back."

"But Jody and I study together."

"Not anymore. After Thanksgiving, you, Jody and I will sit down with her parents and work out rules. If I ever find out she's done anything like this again, Jody will no longer be welcome in our house. And the only reason I'm willing to give her another chance is because she was up against the wall. She loves her siblings, and she knew what serious trouble they would be in if she showed her mother what she'd found. So trying to protect them says she has a heart. The fact she didn't just hand the drugs back to Grace or Gil says she has a conscience. Good qualities, both. Now Jody just needs a little sense to go with them."

"None of this is fair! I was just trying to help!"

"And from this I hope you've learned that helping isn't always *helpful*. Do you understand?"

"I wish Mommy was here!"

So did I, but that was beside the point. "We spoke this

morning, and your mom was the one who figured out what was going on. To be honest, Pet, from what I could tell, she didn't feel one bit sorry for you."

She just stared at me.

I nodded. "There's a rake outside with your name on it. Go introduce yourself. Any time you get hungry, feel free to come back inside and fix something to eat."

She didn't slam the door. Not exactly. I'm impressed by my daughter's ability to come so close without stepping over the line.

This was the right moment to crank up my anger at Robin for leaving me to deal with this mess alone. Maybe I could have done it, too, if I weren't satisfied with the way things had played out. In the next weeks I will make a lot of mistakes while Robin follows Cecilia around the country. But today didn't feel like a mistake. Weirdly, almost more than yesterday, it felt like a beginning.

23

Cecilia

I received three good things from my marriage to Sage. Publicity. Evidence for my fans that I could be swept away by love despite multiple recordings denying the possibility. And the condo overlooking the city of Nashville that Sage and I bought for overflow guests just a month before I began divorce proceedings.

No, I have to make that four things, because I also gained a lifelong friend. Sage and I remain close, although we don't publicize it. We're supposed to be heartbroken, tormented by our failure, even secretly pining for what we lost. Since we can't be seen together for another year or two until we "recover," I've had to say goodbye to the man's back rubs and quirky sense of humor. Sage could make anything seem funny, even our sham of a marriage. I miss that.

Oddly enough I also miss Sage's real love, a squirt of a guy from the hills of Arkansas with a drooping mustache and a wicked grin. The rest of the world knows him as the fiddler in Sage's band, but I wonder how long their secret can last. Surely someone will take note of the way those two look at each other when they think nobody is paying attention.

"What if the world discovers Sage is gay?" Robin, who

has visited me in Nashville but never in this condo, looked up from taking photos of the city off my balcony. "What will they think about your marriage?"

I crossed the narrow expanse to stand beside her, because the view is beyond amazing and I never tire of it. "Sage will tell the world I was an innocent pawn. He'll say he really hoped our marriage would work because he did love me, but even with the sexiest woman in the music world, he couldn't be someone he wasn't."

"That's a suspiciously quick response."

"We settled it beforehand. When Sage finally comes out of the closet, and he may someday, I'll get most of the sympathy."

"You won't be honest?"

"Why start now?" I laughed at her expression. "You always were such a Goody Two-Shoes. If we lived in a better world none of this ever would have happened in the first place. So we just made a little hay out of homophobia."

Robin was frowning. "Would you expose Sage if you thought that would get you even more publicity?"

"Of course not."

"So your standards go like this? It's okay to lie and cheat if nobody's going to get hurt? Otherwise, not so much?"

"Wow, a morality discussion before breakfast."

"Not *my* breakfast. I ate while you were in the shower."

I went back inside to my kitchen, which is not much of a trip since the condo is less than 2,000 square feet. I rummaged through my shiny stainless-steel refrigerator, which is large enough to hold food for half of Nashville. Right now it's nearly empty. One lonely shelf is filled with goodies my house manager, Lenore, selected before I arrived.

I don't take this kind of service for granted. I have people everywhere who will do anything I ask them to. I snap my fingers and food appears—fabulous food, too, tailored exactly to my tastes. It's almost enough to make me forget that once upon a time nobody cared if I ate once a day or once a week.

I removed a blueberry bagel and soy cream cheese, and split the bagel to toast it. Robin leaned over the counter, taking photos, this time of me. How often does the world see a diva toast her own bagel?

I poured a cup of the coffee Robin had brewed. "So what's worse, playing along with a marriage that was never meant to be, or killing and eating animals?" I held up the vegan cream cheese to make my point. "You were right there with me at the Osburn ranch. You know what happens to cute little calves and piglets. Not to mention chickens."

"I admire your persistence, but I'm not going vegan."

"You get my point, though? We make moral decisions every day. But yeah, I'm not a fan of hurting anybody. I make a point of not hurting anyone or anything whenever I can."

After that statement, my significant pause was just a matter of sucking in enough air for the next sentence. "Of course sometimes all of us have to choose who we're going to hurt and who we're going to help."

As if to illustrate, Roscoe wandered in from my bedroom. He was no longer limping, and the pup and I had bonded big-time. Lenore bought him a soft little bed with a fleece blanket all his own, but Roscoe still prefers to sleep with me. I scooped him into my arms and rubbed my cheek against his fuzzy little head.

"I guess I'd forgotten how easily you lie." Robin aimed her camera at Roscoe and me. He was happily licking cream cheese off my fingers.

"You and I got through the system in different ways. You decided you had to be scrupulously honest all the time."

She rested her camera on the counter. "You think so? Do you have a theory why?"

"Because knowing exactly the way things were and acting accordingly was the reality you held on to and still do. You didn't deviate then, because that would have shaken up your world, and you haven't changed much. You couldn't keep a secret if your life depended on it. Me? I figured out early that to survive I had to make choices, so I made what I thought were the best, not the most honest. I looked at outcome. You looked at process."

She was silent for a moment, as if processing now. "You think your way is better?"

"Not for you. We had different beginnings. We both coped. Still do."

"How many concessions did you have to make to get where you are?"

She was asking like an honest woman, but I didn't want to answer like one. "More than I'll ever talk about."

A counter stood between us, but she leaned over it to rest her fingertips on my arm. Roscoe sniffed them, then went back to licking mine.

"There's nothing you could tell me that would change anything." She smiled just a little. "I will always love you."

"Whitney's hit, not mine, bless her tortured soul." I hummed a few bars before I sang the title in my best Whitney imitation.

Her smile bloomed. "No matter what."

Robin was in over her head, but she didn't know it. I wondered what she would think if I was ever completely honest with her. Which of us would the truth destroy faster?

Hal drove us toward Cookeville, the town about an hour east of Nashville where we would meet up with Mick and the others again. Mick wants me to tour a facility on the outskirts that gets excellent reviews from both sides of the foster-care divide. At all levels of government, policymakers who believe children are too quickly removed from their birth families argue with those who believe they aren't removed quickly enough. The number of abused children who die each year is their measuring stick. Policy swings from side to side and is dependent on head counts, funding and the latest sociological study. Not to mention who's in office and willing to make needed changes.

I agreed to do the tour and conduct interviews because I want to see how Children First and Foremost, better known as CFF, manages to straddle that fence and infuriate only the extreme fringes who want everything their way. I'm one of those former foster children who sees both sides. In my case, by the time life completely fell apart, I had no home to remain in and no mother to rehabilitate. Foster care was a lifesaver.

On the other hand, some of the "homes" I was sent to after Maribeth split for good, share the spotlight in my nightmares.

"Such pretty country." Since we left the big city Robin has been ogling the scenery. Mist still hung over a gently rolling green landscape thick with trees, and dotted now and then with livestock and picturesque barns. We were subtly gaining altitude as we drove. Cookeville is located on something called the Highland Ridge.

The crew spent the night in the smallish town, but I knew I would be more content in my own space, and Hal was happy to do the drive from Nashville. I wanted time with Robin, too, and a chance for her to see the condo. We'd spent last night eating pizza with soy cheese and watching some of Mick's older documentaries to get a better idea of what might be coming during the remainder of our time together.

"Sage has a ranch out this way," I said. "We spent weekends there whenever we were together."

"Do you miss it?"

"He was fond of hosting raucous barbecues. Nights of meat roasting on the spit, booze, skeet shooting and whining Dobros never really did it for me. When I had time to spare I wanted to go to Sanibel, but he's not a fan of beaches."

I looked up from the packet about CFF I had been studying. Mick assembled it for me so I could prep for the interviews today. "When we get to Florida I hope we'll be able to sneak away for a few days and pop down. Maybe Pet and Nik can join us, and Kris if he has time. The kids would love it. They're just the right age for collecting shells."

"Kris would probably love having them gone for a few days."

"How is he?"

"Surviving a crisis or two. He just lost his early-evening babysitter."

"What will he do?"

"He didn't ask for suggestions. Thanksgiving's not that far away. Maybe we'll have a good conversation while I'm home."

Or not, but I didn't say that. Maybe a long family weekend *would* put a lot of their problems to rest, and who was I to suggest otherwise? She went back to staring out the window, and I used the remainder of the drive to finish my reading.

Children First and Foremost was established in the mid-twentieth century by a foundation determined to provide a residential facility for girls in the state who need stability and therapy until they're ready for adoption or a return to their birth families. Too many girls have been in and out of the foster-care system for years and are in no condition to succeed in another similar placement. A benefactor donated twenty acres west of the town of Cookeville, and through the years the foundation constructed cottages, apartment buildings for family visits, a recreation complex, picnic grounds with a pool and more.

The foundation is well endowed and adept at fund-raising, which means they don't lack staff. Each girl and her family get the help that's appropriate, regardless of the cost. Some people think that's CFF's secret.

Presently sixty girls ranging in age from seven to twenty live in ten cottages on the grounds. A woman whose no-nonsense gray hair, and skirt, blouse and sneakers, were nun-like in their simplicity, greeted us as Robin and I got out of the car. She introduced herself as Vivian Carroll and told us she'd been the director for the past six years.

"You're in luck today. The middle school the girls attend canceled classes. There's a gas leak in the neighborhood, and it'll take most of the day to repair. So those girls will be home. We've gotten permission for you to interview anyone willing to talk as long as nobody's faces are shown. Mick's trying to decide where to set up first."

I knew this was a lucky break. Otherwise we would have to wait for the weekend or catch the girls right after school. While Robin took photos I thanked Vivian for letting us come. The buildings beyond us were unassuming, like the director herself, but the landscaping made up for it. Towering hardwoods and evergreens outlined paths and shaded cottages. Beds filled with shrubs and fall flowers added color.

"It looks like a happy place," I said. "Is it?"

"Mick tells me you were a foster child?"

"And so was Robin." Robin had wandered off to photograph a welcome sign at the entrance.

"He asked me to save our conversation for filming, but do this for me while we find him. Think about what you needed and wanted when your own family fell apart, and at the end let's talk about what answers you might have found here as a girl."

I probably liked this woman.

★ ★ ★

Toward the end of that day's filming I could answer Vivian's question and did. On camera.

"You asked me to figure out what answers I might have found here as a girl?"

We were standing in the spacious lobby of one of the new apartment buildings, a room filled with plush sofas, and tables piled with puzzles and board games. She had just given me a tour of the upstairs and four comfortable apartments, and the crew was still filming.

So far I had learned a lot. Returning a child to her biological family is CFF's first and most important goal. They work to facilitate reunions and closely monitor them after they take place. While a girl lives on the grounds her family is welcome to stay overnight or for longer stretches, and CCF even helps fund transportation. Weekend parenting seminars are offered, along with anger-management classes. While most families are also working with professionals in their hometowns, parents and siblings can talk to counselors here, as well, or to a social worker who helps them find even more services to make reunification possible.

"Did you find answers?" Vivian asked.

I was careful in my response. "I'm impressed at how great everything looks on the outside. And the description of what you do is faultless. But some of the places I lived looked good enough on the outside, too."

"And they weren't?" She went on without waiting. "Let me ask this. If someone had interviewed you back then in private and asked how you really liked it? What would you have said?"

"You mean the way some of your girls were asked today?"

We *had* asked, and would ask again every chance we got

until we left. The two girls we'd spoken to had been mostly positive about what went on here.

"We didn't coach them," Vivian said.

"Coached or not, they know what they're supposed to say. Foster children can't speak openly. We learn quickly what happens when we try."

"You say *we*. You still think of yourself as a foster child?"

"It's part of who I am. It's a part of who these girls will be for the rest of their lives."

"A lot of our girls have gone on to become more compassionate and concerned adults because of their own beginnings."

I swept my hand toward the stairway leading upstairs to the visitors' apartments. "What happens when a family fails to learn what they need to? Even with all the help you give here."

"Thankfully we have enough staff to make sure a girl will be safe if she goes home. Our caseworkers aren't struggling with the heavy caseloads of some service providers, so we aren't easily fooled. If all else fails we document our findings so that the judge in charge will free a girl for adoption."

"What happens then? Does every girl find a home?"

She didn't smile. "Teenagers are notoriously difficult to place."

"Then some finish growing up here?"

"Although we do keep looking for the right family, some of our young women never find one. So we're their family. They remain here and go to college in Cookeville, or if they go farther afield they're welcome to come back for holidays or weekends. This is their home. We make certain it continues to be as long as they need it."

"Alumni come to visit?"

"Frequently. And some of our employees are former residents."

Those interviews were on Mick's schedule for later in the week.

Vivian brightened. "I think you ought to talk to a girl who will be brutally honest. She's been through the wringer. Most of them have, which is why they're *here*. But the girl I'm thinking about reminds me a little of you."

I had to smile. "How so?"

"Not easily convinced. Not afraid to say so. She questions everything, and while the other girls like her because she stands up for them, the staff has to work harder to accept her." Vivian tilted her head. "Does that sound familiar?"

I just smiled. When she'd introduced herself on camera Vivian had said she was a psychiatric social worker. I could believe it.

"Let me see what I can arrange," she said. "We still have time today?"

"As far as I know."

"Then let's make this happen. I'll go on ahead." She opened the door and ushered us outside. The crew packed up to move, too. We have a second camera operator now, a recent film school graduate who's working cheap so she can work with Mick. Today, though, she looked like a baby bunny trying to outwit a pack of hounds. Everybody looked like they were ready for the day to end.

I was tired, too. Every film requires a lot of standing and waiting, and this one is no exception. Acting can be fun, but this isn't acting. It's even more visceral, which makes it harder.

Robin had been on the sidelines snapping photos. Mick called her over, and I saw them talking, then looking at me. He handed Robin one of his smaller cameras, which to my eyes looked similar to the one she uses, and nodded in my direction. She shrugged, but she took it.

"What was that about?" I asked when she joined me.

"He thinks more than two of us in the room will make the interview impossible. So he asked me to shoot some footage."

"You can do it with that camera?"

"I could do it with mine. But this one's a little beauty, and it does both stills and video brilliantly. He introduced us when we were in Jamestown, and I fell in love. Of course it's just an experiment."

By now we were following Vivian across a bluegrass lawn toward one of the brick cottages, each one a bit different from the others in design, like a real neighborhood. "Can you imagine growing up here?" I asked Robin.

"I spent my last four years of foster care in a group home, so it's not as hard for me as it probably is for you."

"But yours was nothing like this one."

"No, Live Oaks was more like a dorm with rotating room-mates."

The description was accurate. When eighteen-year-old me left Florida for New York, Robin moved to Live Oaks, a residential facility for twenty girls near Tampa. I visited her there whenever I could, taking the long miserable trip south each time I saved enough money for bus fare. There were four girls to a room, and Live Oaks overflowed. There was no place for me to stay, no welcome from the beleaguered staff. At the beginning I snatched sleep at the bus station or the all-night diner a mile away.

Robin's crowded bedroom had seemed familiar. By then I was living hand to mouth in Hell's Kitchen, piled into a one-room apartment with three other women. I had a fold-ing cot, a shelf in a refrigerator that mysteriously turned itself off at midnight and all the cockroaches I cared to meet. But

Hell's Kitchen had suited me. I already knew how to sleep with one eye open.

"You could have come to New York with me," I said.

"You would have been arrested for kidnapping."

"If somebody found us. Or noticed you were gone."

"And where would both of us be today if we'd tried? Live Oaks worked for me. I made good grades, took photography classes at the local art center. They liked to show me off, so my spot there was secure."

She stared into space, as if no matter what she said, she didn't like what she remembered. "But what I liked most? Nobody cared if I bonded to anybody else. There were too many of us, and girls came and went so often we all got lost. I saw a counselor, had a caseworker, but nobody had time to worry if I was making attachments or staying aloof. They were worried about funding, and overcrowding, and what to do with the girls who were stealing jewelry and selling drugs. I flew under the radar, and they loved me for that. My story in life."

"Are you talking about more than the group home?"

"I've been flying under Kris's radar for years. One of the first things I worried about after the accident? Before the doctor told me Talya died? I thought, Kris is going to have to take time off to handle this, and he's not going to be happy."

I didn't know what to say. Robin has never flown under *my* radar.

"It's not his fault," she said. "It's mine. He loves me, or at least he did. But when I'm unhappy, I may not fall mute now, but I still make myself inconspicuous. What's the animal that rolls itself into a ball for protection? A hedgehog? I do that."

"Not anymore. Not since this trip."

"Kris got used to one bargain, and I'm insisting on another."

"If he really loves you, he'll negotiate the terms."

Vivian had bustled into one of the cottages and was already back. Now she waited for us to catch up. Then she started her spiel.

"Hayley's been here for two years. She's eleven going on forty. Her parents are out of the picture, and adoption hasn't worked out. She's a leader, but the adults in her life wish she'd choose better directions."

I was almost too tired for this. I like kids fine. I love Robin's. But I wasn't sure I had the energy to cope with one with so many issues. I could ask the crew behind us to forget it. But what would that say about me? I'd been gung ho so far. I didn't want anybody to think I was scared a child would make a fool of me on camera.

"She knows who we are and why we're here?" I asked.

"All the girls know. But she said she'd talk to you. Her room is interesting. You'll see."

"Can't wait."

Robin narrowed her eyes. She knew I didn't mean it.

We followed Vivian to a living area with cheerful yellow walls that sported framed artwork clearly done by children. The kitchen was straight ahead, painted a soft peach with green cabinets. The room was large enough for several people to work there.

Vivian saw my quick examination. "The girls take cooking lessons. They make dinner under supervision a couple of nights a week. In some of the other houses the older girls make nearly all the meals. We try to make dinner preparation a happy time, when everybody can share what happened during their day."

This was all a little too Martha Stewart for me. "Does Hayley know she'll be on camera?"

"I told her we wouldn't show her face. She was disappointed."

"Sounds like somebody I know," Robin said.

I narrowed *my* eyes. "You can be replaced."

She shot a photo of me sticking out my tongue.

We followed Vivian through a hallway lined with bedrooms. The first, a comfortable-looking suite, belonged to the house parents. Hayley's was at the back. Vivian knocked, then opened the door into a dungeon. At least a Dollar Store attempt at a dungeon.

"Wow." I stepped inside and looked around. Angel hair cobwebs hung across windows, and black crepe paper streamers danced from a heat vent in the ceiling, or were trying to. Clearly they'd been there for weeks. Plastic skulls adorned two dressers, and both girls' headboards were draped in black. A ghost floated from a plastic hanger.

"Somebody doesn't want to say goodbye to Halloween," I said.

"Boo!" A girl sprang out from the far side of the farthest bed. "It's the best holiday. Better than Christmas."

"Bet you're Hayley."

She was slight and dark-haired, with caramel-colored skin. Her ancestors could have hailed from any number of continents, and people who needed labels were probably anxious to pinpoint which one.

"Did I scare you?"

"I was too busy admiring the scenery."

"Hayley, these streamers are collecting dust." Vivian pointed overhead. "They need to come down. Tonight before bed, okay?"

The girl smiled sweetly, but when Vivian went outside to say something to our new camera operator, Hayley tapped the side of her forehead with her forefinger, then put two fingers to the front of it, jerked them away and closed them into a tight fist.

I laughed. Hayley frowned at me, and I slowly signed, *"I bet Vivian doesn't know what you just called her."*

The girl's eyes widened.

"Robin?" I said. Robin was cleaning her camera lens. She turned and I signed, *"How many curse words do you remember?"*

She laughed and said out loud, "Most of the ones you taught me."

"Have you taught this one to Pet?" I repeated Hayley's movements.

"Are you kidding?"

"Pet is Robin's daughter, and she's ten," I said, turning back to the girl. "Robin thinks she's too young. So that probably means you are, too."

"Where did *you* learn to sign?"

"I was a foster kid. Did they tell you that?"

Hayley shrugged. I studied her for a moment. She had a long face, expressive but solemn. By the time she reached her late teens either she would be a heartbreaker or her heart would be broken by constant rejection. So goes adolescence.

"Robin's my foster sister." I nodded in her direction. "We took a class at a local church so we could sign to each other and nobody else would know what we were saying."

"Except the other people who took your class."

"We only used it at home. Drove our foster parents nuts. We just told them we were practicing so we could sign services at church."

"You're not very good. You spell out too much."

"Hey, we only took one class, and I don't have anybody to practice with anymore. Afterward the preacher's son gave me a special lesson in profanity. May I sit on your bed? This has been a long day."

"It's not my bed. It belongs to CFF. I just use it." She perched on the edge, and I joined her.

"Where did you learn to sign?"

"My mother was deaf."

"Was?"

"She died. Do you want to hear my whole sordid little story?"

"I like a girl who uses words like *sordid*. It shows you listen in school."

"Not more than I have to."

"And how much is that? Where do you want to go after this?"

"Anywhere."

I leaned back and turned to see her better. "I've been comparing CFF with the places I stayed. I've got to say, it looks better on the surface. Not so much?"

"It could be worse or better. How would I know?"

"Because you've probably been through worse. Remember your sordid little story?"

"Did they tell you I've almost been adopted three times and none of them took?"

I whistled softly. "Are you going for a record?"

"Stupid people."

I held up my index finger. "One failure for me. I stayed with the family six months. How long did yours last?"

"If I tell you, you'll count months and think you won."

"You must have been a monster to get turned around that fast."

"What's the point of any of it? People get tired of you and they leave or make you leave eventually. I just saved everybody the trouble."

I remembered we were supposed to be talking about CFF, but I really didn't care. "Believe me, I know."

"At least here nobody expects me to get all huggy-kissy. And the food's good."

"Yeah, good food means a lot. But not enough. The worst place I lived had the best cook."

"How did you get famous after all that?"

I suspected that Hayley only rarely asked people about themselves. I'm no expert, but this conversation seemed like a good sign.

"I think I saw getting famous as revenge. I was trying to show everybody I was worth a lot more than they guessed."

"Were you just lucky?"

"Luck has a lot to do with it. I figured out how to be a little different, and people were ready for what I had to offer. I made a few friends, and later they helped me get noticed. But I worked hard, too. Still do." I sat up again. "Why Halloween? You didn't tell me."

"Christmas is for families. The other holidays are, too. But people dying and turning into ghosts and skeletons? You do that all by yourself. You don't need a family."

"That's probably why I always liked it. Only I never figured it out."

"I thought you were going to be all 'Oh, you're so cute, and I'm so glad you're living in such a sweet home for little girls.'"

I made a face. "God, I hope I'm never like that. But I've got to say, the fact that they let you keep those nasty streamers up as long as they did says something good about living here."

"They kind of try."

"Good." I heard a familiar bark. Starla had taken Roscoe to watch a group of girls playing volleyball, but it sounded like my pup was back.

"Do you like dogs?"

"They're okay."

"Can I show mine your room?"

"Does he bite?"

"Not half as bad as you do."

She actually smiled. In the next weeks I would probably meet lots of girls like this one. But I was glad she was my head start.

"You're going to make it," I said. "If I did, you can."

She signed some particularly colorful profanity.

I signed right back.

This time we both laughed.

24

Robin

Pet finally finished the leaves. Jody's family is in counseling to-gether and canceled their annual Thanksgiving vacation in St. Thomas to pay for it. Lynette calls that natural consequences. Natural consequences around here mean Pet rarely speaks to me. There is nothing quieter than a house with a child who's giving you the silent treatment. I'm getting a lot of work done. K

While we waited for the gate to open for our last day at CFF, Cecilia gathered papers strewn all over the car seat during the drive from Nashville. Roscoe was helping. "I'm firmly on the side of this-place-is-okay," she said. "Roscoe's going to be sorry to leave."

Roscoe probably will be, because in addition to charm-ing our adoring crew, he's entertained the girls with the help of CFF's own rescue beagle. The girls named their pet Kit-ten to soothe the feelings of the cat lovers who had wanted a real one, and luckily Kitten welcomed Roscoe into his pack.

"You're going to miss *Hayley*." I finished cleaning a lens in preparation for stowing it in my bag.

"She's a character."

"You two seem to have bonded."

"I'm going to stay in touch with her. Seems like it would be good for her to know I care enough to email occasionally or call."

"What about all the other girls?"

"Is it fair to Hayley to think that way? She's part of a group, so she can't be singled out for a little attention? Lots of them will go back to their biological families. She won't. And as things stand, adoption doesn't look promising. Not until she decides to stop sabotaging it or finds somebody who'll love her anyway."

"CeCe, you aren't just anybody. You do realize that, right?"

"She likes Miley Cyrus better than me."

I laughed at her expression. "That doesn't actually get you off the hook."

"I'm going to give her my public email address, but I'll make sure her mail's forwarded to me." Cecilia's mail is handled by a staff of four. Once she showed me a day's worth, as well as a thick file marked Crazy. Fame comes at a price.

"You start that kind of relationship, you have to stay with it. She's had enough rejection."

"I know."

Relationships really aren't Cecilia's thing. On the other hand her affection for me has never wavered. Maybe she really will keep in touch with Hayley. It might be good for both of them.

I finished organizing everything in my camera bag, which no longer takes conscious thought. I'll always be grateful to Cecilia for prodding me to restart my career, and to Mick for reminding me that intuition is more important than the right lens or the right filter. But when even Kris's perfunctory texts make me homesick, I know I'm ready for a break.

We have weeks of intermittent filming ahead, but the four days here at Children First and Foremost have been produc-

tive. Mick and Jerry brought loosely assembled rushes to Cecilia's condo last night. Donny, who spent most of the week
in New York, flew in to join us. Some footage was brilliant,
enough to make this visit worthwhile, but we're all in agreement that after today we've done what we can.

Like the scenes in Randolph Forge, CFF will be another
feel-good moment for viewers, interlaced with grim statistics
and grimmer visits to less impressive solutions.

Beside me Cecilia checked her makeup, although Wendy
would do the finishing touches inside. We were about to film
a morning meeting. Each cottage begins Saturday the same
way. The house parents serve a special breakfast, and afterward everyone sits in a circle and each girl talks about her
week. They are required to say one good thing about everyone in the room before they air grievances.

Cecilia has permission to sit in the circle and talk a little
about her own years in foster care before she asks questions.
Of course when *At the Mercy of Strangers* airs, hers will be the
only face we see.

Outside the car I lifted my face to the sunshine. I'm sorry
to be heading north tomorrow. Temperatures in New York
City are in the forties, and yesterday sleet sent cars skidding
through streets and onto sidewalks. While Cecilia flies back
to California with Donny, I head off with Mick and the crew
to a program in the heart of Bedford-Stuyvesant. The program is struggling, and the city is threatening to sever con-
tracts for services. We're scheduled to be finished in time for
me to fly home on Tuesday to spend the rest of Thanksgiving week with my family.

The contrast between overcrowded foster homes and my
own will probably be sobering. More sobering for me since
for years I was imprisoned on the other side.

Cecilia glanced at me and as always read my thoughts.

"You're ready for a break, aren't you?"

"Counting the days."

"The kids will be delighted to see you."

I noticed she didn't mention my husband. I'm hoping that once we're face-to-face, Kris and I will begin to plow through our problems. I do know that since firing Grace he's been coming home in time for Elena to pick up her son, and he's working from home on Saturdays, too. I'm not sure what to think of either development, but I still feel encouraged.

"I won't even be home a week. Hopefully all of us make the most of it." I was scheduled to meet Cecilia and the crew in Tampa the following Monday, where we would film until we took an extended break for Christmas. I was looking forward to that, as well.

"Take it slow," she said with sisterly wisdom. Cecilia still gives me advice, even in areas where she needs it herself.

After parking, Hal went back to speak to the guard at the gatehouse. The facility is fenced, and because the front gate is always manned, no extra security was needed. While the girls surely told their classmates that Cecilia was here with a film crew, Mick and the CFF staff carefully kept our daily schedule secret. A few people had gathered outside the gate each day, but they had been dispatched by a local deputy. We're close enough to Nashville that celebrity glimpses aren't uncommon.

My phone buzzed, and I saw my husband was calling. I pointed to the phone. "It's Kris. I'll meet you inside."

With Roscoe in her arms Cecilia continued toward the cottage where we would be filming today. I saw her speak to a few of the girls. The crew had arrived ahead of us to get footage of breakfast preparations, and they were probably already inside.

I leaned against a tree while I took the call.

"Hey," I said. "Hope everything's okay?"

"You're probably busy, so I'll make this short."

"I'm about to be busy, but not this minute."

"I'm at work."

This is my husband's way of saying *he* doesn't want to chat. Like any good attorney he's going to get right to the point.

"Shoot, then," I said.

"I tried to find a way out of this, Robin, but I can't. Do you know when you'll be flying home?"

After that first sentence my stomach was already tying itself into knots. I closed my eyes. "Tuesday the twenty-fifth. Timing depends on how things go in New York. I haven't made my reservation."

"New York?"

I told him a little about what we would be doing.

"That sounds like it could be dangerous."

"More for the kids who live in crowded foster homes than for us. Besides, we both know any place can be dangerous." I thought of Talya, who had seemed perfectly safe until the instant she died.

He was quiet for a moment. Then it was back to business. "Can you please make the reservation for early in the day?"

I forced a laugh. "You're in that much of a hurry to see me?"

"If you can arrange it I just need you here before Elena leaves. If not I'll find somebody for the evening, too, but I need to know."

"You have a commitment the night I get home?"

"I have to go out of town." I had a feeling he wasn't done, and he wasn't. "I won't be able to get back again until Friday afternoon or later. I'm sorry. I really am. But we can postpone Thanksgiving dinner until Friday night or maybe Saturday, when I'm sure I'll be home. I need to pull my weight at the office, and I'm the best person to do this."

I processed this out loud. "You'll be gone for the holiday?"

"Just some of it. We'll have the weekend."

"I see."

"Look, this isn't my idea. But because you're gone every day I'm leaving work early—"

"You're leaving work at a normal hour, Kris."

"I'm leaving work *early* and working at home on weekends. People understand you can't help me right now, but nobody's happy about it. Since you're going to be here to cover again, I need to show I can go the extra mile."

I was struggling to figure out whether I had a right to be angry. Why should I be surprised? Kris's job had already trumped the trip of a lifetime to Prague. Thanksgiving was simply more of the same.

"You're angry," he said, when I didn't answer. "But you need to see this from my perspective. I've given up a lot to let you follow your sister—"

"You've given up a *lot*, Kris? A little time. And for the record, you didn't *let* me take this job. I did that myself. The only thing I asked for was the respect I deserve as your partner."

"This isn't the time to rehash. I need your help. I hope you're willing."

My answer came easily. "Take all the time you need. The kids and I will spend Thanksgiving in Sanibel. Cecilia will be delighted. I'll let the schools know they'll be leaving after classes on Tuesday. Elena can drive them to the airport and put them on a plane to Fort Myers, where I'll meet them. You won't have to do a thing." He started to say something but I cut him off. "I'm sorry, I've got to go now and *follow* my sister. Enjoy your day."

I slid my phone back in my bag.

I didn't have time to think about what had just happened. I looked up and saw that the girls had vanished inside, along with Roscoe, but Cecilia was just yards from the cottage door, backing away from a man I had never seen on the grounds before.

I could tell immediately this was serious because Cecilia rarely backs away from anybody. The man was dressed in a tattered flannel shirt, and his hair was long and greasy. He might have been young or old. It was impossible to tell under a scraggly beard and what might be several layers of grime.

I looked back toward the gatehouse to see if Hal was still talking to the guard. He wasn't. He was heading swiftly toward Cecilia, but he was too far away to intervene. I started forward, too, but Cecilia saw me and held up her hand. Now I was close enough to see that the man was pointing a gun at her.

I could also hear their conversation.

"You don't answer my mail. Not one single letter!"

"My poor sweetie, do you know how many letters I get every single day?" Cecilia had stopped backing away and was now standing her ground. "I tell my assistants to give me the important ones, but sometimes they just don't get it." She smiled her famous smile, as if this was a man she cared about and she was commiserating with him. She didn't look a bit frightened.

"I sent fifty. Maybe a hundred."

She shook her head. "How can they be that stupid? Wouldn't it be clear to *you* how important those letters were? I mean, so many..."

"I'll tell you what they said, them letters. I told you I loved you and we were meant to be together. All the time. I can tell from your songs."

She shook her head in admiration. "A smart man can always read between the lines."

He lowered the gun, but only far enough to rest it against his thigh. "You been singing them just for me."

I saw Donny poised in the cottage doorway, as if he was waiting for exactly the right moment to launch himself at Cecilia's admirer. Hal had pulled up sharply, too, but he had drawn his gun and was holding it by his side.

Who knows why some thoughts race through our heads during a crisis? Yesterday out of nowhere a memory of the accident had returned. Now, again, I remembered the instant when I witnessed the car bearing down on us. Pet and Nik had flashed through my mind. They would lose their mother, but at least they would remember I had loved them. How would Cecilia be remembered?

"I think I ought to sing for you right now," Cecilia said. Instead of moving away, she stepped closer. "You'd like that, wouldn't you? I can look right into your eyes and sing just for you."

I was terrified, but some part of me was also frozen in awe. Cecilia, under the worst possible pressure, was acting as if this man was her salvation, the one she had waited for all these years. When had she learned to act with such skill?

At what point in her life had she learned to lie without blinking an eye?

"I'd like that," he said. "You come right up close and sing to me."

"First you have to put the gun down, sweetie. 'Cause when I'm all done singing, you're going to be so happy, that old gun of yours might just go off in salute. And what if you hit somebody by mistake? That would spoil our day."

He hesitated. I wondered if there was enough logic in his

tortured brain to realize that the moment he abandoned the gun, somebody would jump him.

"I don't think so," he said at last. "I keep it on me all the time."

"You protect the people you love. A man like you would."

"Somebody has to."

"But you could protect me just fine without it, couldn't you?" She stepped a little closer. "Do you really need that gun? You look like a big strong man to me."

I couldn't make myself breathe.

The man cocked his head. "You think so?"

"Oh, I can tell. We could use somebody like you to do security. Then you'd be close to me all the time."

This wasn't what he expected. This poor demented soul had found his way here because he was furious Cecilia hadn't answered his letters. Who knows what he'd hoped for. Fear? Tears? Punishment? Now his expectations were being turned upside down. She had just offered him a job and endless time together. He looked confused.

"I'd like that." He spaced the words, as if he still wasn't sure.

"Are you as strong as you look?" She smiled as if she knew the answer.

"Strong? Sure."

"Come on, show me. Let me feel that muscle. But not with the gun, okay? You're going to take care of me, you can't wave a gun around. We have to be subtle. First rule of a good bodyguard."

He started to put the gun in his pocket. I couldn't believe he would do that for her, but Cecilia stopped him.

"Now I'm all worried you'll shoot off that long leg of yours."

He shook his head, as if dealing with gun-shy women was familiar.

She laughed in delight, and as if her laughter was the final proof she loved him, he set the gun on the ground.

I launched myself in his direction. Donny reached him first, but not before Cecilia had kicked the gun a safe distance. Hal got there next, but Donny, with one sharp blow to the solar plexus, had already knocked the now-howling intruder to the ground. By the time I got there Donny was sitting on his hips, restraining his hands.

"Sheriff's on his way." Hal trained his gun on the intruder. "I've got this now. You can release him."

"Where the hell were you?"

"The guard wanted to tell me they found a section of the fence had been cut. They called the sheriff, but he hasn't made it out here yet."

Donny got up by resting his weight momentarily on his captive's chest. Then he released the man's hands.

By then I was on my way to Cecilia, but Donny got *there* first, too.

She threw herself into his arms, sobbing. He held her close and stroked her hair.

"You're something," he said, resting his cheek on the top of her head and pulling her tighter against him. "You are truly amazing. And you're going to be okay. You're a survivor. You'll get through this, too."

She wrapped her arms around him and let him hold her.

I knew if I moved closer I would be the second intruder this morning. I backed away to give them space and privacy.

I wasn't jealous, but I couldn't remember a time when Cecilia and I hadn't been each other's greatest comfort.

This time she had turned to Donny.

In one of those moments of postapocalyptic clarity, when

adrenaline is surging and the world becomes an entirely different place, I wondered if I had married stoic, logical Kris because I had known I wouldn't need a husband to comfort me and understand my every feeling.

I had my sister for that.

25

—

Cecilia

Hal is calling for reinforcements, and from this moment on there will be two Hals, or whoever, watching over me. Donny says if I refuse, he's done with me. He has too much tied up in my career to see me killed by a crazy fan, and he told me from the beginning that asking Hal to protect me without help was unfair.

I want this trip to feel normal. For this journey into my past I want to forget my photo is plastered all over the globe and people think they know me. Donny says I gave up that right the moment I signed my first big contract. The price of fame. Blah, blah, blah.

Robin claims Donny isn't as worried about his job as he is about me. I'm not sure why she thinks that matters.

We filmed the morning meeting anyway. If I can say one thing about my blighted childhood? Abandonment and foster care taught me to pick up the pieces, reassemble them and move on. Either I reassembled quickly or the pieces would sink so far below the surface that the whole me would never reemerge. The monsters of the deep still try to pull me down—witness those weeks in Australia—but today I'm treading water.

Afterward I found a place to sit by myself, a tranquil pond at the center of the CFF grounds. Weeping willows line the edge, and a pair of swans swim in graceful circles. Last month a girl tried to drown herself here. Her monsters were about to triumph, but someone on staff rescued her.

Other than that? This is a good place to contemplate life or, in my case, finish putting myself together again. Our crew figured that out, and they're leaving me alone for a while, although I suspect there will be long-distance footage.

Cecilia, alone and shaken by her memories. Cut.

Apparently Vivian never got the memo. As she strode in my direction I made room for her on the bench and waited, anticipating an apology.

"You and Hayley are a lot alike," she said as she seated herself.

I turned to see her better. Today Vivian's wearing gray. I've already asked Wendy to buy her half a dozen designer scarves in brilliant colors as a goodbye gift, and to make sure they're too expensive to ignore or give away.

I pasted a polite smile in place. "Are we?"

"The two of you. If you were being run over by a truck you'd roll your eyes like it was nothing. Then you'd pick yourselves up off the ground and walk away."

"I had a good cry. That was a lot for me." And it had been a lot for me to throw myself into Donny's arms for comfort, something I don't want to think about.

"That's more than Hayley's had."

"Why does she need a good cry? Other than the usual reasons, like nobody loving her or wanting her or understanding her?"

"Because she's the one who told Roy Doggett how to get in and find you this morning."

My intruder has a name now. Right out of Central Casting. I summoned the energy to ask, "Hayley?"

"Apparently she's been working on that section of the fence with a nail file, in case she ever wants to make an escape attempt. Handy fellow Roy just finished it off with super-duper wire cutters. His cousin goes to school with her. Hayley sold the cousin your information for fifty dollars."

"That little shit."

"Yeah." Vivian shook her head sadly. "I expected better of her. A hundred dollars, at least."

It was exactly the right thing to say. I burst into laughter, then, unaccountably, into tears.

Again.

Vivian draped her arm over my shoulders as if I were one of her girls. "We both know Mr. Doggett is a sick man, but honestly, if I'd been there, I would have stomped on his chest for the fun of it. And I'm ready to hang Hayley by her thumbs."

I tried to stop blubbering and couldn't. "She…she knows I…care."

"Of course she does. Why do you think she did it? Other than the money, which was also a powerful incentive."

I sniffed, and Vivian reached in her pocket and handed me a tissue. "It's clean. You'd be surprised how many I go through in a day. I carry a wad as thick as a pinecone."

I wiped my nose and eyes, and we sat in silence until I was able to speak again. "Did she tell you she was responsible?"

"Of course not. One of the other girls did."

"Hayley was bragging?"

"No, the other girl saw Hayley and Doggett's cousin make the deal."

"You're sure it was her?"

"I confronted her. And I found the money under her mattress."

"I guess I have to talk to her about hiding places."

"I bet you would know."

I told her something I should have said on camera. "I used to hide food. I got thrown out of one foster home because my stash of graham crackers and moldy cheese attracted mice."

"We get a lot of that, but not the throwing out part. I give every new girl a plastic container with a secure top to hide whatever she needs to. Thwarts the mice."

I was sure the containers got used. Like me, some of these girls just wanted to be sure they wouldn't be hungry again.

"So what are you going to do?" Vivian asked.

For a moment I wasn't sure what she meant. What was *I* going to do? Other than pull myself together?

"She's testing you," she said. "But you should know she didn't expect anything like what happened. She's still a little girl. And even if she's seen a lot, she can't yet project consequences. She had no idea Doggett would show up with a gun. She was shaken."

"How could you tell?"

"I am such an expert."

I laughed again, and this one must have taken, because no tears followed. "What should I do?"

Vivian squeezed my shoulder before she dropped her arm. "What do you want to do? And I'll warn you, turning her over your knee is unacceptable."

"Beating doesn't help."

"Speaking from experience?"

I didn't want to go there. "I guess if I ask her why she did it, I won't get an answer worth anything, either."

"Good insight. I suspect you know that from experience, too."

"I have told so many lies in my life that half the time I don't know what's true and what isn't."

"You know deep inside. And isn't this film part of sorting that out?"

I had to fight tears again, but after a moment I won. "Where were you all those years ago when I needed you?"

"I wish someone had been there for you, Cecilia. Now I just hope this film will encourage more people to do what we're doing here. But for the record? For someone who had to find her own way through the woods, you've beaten quite a path." She stood. "Will you talk to Hayley? She's in her room. Quite possibly for the rest of her life."

"Maybe I'll figure out what to say between here and there."

"If she'll talk, you could listen. And by the way, she is available for adoption." Vivian added the last as if that was just an afterthought and not part of her reason for seeking me out.

"I'm not Angelina. Not even Madonna."

"No, you're even *more* aware of how much Hayley needs somebody. Because you've lived it."

"I plan to stay in touch. Despite this little glitch."

She clapped me on the back. "Good for you."

"I can't adopt every child who needs me."

"Of course you can't."

"She would make my life a living hell."

"She would certainly try." She sent me a smile as she strode away, probably to light a fire under the next person on her list.

I was left to contemplate how I was going to tell the girl who had nearly gotten me killed that I understood why she'd done it and still cared about her anyway.

Hayley looked up when I walked into her room. For obvious reasons there are no locks on bedroom doors here, so when she didn't respond to my knock, I let myself in.

"Did I invite you?" she asked.

I signed something vile enough to get her attention. She shrugged and looked away.

Without asking I went to sit beside her on the bed. She moved away, but not to give me room. She clearly didn't want me there.

I spoke first. "I can't think of a thing to say."

"That's new. Every grown-up in the world has a lecture they reserve just for me."

"Fresh out of lectures. Maybe being scared half to death by your friend Roy chased them out of my head."

"He's not my friend. I never even met him. His cousin paid me, and I told him stuff."

"A lecture just popped into my head. Amazing, right? It goes like this. Girl, don't take money from men for favors. Not ever. Once you start it's really hard to stop."

"Is that what you did? Is that how you got so famous?"

"When the roll is called up yonder I'll have a list of black marks a mile long after my name. But I have never accepted money from any man for a favor."

"You didn't sleep your way to the top?"

"You're eleven years old, Hayley. What a question."

"Did you?"

"No, I did not. Really. I was tempted a time or two, believe me. Once an A and R guy from a label I wanted to record for—"

"What's A and R?"

I figured this meant she was listening, which was what I'd hoped for. "It stands for artists and repertoire. You know, like talent scouts. The people who go to clubs and performances and listen to groups to see if they're worth taking a chance on."

"What did he want?"

"As you put it, he wanted me to sleep my way to the top,

and I told him—" I rethought what I'd been about to say "—no. Years later the same label offered me a great deal, so I made sure they fired him before I signed."

"Do you always get what you want?"

"Far from it. I wanted my mother to stop using drugs, but she didn't. I wanted her to take care of me, even a little, but ditto. And when she disappeared, for some reason I wanted her to come back. That's the one I still don't understand. But she was my mother, you know?"

"My mother hung herself. She didn't pick me up from school, like she was supposed to. So I walked home by myself and I found her."

I didn't touch her, although I wanted to pull her into a bear hug and weep into her hair. There was a catch in my voice, and I know she heard it. "You didn't deserve that."

"Maybe it was my fault. She was always angry at me."

"No, she was always angry. You weren't the cause."

"How do you know? You weren't there."

"Because you were a little girl. So was I when my mother disappeared. But it took years for me to realize my mother's problems weren't my fault."

"I probably won't get that far."

"Hayley, you're a survivor. Like me. You can survive two ways. You can destroy everything and everybody around you and walk over their ashes, or you can start paying close attention to the people and situations surrounding you and choose the ones that are good, without destroying anybody."

"You made the record company fire that man."

"I know. But I looked at the damage he might do to other young women, and I figured firing him would prevent that. The fact that it felt good wasn't the main thing. More or less a side effect."

"So even the second way you still choose who to destroy?"

I ruffled her hair, and she let me. "You really are a brat, aren't you?"

"I work at it."

"I know you do. And I know you didn't understand that Roy Doggett is crazy as a bedbug and might come after me with a gun. I also know that in the long and productive friendship we're going to have, you'll do other things to hurt me, just to see if I'll stay around. I wish we could avoid that, but I'm ready." I stood. "I'll be calling and emailing. I hope you'll respond occasionally."

"I don't get it."

"Get what?"

"Why you think I care."

Both my smile and my shrug were 100 percent genuine. "Nobody will ever understand you better, Hayley. Get used to it."

26

—

Robin

Children are perceptive. They know when storms are brewing. Children are also willing to overlook clouds gathering above them if an adult pretends skies are sunny. Nik and Pet must know Kris and I are having problems. But when I told them I thought it would be fun to visit Aunt Cecilia in Florida over the holiday, they took me at my word.

I guess it helped that Kris bought each of them bare bones smartphones with GPS tracking in case they got into trouble, and he made sure they got on their nonstop flight instead of leaving that to Elena. They have friends who split their time between mothers and fathers. Maybe it seems normal, considering. Or maybe, deep inside, they know this is something they'll need to get used to.

On Wednesday we swam and lazed in the sun, and I let Cecilia and Donny take them shopping for "Florida clothes." My sister's found a certain anonymity here, which brings her pleasure. The locals pretend to ignore her, and because they do, tourists decide they've imagined that *the* Cecilia is buying T-shirts and flip-flops at CVS with everybody else. Of course sunglasses and silly beach hats help, too.

Now, as Cecilia's housekeeper puts the finishing touches

on the only vegan Thanksgiving dinner my kids will likely ever have, Fifi—everyone in the unit has taken up Fiona's nickname—is tossing Frisbees to Nik and Pet. All three of them are just barely holding their own. Nik has been in the water once, and Roscoe, with his matchstick legs, beat Pet to the Frisbee a moment ago and dragged it down the beach.

Mick plunked to the sand beside me to watch the game. "Fifi loves kids. She always wanted a brother or sister. But by the time she was old enough to care, her mother and I knew we weren't going to last."

"I'm not sure Kris and I are going to last." The moment I said it, I wondered why. The words could be construed as an invitation. I feel an undeniable spark igniting whenever Mick is near, and I think he does, too, but neither of us has acknowledged it.

"What's he like?"

"Quiet. Controlled. Responsible." I thought a bit more. "Married to his job."

"That's part of the reason my marriage ended."

"Were you sorry?"

"Not really. If she'd forced me to choose, which I guess in a way she did, I would have chosen my career."

"What was wrong with her that you would have made that choice?"

"Are you asking what's wrong with *you*?"

I was. In our weeks on the road Mick and I had talked about almost everything except our mutual attraction. His films were an outgrowth of his wisdom. And he could be trusted.

"I can't help thinking if Kris wanted to be home more, he could find a way."

"Home with you, right?"

"Right."

"Fifi's mother needed attention. Lots of it. Still does, and Fifi gives it to her."

I had noticed how much attention Fifi gave Mick, too.

"My emotional energy goes into my films," he said. "I couldn't hold her hand every time she needed it. I loved her, but I couldn't stand living with her. She drained me."

Did I drain Kris? I honestly didn't think so. For years I'd asked for so little. We were building something together. We both thought so. Then I made the mistake of asking for more.

"You probably know this, but before I took this assignment I almost died in a car wreck."

"Cecilia told me."

"It changed everything. Afterward I realized I was halfway to invisible. I let that happen, but Kris doesn't see it."

"Because you're still visible to him?"

"No, I think he just stopped looking for me a long time ago."

"Then he's a fool."

I wished it were that simple. "Kris believes that providing for us equals love. His own father is an artist and a political rabble-rouser. They were poor—"

"That figures."

"Kris doesn't want us to be poor or insecure. I understand that. I'm just not willing to live with the consequences anymore."

"What about Kris?"

This was the hardest part to tell. "Since the accident he's closed himself off. He's never once asked me how I'm feeling. It's like he doesn't notice I almost died. He wants to work even harder, but now I won't let him. So he's furious."

"There he was, working all the time to keep you secure and safe, and you almost got yourself killed. Of course he's furious."

I was startled. This was an insight I hadn't reached on my own. "The car was totaled. I lost one of my closest friends, and *Kris* is the one who gets to be furious?"

"You're furious, too, Robin. You don't know that?"

For a moment I couldn't draw a breath. Because, of course Mick was right. I was beyond furious. I was willing to end my marriage rather than remain the same woman who had gotten into that car the night of the accident and given up my seat so Talya could die in my place.

I rested my face in my hands. Mick put his arm around me and his lips close to my ear.

"Your husband is about to lose something wonderful, something irreplaceable. He thinks he's doing everything for you, and he's angry you can't see his sacrifice. Kris wants to take care of you."

"Is that what men do?"

"I don't want to take care of anybody. Not even Fifi. I let her take care of me, and so does her mother. We both have to remind ourselves she needs things. It has to be conscious, and half the time I forget. I don't have a selfless bone in my body. Your husband sounds like he might have too many."

"This is an odd way to defend him, Mick. By criticizing yourself."

"I'm not defending him. He's making a big mistake."

I lifted my head and patted his hand in thanks. We went back to sitting side by side, arms in their proper places. But I was struggling not to cry.

After a few moments, he spoke again. "You want a partner. You want to be a partner. Not all men are cut out for that."

"Kris thinks I'll get this out of my system."

"Does he really?"

I scooped up sand and let it dribble through my fingers. Did he? Because we hadn't talked, really talked, in so long

I didn't know what my husband thought. I was projecting, and it was the best I could do.

Mick knew it was time to change the subject. He stood and offered me his hand. I took it, and he helped me up. I saw Pet looking our way and dropped his hand immediately.

The five of us and Roscoe walked to a point not far away where we watched sailboats on the horizon. Nik hadn't said much since his arrival. He seemed happy and excited to be doing something so exotic when his friends were watching the Macy's Thanksgiving Day Parade and entertaining ancient aunts and uncles. But he hadn't told me he'd missed me, or said anything about what was going on at home. I'd heard all about school, but like his father, with Nik the important things usually go unsaid.

Now he made a point of facing me. "Dad likes the beach."

I wasn't sure how Nik knew this since we'd only rarely gone as a family, and we'd never been to Sanibel, although we'd had a standing invitation since Cecilia bought *Casa del Corazón*.

And why hadn't the children and I just come without Kris? Why had I wrapped my life so tightly around his and let him call the shots?

"He would be here if he could be," Nik said, as if he knew my thoughts.

This was Nik fighting for his family, as direct as he would ever be. I manufactured a carefully noncommittal answer. "It's the pits to have to work on a holiday."

"He said he'll eat at a restaurant."

"At least he'll have turkey," Pet said.

She and Nik made faces. Cecilia had warned them they would be eating tofu for dinner. I happen to know she ordered a roast turkey from a deli and while most of the meal will be comfortably vegan, all the meat eaters will be satisfied.

"Pet, you and I have a pie to make." I looked at my son. "Do you want to help?"

"Aunt Cecilia said I could listen while she and Gizzie work on their song."

"Go for it."

We started back, Pet carrying Roscoe, who'd worn himself out. "What special things do you like for Thanksgiving dinner?" I asked Fifi.

"It's always different. We usually go to a restaurant. I get to choose."

She and Pet, who has adventurous tastes, compared their favorite cuisines while I thought about being juggled between parents on holidays. Nik picked up shells. Mick fell behind to film a phalanx of terns on the shoreline with his tiny GoPro camera. Everything felt so comfortable, so normal, but in reality there was nothing normal about this. At home on Thanksgiving I never had time for a leisurely walk. I cooked all day, determined to give my family and Kris's parents the best. By day's end I was always exhausted.

And I loved it.

Maybe I *was* furious, as Mick had pointed out, but I still missed my husband and the life I thought we'd been making together.

Inside the house Cecilia and Gizzie were cozied up to a grand piano in the sizable great room. Gizzie is closing in on fifty, but he still looks like a kewpie doll, with a froth of orange hair above black-framed glasses. He wore a loud floral shirt, plaid shorts and sandals with straps that crisscrossed halfway up his calves. He was playing snatches of melodies, and Cecilia was stopping him to comment or sing a different line.

All those years ago Gizzie was probably the first person in New York who realized Cecilia had what it took to reach the stars. He's famous in his own right now, but they still collaborate. Their best songs are written together. The theme song for *At the Mercy of Strangers* will probably be extraordinary.

Dark-haired Pat, Gizzie's partner, wearing a suit and tie, was stretched out on the sofa. Donny was reading in the corner.

This was my family for the holiday weekend. An eclectic, exotic mix of talented superstars. I was lucky to have them and glad to be here.

I wondered what cuisine my husband would try tonight. Would he stick with the old standbys mass-produced in some all-American restaurant in Norfolk, or would he opt for Indian or Thai? Whatever he chose I was certain I would never know, just like I was certain that when Kris called to wish our children a happy Thanksgiving, he would not ask to speak to me.

27

Kris

We ordered Thanksgiving dinner at an upscale seafood chain. Merv, me and his company controller, an anemic-looking blonde who seems as depressed as I am. Merv explained he'd invited Josie to dine with us because her family was out of town for the weekend. Like me, Josie had probably been roped into working today, so her family made plans without her. I was itching to point that out to Robin as evidence that women sometimes put jobs before family, even on an important holiday. But our problems are large enough that no example—especially one that's clearly making the example herself miserable—will fix them.

Turkey with all the trimmings was featured on tonight's menu, but I couldn't make myself order a chain version of what Robin does so brilliantly. I wondered if she was cooking for Cecilia and my children. It's unlikely. There are probably others spending the weekend in Sanibel, too. Maybe half of LA's music scene is dishing up cranberry sauce and sweet potatoes served with a flourish by a trio of celebrity chefs. Maybe in a few weeks I can turn on the Food Network and enjoy the meal vicariously.

"Your salmon okay?" Merv asked.

Seconds elapsed before I realized I was the only person at the table dining on salmon. Considering how little attention I'd paid, I could have chewed and swallowed the cedar plank it was cooked on.

"Excellent. And your...shrimp?" Shrimp seemed like a safe guess, although what had once been swimming in the ocean was now swimming in an opaque red sauce on his plate.

"I eat here a lot. This is one of my favorites."

"I can see why." Although honestly, I had no clue.

"My husband is allergic to seafood," Josie said. "And one of my little boys. It's a nice treat for me."

She looked like she'd rather be eating rusty nails, but Merv took her at her word. "Nice of you to stay over and do the tour this weekend."

Her smile was tight enough to suppress whatever she really wanted to say. I flashed an answering one in sympathy.

"So you liked what you saw?" Merv asked me. "We'll finish in the morning, then you can be on your way home. Bet that wife of yours is cooking up a feast."

Josie pushed her plate away, as if her taste for seafood had been eternally satisfied after one skewer of scallops. "What's on the agenda for the morning?"

"I'll show Kris a couple more stores, then we're heading over to the outsourcing facility." Between bites of whatever he was eating, Merv launched into a tirade about the hideous burden of reporting what came into and went out of the facility, the new legal parameters for registration that he hoped to avoid, and ridiculous inspection standards in the wake of a fungal meningitis outbreak that had been traced to another compounding pharmacy chain in Massachusetts.

"We're the good guys," Merv said. "Back in the nineteenth century all prescriptions were compounded by the village apothecary. You and me? We might not even be here to have this little talk if our great-grandparents hadn't been able to count on them. Nowadays, you need a dosage different than the big companies think you ought to have? A different flavor for your kid who won't take cherry antibiotics? How about marshmallow? We can do that. Two medicines in one? We can do that, too, so you don't have so many pills. Something that always worked for you before but's suddenly discontinued?" He turned up his hands. "You need a compounding pharmacy. Right, Josie?"

I was reminded of a doll Pet owned as a little girl. She would pull a string at the back and the doll would recite rotating phrases. Josie looked as if her own string had just been jerked and jerked hard.

"We can provide things like preservative-free eyedrops, because our facilities are sterile." She sighed, although I doubt she realized it.

Merv set off on another tirade on the evils of big drug companies, the FDA, inspectors who were only interested in checklists and the price of equipment that met today's standards. I tuned him out since I'd already heard this and simply nodded whenever there was a significant pause.

I believe there is a need for compounding pharmacies. That's not an issue with me. But I was already uncomfortable with some of what I'd seen on today's tour. Merv's nostalgia for the village apothecary carries over to his shops, particularly the one in nearby Virginia Beach. They're cluttered and dusty. The pharmacist-manager at that Pedersen's should have been practicing golf strokes with his cronies for at least a decade. Did the guy love his job or was Pedersen such a miserly boss he couldn't retire? Had he stayed with Pedersen so long because nobody else would hire him? Was he mentally acute enough to mix medications?

Those questions triggered more personal ones. Would I

keep working well into my seventies? By then, would I have any reason to stop? My kids would be gone. And my wife?

Pedersen excused himself to find the men's room, and Josie and I were alone.

"You would rather be with your family, wouldn't you?" I asked, still caught up in self-examination.

"My God, yes. Pedersen's such a—" She realized what she'd said, and in horror tried to retract it, but I stopped her.

"Does this guy ever stop talking?"

Now we'd traded Pedersen insults. Neither of us could report the other without fear of being reported ourselves.

"Never." She looked as if she wanted to burst into tears, but I was beginning to think that was her normal expression.

"There must be other benefits to your job."

"I'm looking for another one. Job, not benefit." The revelation seemed to make her feel better. "I'm giving notice next week. I'll serve my kids beans and corn bread every night, if it comes to that." She smiled, a real smile this time. "And next year, Thanksgiving turkey."

"Pedersen's lectures getting to you?"

"You know I can't say much."

I leaned toward her. "This will be off the record."

"He'll make a fool of himself if he sues. Don't get involved."

"It's my job to be sure he doesn't make a fool of himself."

"God himself can't pull off a miracle like that one."

I waited, but nothing else was forthcoming. I knew she'd said all she would or could, and by then Pedersen was on his way to the table again, this time ranting about the crowd in the men's room.

Pedersen insisted on dessert. I avoided the pumpkin pie and had pecan, which Robin never makes. I was almost home free. I would call my children from the hotel room and wish them a happy Thanksgiving. Before they left town I'd pro-grammed their new phones so they can only communicate with family members and 911. Even with those restrictions I know they'll be carrying them everywhere for a while be-cause of the novelty.

Robin and I haven't spoken since I told her I would be working today. I'd texted the children's flight times, and she'd texted back to say she'd gotten the information and would be waiting.

And whose fault is that? I have an uncomfortable feeling I'm not going to like the answer once it finally becomes clear.

I'd had the good sense to drive to Norfolk, so tonight I had my own car and didn't have to depend on Pedersen. At the restaurant door I wished my dinner companions a good evening and tipped the valet twice what I normally do, since the young man had been forced to work today, too.

The moment I pulled away I noticed a car that had been lingering in the drop-off area pull away, too. That was nor-mal enough, but for the ten-minute drive to the hotel, every time I looked in my rearview mirror I noticed the same silver-blue sedan right behind me, even when I tested my theory by switching lanes and darting in and out of traffic. I wasn't worried. To my knowledge nobody had any reason to shadow me unless my wife has decided I'm having an affair instead of dinner with a blowhard.

I had chosen a motel near the interstate in hopes I might have a head start for home if we finished our business today. Things didn't work out that way, but tomorrow I would leave as soon as I could. No one would be home to greet me, but I might be able to get some serious work done without Pet and Nik, so when they did return I could spend a little time with them.

I took the exit, sped through a yellow light and made a

sharp turn. I was relieved when I pulled into the parking lot and nobody followed me. I found a slot near the corridor that led to my room, but I kept the engine running. Wise move. When the silver-blue sedan came around the corner, I pulled out again and drove to the front, parking under the roof over the entranceway. I turned off my engine and got out my phone, punching in 911. But I waited to press Talk.

The car pulled up directly behind me and a man stepped out. He held up his hands, then extended them palms first, as if showing me he was unarmed. Not that he couldn't have been hiding a gun in his pocket. This is Virginia, after all, and getting a concealed-carry license is as easy as proving you're twenty-one, minimally competent and moderately law-abiding.

I decided I was safe enough, and I got out to face him, but I moved around my door and placed it between us.

"Want to tell me why you followed me?" I held up my phone as a warning.

He stepped out into the open. "I saw you eating dinner with Mervin Pedersen."

"Last time I checked eating dinner is legal, even normal."

"You're his lawyer, aren't you?"

Quite honestly, I would rather be almost anyone else. You can tell a lot about a man by the way he treats the people who serve him. At the end of our meal Pedersen made racist comments about a Sikh bussing a neighboring table and complained about our meals to our overworked server, as if hoping for a refund or at least free dessert. Once he headed for the exit I had tipped them both in apology. I wasn't about to have a heart-to-heart with this guy, though.

I took the offensive. "How do you know who I am?"

"He ever tell you he was forced to get a protective order

against the father of the woman he killed with his filthy antibiotic?"

I studied him. Clearly *he* was the father, a tired-looking, balding man of about sixty, dressed in jeans and a pastel green sweatshirt. The sweatshirt, emblazoned with the University of Virginia's crossed swords, was sizes too small. Once upon a time it had probably belonged to his daughter.

"No contact," he said, in affirmation. "I just follow him from a distance. Then I talk to the people he talks to."

"You could be sued, you know. For defamation."

"Not if what I'm saying is true. I'm told he'd have to prove it isn't. And me? I just tell all those people what it was like to watch my daughter die and not be able to do a damn thing."

From my research I knew that the husband of the young woman who had died had settled out of court. All the victims had, and Pedersen was still furious he had been forced to pay. In fact, afterward he had fired his lawyers and come to us.

"You settled. Or rather your son-in-law did," I said. "And Pedersen never admitted fault in her death."

"No, that was part of the agreement. I never would have signed it, but then I'm just the father. Her husband wanted the whole thing over. He even tried to give me half." From his tone I could tell he would carve out his heart rather than take a cent that had once belonged to Pedersen.

I was familiar with the amount, generous enough to put this matter to rest, or so I'd thought.

"Your daughter was very sick before she was treated. Pneumonia, right? Complicated by a heart defect? No doctor could say for a fact the tainted injection was the cause of death. How can you say it was if they couldn't? Won't you be a lot happier if you just let this go and move on with your life?"

He stared at me, and I tried not to flinch. I guess neither of us could believe I had said something so stupid.

He finally spoke. "You tell me. Somebody *you* love dies, and you think you just move on? I never had a chance to tell her how much I loved her. By the time her husband called me, she was in a coma. That happened to you, you wouldn't ask yourself every single day what you could have done differently? You wouldn't try to seek justice? What if she was *your* daughter or *your* wife?

My wife *had* nearly died. But I was lucky, more so than this man. Fate had waved her magic wand and someone else had died in Robin's place.

Revelations come at all times in all places. I answered the man's question silently. What had I done? I had distanced myself from the horror, from the recurring nightmare of a speeding car, from my love for my wife. Because when you love somebody that much? Losing her is too painful.

Just ask Michael, who used to live next door.

"I can't even imagine how much this hurts," I said slowly, although I thought maybe I could.

"Pedersen's not stupid, which is a shame. After the first hint of trouble, before anybody could get in to do an inspection, he cleaned every single inch of the facility that manufactured that so-called sterile solution for those antibiotics. He got rid of outdated equipment and threatened his staff if they said anything about the cleanup to the inspectors. But people who used to work there tell me his standards were always lax, and he pinched pennies on supplies and equipment. Room design? Operations? Maintenance? They were all substandard. There were other problems, too, but Pedersen made them go away."

"If this is true, why haven't those people spoken to the authorities? Threats or not."

He cupped his hand and rubbed his thumb over his fingertips.

"A bribe?" I asked.

He didn't answer. Maybe answering was one step too close to slander.

I changed the subject. "Why did he have to get a protective order? Were you threatening him?"

"I was just having a conversation, asking questions, wondering how he slept at night. Pedersen said I made threats. The judge wasn't sure, so forbidding contact was his compromise. I stay back now, but not too far."

"I would venture you do more than follow him from a distance."

"I send regular letters to everybody who counts and talk to them when I can. Virginia Board of Pharmacy. FDA. Professional organizations. But you know how much control they have? Even with the new law? Compounding pharmacies don't come under the same scrutiny as drug manufacturers. Sure, they sent out that warning letter when Pedersen refused to let them test his other products, but that's a slap on the wrist. He needs to be shut down."

"So to retaliate, you follow people around and frighten them."

"I'm not trying to scare you or anybody. I just want you to know what you're getting into. I looked you up on the internet. You're some kind of hotshot, I figure. I just hate to see a talented man putting his energies into the wrong places and people."

"Everybody deserves his day in court."

His smile was wry. "You think so? Pedersen bought everybody off before it got to that. Now he wants to clear his name and get the authorities to stop pestering him."

"If what you say is true, even some of it, if he does brazen this out and sue the FDA, maybe the truth will come back to haunt him."

"You tell yourself that, okay? Right up until the minute the government backs down because they decide it's not worth the fuss. You're that good, you can probably make it happen if you put a whole lot of work into it. Or you can negotiate some kind of truce. What a way to earn a living, huh?"

I thought he was done, but he wasn't. Not quite.

"You have a good Thanksgiving," he said. "I hope you have something or someone to be thankful for today. I hope Pedersen didn't rob you of that much, the way he robbed me." Then he got into his car, backed into the lot and turned. In a moment he was gone.

After a few deep breaths I reparked and made my way to my suite. This motel is not deluxe. The living area is comfortable but not plush, with a sofa that pulls out to make another bed. Years ago Robin and I rented budget suites like this one and put Pet and Nik to sleep on similar sofas. Then we waited for them to fall asleep so the real fun of our getaway could begin.

How long ago had that been?

I flopped on the sofa, but I got up again immediately and began to pace. I stopped in front of the minibar and opened the door. Possibly for the first time in my professional life the contents looked inviting. I pulled out a 50 milliliter bottle of Jack Daniel's and drank it straight, bypassing a glass.

The man in the parking lot had hoped I had someone to be thankful for today. I did, but was I thankful? No, I was terrified. The weight of that fear and, worse, the realization, was a sudden, crushing blow.

I had to make this right or at least begin the process. I didn't want to. I didn't want to be that vulnerable. But what I needed or wanted was immaterial. Because Robin is most vulnerable of all. And how can I let that continue?

I sat on the edge of the bed, pulled out my cell phone and dialed the last woman I'd expected to speak to tonight. I would speak to my children later, but this call was way overdue.

28

—

Cecilia

I love the beach at night. Sanibel has strict prohibitions on artificial light, particularly during turtle-nesting season. Nesting season is finished now, but our beaches remain as dark as nature intended. We like it that way.

When the moon is full and the sky awash in stars, I walk the beach near my house, carrying a flashlight I try not to use. I've learned if I make my way here and stand quietly while my eyes adjust, I can usually pick my way along the shore.

And yes, I carry a cell phone, and I'm careful. I've mentally mapped out every possible escape route. There are other Roy Doggetts in the world.

Tonight when I said I was going for a walk Donny asked to come with me. Roscoe is snoozing. Robin and her children are putting a jigsaw puzzle together. Mick and Fiona are reading. Gizzie and Pat have gone in search of nightlife.

They may have to drive to Miami.

Now Donny was carefully picking his way to the edge of the water so we could head down the beach.

"Cecilia, you actually come out here by yourself?"

"Don't start."

"At the very least Hal or a clone should be walking behind you."

"So far I've been able to make Sanibel a Hal-free zone, and I want to keep it that way."

"You're living on borrowed time."

"Between the causeway, my fabulous security system and good neighbors I'm safe here."

"A pipe dream."

"I need someplace where I can feel normal. The local police know I live here, and they're on speed dial. The only time I ever called they were here in minutes."

"And why did you call?"

By now my feet were wet. The tide was coming in and water was lapping farther up the sand than I'd guessed. I took off my sandals and walked barefoot, although that was risky in the dark.

I took Donny's arm to help with balance. "I heard noises on the roof and at the door. Raccoons, as it turned out. We all had a good laugh. Them more than me."

"I think I'd better move in with you. Somebody with some sense needs to keep tabs."

I wasn't sure why I wasn't more annoyed. Maybe the thought of having Donny nearby wasn't so terrible.

I still had to defend myself. "I have good sense, but I balance it with courage. I don't want to live in a bubble. I sing about life. I need to live."

"Shall I list the celebrities killed by stalkers? Or remind you that Sandra Bullock met hers outside her bedroom door?"

"Not unless you want me to push you into the water."

"I don't want to lose you."

I wondered why exactly. I pay a huge premium on a life insurance policy for which Donny is the beneficiary. If I die, he won't be left penniless for the month it will take him to weed through candidates begging to take my place.

I squeezed his arm. "There's a moon shining over our heads. Do you see anybody on the beach except us? So let's talk about something else. How did you like dinner?"

"The pumpkin tortellini wasn't half-bad."

"And the turkey?"

"The real one or the tofu wannabe?"

"I never miss meat, except at Thanksgiving. I almost tore into the real one tonight."

"Why didn't you?"

I debated my answer, but the truth worked. "I helped with the animals at the Osburn ranch. That was my job in our little *family*. That also meant I was there when they were killed and butchered. I had raised some of them."

"I'm having problems with the part where that was your job. Do foster kids routinely have jobs that traumatic?"

"I don't know. But that placement was…" I struggled for the right word. "Different? *Different*. The thing is, I couldn't really refuse to help, because in theory Robin and I were too far apart in age to be in the same place. The ranch was considered therapeutic foster care, so at the time that rule was more or less overlooked. If I had complained, we would have been separated."

"She meant that much to you." It wasn't a question. He knew.

"Yep, and I was all *she* had, too."

"Then it must have been hard to leave her behind when you went to New York."

"I wanted her to come. I actually believed we might get away with it. Foster kids disappear and nobody notices, especially teenagers. There was a famous case in Florida, about ten years after I left, when a five-year-old girl went missing for a year and nobody at the agency realized it."

"Things are better now?"

"I hope so. Anyway, at the time we had a new caseworker who was still learning the ropes. I thought we could slip between the cracks."

"Robin would have been how old?"

"Fourteen."

"How did you plan to take care of both of you?"

"Before we got that far we both realized it would be better if she stayed behind. The Osburns had separated, and Betty, Mrs. Osburn, planned to sell the ranch and move north. The new caseworker turned out to be a good one. She found Robin a better place to stay. And Robin knew if that home didn't work out, somehow I would come and get her."

"I grew up with a regulation mom and dad and two sisters, lived in the same house until I went to college. I never once took care of anybody except me."

We weren't putting much distance behind us. Walking at night is more like creeping. I stepped on something sharp and stopped. "Let's sit a minute." I shone my flashlight on the ground and found a spot away from the water that looked promising. I limped over and lowered myself to the sand, brushing off my foot as well as the piece of shell I'd stepped on. The skin wasn't broken.

Donny joined me.

"You're such a normal guy," I said. "Maybe that's why I trust you. No skeletons in your closet. It surprises me some nice, normal woman hasn't snapped you up." I added the rest like an afterthought. "Or has that Malibu designer nearly worked her magic?"

"You know I haven't been with her for more than a year."

"Well, you never actually told me."

"Just like I know Sage Callahan is every bit as gay as Gizzie. And you probably knew it before you married him."

I was so stunned I nearly stuttered. "Are you kidding?"

"Kidding that I know?"

"When did you figure *that* out?"

"Right after you said the *I do*s. By then it was too late to talk some sense into you."

"Why would you try? Marriage was a career booster for Sage and me, and the divorce wasn't half-bad, either."

"I hate a business that works that way, don't you?"

"The business that's made us both rich? Not so much."

"Has it ever occurred to you to find a man you can actually be happy with forever?"

"I don't believe in forever."

"Fifty percent of all marriages last. Plus the people who get divorced remarry at an astonishing rate. Love's in the air all over our grand and glorious country."

"More like love is in the smog. When smog clears an awful lot of problems are visible. The same's true for love."

"Not just a cynic when you're singing, I see."

"You've never married."

"I came close a time or two."

"Looking for perfection?"

"I don't want perfection. Just somebody I love enough to do the hard work."

I couldn't claim to know more about that than he did. Sage and I hadn't had any work to do at all. Our situation had been perfectly clear from the start.

I got back to my feet to turn toward home. "I think by now you're what they call a hard-core bachelor."

He joined me. "Everything can change in a heartbeat."

I thought about Robin, who had nearly died between one

heartbeat and the other, and then about her marriage, which had looked so stable and was now on the rocks.

I needed to say something. "I hope only good things happen for you." I wanted to say more, although I didn't know what, but my cell phone buzzed. So few people have my number, I didn't hesitate to pull it out and answer.

I was as surprised by the caller as I was by my conversation with Donny. When I finished, I slipped the phone back in my pocket.

"Kris?" Donny asked. "Is that unusual?"

"He wants to know if he can join us tomorrow."

Donny was standing right beside me, so he had heard my answer. "And you said yes."

"He asked me not to tell Robin. He'll have to fly standby, and he's not sure he'll be able to get a flight out until Saturday. He doesn't want to disappoint her in case things don't work out."

"I'm glad he's coming."

Have I ever been glad to see Kris? I can't remember a time when I've felt even a hint of pleasure. But Robin needs to be with her husband, even if being here together finalizes the end of their marriage.

"They have a lot to work out," I said carefully.

"People who love each other always do."

"That's the hard work you were talking about."

"Exactly."

Then he did something that surprised me. He put his arms around me and pulled me close. Resting his head against my hair he said, "Loving you would be hard work, Cecilia. Not because you're not one of the most lovable women in the world, but because you resist it so vehemently."

I wasn't sure what to do. Then, before I could think too hard, I slipped my arms around his waist and let him hold me. This time I had no excuse. No stalker had found me; no memories had crawled back to hurl me into a dark abyss. A pearly moon shone overhead, and the sky was bright with stars. Even without doing any hard work, I knew that sometimes the moon, the stars and the right arms were all a woman needed. Even a woman like me.

29

—

Robin

Nik might suspect that Kris and I are having problems, but Pet is the one who articulated her fears. On Saturday the children and I biked the short distance to Ding Darling Wildlife Refuge and slowly navigated the eight-mile Wildlife Drive, stopping frequently along the way to look at mangroves and tidal pools, and listen to volunteers who shared close-ups of waterfowl through powerful telescopes. They squealed at alligator sightings—Nik more than Pet—and complained about how tired and hot they were. But nobody complained too loudly.

On the way back to Cecilia's we stopped for a late lunch and a rest at Doc Ford's, named for the main character of a bestselling mystery series written by the owner. Ginny, Cecilia's housekeeper and cook, had loaned me the first book, and I was already hooked. I bought the next two while we waited to be seated and silently applauded the author's marketing strategy. Nik ordered a Cuban sandwich, and Pet and I got fish sandwiches with black beans and rice.

Nik wolfed down his lunch in a matter of minutes, but Pet and I were too tired from biking to eat quickly. My son finished his last drop of ice water and pushed his chair back. "I know the way home."

The way home is simple, so I knew what he was about to ask. "Don't forget, we saw some of the biggest gators along the next stretch of the bike path."

"They'll still be there if you ride with me. I'm not going to freak out and fall off my bike just because I'm riding by myself."

The gators are sun-dazzled, stuffed with local fish and game, and disinterested in bikes or their riders. My son will be perfectly safe unless he decides to stop and pet one, and I know that isn't going to happen.

I gave a thumbs-up. "I guess it's okay. Be careful, and call when you get home."

He leaped to his feet, as if afraid I would change my mind. "Dad would never let me do this." He took off.

That surprised me. So when Kris is in charge, he's even more cautious than I am? I was going to enjoy not being the only one who said no in our family.

Pet and I watched him race out the door, and when our server came back I let her refill my tea and Pet's soft drink, a special treat since we only serve milk and juice at home.

After a few sips my daughter toyed with her straw. "I want you to call me Petra. I don't like nicknames."

"What brought that on?"

"Fifi. That's a pretty silly nickname, don't you think? It sounds like a poodle. Her real name is Fiona."

"Her dad calls her that. I guess the rest of us just fell into the habit."

"I'm nobody's Pet. I want to be sure everybody knows that."

"Well…it might be hard for a while, but I'll sure try."

"Fifi's kind of *like* a pet. She's always doing stuff for her dad. Like getting him things to eat. And this morning she was doing something for him on the computer."

"I think Fi—Fiona is interested in making films, too, and she's Mick's assistant, what he calls a runner."

"I'm glad Daddy doesn't ask me to take care of him. That would be weird. He takes care of us."

Since Mick and I had explored that difference ourselves, I couldn't fault her. In fact I didn't have to look very far beneath her comments to see what was bothering my daughter. She had seen Mick help me to my feet on the beach, seen us sitting close and talking. She's ten, but she's sensitive to nuance. The girl formerly known as Pet is worried.

Am I developing feelings for Mick? He *is* attractive, no doubt. And being with a genius of his magnitude is captivating. But other than a few brief fantasies, which I've carefully cut short, our relationship can and will forever be friendship. I'm still married, even if my husband is out of the picture these days, and even if I wasn't, I need more from a relationship than a man like Mick can ever give.

"Your dad wants the best for you," I said carefully.

"And you."

"I know it's different having all of us separated for a while, but you and Nik will always be our top priority. No matter what."

"He's unhappy with you being gone."

At least Kris was home often enough now that she had noticed. I was walking through a minefield, but I gamely picked my way.

"I'm not always happy being gone, either. I miss you, but I like working again. I hope you can join me for a few days on the road and be *my* runner."

We had already talked about that possibility, and she had been excited. Now she looked worried. "I don't know. Hasn't Daddy been left alone enough?"

I felt the slap, but I didn't react. "He's not alone. He has you, he has Nik and he has work. He and Nik will do guy stuff while you're away. Then, if Nik can join me for a few days, you and your dad can do stuff *you* like."

"Are we going to spend Christmas together?"

"That's certainly the plan."

"I'm going to tell Daddy he can't work if you come home."

"You let your dad and me figure this out. You aren't responsible for anything, including anybody's work schedule."

She gazed at her half-eaten sandwich. "*Are* you going to work it out?"

I couldn't be less than honest, because I didn't want her to come back later and accuse me of lying. "We're going to try hard. That's a promise."

"I don't want you to get divorced."

"Nobody wants that." I hoped that was true.

"Good." She took a bite, filling her mouth to prevent more conversation.

The time had arrived to change the subject. "So if my calculations are correct, you can get back to your normal routine now that Thanksgiving is over. You and your dad are going to get together with Jody's family and figure out how things should go from now on, right?"

"She's mad at me. She says all this was my fault because I didn't hide the…you know, well enough. But she knows that's not true."

I envisioned my daughter as a woman. If she's this insightful at ten, what will she be like at twenty or thirty? For the first time in my life I wished I could show my own mother what she had produced. Not me, since clearly I had not been enough to stop her from leaving, but by *having* me, she made life possible for this lovely little girl who is both smart and kind. Sadly, Alice will never know.

"What are you going to do?" I knew Pet had to figure this out on her own.

"I told Jody I'll still be her friend when she stops being mad. She thinks she has to choose between Grace and me, but she doesn't."

"Do you think maybe she's embarrassed?"

"I'm kind of embarrassed, but we didn't tell anybody else at school. So that's good. When she's back to being my friend we can be embarrassed together."

I hope the news blackout lasts.

We talked about her new friend, Anupa, who was from India and a vegetarian, like Cecilia. We moved on to school and visiting me when the crew was back together. On the way home we rode side by side whenever we could and continued the conversation.

The reality of having her right beside me made me realize even more than before how much I had missed my daughter.

Back at the house, *Petra* went to listen to Gizzie and Cecilia work on their new song. Nik—how long until he demanded to be Nikola?—was already there, sucking in as much as his preadolescent brain would hold. I took the free time to work on editing photos; then, when nobody else wanted to join me—both my worn-out children were napping on great room couches—I decided to take a long walk on the beach by myself.

The sun sets early in November, and it was already on the horizon when I finally turned to go back to Cecilia's.

I was nearly there when I saw a man walking toward me on the beach. He was built like Kris, long-legged, broad-shouldered, with an easy, natural gait. The sky was a kaleidoscope of color, and he was silhouetted against the setting sun. I paused and shaded my eyes, but not until he was closer did I know for sure.

I started forward, although I didn't run. I had no idea why my husband had come or what he had flown this distance to say. I just knew I had to meet him halfway.

"Robin..." Kris walked faster until I was in his arms. Then he kissed me. Not in greeting, but as if he would never—*could* never—get enough of me again.

30

—

Robin

On Sunday the Thanksgiving house party broke up with a staggered exodus. Mick and Fiona left first to drive north to Tampa and finalize arrangements for filming there next week. Gizzie and Pat left after lunch. In the late afternoon Kris and our children drove to the airport with Donny, who was heading to New York for a few days.

I am still stunned that my husband traveled all this way to spend less than a day together, and equally as stunned that somehow he managed to get a seat on the same flight home as our children.

We had no real time alone to talk, which seemed okay with him. Maybe he still doesn't know what to say or doesn't want to spoil the reunion, but that kiss and the "I love you" that followed sparked hope that when we do have time and space together again, we will work out whatever we have to.

We also had no chance for anything more intimate, since there are only two queen-size beds in Cecilia's guesthouse. A grumbling Nik moved over to let Kris sleep with him, while Pet and I continued to sleep in the other. He did manage to get me aside before he left and tell me he was going to take off as much of Christmas week as he could. I promised I would get home at the first opportunity. He kissed me goodbye in front of the children, which was the best thing he could have done.

Cecilia and I are scheduled to leave on Tuesday morning, but Sunday evening, while we ate Thanksgiving leftovers in an otherwise-empty house, she suggested a road trip.

"Hal's flying in tomorrow evening to drive us to Tampa on Tuesday. That gives us most of Monday without a chaperone. You still have your rental car. It's about as anonymous as a car gets. Let's see some sights and have lunch out."

I appreciate how constrained Cecilia's life is, and I know she and Donny argued about protection this weekend. Hal's appearance tomorrow is a compromise. I suspect the other part of the compromise is that she's supposed to stay put between Donny's departure and Hal's arrival.

I answered cautiously, because this *was* Cecilia across the table from me. "Where do you want to go?"

"Somewhere nobody will expect to find me. How does the Everglades sound?"

Even in November it sounded sultry and bug infested, but the idea of sightseeing rather than staying put in the house had appeal. Because of the holiday Sanibel is busy enough with an influx of tourists that Cecilia would probably be recognized and approached if we tried to have lunch or shop in town.

"Are you thinking about one of those airboats through the swamps? Hiking?"

She made a face. "Ginny says Everglades City is a cute little town, and we can take a tour boat from the visitors' center or rent a kayak. It's not the kind of place anyone would expect to find me."

I knew that last sentence was supposed to make me feel better. "If we keep sneaking away together I may have to take up karate. It might be a while before I'm up to Hal or Donny's level, though."

"We'll be okay."

"Hats and sunglasses. I know."

She smiled, calculating that even I would be smitten and fall under her spell.

The next morning we set off after breakfast. The weather was gorgeous, midseventies, clear, with just enough breeze that the sun felt good. I was sorry I hadn't rented a convertible, but my gray Toyota had a moon roof, and we opened it as wide as it would go.

Once we were off the island heading south, Cecilia seemed to relax. "I'm not looking forward to filming this next part."

I knew what was planned. Cecilia's mother abandoned her for good in Tampa, and somehow Mick had secured permission to film the apartment where she and her mother had lived. "Lived," of course, isn't an accurate term. She only rarely speaks about that time in her life, but I do know that when the police arrived in response to a tip, no food or water was in sight. Cecilia had been drinking from a saucepan she kept outside to catch rain.

My sister has always been a survivor.

Cecilia views sympathy as criticism. I phrased my reply carefully. "Reliving that time in your life won't be easy."

"I barely remember the apartment, if that's what you want to call the rooms we shared with her boyfriends and anybody else who showed up. Mick says a year after the police took me away, somebody bought the building, chased out all the druggies and did minimal renovations. That's the only reason it's still standing. The guy who bought it believed the neighborhood was due for a resurgence, and the building has historical significance. Lucky for Mick it fell on hard times again a few years ago. Whatever I say, at least the place will look authentic."

"You're sure you want to do this?"

"They say you can't go home again."

"Was that ever home?"

"I think sometimes you have to at least stroll by so you can move on."

Her logic was convoluted, but she'd given this the required thought.

How would I feel about revisiting my own past? I made a guess. "I could go back to my grandmother's house, only I would probably have nightmares for a year."

"This trip may be the stuff of nightmares, but don't you think facing up to them will finally make them go away?"

Most of my recent knowledge of psychology comes from magazines and internet quizzes, but there seem to be two theories on that and I repeated them.

"Some people think if we wallow in the past, eventually it will cease to have power over us. Others say if we just tell the past to take a hike, it will. Maybe not always, but that last one's worked pretty well for me."

"Really? And you don't think your past is right there guiding every step?"

I know criticism when I hear it. That's one thing I learned from my grandmother. My answer had an edge. "I think if it were, I wouldn't have been able to function, much less make a success of most things I've tried."

"I'm not saying you're not a success. But don't you worry sometimes that you try so hard to be perfect because of the voices in your head? And maybe I'm really talking about myself, not you. Blocking worked for a long time, but some days now the voices are too loud to ignore."

Pacified, I wondered why. Cecilia has everything she's

ever wanted. She doesn't have a man in her life—at least not that she acknowledges—but has she ever wanted one? Even in high school she kept boys at a distance, and she's never shown any romantic interest in women.

Since she rarely spoke this frankly, I took her words seriously. "When I stopped talking all those years ago someone finally got me into therapy. That made all the difference. Why aren't you seeing somebody? After what you went through in Australia, don't you think that might help?"

"I'm a do-it-yourself kind of woman."

"No, you just don't let anybody in if you can avoid it."

"I live in a world where most people can't be trusted. If I don't let them in, when they finally disappoint me, it's no big deal."

"Starting with your mother."

She was silent so long I thought she was angry, but when she spoke her voice was soft.

"There's such a long history, I don't know when it started. Maribeth. The men she brought home. I had to find a place to hide in every building or house we lived in. First thing I did every time we moved. Just in case."

I took my hand off the steering wheel and grasped hers a moment. "Are you going to say that on film?"

"I don't know. I don't know what will happen when we go back to that place."

"I'm glad I'll be with you."

For the rest of the trip, by unspoken mutual consent, we chatted about the photos I'd taken, about the new album she wants to record and about my family's visit. I told her that Pet was now Petra.

"Whether she's Pet or Petra, she'll always stand out among the Emmas and Madisons." As she spoke Cecilia tucked her hair under a cap that said Jean's Bait and Tackle and detailed a tarpon midleap. The opening in the back had a ready-made brown ponytail threaded through it.

She glanced at herself in the sun visor mirror and straightened the cap. "Do you know why you gave your all-American children Czech names?"

"Because I wanted them to feel connected to the roots they do have. I don't know anything about my own background, but Kris knows everything about his."

"That answer came easily."

"I gave their names a lot of thought. I have this crazy sister who thinks names are important. I learned from the best."

She looked delighted that I had paid attention.

Everglades City sits, not surprisingly, at the edge of the Everglades National Park, and a hop, skip and jump from Big Cypress National Preserve. It's a different view of Florida, not immune to wacky souvenirs and wackier characters, but also a sanctuary of sorts for what's left of Florida's wilderness. As we drove in I saw that the town itself was small and picturesque, a fishing and boating community flanked with quaint seafood restaurants along the Barron River, which flows into Chokoloskee Bay. I wondered how long it would stay this way.

I parked on what looked like a main street and we got out. Cecilia had continued her transformation with molded gray sun goggles embedded with crystals at the temples. Not exactly what people here might buy at the local drugstore. She saw my head cocked in examination.

"Too much?"

"You think?"

"They're gray."

"They're also worth more than the locals make in a week. Keep the hat, lose the glasses."

She dug through a canvas bag that probably cost more than the glasses but had the grace not to flaunt it. She gestured to the new pair once they were in place. Square tortoiseshell frames and impenetrable black lenses, as if she'd picked them up on the set of *Mad Men*. For all I know she may have done a guest appearance.

I gave her a thumbs-up. "If we're lucky, somebody will think you picked those up at an estate sale."

"Do I look like me?"

She wore an oversize T-shirt and baggy cargo shorts with a million pockets. She still looked gorgeous. "How would I know? You always look like you to me."

"It's too early for lunch. What shall we do?"

We took a short stroll around town, picked out vacation homes we wouldn't mind owning—dangerous to do with my sister, since on vacation she buys real estate like most people buy sunscreen. Then we returned to the car and drove to the Gulf Coast Visitor Center to see if we could hop a tour boat for a closer view of the Everglades and the Ten Thousand Islands.

Two hours later, we disembarked after viewing too many manatees and dolphins to count, and an entire spoil island covered with white pelicans. The crew had tossed admiring glances at Cecilia—and even a few at me—but not as if they recognized her.

"I checked out places for lunch," she said after deciding that climbing the observation tower wasn't in our best interests.

I rested fingertips on my forehead and closed my eyes. "My psychic vibes tell me every joint in town specializes in seafood."

"The place we're going makes its own veggie burgers."

"Which I won't be eating."

"At least *I* don't have to spend long periods of time trying to choose between oysters and shrimp."

"No problem," I said as we got back in the car. "I'll have both."

Captain Henry's reminded me of every coastal seafood restaurant I've ever visited, happily dilapidated and adorned with colorful weathered buoys, mounted swordfish and other local artifacts. We were too late to get a seat on the river, but one row back we still had a good view of the heavily forested bank across the water and tall palms against an impossibly blue sky. Boats cruised by on their way out of port, some rigged for commercial fishing, some for recreation. An osprey nest topped a channel marker, and one of its architects dived for fish.

The restaurant wasn't crowded. A young man brought us ice water, menus and place settings, and took our orders for sweet tea, an addiction neither of us has outgrown. He promised our server would be with us right away.

"This is nice." I turned to my sister. "A good idea."

"I'm glad you think so."

"What made you choose this one? Only place with veggie burgers or the view?"

She didn't have time to answer. A woman came to our table and smiled at both of us. A quick glance suggested she might be in her fifties, but she was slender, tanned and pretty in white knit Capris and a polo shirt with Captain Henry's embroidered in red. Her hair was short and brown, with enough blond that I guessed highlights were her solution to going gray, one I might try myself in a few years.

She must have given her opening spiel a million times, because she fell into it as if by habit. "Welcome to Captain Henry's. I'm Al. I thought you might want to know the day's specials before you get too far into the menu."

I smiled up at her, and suddenly *her* smile faltered. She fell silent and stared at me.

"I'm a vegetarian," Cecilia said, as if nothing unusual was happening. "Actually a vegan. Can I get the veggie burger without cheese? And is there anything else I ought to know about the menu before I order?"

Al looked like a woman searching her memory banks, and I wondered if she had recognized Cecilia and was trying to figure out how to respond.

"I'm sorry?" She glanced at Cecilia. "What did you ask?"

Cecilia repeated her question.

"I'll be sure there's no cheese on the burger. And we make our own here. There's nothing about it or the fries you'll object to."

Cecilia gave a nod. Al turned back to me and cleared her throat. "Would you like to hear the specials?"

Something was happening here. She looked as if she wanted to cry.

"I think I would like fried shrimp and oysters, if you have them. I haven't had a chance to look."

She was still staring at me as if she was looking at someone else. "We can certainly do that."

"Then I'm set. No fries, though."

She listed sides, and I chose coleslaw, reaching back into my Florida roots.

She left, and I turned to Cecilia, who was watching her departure. "Remember Betty's coleslaw?" Our mutual foster mother had only come to life in the Osburn ranch kitchen. Her signature coleslaw, with pineapple, coconut and tiny colored marshmallows, had been my favorite, although now as an adult I never make it. Betty's coleslaw would be a reminder of sultry afternoons sweating away in the kitchen while she listened to country music at top volume to avoid saying anything to me except "chop this" or "stir that."

"She recognized you."

I had been thinking about Betty, so Cecilia's words made no sense. "What are you talking about?"

"Al." Cecilia didn't elaborate.

"You mean she recognized *you*."

"No. You. She just left by the front door. She won't be back."

"Why? She seemed fine." Although actually the woman hadn't seemed fine at all. She had seemed…what? Unhappy? Preoccupied?

Worse. Al had looked as if she had just seen a ghost.

I had a sudden and terrible insight. And since I don't believe in coincidence, I had a feeling my sister knew everything there was to know about Al's reaction.

I had been toying with my fork, but now I dropped it on the table and leaned forward. "Why don't you tell me what's going on, CeCe? Exactly why *did* we end up in Everglades City instead of a dozen other places we could have gone today? And don't tell me you're a fan of swamps."

"I don't think I'm the only one who needs to face her past, Robin. Please understand I did this for you."

"Just tell me what's going on. Who is that woman?"

"I didn't expect her to be our server today. That was unplanned, and I'm sorry this was all so in-your-face."

"The truth, please."

"She's the owner, or one of them, married to Captain Henry himself for almost twenty years. But you're her only child, Robin. Al is the former Alice Swanson. Your mother."

31

—

Cecilia

For our stay in Tampa, Starla rented a Mediterranean-style home that's large enough to house everyone working on the film. Most of the lavish lakeside residences inside this gated community are seasonal, so their owners only trickle in after Christmas, but the gate is still an extra level of protection unless another preteen wants to work a business deal this week.

Mick thinks the house is safer than the most secure hotel, and to make sure another stalker doesn't sneak in, Donny hired a second Hal, smaller, shorter and older but amazingly quick on his feet. Since his name is Russian and requires phlegmy consonants beyond my capabilities, I call him Ivan the Terrible, which is the only time he ever smiles.

There's plenty of room in my second-floor suite for Robin, but when we settled in last evening she declined the honor. She's still angry and has said very little since she insisted on paying the startled cashier at Captain Henry's for the meal they hadn't yet served and left the restaurant yards ahead of me.

By the time I reached the car she was already buckled in and the Toyota's engine was revving as she angrily pumped the accelerator. No matter. She was so upset I could have heard her over the roar of a jet.

"I know you have a skewed view of the truth. I'm pretty sure you didn't get where you are today without playing fast and loose with it more times than I want to know about. But I never, *ever* expected you to pull something like this with me!"

I buckled up, too. "I was afraid if I told you I'd located your mother, you wouldn't come."

"And how did that work out, CeCe? Looking for her even after I've told you I wanted to forget I have a mother? Throwing our miserable past back at me, and at Alice, too?"

I'm good at smoothing over problems, but this one wasn't going to smooth easily. I floundered a little. "Listen… I admit things didn't go quite the way I planned. I had no idea she would recognize you. I was going to let you know as gently as I could. I wanted you to decide what to do, acknowledge her and introduce yourself, or just take one good look. I thought that would help you put what she did behind you. The fact she recognized you has to mean she's kept up with you, right?"

"Or maybe looking at me was like staring into a mirror. My God, we look alike, and I didn't think twice about it when I was talking to her. She was barely sixteen when I was born!"

"Lots of people look alike. At some point she must have traced your whereabouts, done some research. It wouldn't have been that hard. Maybe the Department of Children and Families gave her some clues, and you have a photography website with your picture."

She spaced her words like bullets at a shooting range, and her aim was true. "I am not a little girl. The days when I needed you to help make my decisions are *over*."

"Well, I thought you were wrong about this one."

She pulled out to the street. I was glad there was so little traffic, because her hands were visibly shaking, and I hoped we didn't end up in a ditch.

"You know what? I wish *your* mother was still alive, CeCe. Then maybe you could actually put yourself in my place."

And that was all she said, even when I tried to draw her out.

Oddly enough, today Robin is going to get her wish. Because today we're going to resurrect Maribeth, or at least my final memories of her.

Donny flew in early this morning, and now the two of us are sitting on a concrete bench by the lake. A pair of sandhill cranes just flew overhead, and on the opposite bank, barely in view, a gator is sunning itself. This is a Roscoe-free zone, since my pup's exactly the right size for a gator snack. He's snoozing inside. The crew fights for the privilege of watching over him.

I'm not sure why I decided to tell Donny about Robin's mom. He listened while I matter-of-factly presented what I had done. Now I was waiting for him to react.

He finally spoke. "So at what point did you decide you always know best? Before or after you became such a phenomenon? Because most of the phenoms I know have to make so many huge decisions they stop realizing other people have valid opinions, too."

"Robin's not just anybody. She's my sister. Nobody knows her better than I do."

"She knows *herself* better. And Robin knows exactly how she wants to handle that part of her life."

"But she's always wondered about her mom."

"She's said so?"

"I know her."

"Cecilia, you can't know what she's thinking. Or—especially—what she's feeling. You hardly know yourself."

I felt as if he'd slapped me. "What's that supposed to mean?"

"It means you're beginning to come to terms with a lot you've been repressing. And you just let that spill over to the person you love best in the world. But you and Robin are two separate people, and love doesn't give you the right to make decisions for her."

"How do you know so much? Who the hell do you love, Donny? You speak from experience?"

"I do."

He didn't go on, and I didn't really want him to. But I did make myself a little more vulnerable. "I'm afraid she's going to pack up and go home."

"And that would be upsetting on all kinds of levels."

"Stop being my psychiatrist."

He took my hand and threaded his fingers through it. "How about your friend?"

"You can't be my friend. You're my manager."

"As if anybody could manage you."

It was the right thing to say. I couldn't stifle a laugh, and he squeezed my hand, but he didn't drop it. "So how do you keep her from leaving?"

"I don't know."

"Of course you do."

"Listen, I'm not going to apologize. I thought I did the right thing. I'm still not sure I didn't."

"That would definitely not be a good start."

We sat in silence, our hands entwined, even though I knew attaching myself to him in any way other than financially wasn't a good idea. There have to be borders between our lives if we're going to work together. Unfortunately, at the moment I couldn't imagine my career without Donny beside me. On top of that, I couldn't imagine sitting on that bench without Donny holding my hand.

"So you think I should tell her I made a mistake?" Just the possibility made my head ache.

"If you admit to yourself you did."

I thought about my life. I don't make mistakes. Mistakes are like boulders rolling downhill. They destroy everything along the way. I know this for a fact.

I tried a different strategy. "Robin knows I don't apologize."

"Maybe Robin doesn't know *you* any more than you know her."

"This is getting complicated. I don't need this today."

"Then why don't you settle it before we leave for the apartment?"

"I'm not sure this is a good idea."

"The apology? Or filming the slum where your mother abandoned you?"

My throat felt swollen, as if the air that needed to pass through was going to have to slay dragons first. One breakdown. In a foreign country yet. I've told myself falling apart in Australia had next to nothing to do with my messy past and everything to do with exhaustion. But I'm not exhausted today. I am two steps past petrified.

"Neither," I said.

"I'm not trying to psychoanalyze you, but to do what I do I have to understand people. And it seems to me that if you apologize to your sister, that will put you on a more equal footing. You really don't have to take care of her anymore. She's doing a good job by herself. Standing up for what she needs? Easing the reins at home so Kris can step in and be the dad she wants him to be? All very grown-up and sensible. As was her decision about finding her own mother."

"I just wanted her to be able to close a door I can't."

He squeezed again.

Words spilled out without permission and refused to halt. "I hate Maribeth. You have no idea how much. But every once in a while? I remember something good. When we were abandoned by the king of scummy boyfriends after her stint in rehab, she started going to Narcotics Anonymous meetings. She took me with her, and I remember some of the other kids, messed up and embarrassed to be there, but all of us so pathetically hopeful. Maribeth got a job waiting tables, and we rented a big airy room in an old house. She bought yellow curtains at a garage sale, and a pretty ceramic bowl for fruit. After work we took walks and pretended we lived in the houses we saw. I remember an ice-cream sundae."

"Good memories are like a wedge that keeps the door open."

It wasn't a question. He understood.

I didn't even have to nod. "That's pretty much the sum total of the good ones. She started using again soon after the yellow curtains and the sundae, and never stopped. But she left me with enough glimpses to know that inside that drug-riddled body was a woman who could have been more if she'd made different choices, or maybe even if my father hadn't died."

"You feel sorry for her?"

I spat out the answer. "Not one bit."

"But you still miss her."

I started to protest, but the words wouldn't emerge. I'll share a secret those of us who have been abandoned know, and it binds us together in the saddest of ways. Despite everything our parents did or didn't do for us, we miss them until the day we die, and worse, we will always be certain, deep inside, that we were the cause of their desertion.

He took my silence for what it was. "You came through worse times than Maribeth did, but you made a success of yourself. It's hard to imagine why she couldn't get by. But nobody can answer that. She didn't, and as retribution, she left you with a few good memories."

"I hate her the most for that."

"Do you work so hard to take care of Robin because nobody took care of you?"

"You think that's a new insight? One I never had before?"

"No, but maybe it's the first time anybody's mentioned the possibility out loud."

"I can't figure out why I haven't fired you."

He drew my hand to his lips and kissed my fingertips before he dropped it. He stood. "Don't try. I'll take you to court."

I watched him go. Was I going to make a hard day harder by apologizing for something I believed was right? Apologies aren't something I've practiced. Are apologies like mistakes? Once begun, they can't be stopped or controlled? Another boulder plummeting down an endless mountain?

I looked toward the house and saw Robin talking to Donny, who was pointing toward me.

The bastard.

I stood when she got close enough that I could read her expression. She looked outwardly composed, but I know her well enough—and yes, this time I really do—to see she was still angry.

"I really blew it. Is that good enough?"

"Not nearly."

"I haven't had much practice apologizing."

"Get some."

"I thought I was doing the right thing. I thought you needed closure. I sure need it."

"I'm not you."

I might be getting into the swing of this. "I'm sorry I tried to fix something that's none of my business. I thought it was a gift, something you just didn't realize you wanted. I guess I still feel responsible for you. Donny says I need to take care of you because nobody took care of me."

She looked surprised. "He said that and lived to walk back to the house?"

"I'm not sure why."

"You really did blow it, CeCe."

I bit my lip—gnawed it, actually—until I could speak. "Yeah. Will you forgive me?"

"Did you arrange that touching little scene with Alice before we got there?"

That puzzled me. "Are you kidding? You saw her reaction. Afterward you and I even talked about why she recognized you."

"When you pull a fast one on somebody, they begin to doubt everything you say or ever said. You see that?"

I gave the shortest nod in history. "Okay, but no, Alice was every bit as surprised as you were. And it never occurred to me she would recognize you or even wait on our table."

"That's the problem with surprises. They zoom out of control."

"I like control."

"You like controlling everyone and everything. Me included."

"I'm sorry it turned out the way it did."

"You mean my mother walking out on me again?"

I hadn't thought about it that way, not exactly, but that's what had happened. Alice had abandoned Robin *again*. This time because of me.

Unlike most of my colleagues, I watch my level of profanity. I figure there are better ways to express myself, but this time even Robin blinked at the string of words that followed her question.

"Whew." She fanned herself.

"I set it up," I said. "This time I set it up myself. I can't believe it. I let her abandon you again on my watch."

"You set it up, all right. But you don't know the ending."

I'd been about to apologize again. Maybe I was finally getting better at it? But her words stopped me. "Ending?"

"When I went to pay for that meal we never ate? Alice left a business card at the counter, attached to the bill—which was comped, by the way. There was a note on the back that said if I ever forgave her long enough to call, she would like to talk to me."

I wasn't sure what to say.

Robin went on. "I'm not glad you did this, CeCe. Just so you know. It was wrong, through and through, an awful thing to spring on me. But the outcome is surprising."

"You're going to call?"

She shrugged. "Not right now. Maybe not ever. But it's a different ending than I thought I would have. If nothing else Alice seems to feel remorse. It's possible that's all I need."

I started to argue, but the words stayed put. Because Donny's right. Robin is a grown-up, and she doesn't need me to take care of her or even give advice she doesn't ask for.

Instead I changed the subject. "Donny said if I apologized, you and I would finally be on more or less equal footing."

"Donny says a lot to you none of the rest of us can get away with. But for the record, we've been on equal footing for a long time, only you refused to see it."

"I'm not enjoying this."

"Get used to it." She stepped forward and put her arms around me. And she held me when I started to cry.

32

—

Robin

Cecilia has always had more courage than I do. Last week she walked through the squalid rooms where her mother abandoned her as if she were a gracious first lady giving a tour of the White House. She grimly did five takes over two days, and she only broke down once.

On the final one she took us down the hall to the broom closet where as a child she hid when she needed to be safe. She showed us how she wedged the door shut from the inside so nobody could find her.

And she told us she slept in that dark, roach-infested closet as often as she slept on a filthy mattress on the floor of the apartment.

For anyone who questions whether my sister deserves the good things that have come her way as an adult? Take a look at the moment when she opens the closet door and bursts into tears.

Now a week later we were at the airport in Tampa, and Cecilia, who just got back from a quick trip to LA this morning, is on her phone in the parking lot talking to Hayley while I say goodbye to my daughter.

As a break from the more difficult scenes, Mick and crew

spent a few days filming in this area, and even though I'd just seen her, the lighter schedule seemed like a perfect time to invite Pet to join me for a long weekend. Even Kris, who had to make more trips to the airport for pickup and delivery, agreed she would get more from being on a film set than from her class unit on messages in the media.

Ten is not too young to understand the inner workings of a parent. When I wasn't needed for photos, I drove Pet on a tour of homes I had lived in, including a drive-by of my grandmother's, a last-minute decision I was afraid I might regret.

When I left foster care I was presented with the life book with information about my childhood and education that had followed me from placement to placement. So even though I was a child when I left my grandmother's house, I had the address. Secretly I hoped the house had blown away in a hurricane, but as expected, when Pet and I pulled up it was still standing. The little bungalow looked as if somebody cared about it, because the shrubs were neatly trimmed, exterior shingles replaced and the shutters had been recently painted. Of course the house is smaller and more ordinary than the one in my memories.

I tried to phrase my own reaction in a way that would convey some of the truth to Pet without worrying her. "You know my mother was really young, and she left home for good while I was still just a toddler. When my grandmother was well enough she took care of me until she died."

"What was she like?"

"Very orderly. Things had to be just so. And she was hard to please. Actually, nothing much pleased her, because nothing's ever perfect. That's a hard way to be and a hard thing to live with."

"But you were her granddaughter. She loved you, right?"

I struggled to tell the truth without telling all of it. "I think she must have been tired and worried most of the time. She tutored Latin students after school. She made sure they really knew their stuff. There wasn't much energy left over for me."

My daughter perked up at the mention of Latin. "Priests speak Latin. Do you?"

To this day, when I hear the occasional snippet in church, a cold chill streaks down my spine.

I didn't tell her that. "I don't remember much."

"If she hadn't died, you would have stayed here. Were you sad to leave?"

I pondered the possible answers. "Scared more than sad, because I didn't know what would happen to me. But to be honest, I wasn't sorry to say goodbye to this house. We can't always love the people we're supposed to. Sometimes it's just not possible. My grandmother was very different from yours. I'm glad you have Maminka, and Táta, too. When you have grandchildren, you'll be just as loving."

"I'm sorry your mother left you."

Of course Alice had been on my mind since the day in Everglades City. How could I explain her to my daughter so Pet could sympathize, at least a little?

"I'm sorry, too," I said carefully, "but she was still a child herself. Younger than Grace. She didn't know how to be a mom."

"I don't want to talk about Grace."

I tried not to smile. "I can't imagine being a mother at sixteen. Can you?"

Pet made a face that said everything.

As I put the car in gear to leave, the front door of the house opened and two young boys shot outside, followed by a young woman in shorts and a tank top, who was obviously their mother. She grabbed one by his T-shirt, swung him around and lifted him into her arms for a bear hug. I was grateful to see love in full bloom where it had never been planted during my childhood.

My grandmother doesn't haunt the house the way she still haunts me.

As we drove away we chatted about the things we saw until I parked in front of the Davis house, where Cecilia and I first met.

"We can't film here," I told Pet. "The new owners said no, and apparently they've done so much renovation, it's not the same inside, anyway."

"It's small."

"It used to be a lot smaller. One bathroom, two bedrooms, but a big living room with a piano, which is the reason your aunt discovered she has such a gift for music. She'd never seen a piano she was allowed to play before, but she told me her first day in this house she sat down and after a few minutes began to pick out the melodies to songs from the radio and sing the words. The Davises knew how unusual that was and started her on lessons. By the time we left here, she'd sung solos in the school choir and starred in the middle school production of *Annie*."

That had been typecasting, of course. The little red-haired orphan girl. Cecilia probably hadn't been above exploiting either the hair or the status to get the part.

"What about you?" Pet asked.

"They made sure I always had a camera and film, too, and even built a little darkroom in the laundry closet. That was back in the day when we still used film cameras, and Mr. Davis helped me develop whatever I shot. They were good people."

"Did you and Aunt Cecilia get along right away?"

"We shared a room. The first thing she asked me was if I liked playing with matches."

"That's weird."

"The last girl who shared her room set Cecilia's bed on fire. Luckily it smoldered awhile before the blaze really caught, and she woke up in time."

Pet's eyes widened, and I wondered if I had gone too far. Describing foster care to a child, the free fall from living at home to living with strangers, isn't easy. I decided to go just a little further.

"The Davises were really good foster parents. They tried to help her, but after the firefighters hauled the mattress outside, they found a whole stash of matches hidden in her closet. They realized she needed to be somewhere more secure where she could get serious help. So they took me in, instead."

"What happened to her?"

I didn't know, but I could guess. Outcomes for foster children are often grim. Cecilia and I skew the graphs.

But then, we'd had each other.

"I hope she got the help she needed," I said.

"If she hadn't done that—set the bed on fire, I mean—you never would have met Aunt Cecilia."

"I can't imagine life without your aunt, can you?"

"You love her more than I love Nik. I wish you'd send Nik somewhere more secure."

I laughed, because while they fight, Nik and Pet stand up for each other when the going gets rough. Once the storms of adolescence blow over, they'll be friends forever.

"The Davises were strict but always fair. And fun to be with. Cecilia hated my wardrobe. My grandmother had very plain taste in clothing. Everything I owned was either brown or gray, except for a red sweater that a previous foster mother had given me. I walked into the Davises' house wearing that sweater and Cecilia said I looked like a robin. Brown feathers, red breast. The name stuck."

"Robin's not your real name?"

"I changed it legally when I turned eighteen."

"What was it before?"

"Roberta Ingrid. My grandmother always used both. 'Roberta Ingrid do your homework. Roberta Ingrid eat your dinner.' Long names for a little girl."

She thought about that and came to the right conclusion. "You didn't want to remember your grandmother every time somebody said your name."

"Do I look like a Roberta Ingrid to you?"

Another face, and we both laughed. "Anyway, Cecilia said *Robin* was close enough that I wouldn't forget who I was. She and Mrs. Davis took me shopping on my second day there, and Cecilia picked out new clothes for me and supervised a haircut."

"Aunt Cecilia sure is bossy."

I rolled my eyes. "Tell me about it."

I'd finished the story as we went back to the mansion by the lake. "I looked like a new person, and that's what I needed. New name, new clothes, new hair, new place to live. New sister."

"I wish I had a sister."

"You're stuck with Nik."

Now we were once again saying goodbye at the airport gate. My daughter, who would never be tossed on the winds of foster care, was heading back to Virginia, to Kris and Nik and the life she'd always known.

The gate agent asked families with children to come forward, and we both stood. Reassurance seemed important, even though Pet didn't look one bit flustered. "Your dad texted again this morning to say he'll be right there to meet you when you get in. And don't forget I'll be home in less than two weeks, and we'll have Christmas together."

"Daddy said maybe this year we can go to a tree farm and cut down our own tree."

"Did he?" I was as surprised as if Kris had promised a trip into outer space to find the perfect stars to trim it.

"He said we used to do that."

"When you were really little."

"I hope it snows."

I didn't, but I smiled and gave her one last hug. "Now scoot, and don't forget to call when you get there. Or I'll worry."

I watched her hold out her ticket to the agent and, after she was cleared, enter the Jetway. My daughter the world traveler was completely at ease.

Kris and I had spoken twice since our reunion. Maybe we share the opinion that a telephone conversation isn't the best way to dissect marital problems, or maybe we're both so tired of conflict we just prefer chatting about daily routines. But I was cautiously hopeful that our Christmas might be a good one.

When Hal drove in from the cell phone waiting lot, Cecilia had her eyes closed and her head—coiffed in loose corkscrew curls—resting against the backseat. While I was in jeans and a long-sleeved T-shirt, she was dressed for the camera, a sparkly tank top that showed just enough cleavage, a silky turquoise jacket that seemed to float even when she was sitting absolutely still, calf-length skirt and sandals with ridiculous heels and colorful butterfly wings resting behind her ankles.

"Hayley okay?" I asked as Hal pulled away from the curb and I fastened my seat belt.

"As okay as Hayley can be. We need to move to Skype so I can see what she's signing when we chat." She opened her eyes one millimeter per second. "I'm going to spend part of Christmas in Nashville so I can visit her."

"At CFF?"

"Do you think it's a bad idea to bring her to my condo for a night? Not Christmas Eve, they'll have something special going on in the cottages then, but maybe the day after Christmas. There's always such a letdown after the holiday."

"I don't know. It's tricky. It's like a promise, isn't it? A lot more than phone calls."

"Yeah, but maybe it's just a promise I'll be there sometimes when she needs me."

"She needs somebody all the time."

"But she doesn't have anybody like that. Isn't something better than nothing?"

"Unless *something* sounds like it's going to be more than it is."

"This is so confusing. I hate confusing."

I realized how true that was. Cecilia likes to have everything neatly tied up. She makes decisions and doesn't look back. And even though she hasn't said so, Hayley is an unmade decision.

Today we were going to film a segment on adoption. The agency where we were headed hadn't been around when Cecilia and I were in foster care. Adopting Children Today, or ACT, specialized in finding permanent homes, with a success rate that was far above average. The director, Travis Simpkins, who I'd met yesterday, was young and enthusiastic. Travis and his staff worked tirelessly, and they wouldn't be happy until every child who needed a family found one.

Which meant a life of eternal disappointment.

"You'll like Travis Simpkins," I said. "Maybe you can get him alone for a few minutes, tell him about Hayley and ask his opinion."

"He'll draw up the necessary papers before I finish my first sentence."

"I think he's more interested in finding the right parent than just any parent."

"I am not just any parent!"

"Well, not everybody who comes looking for a kid is famous and gorgeous."

"You know that's not what I mean."

"Really? What else do you have to offer?"

She closed her eyes again. "I'm taking a nap."

I laughed and closed my eyes, too.

ACT spends more time and money placing children than they spend on appearances. The agency is housed in a down-at-the-heels three-story building on the outskirts of downtown shared by insurance agents, podiatrists and a dog groomer, who has the entire first floor. Howls and barks echoed through windows flung wide-open as Travis, a barrel-chested guy in a tropical shirt and flip-flops, came into the reception area from an office the size of a powder room and enthusiastically embraced us both.

Mick and a bare-minimum crew had already followed Travis for a morning. Pet and I had taken photos at the same time and I was scheduled to come back tomorrow when a family who was working with Travis came in for their second interview.

Travis took us back to his office. Today the only person from our crew was Jerry, with one of his larger cameras already locked in place on a tripod. Earlier he had set up the sound, and in addition to sunshine filtered through a curtain at Travis's window, he had softly lit the room with a standard lightbulb surrounded by what he called a China ball. I knew it as a Japanese lantern, and he used this trick often.

"We have to go somewhere else to finish this," Travis said, after we talked a little while. "I can't stand being cooped up in here when I don't have to be. Mick suggested a park across town." He turned to Cecilia. "Did he mention that to you?"

She gave a short nod. This was news to me, but I had been busy with my daughter for the last few days, and I had probably missed other things, too.

Cecilia caught my eye. "I spent a lot of time at the park he's talking about. That was the year I officially proved I was unadoptable. I was allowed to play there by myself after school. They liked getting me out of the house. Anything else fun was off-limits."

"Nobody is unadoptable." Travis swiped his hand through the air in emphasis. "Although some people shouldn't adopt."

"Sometimes I still wonder why I didn't try harder to follow their rules."

"Because you were a perfectly normal messed-up kid," he said without missing a beat.

Cecilia and Travis fist-bumped, and I knew she had decided he was okay. That would make today easier. Cecilia is cautious, although not everybody sees it. She knows how to get along with almost anybody, but she doesn't always try.

He turned to me. "Robin, Mick told me you were also a foster kid. You didn't mention that when your daughter was here."

"She knows. I just don't make a point of it."

"You weren't adopted?"

I knew what he was asking, but I smiled. "Why, are you going to try to find me a family?"

He had a penetrating, almost frightening laugh, like a wild dog who's just heard a good joke. The man was friendly, but in defense of his kids I thought Travis could turn into a predator when necessary.

"You might be surprised how many people *are* adopted as adults," he said. "Last month I went to a wedding for a young woman, twenty-two, who was adopted by former foster parents a week before the ceremony. They'd always wanted to adopt her, but she had family members who objected. When she announced she was getting married, they told her nothing would make them happier than finally becoming the official parents of the bride. Her father gave her away. Everyone was delighted."

"Can Cecilia adopt me?"

"I more or less did," Cecilia said. "And did a pretty good job of raising you, too."

I answered more seriously. "There were long periods of time in my childhood when I didn't speak. Nothing good ever came from speaking, so I quit. One psychiatrist decided I was autistic. The diagnosis stayed in my records too long, and at the time, nobody thought finding a permanent home for an autistic child was possible."

"Neither of you was served well by the system."

Cecilia made a noise low in her throat. Of the two of us, she had been served most poorly.

On some level I was aware that Jerry was still filming. I guess I'd known from the beginning that I might be in front of the camera as well as behind it. I'm too much a part of my sister's past to be excluded. But I value presenting the facts about foster care more than I value my privacy. If Cecilia, with all she had to lose, can tell her story, I can tell whatever part of mine might help.

"Let's go see if we can make some sense out of what happened to both of you," Travis said. "And I'll tell you what we do to make sure our adoptions stick."

I already knew a little. It seemed to come down to working constantly. "Will you burn out? Because the best caseworkers Cecilia and I had found other jobs pretty fast. The workload was too difficult, and the lack of progress was worse."

Travis met my eyes, and I could see that on a personal level, he knew exactly what I meant. "This is my life. When everything starts to get to me I lock myself in my office and attack paperwork for a day or two. That usually sobers me up. Because even one small island of success in a river of failure is worth whatever we have to do to achieve it."

He gestured to Cecilia, then to me. "And, you know, one of those successes could be somebody like either of you. Isn't that worth whatever price I have to pay?"

33

—

Cecilia

I remember this swing set, although I'm sure that all these years later everything about it has been replaced countless times. It still sits in an overlooked corner of this spacious public park, flanked by bushes and far away from baseball diamonds and soccer fields. It's as private as a public space can be, which is why filming here today was our little secret.

I've never forgotten how it felt to pump my legs and fly through the air, wishing the whole time I could let go and soar into the clouds and away from life with my new mother and father.

Mother and Father. Never Mom and Dad.

Today I was forced to remember those months with the Ruskillion family, who had lived just blocks away. From my first day to my last in their home, every movement I made, every word I uttered, was heavily scrutinized. After all, a child with my background couldn't be trusted to do anything the right way. I had to be schooled in everything. Manners. Dress. Thought.

Gratitude.

Gratitude was a big one for Mother and Father. It was their Christian duty to share all they had with the unfortunate.

Why wasn't I more grateful they allowed me to share their life? I had my own room—without privacy, of course, since they removed the door before bringing me home, but still mine. I had three healthy meals a day, and they were right there to make sure I ate every bite, even if the taste or smell made me choke.

I also had a sister. Now, as darkness fell and stars gathered to light the canopy overhead, I wondered what ever became of Gretchen Ruskillion, their biological daughter. Gretchen was two years older than me, and the Ruskillions thought having a little sister would be good for her. In the many years since, did she ever see me in concert and wonder why I looked familiar? She wouldn't remember me as Cecilia. From the moment I entered their home the Ruskillions called me Hope. In the beginning, did they really "hope" the adoption would be successful?

Unfortunately Gretchen had not, as "hoped," been happy to have me in the house. Every moment her parents' backs were turned she tormented me, and then lay whatever new scheme she'd concocted at my doorstep.

Gretchen did me a favor, though. I'm not sure I would have survived the Ruskillion household with my spirit intact.

As I arced forward again Donny materialized out of the shadows beyond the swing set. "Don't you know bad things happen to good girls alone after dark?"

I was delighted to see him—and worried at what seemed like my extreme reaction. I let myself drift to earth. "Hey, when did you get here?"

"I came straight from the airport."

"Ivan and Hal are somewhere out there. I'm fine."

He lowered himself to the swing beside mine and pushed off. "I sent them home. And you're not fine. If you were, you would have gone back to the house by now."

I wasn't about to argue. I knew from the beginning that I wasn't going to be fine on this journey. Maybe, with luck, I'll be closer to fine when it's over.

Or I can check myself into a locked facility and weave pot holders until my money runs out.

Donny gained momentum and height. "This is where you hung out when things got rough at home?"

I pushed off again and pumped my legs until we were in sync, rising and falling at the same speed. "Never *home*. I never once thought of it that way."

"How long were you with these so-called adoptive parents?"

"They kept me for maybe six months. Then, when it was clear I wasn't going to learn any good tricks, they snapped on my leash, took me back to the pound and said they didn't want a puppy after all."

"That must be what it felt like."

"Mostly it felt like relief, but suddenly there was a whole sheaf of notes in my file about how I was unadoptable and should be relegated to perpetual foster care. One of my prime sins was bed-wetting, which mysteriously stopped the moment I left the Ruskillions' house. But I doubt anybody noted that. And besides, I didn't want to leave the Davises, and I told them so every single day. I think they purposely underplayed how well I was doing so I wouldn't be sent somewhere else."

"But eventually you *were* sent to another foster home."

I wished he hadn't brought that up. "Mr. Davis had a heart attack, and they had to move north to be closer to their children. I think they hoped to see me to adulthood, and they were genuinely sorry. While they were still alive Robin stayed in touch."

"Not you? Why not?"

"Connections are tough."

"Except Robin."

"Except Robin."

We swung in silence for a while before he spoke again. "What did you think about when you were here at the park?"

"I plotted how I would run away and find my mother." My throat tightened, but I plowed on. "At that point I still believed maybe she'd forgotten about me for a little while, but now she was looking and didn't know where I was. I knew she couldn't go to the police. She wasn't a big fan of cops, if you can imagine that. But what if she was trying to find me and didn't know how?"

"It might even have been true."

"Yeah. That's the funny part."

"Not so funny."

"Of course there was an obvious solution. Maribeth could have gone into treatment again and then presented herself as a changed woman. She might even have regained custody, or at least visiting rights, after she did penance and possibly a little time in a cell."

"From everything you've told me, that was beyond her."

"Not in the imagination of an unloved ten-year-old."

Donny dragged his feet on the next few arcs, and I followed suit. Once the swing had stopped he stood.

"It's dinnertime." He held out his hand.

"I'm not all that excited about heading back to a house full of people right now."

"I know. I'm taking you to my place."

I let him help me out of the swing and then looked down. "I think I lost a shoe."

"Can't have gone too far. Stay put."

He turned on his smartphone for light and swung it over the ground. The sandal had flown wild and free but not far.

He brought it back, then knelt in front of me while I lifted my foot and slipped it on.

Just like Prince Charming. It fit perfectly.

"You're not staying at the house?"

"I'm renting a little cabin on the Hillsborough River. Not too far from there. Privacy sounded good."

"You could have stayed in LA, Donny. You don't have to be with me every step of the way."

"I *haven't* been with you. I missed today. I didn't want to miss tonight." Something about the way he said it sent shivers everywhere it shouldn't have.

"Because I've ordered dinner to be delivered in an hour," he went on after giving me just enough time to worry. "And I'm told the lights from the city are something to behold once the sky is really dark. I'm sorry we missed the sunset."

"How did you do all this? Find a place? Order dinner? Find me here?"

"I have people. You have people. Always the twain shall meet."

"You *are* my people. At least my head people."

"That doesn't hurt." He touched my cheek. Quickly. Softly. "Nothing's expected tonight except showing up and sitting with me to watch the stars come out."

"There's no boiled cabbage on the menu?"

"Not that I know of. Is that a deal breaker?"

"There are exactly 639 ways to boil cabbage. Mrs. Ruskillion knew every single one of them. Luckily I was only living in their house for 184 days and was spared the other—" I did a quick calculation "—455."

"I'm going to hunt those people down."

"My hero."

He put his arm around my shoulders and guided me toward the parking lot. "You're going to get in my rental and close your eyes. I'm going to put the top down—"

"You rented a convertible?"

"My last bit of ammunition in case you refused to come. As I said—"

"'I'm going to put the top down,'" I repeated, to be helpful.

"And you're going to shut your eyes and let the wind blow all thoughts of the Rapscallions out of that overactive brain of yours, okay?"

I smiled at the name. "You're saying it will take decades to get to your cabin?"

"Let go of them."

"I bet they haven't given me a thought. Not in all these years."

"They will when I find them and send a personal copy of the film. I'm hoping you'll autograph it."

I laughed, and somehow, my heart eased. Not because Donny would ever do it, but because he wanted to.

I woke up sometime later as we pulled to a halt and a gate whirred in front of us.

"You went out like a lamp at bedtime," Donny said.

From the dashboard clock I saw I'd slept about twenty-five minutes. "I love this car. I love having the top down."

"You may not buy a fleet of convertibles."

"You're not my business manager."

"He and I speak frequently."

I laughed because Donny only did his job and never overstepped his boundaries. "I'm starving."

He pulled into a parking space as the gate closed behind us. "You eat like a bird. Two lettuce leaves instead of one?"

"I eat like somebody who has to make seven costume changes when she's on tour."

"You're not on tour right now."

"I'm on camera, which adds ten pounds." I smiled at him. "But not tonight."

"Good girl. And for the record, I think you're losing weight. None of those costumes will fit if you don't put a few pounds back on."

Donny knows as well as I do that every tour demands new costumes, but I was glad he was paying attention. And not because I want him to take care of me. Because, well, he's looking.

We got out and started toward the water. The cabin probably started life as a boathouse. Perched at the end of a short dock it was almost as good as a houseboat. Lights were coming on up and down the river, and the surface glistened and rippled under a rising moon. The cabin itself looked like a rickety bait shop. I loved it on sight.

"Your people did good."

"It's nicer than they told me. So you like it?"

"I love it."

He pretended to sound stern. "You don't need a house here, and as far as I know it's not for sale."

"I'm not nearly as free with my money as you like to pretend."

"Actually you're an amazing businesswoman."

I took his arm, warmed by the praise, and we strolled down the dock. He punched in a code to unlock the door, and we stepped inside. While the outside was bait house—chic, the inside was beautifully updated. The walls were bead board painted a soft white and dotted with watercolors of aquatic life, and the ceiling had been raised and angled to give the illusion of more space. French doors to the dock flanked both sides, and tall windows faced the water. The boathouse was tiny, but not an inch of space was wasted.

I nodded toward a small flat screen on the wall between windows. "They don't need the television. The view is entertainment enough."

"Looks like I landed on my feet. I'm looking forward to seeing the river in daylight."

"We only have one more day here, or at least I do." Mick wanted me to spend more time interviewing Travis tomorrow at the home of a child he'd placed, then I was done until after Christmas. The crew would film some short segments that didn't include me.

"What are your plans for the holiday?"

He knew my plans until Christmas week because he would be with me for some of them. I'm scheduled for interviews, a guest appearance and performance on *The Today Show*, more discussions with Cyclonic about the album I hoped to record, meetings with several producers to nail down the right person for the project. Gizzie and I are going to spend a long weekend trying to finalize the theme song for *At the Mercy of Strangers*, as well as other music for the soundtrack. Every day a new audio file turns up on my computer. I love technology.

"I was thinking about Nashville at some point," I said. "To see Hayley. What about you?"

"I'm going home."

I don't know a lot about Donny's childhood. Since we've been on this odyssey together I've learned that he grew up with two parents, two sisters and that he has at least one niece. From previous conversations I know he started life in Indiana, or maybe Iowa. Not knowing details is part of staying professionally distant. It's tough to fire somebody if you know their mom is having chemo or their sister's house just burned to the ground.

I wandered, touching this, then that. "Have anything to drink here?"

"They were supposed to stock the fridge. Let's see."

We found a fully stocked bar. Better yet, I found two cans of Diet Dr Pepper.

I squealed in delight and found a glass. "Okay, you know my secret, but my reputation will be ruined if you tell anybody." I popped the top and toasted him once my glass was full. He added vermouth to club soda and toasted me back.

We settled on the sofa with a bowl of cashews and another of raisins. I was ready for information. "Tell me about your family. Exactly where is home for everybody these days. Where will you go?"

He angled his body to see me better, but he didn't answer. Finally he sighed. Then he reached for my glass and set it on the table in front of us where his resided. He threaded his fingers through my hair and nudged me closer, his hand warm against my cheek. "Indiana. And I want you to come with me."

He waited, as if he knew I had a decision to make.

I bit my lip. "Promise if you kiss me, we can still go back to the way things were."

"We can't, Cecilia, even if I don't kiss you. Even if you spend Christmas alone."

He was so close I could see the gold flecks in his eyes, warming to something even more elemental. I removed his glasses and set them on the table beside me. "When did you decide this was inevitable?"

"An exact date?"

"Close."

"When I realized you married a man you couldn't love and I had another chance to be the one you could."

My heart lifted, and I was filled with longing. Because weren't those words a declaration? That I was wanted by a good man like this one? A man who has seen me at my worst and still cares? A man I have tried to pretend I don't desire?

Of course fear followed quickly. Even Donny, who lived through Australia with me, knows so little of the truth. I struggled to be as honest as I could. "I don't know if I can love anybody. I think maybe that part of me died a long time ago. You're asking for trouble."

"Nobody knows that better."

"I would miss you so much if this explodes in our faces."

"Let's assume it won't."

"Can we take things slowly?"

"Like five years slow?" He moved closer. "I'm just going to kiss you tonight. Slow enough?"

I wasn't sure which was stronger, fear or desire. Because for the first time in my life, how this turned out really mattered.

So *I* kissed *him*. Because even though I lie as often as I tell the truth, he needed to know how much I wanted him.

Sometimes you have to launch yourself into the void and hope there's somebody there to catch you.

34

—

Kris

I remember teacher planning days. As a kid in school, having an extra day to do whatever I wanted? Awesome. As a working parent? Not so much.

Today Nik has the day off, although for some reason Pet doesn't, so I spent yesterday debating how to handle it. Robin won't be home until tomorrow night. Nik's best friend is scheduled for a mom-enforced shopping trip, and this close to Christmas I don't want to ask Elena to arrive early. He's old enough to spend the morning alone; he can probably sleep in until Elena arrives, but aren't there better ways to deal with it?

Nik was sullen on the trip to Tysons Corner that he didn't want to take. "I don't want to be a lawyer."

"I don't blame you."

Off the toll road I wound my way through traffic toward my office. I got my son up early enough to leave for work with me, but of course, he dragged his feet, hoping that I would change my mind. I didn't. Now we were late enough that the traffic in Tysons was bumper to bumper.

"You just do paperwork all day?"

"Meetings, too. Lots of phone calls."

"Great. This is going to be so much fun."

Actually Nik has the makings of a terrific lawyer. He questions everything. He never accepts anything at face value, and he doesn't believe most of what he's told. Empathy doesn't come easily, and he keeps his distance until he's certain a situation requires it.

Oh, and he plans to make a lot of money at whatever he does. Not that finding a good job is easy for lawyers these days when law schools are graduating more than the world really needs.

I finally got through a green light after watching it turn red three times. "You like the music business, right?"

He grunted, which was not exactly the "Yes, sir" I'd been taught by my old-world parents, but expressive enough under the circumstances.

"Would you like to be a personal manager like Donny?"

"Who wouldn't?"

"He has a law degree. Did you know that?"

Another grunt. I was amazed at how well I was learning to interpret. "He went to UCLA Law and worked in a big entertainment firm until he went out on his own."

"How do you know all that?"

"I asked him." I like Donny. Even if I'm not crazy about Cecilia, I admire her ability to surround herself with the best people. Like my wife.

"Is that a good way to get into the industry?" Nik asked.

I liked the way this conversation was shaping up, as well as his use of "industry." My son has been giving this a little thought.

"It's certainly one way, plus if you don't like doing the legal stuff day in and day out, you can branch out, the way Donny did. But entertainment law in itself would be fascinating. Imagine the people you'd meet."

"So if you go to law school, you don't have to be a lawyer?"

That question took us all the way up the elevator in my building. We finished as the doors opened again on Singer's floor.

Buff and another partner were standing, heads together, just a few feet away, and when Nik and I emerged, I introduced my son to the other man, someone I rarely work with.

"Nik's going to see what I do here," I said.

Buff's expression was pleasant if nothing more. "Bring your son to work day?"

"I had a day off," Nik said. "I figured I'd see the place where my father really lives."

The two men laughed. I squeezed Nik's shoulder—maybe a little too hard. "I'm going to show him around."

Buff touched my arm. "We need to talk when it's convenient."

I knew about *what*. Yesterday afternoon I'd carefully crafted a memo about my experience in Norfolk and my decision to no longer be associated with Mervin Pedersen or his case. I strongly recommended that the firm drop him as a client.

Quite possibly this was not, after all, the best day to bring my son with me.

We made arrangements to meet in his office at eleven. Nik and I strolled down the hall.

"Great sense of humor," I told him. "Me living here and all."

"Not too bad, huh?"

"Our first and last stop is the law library. You can spend the morning researching statutes on the disposal of dog waste."

He didn't, of course. We spent the rest of the morning touring the offices and talking about what I did and why. Just before eleven I took him to meet one of our associates, who is working with a songwriter on a new intellectual property infringement matter. The songwriter believes a melody he composed was stolen and recorded, and Jeanie is helping him document his case. I introduced Nik and asked if she had a few minutes to tell him whatever she could.

When it was clear Jeanie was enthused enough to keep Nik busy for at least a few minutes, I headed down the hall.

You can tell how well regarded an attorney is by the size and placement of his office. Mine has a large window and enough room for a leather couch along the only wall not covered with bookcases. Buff's corner office is twice as roomy with twice as many windows, original artwork, wing chairs in addition to a couch and a small mahogany cabinet in the corner, which hides a well-stocked bar.

When I stepped in he nodded to the bar, but I shook my head. I have no intention of acquiring a taste for liquor in the middle of my workday. It's hard enough to stay focused.

"I got your memo," he said without more preliminaries. "I had to read it three times to be sure I understood."

"Wasn't I clear? I'm sorry."

"You were clear. I just couldn't believe it."

I took a chair in front of his desk. That he hadn't come out to sit on the sofa was a sign I couldn't misinterpret. I'd just been called to the principal's office.

I took the initiative. "This is not a man the firm should represent. He'll drag us through his own contamination, and we won't win. In the short time I was there I encountered an employee, soon to be an ex-employee, who will probably testify against Pedersen and his practices if given the opportunity. I'm sure there are others. He has more money than sense or ethics. He's angry for no good reason, and he wants retribution. He won't get it. At best he'll get publicity, but it won't be good. I would guess when the proper authorities find time, money and legal precedent to go after him, they will, with guns blazing."

"Back up to the more money than sense part."

I knew where Buff was going. Singer could be absolutely honest with Pedersen, and he would still want us to represent him. He wanted his day in court, even if we promised he was going to lose. And he had that right. This is America, and "land of the free" means we're *free* to bring lawsuits, even if they are certifiably crazy. We're also free to spend our money any way we want.

I elaborated on my memo. "I've represented people I don't like, and I've represented people with little or no chance of winning. This time it's a doubleheader. Pedersen's a dirtbag. His facilities are substandard, and his employees are forced to cut corners on safety. I don't want any part of it."

"What if I tell you we're going to work with him anyway? Because that's what we do. We aren't going to do anything shady or unethical in representing him, but we *are* going to do it to the best of our ability, and Pedersen wants you on the team."

"Then I'll tell him I've suddenly discovered I can't give his case the thoughtful preparation it needs, and I hope he understands. I'll be glad to make that phone call."

Buff was tapping a pen on his desk. "That's your final word?"

"I hope so."

"This doesn't look good, Kris. Some people will think you're just too busy with your personal life to take this on, and they'll think you're slacking."

"I hope everybody will be told up front why I'm not doing it, and I hope the firm will reconsider its own decision to work with him."

"That will be *my* decision, not the firm's. And I haven't yet decided."

I stood, because there was little else to say. "I've billed as many or more hours in my years here as anyone else in the office. And this month I didn't let up, despite being busy at home. The facts are there for anybody to see. I hope they take a look."

"Backbone's a good thing for an attorney."

"For human beings in general."

"Backbone tempered by common sense is better."

"My backbone and my conscience agree on this one, Buff." I nodded and left. In the hallway I could almost feel the cold chill that would probably greet my decision once it was widely known. Depending, of course, on how Buff explained it to the other partners.

Jeanie and Nik were still chatting away when I went to fetch him to go home. I couldn't remember when I last left the office before five, but by the same token, I couldn't remember when I had so thoroughly jinxed my career, either. Some kind of celebration was called for.

I was gathering my things to go, and Nik was muttering about the boring books on my shelves, when my phone buzzed. When I hung up a few minutes later he was standing beside my desk.

"Who was that?"

He actually sounded interested. "My friend Howie. He teaches at GW Law. You met him this summer, remember? He and his wife came to dinner." Robin made a wonderful couscous dish, and Howie went back for thirds.

"You're going to teach a class?"

"I might. I've been doing guest lectures for his classes. Now he wants me to teach my own as an adjunct professor." Adjunct means the pay and prestige will be minimal, but Howie also mentioned that a faculty position might open next year, and teaching this spring could help pave the way. If I was interested.

"You must like teaching. You sounded..." Nik shrugged. "Different."

I examined my son, the one with the supposed empathy problem? Nik had picked up on my tone, maybe my posture. And I guess I did laugh more than once.

"I do like teaching. I like it better than anything else professional that I do."

"Then why don't you do that instead of this? If you like it? Aren't we supposed to do things we like and get paid for it?"

"It doesn't pay nearly as well."

"Yeah, making money is good." He picked up a paperweight and tossed it from hand to hand. "I guess I want to be happy, too."

I was raising a wise young man. Of course most of the time Nik hides it well, but when the chips are down, out it pops. I memorized the conversation for Robin. In the coming years we'll need to document each and every case of mature behavior on the part of our children to tuck away as reminders.

On the way to the garage we talked about Jeanie's case and what he'd learned. Out on the road I gave him a tour of the area. Two popular upscale shopping malls are situated nearby, and the streets between them are lined with freestanding stores. With only ten days until the holiday, Christmas is everywhere. Office buildings and shops are thoroughly saturated in green and red, with silver bells tinkling in a bracing breeze.

"What's a model-train store? A whole store for model railroads?" Nik pointed to a shop at the end of the row.

"Right. The kind of place a kid goes to drool over train sets he can't afford. I went weekly when I was your age."

"You did?"

"Sure. Train sets are great. Like the one I had as a boy. You've seen it."

"No."

I pulled into a parking slot near the store in question. Model Train World sat companionably beside a stationery store. Does anybody really use stationery anymore?

"You've seen my train set," I said. "I'm sure you have."

"No."

"When your grandparents moved from the house where I grew up they boxed everything of mine they found in their attic and shipped it to us. Train set, too. You were pretty young, but I'm sure I showed it to you."

"No."

Judging by his unswerving devotion to his own opinion, I could see law school was becoming inevitable. "Okay. I didn't show it to you. I'm sorry."

"It's up in the attic now?"

"It's not much of a set." Of course any little boy—or girl— would adore it, cheap and incomplete as it is. Especially a child, like my son, who loves hobbies and collecting in general.

I had loved every single piece. Somehow, in the midst of my important life, sharing my beloved train set with my son and daughter simply slipped my mind.

For a moment I found it hard to speak. I cleared my throat. Nik, Pet and I had cut a Scotch pine at a local Christmas-tree farm yesterday, and now it stood undecorated in its designated corner, waiting for Robin to come home and help. "We'll find that box tonight. What say we set it up around the Christmas tree?"

His face lit up. "Really?"

"Well, I had to save pretty hard for each piece. I used to haul out trash for elderly neighbors. There's not a lot to it. Let's check out the store and see what's there. Maybe buy more track?"

"Really?" he repeated. "How cool is that."

Nik is almost too old to appreciate this. In a few years he'll roll his eyes when I bring the train set out of the attic to set it up under the tree. I nearly missed this chance to share something that once meant everything to me.

How many other things have I nearly missed? How many others are gone forever?

"I collected O gauge trains and track. Do you know what that means?"

"I don't know anybody with model trains."

"Remember how much you loved reading *The Polar Express*?"

"Did you ever see the movie? It's scary."

"Maybe we can watch it tonight while we set up the train."

"Yeah, Petra would like that."

"You're doing better on the name change than I am. I still call her Pet."

"She doesn't mind because it's *you*."

I opened my door, and by the time I went around the car, Nik was standing in front of the store, nose pressed to the glass.

Today I took a stand that will lower my status at work, but at this moment my status with my son is at an all-time high. And really? The relative importance suddenly seems clear.

For the first time since she walked out our door, I was grateful to my wife for taking her own stand. I just hope it's not too late to tell her.

35

Robin

I'm not sure where Cecilia is spending the holidays. In our telephone chats she's been purposely vague. Hayley will figure in somehow, and Donny? That's where the vague part comes in. As good an actress as she is—and as good a liar—there's a hitch in Cecilia's voice when the subject of Donny comes up. If she hadn't flown back to LA almost a week ago and I could look her in the eye, I wonder what I would see?

I'm afraid to hope.

I'm also afraid to go home, because I'm already worried about leaving again. Part of me is afraid if things go badly I might be compelled by my disintegrating marriage to head out for good. Another part is afraid if things go well I won't have the energy or desire to leave, and I'll fall right back into my old life. But it's too late to worry. The airport shuttle driver just pointed out that we've almost arrived. We're now officially in Meadow Branch.

I left northern Virginia six weeks ago when fall nipped the air. Winter is an iffier proposition. Almost anything can be considered normal in December. Today, according to the driver, the sun shone and temperatures reached the low fifties. Tomorrow rain will wash away patches of snow visible on hillsides and rooftops. If we're lucky it won't turn to sleet or ice. Ice storms can shut down everything for miles around.

Of course if that happens, Kris won't be able to go to work.

I was scheduled to come home tomorrow, but we finished filming earlier than anticipated, and everyone else caught flights last night. With the holidays looming planes are packed, but this morning I was able to change my ticket at the airport. I didn't warn my family.

I'll be an early Christmas present.

"Pretty community," the driver said. I was his final passenger; the others had already been deposited at homes along the route.

Almost every house we passed was decorated for the holiday, and as darkness fell, outdoor light displays were beginning to twinkle. Fully decorated trees glittered in living rooms. As we turned onto my street I saw that our new neighbors had chosen fresh pine garlands and tastefully simple candles to adorn window ledges. In former years Talya decorated with a Happy Chanukah rope light across a front window and a lit Star of David on their front door. I smiled, remembering that Talya had faithfully removed them before her strictly observant in-laws came to visit.

I hope to persuade Michael and Channa to come for Christmas dinner, the way they always did when Talya was alive, but I'm afraid too short a time has passed for a return visit to Meadow Branch.

I told the driver to slow. "It is pretty, isn't it? This is beautiful country."

"Yeah, you're lucky to live here."

I thought about the places I lived in my childhood, one still to revisit. "Very lucky."

I pointed out my house, and he pulled into our driveway. If Kris put up our lights—or more likely remembered to hire someone else to do it—no one had yet switched them on. Our curtains were drawn, and no wreath adorned our front door. Compared to other houses in the neighborhood, ours looked like the domicile of Ebenezer Scrooge.

I had hoped for a bright splash of joy, for obvious changes here, but if things really were different the exterior of our house offered no clues.

The driver got out to retrieve my suitcase, and I had to follow. This was my home, my family, but I felt like a stranger. The life I'd known here had been shaken and rearranged, and I wasn't sure where or how I fit.

I thanked and tipped him, then I slung my backpack and camera bag over my shoulders, grabbed the handle of my suitcase and started up the front walk. The door flew open.

"Mommy!" Pet launched herself at me and I just barely caught her. "You're here!"

The house might not look like Christmas, but my daughter, dressed in a green sweater and red leggings, looked like a Christmas angel. I kissed her hair. "I got an earlier flight."

"You should have told us! We could have picked you up."

"She's right. We could have." Kris was now standing behind Pet, who stepped back to smile up at me.

"Merry Christmas." I smiled, and better yet, so did my husband. At that exact moment the Christmas lights strung along our eaves flicked on. Anxiety unraveled and trailed away.

Kris held out his arms and we hugged, sandwiching our daughter between us. Nik arrived and squirmed into place. I wondered how many more years of this were ahead. When would Nik, then Pet, find this silly? I was grateful that they didn't tonight.

Kris stepped back. "You surprised us, so we'll surprise you."

Pet's never been good at surprises and she couldn't wait. "Maminka and Táta are here!"

Kris's mother appeared in the hallway. "Červenka is here?"

Kris and I had known each other for only a few months when he introduced me to his parents. From the beginning Ida called me by the Czech word for *robin*. Not as a reminder I wasn't Czech, but because she loved me on sight and decided I needed a Czech name before I joined her family.

The others stepped out of the way, and I went straight into her arms. "I can't believe you're here!" I hugged her hard. Ida is a little shorter than I am, and pillowy. Hugging her is like cuddling deep into a feather bed.

Her English is good, but her accent is strong. Gus, who spoke excellent English before emigrating, appeared behind her. "If the mountain won't come to Muhammad, then Muhammad must go to the mountain."

I moved forward and hugged him, too. Kris's father is tall and strong, and when Gus hugs you, deep breaths are impossible. "Tell me I'm not dreaming. You're supposed to be in Prague!"

"We'll go back after the holidays. There are planes between here and there."

Kris had come up behind me, and now I felt his arm around my shoulder. "They've come for a week. Then Lucie has invited all of us to spend Christmas Eve and day with her family."

Lucie and her husband live in Chicago, and their four children are still with them or in college nearby.

Gus answered the question I hadn't quite asked. "They canceled their trip when they learned we wouldn't all be together, so we decided we could come and surprise you here instead. There is hope you will come at Easter?"

Kris squeezed my shoulder. "It's on my calendar, Táta. Engraved in stone. Now if Robin can put it on hers?"

I looked up at my husband, and his eyes were warm. He hadn't simply assumed I could make the trip. He wanted me to know that.

When I answered I was still looking at him. "Nothing could stop me."

Ida and Pet, arms around each other's waists, could barely contain their excitement. "We have been making Christmas for you," Ida said. "We have made so much already, but there is more to make. And our Petra will show you the many cookies we plan."

Pet was so excited her cheeks were flushed. "We're making beaded snowflakes for the tree. Maminka is teaching me, but we didn't decorate it yet. We waited for you."

"Come see the train, Mom," Nik said. "Dad and I put it around the tree. It used to be his."

"A train, Kris?"

"From my childhood." Kris looked embarrassed, and pinched his thumb and index finger together in emphasis. "With just a few small additions."

Nik was already on his way into the living room. "We went into this store and bought the Polar Express, and lots more track and—"

Pet grabbed my hand. "And a little Christmas village with carolers and a snowman and Santa Claus."

"Baby Jesus brings presents, not Santa," Ida said. "And he will bring them to Chicago this year. On Christmas Eve." She stopped. "Unless you don't want to go to Lucie's, Červenka? Perhaps you are too tired and need to stay home with your family?"

Lucie prides herself on celebrating Christmas the way her ancestors did. I've seen photos, been given recipes, but we never celebrated the holiday with her family. It would be crowded, crazy, foreign to me and absolutely wonderful. I looked at Kris. "You can take those days off?"

"I have more time off than I expected to."

I filed that away. "I would love to go."

"We will bring the cookies," Ida said. "Lucie will make carp and potato salad, and I will help with the dinner."

Other Christmases flashed through my mind. Not the ones here, with Kris and my children, which have always been wonderfully memorable. But cold canned ham at my grandmother's table served with corrections of my many etiquette lapses. Christmas at one of my emergency foster homes, where the family's biological children sat with their parents in the dining room and I sat in the kitchen with the other foster child, who ate my slice of turkey. Christmas with the Davises, who always took us out for dinner at the local Chinese restaurant because we loved it so much. Christmas at the Osburns, where Betty and I spent most of the holiday roasting chickens to feed her visiting relatives, chickens that poor Cecilia had nurtured and then been forced to slaughter.

"I knew I married your son for a good reason," I told Ida. "It was a package deal. I got all the rest of you in the bargain."

"I told him that first day if he did not marry you, he was *zbláznený*!" She tapped the side of her skull in emphasis.

"A better interpretation? Infatuated." Kris smiled at me. "Still holds true."

I did my best to pronounce it. "A good word, then."

Nik grabbed my hand. "You've got to see the tree and the train."

"I absolutely do." But first I stretched on tiptoe and quickly kissed my husband. "Merry Christmas, Kris Kringle," I murmured.

So what if the mythical Kris Kringle was probably German

not Czech? My own international Santa Claus had brought me what promised to be one of the best Christmas gifts of my life. This was my home, and no matter what had happened in the past weeks, I was truly welcome.

36

—

Kris

I love my parents, and having them here is both a surprise and a joy. I should never have canceled our trip to Prague, and I hope I'll be as understanding when my own adult children do something that hurts me. No one can say I don't have wonderful role models.

That said, I'm lying on the pullout couch in my study, staring up at the ceiling, because we don't have a guest room. Just above me Robin is sleeping in Pet's room. I insisted my parents take the master suite, which is most comfortable for them. Still, I am uncomfortably aware my wife and I have been separated for too long. I miss her warm body against my own.

The house has been quiet, but now someone is banging around in the kitchen, and I wonder if Robin, like me, is having problems sleeping. I debated warning her about my parents' surprise appearance, but I knew she would be delighted to see them. From the beginning they've treated my wife like a daughter, and without parents of her own, that's been particularly special. I sometimes think if Robin and I ever got divorced, she would get Maminka and Táta in the agreement, and I would be the orphan.

I got up and made my way to the kitchen, but it wasn't Robin rummaging in the refrigerator.

"Táta?"

My father, in striped blue pajama bottoms and a white T-shirt, turned and looked at me with surprise, as if I were the intruder. "Did I wake you?"

"I was already awake. Can I get you something?"

"I couldn't sleep. Jet lag? It takes longer to adjust to any change at my age. I thought I would try warm milk."

"I bet you'd rather have *Slivovice*. If I'd known you were coming I would have scoured DC for a bottle."

"I'm not so fond of what's available in this country."

When I was a boy, the moment plums came into season in Ohio Gus made plum brandy. As a special treat I was always given a sip once the batch was properly fermented. No commercial version I've had in the years since comes close, but sadly Gus stopped making his own a decade ago.

"I have Irish whiskey to put in the milk," I offered.

"I drink little these days. I'll take it straight."

He stepped aside and I found the milk, took it out and poured two mugs, adding a dollop of honey before putting both in the microwave to warm.

"We have evicted you from your bed," Gus said. "And your wife newly arrived."

This was as close as we had ever come to discussing sex. My mother worked as a pediatric nurse in Czechoslovakia; sex was her domain, possibly because of her medical background, but more likely because Gus avoids talking about anything personal.

I stood with my back to the stove and crossed my arms. "We're happy to let you have our room."

"Červenka looks well."

I wondered where this was going. "She does look great, doesn't she?"

"Her leaving the family? Was this difficult for you?"

I measured my words. "It's taken some getting used to."

"It's good she has her own life. You certainly have yours."

"As you had yours." The microwave dinged and I opened the door and took out both mugs, setting them on the counter so my father could take his.

"I had too much of a life," Gus said, and followed the words with a sigh. "So much to say and do, so little time for either. And in the end, not that much worthwhile came from it."

I leaned against the counter. Because this was so out of character, I knew more was coming. "Aren't you getting the recognition you sought? Would they have invited you to teach at the Academy of Fine Arts if you weren't respected?"

"'For what is a man profited, if he shall gain the whole world, and lose his own soul?'"

I stared at him. "You? Quoting the New Testament?" Even though I was sent to a Catholic school, my father is a freethinker who refuses to attend church unless his presence at a baptism or First Communion is absolutely required.

"I was raised on the New Testament. Some things are not forgotten even when not all are believed."

"Táta, are you ill? Is that why you came back?"

My father has a wonderful smile that I'm just vain enough to hope I've inherited. "If I were ill, Kristoff, would I be here having fun with your family? Wouldn't I be on a ward somewhere letting doctors pump poison into my body?"

"I have no idea, but I'll ask Maminka in the morning. She's much less likely to squirm away from the truth."

"So if I talk about regrets, I must be dying?"

I didn't know what to say. He nodded. "I am as well as a man my age ever is. Little aches, little pains, the occasional upset stomach, and sadly only a little wine and *Slivovice* agree with it these days. But who knows how many years are left?"

I thought of Robin, whose own years nearly ended in October. "None of us knows that."

"I have had a good life. Difficult at times, but that is always to be expected. And for the record, recognition was never my goal. My world needed to be fixed, and I tried with the only talent I had."

"I don't think fixing the world and losing your soul are synonymous. Don't people who try to fix the world find a special place in heaven?"

He gave a snort of disbelief. "Who could believe in a God who picks and chooses? I want no part of heaven. I just want to know I did my best. And my art? It was always the best I could do. But taking care of my family? Never quite."

I was stunned. I sipped my warm milk and stared at this stranger. "We survived," I said at last. "We ate. We had a roof over our heads."

"You think I'm talking about money?" He sounded honestly curious.

"*I'm* talking about money. Not having it was a fixture of my childhood."

"It never seemed important."

"Yes, I know."

"Is that why you work so hard? To give the family things?" He gestured around the kitchen.

I dodged the question. "If we aren't talking about money, what *are* we talking about?"

"Time. Attention. I was always thinking of the next painting, the next subject. It is true of creative people, but that's not an excuse. I missed much. I should have tried harder."

I'm not creative. If the seed exists, I chose not to water or feed it. But more likely, in this way, I'm my mother's child. She worried about paying bills, and she worked tirelessly to be sure she could, even when rudimentary English forced her to do the lowliest jobs in American hospitals.

"It's not just creative people," I said. "It's easy to get obsessed with other things and forget the people around you."

"I never forgot you. I just forgot you might need more from me."

I considered that, considered it long enough that I finished my milk before I spoke.

"Táta, I had regrets, like any son, but whatever I had of you was worth more than three fathers put together. I was lucky even when you weren't paying attention."

Tears filled his eyes, something I had only rarely seen. "I am afraid I taught you poorly. Now *you* are too busy, Kristoff. I worry."

"I think I'm on a different path these days."

"You need to spend time with your wife."

I wondered if I was asleep and this entire exchange was a dream. My father had apologized for a lifetime of perpetual distraction, and now he was giving me marital advice. This in a family where feelings are never discussed.

I shook my head, as much to see if it needed to be cleared as to disagree. "Robin would be furious if you left to give us more time alone."

"No, I have given this some thought. *You* should leave. Here's what I have in mind."

He outlined his plan, and I listened, nodding. "You clearly haven't forgotten me tonight," I said at last. "I'll take your advice."

"You have been the best of sons. And you are a good man, if a distracted one."

"I had a great teacher on all counts."

He smiled, then the evening ended in an extraordinary way. He embraced me, and I know it was a moment I will remember on my deathbed.

37

—

Robin

I stared out the window as Kris pulled up to an unfamiliar curb. A light rain had just stopped, and the DC streets were glowing like freshly shined shoes. "Really?"

He smiled at me. "Really."

Kris and I rarely eat out. Before I left him in charge of the family, he spent so little time with our children that I didn't want to take him away for an evening. Tonight, though, he suggested we do some Christmas shopping and catch a quick bite in the city since his parents would cherish time alone with their grandchildren.

The downtown Ritz-Carlton is not a quick bite kind of place.

A valet was waiting to take our car, and a doorman started toward us to assist me. Kris left his keys in the ignition. "I've had business lunches here but never dinner. I've always wanted to bring you."

"Won't we need a reservation?"

"Got one."

Kris is not one for surprises. On holidays he asks me what I want, and he buys exactly that, most of the time online.

Now I was glad I'd dressed up enough to get by in what was probably an upscale dining room.

I smoothed my palms over my dark wool trousers. "I'm lucky I didn't wear jeans."

"You look wonderful in anything."

Compliments, too? "We'll still have time to shop?"

"Plenty of time to do everything we need."

I was doubtful, but since I'd shopped in Florida and mailed the gifts to a neighbor who was holding them for me, I wasn't worried. Maybe Kris needed help buying gifts for his parents or his sister's family, but otherwise I'd bought enough to keep everyone in our immediate family happy.

After the valet slid into the driver's seat, I followed Kris inside. "I'm going to find the ladies' room. Shall I meet you…"

"I'll wait in the lobby."

The lobby would be a pleasure to wait in, dark wood, crystal chandeliers and fawn-colored marble polished to a sheen. A quick survey indicated that the dining options consisted of a secluded bistro or a lobby lounge, so I wasn't underdressed after all.

Even the restrooms in a hotel like this one are lovely places to linger, but I finished up quickly, giving my hair a quick comb and straightening my sweater. I hadn't known what to expect from time alone with my husband, but the evening was shaping up nicely.

Outside Kris stretched out his hand and led me toward the elevator. Since the bistro is on the first floor, I wondered if there was an undiscovered option upstairs.

When the car arrived we stepped inside and found we were alone. He pulled me close and kissed me.

The evening was shaping up *very* nicely.

By the time we reached the sixth floor, I had a good idea what was happening. Arms around each other he led me down the corridor and pulled out a key card. In a moment we were standing in the living room of a suite with a spectacular view of Washington, a lovely city made even more glorious for Christmas.

"How hungry are you?" he asked.

"For you, or for dinner?"

"You choose. One before the other?"

"You win easily."

He drew me close and kissed me but immediately afterward backed away to see my face. "I promise I planned to start tonight by telling you how much I love you, and how sorry I am for acting like such a jerk."

"I can't wait to hear it. Later." I rose on the balls of my feet, and circled his neck with my arms. "Why don't you show me why I should forgive you?"

He swung me up and carried me to the bed.

He looked proud and only a little winded after he dropped me on the down comforter. I laughed as he sprawled beside me, panting. "I bet you're glad the bed was close."

"Tonight I would carry you across a desert."

"Good thing it's not required."

And that was the last thing we said for a long, long time.

Kris fell asleep after we made love. For a while I propped myself on one elbow and watched him breathing gently in and out. His hair was tousled, and he had one arm flung across the pillow where I had been. When it was clear he wasn't going to wake up for a little while, I found the in-room dining menu and ordered an assortment of dishes to be brought up in an hour, when I knew we would be ravenous.

I was in the soaking tub, enjoying steaming water and a view of the city, when he joined me. He winced as he eased in. Then he opened his arms so I could lie against his chest, arms around me.

"This was the most wonderful idea," I said. "But do your parents expect us back tonight?"

"My father suggested it. He knows how long you've been away and how much we need some privacy."

"Gus?" I was happy to be here with Kris but a little sorry he hadn't come up with this plan on his own. "Well, it was a good idea, no matter who thought of it."

"Hey, I thought of it first. The minute I opened the door and saw them standing on the steps, I thought of it. But I was thinking more along the lines of escaping to Hawaii for a week and not telling anybody where we'd gone."

I smiled, although he couldn't see it. "Next trip."

"After canceling Prague I couldn't find words to ask for a favor that included me disappearing. No matter how badly we needed it. But you'd better believe I leaped at his suggestion."

"I'm glad you did."

His arms tightened around me. "He also apologized for being such a distracted father."

I wondered what this meant to Kris. He loved Gus, and on some level admired his commitment to his art and the causes he held dear. But resentment simmered, too.

I turned just a little, so I could see his face. "Did that help?"

"I don't know why it should have. I'm an adult. He didn't beat me, never screamed at me and he always wanted the best for our family. But admitting he was distracted?" He looked rueful, as if his logical brain wasn't quite sure how to process this. "It makes a difference. Just to know he realizes he wasn't always there for us when he needed to be. Whatever resentments I held on to are draining away. I can look at him, one flawed adult at another..."

"And love him for the man he is."

He looked grateful I understood. "And he's quite a man, my father."

"He certainly is."

He tilted my face to his and kissed me. "And speaking of flawed adults? If my father can apologize for being distracted, how much more do I need to apologize for acting like a kid when you decided to go back to work, Robin? Can you ever forgive me?"

I asked a dangerous question, because without an answer, the apology wasn't complete. "What was behind it? Do you know?"

This was the kind of question Kris hates, the kind that requires him to think beyond facts and examine his heart. To his credit, he didn't look away.

"You already know part of it. I was stressed. I felt like you were manipulating me. I felt like you didn't appreciate how hard I work to give you and the kids security."

"I do know that."

"But it went deeper, something I've had time to face. I almost lost you for good, and then you just picked up and left and I *did* lose you. I wanted you safe where I could make sure you were okay every night. For a long time I couldn't even think about what almost happened, about Talya and the accident and how awful all of it was." He looked away, as if that was required to go on. "I had nightmares for weeks. I saw that car heading toward you, and I couldn't get to you...."

I didn't know what to say, and in fact, there was nothing that *could* be said. I couldn't change what had nearly happened. The accident would always be with us.

He finished. "I think I was so afraid of losing you that when you left... I pushed you further away. Maybe I thought if I was in control of losing you, it wouldn't hurt so much? It doesn't make sense, but it's as close as I can come."

"Close enough." I stroked his cheek until he met my eyes. "Closer than either of us usually goes. We've lived together all these years, shared our home and children, and there's still so much we can't say."

He covered my hand and held it in place. "Just give me more time to work on that?"

I thought about all the ways we can't speak, all the ways we can't say what we should. As a child I found the most obvious way when I fell mute, but now it was time to work on the others. "I have so much to tell you. And I know you have so much to tell me. We could talk all night and not get to all of it."

"We can try."

"I ordered dinner."

"Right away?"

"No."

"You're just full of good decisions. Making sure I'm closer to my children again. Giving me time to process all this without pushing me. And best of all?"

I was still processing *that*. He'd said so much in such a hurry. "And?"

Laughter rumbled deep in his chest. "Giving us more time in this tub before room service arrives."

I ran my fingers over his chest. "I just had a feeling if I hurried dinner, the food might get cold."

38

—

Robin

I am an inveterate maker of lists. Since I learned to print I've probably made thousands. I sometimes think this obsession is a piece of my grandmother lodged inside me, but more likely as a child I was so afraid I might forget one of her demands, I had to write them down. Keeping such a long list in my head would have been impossible.

Maybe lists keep criticism and chaos at bay, but lists can also be a source of pleasure. An example.

Ways life in Meadow Branch has changed:
1. My husband makes a wicked spaghetti sauce.
2. He also makes enough to freeze leftovers.
3. My children eat my husband's cooking.
4. Everybody puts dinner on the table.
5. Everybody cleans up after meals are eaten.
6. Everybody does laundry.

I could go on. After Christmas in Chicago I had almost a week at home with my family. Kris only went into the office twice, for a few hours each time. If he had to work at home, he waited until the children went to bed or worked before they got up. Mostly he just didn't work.

In one of our conversations I learned about Pedersen Pharmacies and Kris's decision to absent himself from that case. I also learned about the fallout. Some matters Kris hoped to be involved in are now in the hands of other partners, and his Christmas bonus was smaller than anticipated. My husband is no longer the fair-haired boy, and he seems curiously unconcerned. He promises this is temporary, but from what I can tell, he decided to take full advantage of the career lull and simply enjoy the holiday.

And we did enjoy it. Leaving this morning is difficult. I said goodbye to my children when they left for school, but now it was time to say goodbye to my husband.

As we neared the airport I told Kris to drop me off at the departure gates. I was flying back to Tampa, where I would meet the crew and stay two nights before heading to Cold Creek and the Osburn ranch. Instead he took a detour and parked, then grabbed my suitcase and hefted my camera bag over one shoulder. "I have a new appreciation for what you do," he said, pretending to list to one side once the bag was in place.

"When I come home I'm going to start working out."

"You'll need to if you keep doing this."

In our time together I had told him about the past weeks, but I hadn't brought up my professional future, at least not directly. Now I did. While I was away he would have time to consider my words, and so would I.

"Once filming is finished I don't know how much traveling I'll be doing. Selecting the best photos and working with the writer who'll do the copy for a book is going to take time. Assuming we finalize a contract."

"Do you think you'll freelance after that?"

Kris knows, from my stories, that being back in the field with my camera has had ups and downs, but I think it's also been clear how much it's meant to me.

"Mick's put me to work a few times with some of his video equipment when he needed another camera operator. He liked what I did. Making films may be in my future, Kris."

"With him?"

"Probably closer to home. His next project is in Southeast Asia. But he has friends he'll recommend me to if I'm still interested. I'll have to start from the bottom, do some classes and workshops to catch up with technology. I won't make a lot of money, even once I know what I'm doing, but I think I would like to branch out. The more skills I have, the choosier I can be."

He didn't say anything else until I was at the kiosk to finalize my flight to Tampa. But from what he said next I knew he'd been thinking. "Whatever you decide, we can work out logistics. The kids are getting older. Plenty of help's available."

"And my husband's turning into a pretty good cook."

He put his hand over mine as I withdrew my gate pass. "I may be making changes, too."

"Singer's not bringing down the ax, are they?" This had happened to others of his colleagues. Kris had defied Buff, who didn't take rebellion lightly.

"The jury's still out, but I don't think they will. In the meantime I've been offered a chance to become an adjunct professor at GW Law, and I could be in line for a permanent slot just down the road. If that happens I can probably stay on at Singer, too, although probably not as a partner. But even with that, I won't be earning nearly as much as I am now. Professors aren't among the highest paid professionals."

I thought it was just like Kris to be so offhanded, and only to mention something this important as I was leaving. His nonchalance was a clear sign he had strong feelings and was having his usual problem expressing them. But he *was* trying.

"Do you want to teach?"

"I love teaching. I've just never given enough thought to what I love."

"Then you should do it."

He looked so relieved, my heart brimmed with love. He leaned over and kissed me, and we held each other for a moment.

When he backed away, he wasn't smiling. "Look, I don't think this next leg's going to be easy for you."

I didn't want to assure him everything was going to be fine. Burying feelings had brought us to the brink of a real separation. I was determined not to let that happen again.

Following Cecilia's journey through foster care wouldn't be complete without a look at her final foster home, *my* final foster home, too. From the beginning I had wondered if "complete" was really important enough to expose us both to memories of what had been a disastrous placement from start to finish. I planned to keep my voice light, but that's not how it emerged.

"I have never yearned to see the Osburn ranch again."

"While we were in Chicago I talked to Lucie. She's practically an empty nester these days, so she's available to come and stay with the kids so I can join you at some point. They would love it, and so would she."

"You would come to Florida?"

He touched my hair, stroking it back from my cheek. "I'm going to wait until you decide you need me most. Will you let me know? She's on call."

"And work?"

"I'm sure I have a few days of vacation coming."

Kris probably has years coming, but nobody at the firm

expects him to take them. Knowing that taking time off now won't help salvage his career, a good wife would pretend she was fine.

But I am no longer a good wife.

"I may take you up on that."

"You *will* take me up on it. Okay?"

I blinked back tears. "I've never wanted to mix our lives with my past."

"Your past made you the woman you are. And since that's the woman I love? I'm going to miss you, Červenka."

I smiled through tears at the nickname.

He stepped away. "The more warning you give me, the easier it will be to get Lucie here and book a flight to Tampa. Okay?"

"Call me every day?"

"Without fail."

"I'll let you know when to come."

He left me at security and I waved goodbye. Last time I had been in this airport my marriage was teetering. This time Kris and I were on our way to finding a balance we could live with.

I was just removing my shoes to be ready for the conveyor belt ahead when my phone buzzed. I wondered if Kris had forgotten something. But the message wasn't from him. It was from Donny.

Cecilia has disappeared. No foul play. Do you know where she might have gone?

39

—

Robin

Cold Creek, Florida. Population 3,129. The number on the welcome sign surprised me when I drove into town. Why would anybody live here? Cold Creek is a blip on the map, a quick stop for travelers on their way somewhere more inviting, a place to fill their gas tanks or slurp a Strawberry Cheesecake Blizzard at the Dairy Queen. During the two years I lived with the Osburns, the Cold Creek Dairy Queen had a reputation as the best for fifty miles. Since during those years I never traveled far from the ranch, I can't speak from experience.

Probably half of those 3,129 souls are spread through the countryside, and the others live in the town that meanders a few blocks in all directions from the spot where I'm parked. The ubiquitous Dollar Store anchors one block, along with what looks like a descendant of the Blue Heron Café where Jud Osburn ate lunch and flirted with the servers whenever he came into town. A Southern Baptist and a Methodist church bookend the next, and a bar with a neon bronco bucking in the window sits between a vacant lot and a movie theater.

The week before it closed the theater probably showed Hopalong Cassidy flicks and newsreels. Since it was vacant and moldering when I lived here, it's hard to believe the building still stands. But right now I'm parked in front of it, watching the street. Nothing and no one is moving, and I wonder if the Christmas lights, still strung between telephone and electric poles, will be seen by a single soul other than me if they snap on tonight.

I know Cecilia isn't going to materialize on the sidewalk with a soft-serve cone in one hand and a pack of two-for-one trouser socks in the other, but I'm taking a few minutes to gather courage for the next leg of my journey.

Cold Creek is Florida cattle-ranching country. Arcadia, about thirty miles west of here, holds a championship rodeo in March. Okeechobee, about thirty miles east on the northern rim of Lake Okeechobee, has an annual cattle drive through the center of town. I know these things because my smartphone tells me so. If rodeos and cattle drives were held when Cecilia and I lived with the Osburns, they attended without us. Who knows what that much fun might have done to us?

Who knows what this trip back in time will do?

My sister has disappeared. She isn't answering her cell phone and clearly doesn't want to be found. Donny is worried she's come to Cold Creek ahead of schedule, perhaps to ease herself into this final segment of filming. He's flying out as soon as he can get on a plane, but nobody in the world is better equipped to find her than I am. We've known all along that the Osburn ranch would be the most difficult of difficult venues for both of us.

I wonder if Cecilia *is* testing her own reactions or if she's simply decided to cancel this portion and gone somewhere else to recover. If so she'll let us know soon. Most likely I'll celebrate, because that means I can leave, too. Surely Mick has filmed enough of Cecilia's personal history to illustrate whatever he ultimately decides to say about foster care.

For this leg of the journey I rented a small SUV, since Donny reported that the roads at the ranch are in bad condition. Before deciding to shoot here Mick consulted a location scout to determine we would be safe. For the past ten years the property has been unoccupied, but apparently at some time work was done to shore up the house and barn. Four years ago an investment company bought the acreage after minerals from new wells caused so many problems, the citrus conglomerate that had tried to bring the land back to life moved to another site. Getting permission to film had required few negotiations.

Back in the day when rain fell regularly, Jud and Betty tended their own small grove. Fresh squeezed orange juice still brings back memories of breakfast at the Osburn table. Three-hundred acres was a small spread compared to others in the county, but the Osburns tried a little of everything. Citrus, Mulefoot hogs, truck farming and their lifeblood, Cracker cattle, a unique strain, like the Mulefoot, that Jud bred to sell. We foster children were a cash crop, too, like the other animals they raised—only we slept in the house. There were so many nights when Betty and Jud were screaming at each other that I wished I could sleep in the barn, too.

With nothing else to see in town I started the car and pulled out to the street to head for the ranch. The same location scout had determined there were no acceptable hotel accommodations here, and the drive to anywhere larger was too long to be sensible. Mick had rented campers to be delivered and set up tomorrow at a private campground a short distance from the ranch. We would have the place to ourselves.

In the meantime the rest of the crew is gathering at the house on the lake in Tampa for meetings. Cecilia and Donny were supposed to arrive tomorrow evening. Now I've asked

Donny to stay there until he hears more. For all I know, he's part of Cecilia's problem.

The scenery, if not the route, was familiar. I passed green fields fenced for cattle with moss-draped oaks for shade, and occasional stands of cypress, scrubby pine, palm and palmetto. As I turned off the main road and began to wind my way through the countryside I glimpsed a pond and a prefab home with a plowed garden stretching far in front of it. As a young teen, I never drove these roads, so I let my smartphone guide me.

Although it wasn't yet dark, a thin, eerie mist was already glazing the landscape. In my past, on the hottest of mornings, Cold Creek, which meanders along the edge of the Osburns' property, breathed tendrils of dancing vapor into the warmer air. The creek is fed by a spring miles away, and the Osburns used it for irrigation, although even then the creek grew shallower each month. In the years since, because of persistent drought and increased tapping of the aquifer, the output has diminished to almost nothing. The scout had informed Mick there would be no pictures of Cold Creek to establish setting. At the moment the creek is dry as dust.

Fifteen minutes from town I stopped at the entrance to what had once been the Osburn ranch. No gate marked the gap in a three-rail fence that was tumbling to the ground. When I lived here tall posts flanked the entry, but now only a cattle guard announced that livestock had once grazed their way across these fields. I could see the house in the distance, and even from the road I could tell by the sagging roof that it was on the way to oblivion. Never well tended during our years in residence, neglect was hastening its end.

I drove across the guard and down the long, rutted trail to the house. The Osburns' citrus grove on the right had been leveled. The barn, still standing, was in the distance on my left. Other outbuildings were now heaps of wood and stone.

I half expected to see Cecilia's car, but mine was alone. It would be like my sister to park behind trees or a tumble-down outbuilding to hide her presence. She'd made every attempt to keep her whereabouts a secret, so why stop now? I only hoped that wherever she was, she was alone and un-recognized.

I parked and got out. I didn't expect a response, but I shouted, "Cecilia!" Then I repeated it again, and once more out of frustration.

In the patch of woods beyond the house a Chuck-will's-widow answered, the call so much like Virginia's whip-poor-wills. Betty, who didn't have another ounce of sentiment in her body, loved birds. She never made a point of teaching me anything except what I had to know to work in the garden or kitchen, but she spoke so seldom that when she mentioned the name of anything, I remembered it.

The sun was sinking, and in an hour it would be com-pletely dark. This land was so filled with ghosts, I wasn't going to linger, not even for Cecilia, but I took a deep breath and walked up to the porch, then navigated sagging steps, cell phone in hand in case I needed to summon help. The front door, which had always stood open to capture a breeze, sagged on one hinge, and the screen door was nearly rusted through. I reached into a gaping hole and pushed the door. To my surprise it swung open with a loud creak.

A noise, a blur, and suddenly something streaked past me. I screeched, but by the time I opened my mouth the animal, most likely a raccoon or a possum, had zipped beyond, dis-appeared down the steps and, probably hidden itself under the house.

When my heart was beating normally again I shouted "Cecilia" into the hallway. I didn't expect a reply. If my sister was inside, the animal I'd just encountered would have left with her arrival, and the door would have been standing open.

I retraced my steps to the car, but I leaned against the passenger door and scanned the slowly dimming landscape. I tried to think where, if she had been here, she might have gone. Buzzards circled behind the house where a pond had once watered livestock, and while I was sure their presence was unrelated to my search, I got into the car and drove the overgrown, corrugated road toward the barn, stopping halfway in between to get out and peer into the distance. The buzzards had already dispersed, most likely on their way to something more promising, and my unanswered shouts were a lonely echo.

I drove past the spot once occupied by Betty's flourishing vegetable garden and glimpsed the remnants of a new citrus grove, row after row choked by weeds, with only a few trees clinging to life. The grove was smaller than the garden had been. The rows didn't even extend to the garden's edge, where compost bins had rested against deer fencing and chicken wire. I'd spent so many hours of my early teens at this spot, tending and picking tomatoes, hoeing and weeding, sprinkling fertilizer and spraying insecticide. In the years since I've been a staunch advocate for better conditions for farm workers.

I parked fifty yards from the barn. Up ahead a fallen tree blocked a piece of the road, but now that it was dusk I couldn't tell how badly. I climbed out again, but I didn't move closer right away. The house was in sad disrepair, most likely beyond hope of renovation, even if anyone cared enough to try. The barn looked as if it were one puff of wind from collapse.

At one time this barn had been the center of ranch life, home for the horses Jud used for hauling logs and moving cattle from one pasture to another. The chickens were housed here, too, with a fenced coop opening to the outside. The expansive pigpen was attached to the other side of the barn, with separate sections for the boar and for the sows with piglets, as well as an indoor area for shelter and segregating the hogs when the pen was cleaned.

Cecilia was in charge of feeding and cleaning up after the horses and hogs. Jud delighted in making her do the dirtiest chores, and the little Betty said in protest never affected him. Usually, in fact, he suggested that if Betty thought the work was too much for Cecilia, maybe I should take over.

I was terrified of his boar, and of course he knew it. Jud was proud of his black Mulefoots, a unique heritage breed suited to the area. At their peak the hogs might reach weights of more than 600 pounds, and Jud's prize boar had been at least that. The boar was mean tempered and aggressive, but then so was Jud's bull, a speckled black-and-white monster with twisting horns. Armed with a cattle prod, Jud liked to pit himself against both, just to prove he was in charge.

Cecilia used to pray out loud that the bull would gore Jud when nobody else was around to rescue him. I was less vocal. I prayed silently.

Many farmers care about their animals, even if they are raising them to slaughter. They provide the best conditions, sometimes even affection, and do what they can to give them good lives. Jud was not one of them. He enjoyed suffering. He employed the most minimal standards in everything he did, and he had no empathy for any living thing he controlled. No priest will ever convince me that hell exists, but if I'm wrong, I will know where to look for Jud in the afterlife.

I pushed away from the car and hiked to the tree, which was not the roadblock I'd feared. I couldn't believe Cecilia had driven around it, yet she had spent so much of her time with the Osburns in this very place that the possibility existed. I shouted her name and listened, but as before there was no answer. Giving the barn a wide berth I circled it on foot, but no car was parked behind it, and through a gaping hole on one side I could see into the surprisingly solid interior. I was alone here.

For the next half hour, as the sun sank closer to the horizon, I drove what I could of the farm roads, through and around fields overgrown with scrub, more ill-considered groves, along the bank of what had once been a flowing creek. Tire tracks are quickly erased on a sandy roadbed, but I saw no signs any vehicles had been here recently. I ended up on the driveway back to the main road, convinced Cecilia wasn't here and probably hadn't been.

As I was about to start back to Tampa I remembered the only other place where she might have gone, the place she most liked to escape to.

The place that had nurtured and fed her love of music.

At the road I turned west and hoped I would find what I was looking for. Both the place and the sister.

40

—

Cecilia

Robin and I aren't the only foster children who crossed the cattle guard at the Osburn ranch. Before us Jud and Betty raised four teenage boys. One had "emotional problems," and to keep him, the Osburns were required to take special training, which also increased their stipend. I can only conclude this area of Florida was so lacking in foster-parent candidates that the state was pathetically grateful to anyone who applied.

Jud once told me that the boys liked the ranch because nobody watched them too closely, and he made sure they got a six-pack on Saturdays if they did a good week's work. Sometimes I wonder what happened to those young men after they turned eighteen and were booted out of care. Maybe Mick will make it his business to find out, but with Jud as their role model, I don't think he'll find them teaching school or preaching the word of God.

God comes to mind because I'm sitting on the steps of what's left of the Cold Creek Mission Church of Christ, down the road from the ranch. I used to come here on Sunday evenings to listen to the choir. At first I stayed outside in the woods, not sure I would be welcome. The congregation was African American, and this area was not noted for integrated worship. After several months I was discovered by an old woman who was late for the service. She spotted me hovering, and when she confronted me I told her the truth. She marched me inside, where I remained.

Attending choir practice was out of the question because on a weeknight I would have needed to explain my absence to the Osburns, who were racist to the core, but when the director heard me singing hymns from the back row she taught me some anthems so I could join in. No lessons I have taken in all my years since have shaped my voice and love of music more than those.

Years have passed since this patch of scrub and sand rang with music, but I can remedy that. "He Will Remember Me" is still one of my favorites.

"When on the cross of Calvary…"

I got almost all the way through to the end without choking up, but I knew I wasn't going to finish. I rested my head in my hands.

A minute later I heard a familiar voice.

"Nobody sings that song better than you."

I straightened and watched Robin, in jeans and a blue windbreaker, pick her way down the scrub-choked path. I hadn't heard a car, and I didn't see one now. She probably parked beside my rental, hidden in the woods along the road. Sunset was just beginning to tint the sky. In fifteen minutes or less we would be in total darkness.

She joined me on the step, gingerly lowering herself until she was settled. I held my breath in case her weight sent what was left of the rotting boards crashing to the ground, but they held.

This is the time of day photographers call the magic hour. The light is perfect, and Robin usually has a camera in hand, no matter where she is or what's going on around her. Now, though, her hands were empty. There would be no visual record of whatever we said.

She spoke when I didn't. "I wonder what happened here. Where did this congregation go? Did they move? Or lose so many members they just closed the doors one day and walked away?"

"They have a tidy little concrete block building closer to town. Fifty-six members, last time I checked."

She thought that over. "I wonder how they got that tidy little building."

"Hard work and prayer."

"And an anonymous donor?"

"Not me." I didn't give the congregation money for a new church. When this building reached the point of no return they didn't need a white girl's charity to keep their spirit and faith alive. Of course, in the interest of local education and the preservation of their musical tradition, ten years ago I did set up an annual scholarship. Each June one senior who sings regularly with the Mission Church choir is awarded a four-year scholarship to any Florida university. It's nothing compared to what they did for me.

"I remember coming here with you sometimes," Robin said. "Sundays. Our day of rest."

"I used to tell Betty and Jud wild tales about where I was going on Sunday nights. As long as I didn't ask them to take me, they didn't care."

"By Sunday evening Jud wouldn't have noticed you leaving anyway."

Jud had rewarded *himself* with end-of-the-week six-packs, too. He'd always indulged somewhere away from the ranch, with somebody other than Betty. That was the only reason I was able to leave Robin behind on the Sunday evenings she didn't want to come here with me.

Since Robin wasn't bringing up the obvious, I did. "Did Donny call you?"

"He's worried."

I tried not to imagine that. "I left him a note."

"Right. Something like 'I need time to think.'"

"I was more gracious than that."

"Oh, right. '*Sorry*. I need time to think.'"

I couldn't argue. Those were my exact words.

"I got his message as I was going through security. When I called he was halfway to frantic. How did you get here?"

"A friend of Sage's with a single-engine plane. He was delighted to make the trip. And Donny should know I would never leave everybody in the lurch without a word."

"You took *off* without a word. And forget the note, okay? It didn't do much for him."

"I'm tired of having to account to somebody every minute of my life. I needed time to think. I deserve that, right?"

"Tell me that having somebody to account to is worse than not having anybody who cares. Ever. Want to be in that place again?"

"I always had you."

She rested her hand on my shoulder for a moment. "Well, here I am again."

I felt my resistance unwinding. "I know I should have warned him, but this was an impulse. I wanted some time to think about what's coming. Is that hard to understand? Don't you need that, too?"

"Sure, coming back here was on my mind over the holidays." She paused. "How did yours turn out, by the way?"

"Nice job of sliding into that."

"Did you see Hayley?"

I glanced at her. "Why?"

"Because I'm your sister and I haven't talked to you since Christmas Eve, when you were pretty evasive."

I didn't want to talk about the holidays, but while most people think I'm the relentless one, Robin comes in a close second. "She spent the day after Christmas with me at my condo. Roscoe, me…and Donny."

"Donny spent Christmas with you?"

"He spent it with his family. He flew in on the twenty-sixth."

"He invited you to go wherever his family lives, and you said no. Am I wrong?"

I didn't answer.

"A little too close for comfort, huh?"

"Things are moving too fast."

"Says the woman who met Sage Callahan and married him a few months later."

"And look how well that turned out."

"CeCe, you didn't *expect* that to turn out. Donny's a different story."

"You should take up marriage counseling. Just as soon as you get your own in shape."

"It kind of is."

I glanced at her. "Really?"

"Kris made some big changes. He apologized for the way he behaved. He even offered to join me here when I need him most."

"Was it a prelude to sex?"

She poked me with her elbow, and the step squeaked beneath us. "Postcoital pillow talk, if you must know. The apology was genuine."

"I'm glad."

"Are you?"

This time I shifted so I could continue to see her face. "What's that supposed to mean?"

"Well, isn't it easier when we're both having problems with the men in our lives?"

"Donny is not the man in my life."

"But he would be if you'd let him."

"No, it's not easier. I'm not that selfish." At least I hoped I wasn't.

"So how did it feel? Hayley, Donny and you. Exchange gifts? Sing Christmas carols? Roast the Christmas goose?"

"Tell me about yours."

"Tell me about yours *first*," she corrected. "I told you a bit on the phone. Kris's parents surprised us. Ida gave me gorgeous vintage cookie molds that have been passed down through her family so Pet and I can make authentic bear paws every holiday. Christmas in Chicago was wonderful, although carp for Christmas dinner isn't a custom I intend to follow. Kris took a lot of time off afterward." She smiled a little. "The highlights. Now it's your turn."

"Hayley gave me three Christmas ornaments she made in art class at school. All these little beads and tiny narrow ribbons. She's very creative. She and Pet would get along."

"What did you give her?"

"I had to be careful. But most of the other girls in her house went home to their families, so it only seemed fair she got something nice."

"And?"

"Purple UGG boots. Shiny bows in the back. She looked at me like I was nuts, and then she wouldn't take them off. I think she's probably sleeping in them at night."

"Perfect."

"She was a brat, but not as bad as I expected. She's reading Anne Frank's diary. Remember when you read it?"

"You warned me about the ending. Did you warn her?"

"She read the ending first. Hayley's not a fan of surprises. None of the ones in her life have been good ones." I didn't like the way that day had ended. "I hated to take her back to CFF, but I don't want her to get the wrong idea."

"Or the right one?"

I ignored that. "She and Donny got along. He's good with her. He doesn't react at the most outrageous things she says, but he gives her all kinds of attention when she's being appropriate."

"Does he give you attention when you're being appropriate?"

"So few chances."

"He stayed with you?"

"I have plenty of room." I shifted just enough that we were almost eye to eye. "We aren't sleeping together. Is that what you want to know?"

"Of course I want to, but it's none of my business."

"My reputation is a lot more exciting than I am. He's going to be disappointed, and the minute he is, our working relationship will be over."

"What part of that do I address first?"

"No part. Please."

She frowned. Then she shrugged.

"It was all so normal, Robin. You know? Like people all over the world. The three of us laughing, getting dinner together, opening gifts. Donny found 78s of all the old songs I want to record and some other good possibilities besides. I don't know how he did it, but now I have a stack to listen to and one of the original Gramophones to play them."

"It's normal to be with people you care about."

"I don't care about that many."

"You tell yourself that."

"I care about you." I realized this was the right time to set the record straight. "I care enough that I have to tell you something. Something about the years we lived here. That's one of the things I needed to come here to think about."

Robin went very still, as if she was steeling herself for a blow. She was just fourteen when we left this place, but I know she remembers a lot.

"Did you ever wonder how we ended up at the Osburn ranch?"

"The Davises told the agency we were close and should be kept together. That's what I remember."

"It's true as far as it goes." I stared into the woods again. "But most of the time the foster care system doesn't even keep *biological* siblings together. A lot of the time brothers and sisters are separated. Sometimes they don't see each other again until they're adults, although I think that's changing. They try harder now."

"They certainly need to."

"But even now they don't place unrelated girls as far apart in age as we are in the same home. The only reason we were together in the first place was because we both needed a therapeutic home and the rules were different."

She absorbed that. "What I *do* remember about those days is that a lot of things were unusual. Good foster homes were hard to find. Rules were stretched and broken."

"Yeah, they were." The light wasn't going to last much longer, and we had to walk back to our cars. I was sorry I had started this part of the conversation, but there was no way she would let me stop now.

"Do you remember Nathan Johnson? He was Mr. Johnson to us."

"One of our caseworkers?"

"Right. He was the one who placed us with the Osburns."

She raised a hand high over her head in illustration. "The tall one, right? Skinny and tall. When he wasn't around you called him Ichabod."

"Yeah, that's the one."

"What about him?"

"One night when we were still living with the Davises, I heard them talking. I got up to go the bathroom or get a drink. I don't remember, but they were talking in low voices. Low voices mean secrets. By then I knew secrets were useful."

"Ammunition?"

"If needed, and *only* if needed. You would be amazed at the secrets I've kept about friends in the music biz. Things the world would love to know and doesn't deserve to."

She knew I was delaying the inevitable. "The light's fading. What did you hear that night?"

"That Mr. Johnson had been accused of molesting one of the girls on his caseload. The girl herself accused him. He was suspended while the state investigated, but there was no proof, just the girl's word, and nobody thought she was trustworthy. Some of what she said didn't add up. Nobody else on his caseload came forward. So he was reinstated. But the Davises found out. That night they were discussing how to be certain he was never alone with either of us. They thought he wasn't guilty, but they wanted to protect us, just in case."

"They loved us."

"They sent us away." I held up my hand. "I know. They had no choice. But that's still what I remember."

"It hurt. I remember, too."

I shuffled through everything I had to say next. "I filed away what I heard that night, just in case. And six months later, when the Davises told us they couldn't be our parents anymore, I dusted it off. The thing is they also told me they were going to make sure our status was changed. We were both doing so well we didn't need to be in a therapeutic home anymore, and they'd already told Johnson and asked him to make that happen. Only, I knew changing our status meant we wouldn't stay together. Because of our age difference. And the chance we would have been together whatever our status was?" I shook my head. "It wasn't anybody's priority."

"I'm not putting these pieces together."

"I wasn't going to let them separate us. We were sisters, even if nobody saw it that way except us."

"But how…?" Her voice trailed off. I thought maybe the pieces were beginning to merge.

"When Mr. Johnson came to tell me we would be moving soon, but we wouldn't be living together, I was ready. I told him if he tried to separate us, I would tell the Davises he had molested me. And with one complaint just behind him, this time he would lose his job and any chance of another. I'd invented a very realistic scenario, and I told him all the details."

"You didn't." She hesitated, but not for long. "You did, didn't you?"

"Please believe me—I'm not proud of it. But I was desperate. Even then I knew I might be ruining a man's life. I just couldn't let him ruin ours."

"What did he say?"

"He told me he wouldn't let me blackmail him, but since it was clear I felt that strongly about staying with you, he was going to see if somehow he could make it happen. Of course the blackmail was what did it, and I wasn't fooled. He didn't care how strongly I felt, but he did care about his reputation. And not going to jail."

Robin got to her feet and began to pace. "It was that important to you?"

"How important was it to you? Can you remember?"

She stopped in front of me. "I don't like thinking about that time."

"That makes sense."

"I didn't know any of this. I can't guess how I would have felt."

"Sure you can."

She looked defeated. "If they had separated us, I probably would have run away to find you."

"Me, too."

"So somehow he managed to find us a place."

"The only place he *could* find. The Osburn ranch, where the foster parents had taken the necessary classes and had a temporarily empty house. Johnson made sure our status stayed the same, so we could be placed together. Then he convinced Betty Osburn that two girls would be an asset, that she could teach us the life skills we needed, and we could help with her chores."

"And that's how we ended up there? You blackmailed our caseworker and he manipulated the system?"

"I prefer to think I made him see reason."

"Whatever you want to call it, *you* were the reason we ended up at that ranch."

I watched her pace again, and after a minute I stood and blocked her path. "If it's any comfort, I've spent so many hours wondering what might have happened if I'd just let things play out. Would we have ended up in good homes, maybe even been allowed to visit each other? Would we have grown up to be different women? Maybe I would have gone on to college, and maybe you would have blossomed with parents who saw your talents and made sure you developed them. Parents like the Davises, not the Osburns."

"That's a waste of time."

"Is it?"

"There's no way to know what would have happened."

"Sometimes I think the best, but maybe things would have been worse. Much worse. Maybe we never would have seen each other again. Maybe you would have ended up somewhere awful with nobody to protect you."

"The way you protected me."

"At least I was with you to try."

"And what did you get, CeCe? Was staying together worth those two years at the ranch? With Betty and Jud screaming at each other every night, and Jud getting drunk whenever he could. With all the work we both had to do and the loss of any kind of normal life? You suffered the worst of it."

For a moment I just stared at her. Then I recovered. "We both suffered. What do you mean?"

"Jud was meaner to you. Betty protected me when she could. She kept me busy so he wouldn't make me do his dirty work. She kept me away from him when he was in one of his moods. But nobody protected you. And I was only fourteen when I moved to the group home. Maybe that wasn't heaven, but at least I had a semblance of an adolescence until I graduated. There was nothing normal about those last few years of high school for you. Not once we got to the ranch."

"Maybe all the hard times are why I'm successful. Maybe *that's* what I got."

"Maybe, but that's not the only thing. Because the big thing you got from all the lies? You got to keep the one person who would love you forever, and you made sure that she was going to be all right. No matter what else you did or who you hurt."

"How can you forgive me? Considering…everything."

"Would you do it again? Especially not knowing what waited for either of us if you didn't?"

"Knowing as much as I do? I would run away and drag you along with me."

"And who knows what would have happened then? Children have so few choices. You and I had fewer than most, but you didn't let that stop you. You stared down the system and got what you wanted." She put her arm around me. "Me."

"*Can* you forgive me?"

"My mother was sixteen when she abandoned me. *You* were sixteen when you *refused* to abandon me. How can you imagine I wouldn't forgive you? Even if we had to live with the Osburns."

"I'm not going to cry."

She gave me a hard hug. "Are you coming back to Tampa? We can leave your car in town or at the ranch, and I'll drive. You'll have the whole trip to figure out what to tell Mick about filming here. If you tell him to forget it, I don't think anybody will be surprised. You've already been through the wringer."

I wondered if there had been enough revelations. The film would be outstanding no matter what I did next. The way people viewed and thought about the child welfare system would change because of all Mick would bring to the finished product. I really had done my part.

How much of the truth would set me free? All? Or if I continued keeping secrets to the bitter end, would I never be free again?

I had to say something. "I don't know how much I'll admit about Nathan Johnson, so please don't repeat what I told you. He wasn't much of a caseworker, but he's probably still alive, and he doesn't deserve to have that episode in his life rehashed on film. I'll give it some thought."

"We have to go. If it gets one bit darker we won't find our cars."

"I guess I'll leave mine in town. It will be easier for the rental agency to locate."

We started toward the woods, but Robin wasn't finished with our conversation. "Call Donny before you get behind the wheel. I can meet you in town. In front of the theater?"

"He's not going to understand."

"Then it's your job to make him."

"I don't think there are enough words in the English language."

"CeCe, sometimes it's not about words."

We started back toward the road, but I turned for one last look. The light was dying, and the old church was barely visible. I bowed my head in tribute, but no words came. I hope Robin is right. Maybe sometimes words are unnecessary. Maybe sometimes it's just about whatever is in your heart.

Or whatever should be.

41

—

Cecilia

Before my flight I left Roscoe with my Nashville house-keeper, Lenore, who loves him nearly as much as I do. A dog makes no sense for someone who is rarely sure where she's going to be, and Lenore would take Roscoe for good if I asked her. Considering how much I miss him already, I don't think that's going to happen.

A dog is an encumbrance. So is a girl sliding into adolescence, toting a lifetime of rejection behind her. So is a man. Until now Robin has been my only encumbrance. That's been hard enough.

When I called from Cold Creek, Donny didn't answer his phone. He was probably on a plane, so I left him a message and didn't hear back on our drive to Tampa. But something tells me that the encumbrance banging on the door of my suite isn't Robin or anybody else on the film crew.

"You're going to wake up the whole house." I ushered Donny inside. I had known better than to change for bed. I didn't want to look soft and cuddly when I faced him. In reality I'm hard as nails, perfectly capable of making my own arrangements when required and doing what's best for myself. Hopefully Donny will catch on.

He looked exhausted, hair and shirt rumpled and cheeks in need of a shave. I was exhausted, too. We probably weren't going to compliment each other, so I launched in to get this over with.

"You got my message. I'm sorry I frightened you, but I really am capable of figuring out what I need and what I have to do to get it."

"How long ago did a stalker with a loaded gun find his way through the security fence at CFF?"

"If I'd told you what I wanted to do, you would have insisted on making all the arrangements and coming along. Want a drink?" I pointed to the liquor cabinet.

"I don't want a drink. I want an explanation."

"Really? And you think I'm required to give you one? I got here safely. I gave myself some much-needed time alone. Until you sicced Robin on me, that is."

"Sicced her?"

"You sent her to look for me."

"For the record, I didn't send her. She volunteered when she learned you were missing."

"I was *not* missing! I knew where I was."

He cocked his head as if examining a crazy person. "You always know where you are. That's part of inhabiting your body. You take it with you everywhere. Even *you* can't leave it behind."

"You know what I mean, Donny. I didn't just wander off. I made plans. I executed them perfectly. I did what I thought I needed to."

"You can't see this might worry me?"

I was trying to hold on to the conviction I'd done nothing wrong. I crossed the room and flopped on the sofa. I didn't invite him to join me, but that didn't stop him.

The sofa is L-shaped. He sat kitty-corner so he could see

me, but he stayed several arm's lengths away, as if to keep from shaking me. "Lenore told me you left Roscoe and were heading to Florida. So I knew you hadn't been kidnapped. But that's all I knew."

"I left you a note. She gave it to you."

"Just for the record, you're speaking to two different people here. Your personal manager who always needs to know where you are and if you're safe. And the man who loves you. That one always needs to know where you are and if you're happy. And if you ditch him with nothing more than a couple of lines, then that man is pretty sure you aren't."

I was still mulling over the "who loves you" part. Until now Donny has been very careful not to use that particular four-letter word quite that way. He's made his feelings clear, but somehow saying the words directly changes things. I wasn't sure why, and there was no time to figure it out.

"How can you think I *could* be happy? This whole film is guaranteed to make me unhappy. If there was a script, that's what every single stage direction would say. Cecilia blah, blah, blah, feeling miserable."

"The film was *your* idea, yours and Mick's. And if you recall, I've made a million accommodations so it can happen. I've canceled everything from personal appearances and interviews to meetings at a major studio where you're being considered for a part in an important film. I've misled reputable reporters along with paparazzi to get you safely through airports, and in and out of towns and cities. I've made promises to promoters and Cyclonic executives that I'm pretty sure I won't be able to keep. I've traveled with you when I should have been in negotiations somewhere else."

"I believe that's why you earn the big bucks."

He leaned forward. "You think any of this is about money?"

I looked away. "I appreciate everything you've done, but nobody, not even you, gets to control me."

"Let's back up. What does 'not even you' mean? The manager or the man? Because it's the second one you're reacting to. If I were just your manager you would have called, told me what you were doing, told me to shut up when I argued and gone on your way."

"You're not that easy to order around."

"What do you think I would have said? That you couldn't go? That I know best and you have to listen? I would have been fine once you explained how you were getting here and why you wanted—"

"I didn't want to explain! I'm not even sure I understand, okay? I just know I had to go out to the ranch by myself. Without you. Without Robin. Without anybody. I just needed to be there alone. And I didn't want a discussion. I wanted to go. Period. And I did. So I'm sorry if you're upset. I'm sorry if I worried you. But there is nothing in our relationship that requires me to keep you up-to-date about everything I think or feel. And if you got that idea somehow, now's the time to put it behind you. I'm in charge. I always will be."

Donny took off his glasses and rubbed the bridge of his nose. I waited for his next salvo, but he was silent.

"I know you think you love me," I said when the silence became unbearable. "But that can't change anything."

"No?"

"The only way this can work is if you separate your feelings from our business arrangement."

"If *I* do. What about you?"

"Could there be a worse time for this?" I grabbed a pillow and hugged it close. "I don't have the strength to deal with you right now. I'm having enough trouble dealing with me."

"Oddly enough I thought having my support would make that easier."

"Support, sure. But not demands."

"Demands?" He perched his glasses on his nose again, but he stared well past me. "Cecilia, letting me know where you go isn't a demand. It's the courtesy people in love show each other. That's all I need. Just that. A phone call. A brief explanation. Trust that I'll understand and help if I can, or not, if you prefer it that way."

"You want a lot more than I'm capable of giving anybody. You refuse to see it. Nobody should understand better than you, Donny. You were in Australia. You saw what happened then, but you refuse to see what's happening now."

"You are capable of so much more than you believe."

"You're kidding yourself." I tossed the pillow on the sofa, got up and started for the door. "We've both had it tonight. We can finish this in the morning. If I can get one, I need a good night's sleep."

"This isn't going to work, is it? You're going to make sure it doesn't."

I turned. "What does that mean?"

"I can't be your manager anymore. You were right about that. It won't work. The minute I tried to make it more, I made it less. I made it impossible." He got up. "You need to finish your responsibilities here, then we'll settle all the business stuff, or our lawyers will. I'll make sure it's not any messier than it has to be, and if you want me to recommend somebody to take my place, I will. But I'm sure you've had your eyes open and know who you want next. After all, as you say, you're in charge."

I stared at him. "I'm not asking you to stop working for me. I just want you to back off on the personal stuff right now. I'm too confused. I'm a mess."

"Anything but. You know exactly what you're doing, and you're getting exactly what you want. You're pushing me away. And don't pretend you didn't know. For once be honest. Either you don't love me and know you never will, or loving me scares you too much to let it go further. In the end, I guess which it is doesn't matter."

"Can't you just give me some time?"

"To do what? Work out your whole life without my help? And then what? You won't *need* my support? You won't have to show me the real woman, the one the world doesn't know a thing about? Is that what love means? Waiting until you're back on both feet and hiding in plain sight?"

"You have no idea who I really am. You think you do, but nobody, not even Robin, knows."

"I think Robin and I have a pretty damned good idea." He brushed past me and opened the door. "I'm going to stick around and see the filming to conclusion because that's my job. But I'll back off. You let me know when you want my help, and I'll make sure you get it. At arm's length. Where you are most comfortable."

He didn't slam the door. He closed it softly, with much more effect.

I stared after him, and I asked myself, the way someone asks a stranger, how I felt. Because Donny is right. Whether I understand it or not, this is the way I knew our relationship had to end. And it's like him to see it first and take the initiative, so the burden won't be on me.

But if I forced this, why did I feel sick? Why did I want to go after him and tell him how wrong he is, that I need him the way I've never needed anyone before? Why did I want to tell him that of all the men I've known, he's the only one I've ever had a prayer of loving? Donny is the only man who

42

—

Robin

If a bystander asked me to make a bet on who was about to win the argument escalating in front of me, I would decline. Watching two strong personalities locked in combat was fascinating. Who would be foolish enough to favor one over the other?

The challengers? Mick and Cecilia, halfway between the Osburn ranch barn and house. Both, at the moment, holding their own.

Cecilia was appropriately dressed for a ranch, although more California dude than hand-to-mouth working. Her hair curled halfway down her back, clipped back from her face with broad turquoise barrettes. She wore faux-leather cowboy boots embroidered with palm trees, a studded denim shirt and wheat-colored jeans tailored to every curve. By itself each item costs more than all the clothing we bought together during the years we lived here.

She was speaking softly and slowly, as if to make her point with as much tact as possible.

"I understand where you're coming from, Mick. I know you think if I go inside without the crew, you won't get the shots you really want later. They'll be hashed over and edited in my head."

Mick's voice was equally melodious, but an edge was forming. "Cecilia, if you understand, why are you insisting?"

"Because I'm a better actor than you give me credit for."

"I know how good you are." Mick, wearing his usual jeans and T-shirt, looked casual enough, but the easygoing filmmaker has a ramrod backbone, and today he needed it.

"Then you know I can do this." I watched Cecilia rest her hand on his arm. I could almost feel her fingertips digging in. "More important, though, you need to know that I'm not going in there at *all* unless I can go in without the crew first. You know what a good sport I've been. And you've been amazing. You've made this doable, and I appreciate every single accommodation you've made for me. But honestly? This isn't a request."

Mick made one more stab at getting his way. "I know this will be hard. But I'd like to see how hard on film. Remember, at the end you have the right to edit out any shot you don't want viewers to see."

She smiled her Cecilia-onstage smile and clasped her hands in front of her. "No."

And so, it was over. When Cecilia makes up her mind, that's it.

Donny stepped forward, but I noticed that he angled his body away from my sister's, as if to keep her out of his sight line. "Mick, you're sure the house was thoroughly checked? She'll be safe in there by herself?"

"*We'll* be safe in there," Cecilia corrected him. "I want Robin with me. And, Mick, to make you a little happier, Robin can bring her camera."

This was news. As usual Cecilia had left me out of negotiations. "Wait a minute," I said. "Nobody asked me."

Cecilia glanced over her shoulder. "Mick assured me it's safe. Somebody's done some work in the past months to make sure it doesn't tumble down with us inside. Will you come with me?"

"That's better."

She smiled her wheedling smile. "It would mean a lot."

I wasn't looking forward to being in the house. Last night I'd lain awake for hours, sorry my memory banks were still filled with Osburn ranch images circa 1990. But I have to go inside at some point to take photos. I've known this moment was coming. And going in alone with Cecilia? Maybe that would help us both put ghosts to rest.

My nod was more like a tic, but she smiled a more natural smile at me, although not at Donny.

Everyone had eaten together in Tampa before packing up to move to the ranch for this final shoot. The campers arrived at the campground yesterday as promised, and this morning we spent a little time after our arrival moving in. My children would love overnighting in mine, with everything in miniature and easy to reach. They would love it, but I'm so grateful they're not here. Because what would I tell them that they could hear?

Yesterday I was busy with crew meetings most of the day, and Cecilia stayed out of everybody's way. I don't know where Donny spent his time, but I didn't see him until breakfast this morning. It's pretty clear from the way they're avoiding each other that he and my sister aren't happy.

"When do you want to do this?" Donny's expression was carefully blank.

Cecilia looked as if the real answer would be "never," but she caught my eye. "Are we ready?"

"Let me get my equipment."

"Not a lot, okay? Just a few photos."

She didn't want me to be distracted. That was easy to see. I was sorry, since distraction sounded like a good thing. I promised to meet her back at the house in ten minutes.

She and Mick walked toward the front porch and I started back to my car, where I had stowed my equipment. I had kept my rental car, although I hadn't needed to. I could have gotten here in the crew vans with everyone else, but the car was my security. If necessary I could leave anytime I wanted. Apparently Cecilia felt the same, because she'd fetched hers from town this morning instead of asking the rental agency to take it back. I'm not sure where either of us thinks we'll go, but knowing we can go somewhere makes this easier.

Donny joined me, and we walked in silence for a few moments before he went right to the point. "I've given Cecilia notice. I don't know if she'll tell you herself, but I wanted you to hear it from me."

I was stunned enough to stop walking. "That's crazy. The two of you are great together."

He looked tired, as if he'd gotten as little sleep as I had. "It just isn't working. She needs somebody more objective. I can't back off the way I used to. And that's what she thinks she needs."

I had no idea what to say. This seemed like a disaster in the making, but Cecilia is an adult, and she wouldn't appreciate interference. We respect certain boundaries—although *I* respect them more than she does.

"I'm sorry." As hackneyed and pointless as that was, it was the best I could do.

"I'll ride out this Florida trip, then we'll work out details in California. She'll have the best people knocking down her door for an opportunity to work with her. She'll be fine."

"What about you?"

He lowered his head as if his neck was too stiff to hold it.

"I'm not sure what I'll do. I can retire ten times over, but I like the work. I might cut back, but I won't quit."

"I've always felt she was…" I grasped for the right word and found it. "Safe. Safe with you. Once you came on the scene I stopped worrying so much."

"What did you worry about?"

"She's so alone. Except for me it's always been Cecilia against the world."

"That's the way she wants it."

I rested my hand on his arm. "No, it's not. She's scared to death to have it any other way because she doesn't know how to handle anything else. You can't know what life was like for her growing up, Donny. You probably have more of a feel now, but nobody can ever fully understand."

"Even you?"

"Not even me. And she'll never understand what *I* went through, either. For years I hardly spoke. Can you imagine Cecilia not speaking? She would have shouted louder and louder until somebody heard her. That's who she is. She always takes matters into her own hands, but this time, she's made a big mistake."

"I just wanted you to know what's going on."

He turned toward the house. I wondered what Cecilia was feeling right now.

In ten minutes I was back where I'd promised to be. Off to the side Mick and Donny were in conversation, and Cecilia was staring up at the second floor.

She didn't turn to greet me, but she knew I was there. "Apparently it's not as bad inside as we expected. After Betty sold the property another family moved in and probably shored up the foundation. Then the citrus growers decided not to tear down any of the buildings. They planned to use the house for administration purposes and did the bare minimum to keep it from collapsing."

"The place is a time bomb. There aren't enough nails and manpower in the world to keep it standing much longer."

"Termites wreaked havoc. For starters."

"What about the new owners?"

"The land is owned by an LLC out of New York. Mick's not sure why they bought it or what they're planning, and he's only been able to communicate through their attorney."

"God knows why they want it."

"You have to look at it through a different lens. Not the one from 1990." She changed the subject. "He's asked me to be the narrator, at the very least for the parts we've been involved in. Better yet the whole thing if I can carve out enough weeks in my schedule. I'm going to try."

I'm not sure what made me probe further. "Donny thinks that's a good idea?"

"Not Donny's decision."

"Did I mention decision? I was talking about advice. Counsel. Wisdom."

"Apparently he's talked to you."

"Uh-huh." We see right through each other.

"I don't want to discuss it, okay?"

"For the record, discussing anything to do with feelings is always pretty much off the table, so I was prepared."

Her voice wasn't quite steady. "It's a business decision. And he's right. We've been together too long and objectivity is wavering. It's better this way."

"Right. It's all about business."

"Let's get this over with, okay? Before I throw something at you."

I slung my arm over her shoulder, but I squeezed. Hard.

"We might be standing in front of the Osburn house, CeCe, but one thing has definitely changed."

"Yeah?"

I squeezed even harder. "You can throw anything you want, but these days I can catch."

43
—

Cecilia

The first thing that hit me when Robin and I picked our way across the porch and slipped inside the Osburn house? All hints of life have been removed. The place is now a hollow shell.

During our years here the house was shabby, with '70s geometric wallpaper peeling from the high humidity and scuffed vinyl flooring dotted with rag rugs. Now both paper and vinyl are gone, and as we moved farther inside, bare pine boards creaked under our feet and the smell of mildew grew stronger.

Betty Osburn didn't have much to work with, but in her day, the house smelled like lemons and Lysol. The cobwebs now adorning every corner were banished with a dust mop, even the ones so high she had to lean precariously over the banister and wave them into submission.

I was never sure whether to pray the banister would give way and send her tumbling to the floor or pray it wouldn't. Because as vile as Betty was, Jud was so much worse.

"The smell." Robin coughed. "What is that?"

I outlined a list of possibilities. "Mildew, mold, dead rats in the walls, bat guano in the attic? Who knows?"

"Should we try to open the windows so the crew doesn't smother when they come inside to film?"

"Mick said they tried opening one. The sash disintegrated and the whole window crashed to the ground. Now there's a hole in the wall, and they had to board it up."

"Imagine rain pouring in through the side of the house and not just what's left of the roof."

I managed a perfunctory smile. "Do you remember the first time we walked through this door and stood here?"

Robin stared into space—or the past. "A week went by before I could form a sentence."

"More like two."

"If you hadn't been right here standing beside me, I might have been silent the rest of my childhood."

I was warmed by that, although I was determined not to show emotion inside these walls. I pictured vampire ghosts hovering everywhere.

I gave her my version of that day. "I kept telling myself things could be worse. That if we hadn't come here we might have ended up miles apart and never been told where the other was living."

"Jud came in behind us wheeling our suitcases."

The suitcases were a farewell gift from the Davises. Previously both Robin and I packed our belongings in black plastic garbage bags, a foster child's best friend.

Now I could almost feel Jud creeping up behind me. I steeled myself not to look. "I think that was the last time he did anything for us, don't you?"

She didn't laugh, because, let's face it, nothing about that was funny. "Our caseworker was with us."

"Right. Ichabod dropped us off and left. I can't remember how many times after that we actually saw him. At some point he quit his job and somebody equally disinterested took over. Remember her? At least she was honest about not wanting to do her job well."

"What do you mean?"

"The woman who took his place. Debbie? Does that sound right?"

"Who knows?"

"Debbie said Ichabod warned her about me, so she planned to take everything I said with a grain of salt. She said I might as well not lie."

"I don't remember that."

Robin didn't remember because I never told her. At the time the story would have made no sense, unless I told it all.

"Where shall we go first? You spent a lot of time in the kitchen. Want to go there?"

Robin raised her camera to get a photo of the cobweb-draped stairs. "Let's get this over with and get out of here."

The kitchen was at the end of the hall. We passed the ranch office on the left and across from it the room Betty called the parlor. A velvet love seat, perpetually protected by clear plastic, had rested against one wall until the sad day Betty discovered mice were building a nest in the cushions.

At the time the destruction seemed only fitting. Nobody but the mice ever used the parlor anyway. Having a room for company that never arrived was Betty's vision of a better life. I guess we all need our fantasies.

With a push the kitchen door creaked open. While the rest of the rooms in the house are small, in our day the country kitchen held a table for twelve. The Osburns rarely needed one that large except when Betty's extended family came at holidays, or when extra farmhands arrived to move livestock or help with the harvest. Then all the chairs were filled. At those times Robin worked in the kitchen every single moment she wasn't in school.

Now the kitchen was empty of furniture. Cupboard doors hung open; the sink was black with grime and so were the windows.

Robin trailed a fingertip along the edge of a scarred countertop, then wiped it on her jeans. "At least the food was good."

"And as a special bonus we knew the name of every animal we ate."

"Good thing we didn't make pets of the mustard greens or field peas, or you wouldn't eat anything these days." She started forward, careful not to trip over the linoleum tiles curling toward the ceiling. "I helped Betty make a million meals here."

"And gallons and gallons of sweet tea."

"Lemonade with real lemons, remember? Coffee. The coffeepot was on all day. Jud needed lots of coffee to sober up."

"Too bad it didn't work."

"I don't know—when he was sober he was worse than when he was drunk."

"Back in the day I researched that carefully. Jud was at his best when he had two beers. I used to watch and wait, and after the second, if we needed something, that was the time to ask. After three he turned mean again."

"These days we would have a *guardian ad litem* to talk to. The whole system is better. Caseloads are smaller. Foster parents have better screening and training. Agencies try harder to work with families before kids are removed."

Robin sounded a little desperate, as if she needs to believe children are no longer powerless, that somebody who cares is there to listen and help. I know things are better, but I still worry about every single kid who's caught up in the system. And there will always be kids, no matter how hard caseworkers and therapists try, and how much money is allocated. Because people who should never have children and don't know how to take care of them will continue to have them, right up until Judgment Day.

Robin had wandered to the empty space where the table used to be, and I joined her.

"Betty never sat at the table," I said. "Do you remember? She stood there." I pointed behind her. "At the counter. Back then it was L-shaped. She stood in front of it with her plate at her side, and she ate standing up so if Jud or one of the workers needed something, she could get it."

"She told me standing was easier than getting up and down. And when she was sick or gone for some reason, Jud made you take her place."

I had forgotten that, but Robin was right. I hadn't been required to take Betty's place often. Unless she was on the verge of dying, she made it downstairs for meals. TLC wasn't part of Jud's philosophy.

"Why do you suppose she stayed with him?" Now Robin trailed her finger over pockmarked plaster that had once been covered by wallpaper with multiple repeats of smiling fruits and vegetables. "Didn't the ranch belong to her? Couldn't she have kicked him out and sold it? If she loved this place, she never let on."

I knew the answer. "The property came down through her family, but Jud convinced her to title it in both their names. So if she just walked out the door, most likely he would have gotten half."

"How on earth do you know that?"

"Jud told me once. He said…" I did my best Jud impression. "That woman knows I'll be as hard to get rid of as a bedbug. And I'll suck a whole lot of blood if she tries."

"Please don't ever do that again. I'd almost forgotten what he sounded like."

"Lucky you." I peered into a cabinet, then I opened a drawer and watched something large and multilegged scurry over the back and disappear. I slammed it shut. "After he left she did sell the property. Because here we are. And she's not."

"She's living in Connecticut."

I spun to face her. "How do you know?"

"She sends me Christmas cards."

That took a moment to sink it. "The Davises wrote you until they died."

"Betty does, too."

"You never mentioned that."

"Did you want to know? The way you felt about her and him?"

"Why don't you tell her to stop?"

"That takes energy."

"Why? Why would she do that?"

"Maybe she feels bad about those years. Maybe she's changed now that Jud's out of her life."

"She says that?"

Robin started back through the doorway, the way we had come. "I don't know what she says. I can't make myself open the envelopes."

"Really?" My voice rose a half step. "Have you ever thought maybe Jud turned up? Maybe they're together again?"

"CeCe, he deserted her twenty-five years ago. She despised him. Do you think even if he tried, she would take him back? Ever?"

"Some women will do anything to keep from being alone."

Robin answered from the hall. "Maybe I was only fourteen when I left here for good, but I do remember he had some kind of heart condition. He was overweight, had high blood pressure. Prediabetic. While she was adding salt and butter to everything in sight Betty muttered all the things that were wrong with him, like a voodoo curse. She used to say Jud was one sparerib away from a heart attack. She never said it like she worried."

"One more six-pack, one more pack of cigarettes, one more pound. And yet he survived it all, at least while he lived here."

Robin's voice began to fade as she walked deeper into the house. "Do you think if he lived long enough to see you on an album cover or a television special he would have stayed in the background? Jud would have been the first one at your door with his hand out in return for a promise he wasn't going to tell stories about you."

I followed, glad to leave the kitchen behind. "Let's go upstairs and get that over with."

"What about the office? You spent a lot of time there."

"We can do that on the way out."

The stairs were rickety but safe. Treads had been replaced, but neither of us trusted the railing. The upstairs had three bedrooms. Jud and Betty slept in the middle room just in front of the stairs. Our rooms were smaller, Robin on one end, me on the other. A storeroom that was also the entrance to the attic stairs stood between her room and the master. Mine was separated from the Osburns' by the upstairs bathroom.

"Your room first," I said.

"I hated mine. I was always scared of the dark. I wanted to share yours. Jud wouldn't let me."

I looked away. "Something about square footage. And agency rules."

We stood together in the doorway of the empty room that had been hers. It was only a little larger than a walk-in closet, but it had satisfied the state's requirements. Robin's bed had rested against the back wall, with a dresser under the window and a spindle leg chair to sit on. There was no room for a desk. She did homework at the kitchen table.

Now that we were upstairs the stench was worse, and the hall floor and ceiling were water stained. The roof was no longer doing its job, and the attic was hosting a mold festival.

"There was an air conditioner in the window." Robin gestured. "Remember? If it wasn't on, you would turn it on when you came to say good-night. It rattled like a freight train, but even when it was cool outside and only the fan was blowing, the noise helped me sleep. When I moved to Live Oaks they had central air, and for months I tossed and turned because of the noises."

I remembered making sure the old window unit was on every night, and I remembered coming in to make sure she was all right before I went to bed. Robin always had an active imagination. After we left the Davises' house she was scared of monsters, and I rescued the chair for her to prop under her doorknob to keep them away.

I didn't like thinking about that. "We shouldn't stay up here too long. Breathing this air isn't good."

"I hated this room, but spiders didn't. It was like their clubhouse. I never got used to them. Jud liked to tease me. If I complained, he'd capture one and drop it down my shirt, just to hear me scream."

I tried to breathe. Between the mold and fury, air wasn't seeping into my lungs. I felt dizzy and for a moment I thought I might pass out. I rested my hands on my knees and bent over.

"CeCe?"

"I'm…okay." I took a breath, then another. "I just… I hate this place."

"We ought to go."

"I need to see my room. Then the office, then out."

I straightened. Robin looked concerned, but she didn't argue. We followed the hall to the other end. She waited, and

I pushed open the door. I didn't say anything. I just stared. She took several photos, not of the room but of me. A professional to her toes.

Finally she spoke. "Somebody must have had boys."

Electric-blue walls were covered with peeling posters of football players. But the room was otherwise bare except for slime growing on the outside wall. I reached for the knob and slammed the door shut.

I was trembling. "I've seen enough."

"I really think you should go out—"

"The office. Then out. Please."

She was frowning, but she didn't protest.

The air downstairs almost smelled fresh in comparison. I didn't waste time. I went to the office, pushed the door wider and went in.

As hard as it was to believe, Jud's vintage desk was still exactly where it had been twenty-five years ago. Betty hadn't taken it, and the series of renters and owners who had come later hadn't disposed of it. It wasn't a valuable antique; it was scarred and battered by careless usage, but it was substantial. One side held two file drawers. The other had regular drawers once filled with office supplies.

"There were three file cabinets against that wall." I walked over and framed the space with my hands. "A bookcase over there with nothing much on it." I nodded to the adjoining wall. "Jud wasn't a reader. Old copies of *Farm Journal* took up one shelf. A couple of veterinary textbooks and framed photos of him in his rodeo days another."

"Rodeo," she said, as if she was remembering.

Whether she did or not, I recapped as she looked through the desk. She didn't stop me. "That's how he and Betty met. He was riding the circuit somewhere in Arkansas, and she was visiting family in Fayetteville. I guess they both thought he was big stuff. He got thrown off a bull and broke something or other, and she nursed him back to health. He liked her cooking, so he married her. He liked that she had land coming to her someday, too. Her family was scattered all over this area. The year after they married she inherited the ranch from her father and they moved here."

"You remember a lot."

"He talked more than she did. In fact he talked about himself all the time. And I had the pleasure of his company whenever he saw fit to come out to the barn."

Robin said the next without enthusiasm. "He always wore a tooled leather belt with a rodeo belt buckle. The buckle was brass, maybe with some silver plate. He used to brag about winning it somewhere in Texas. He liked to show it off. There was a cowboy riding a bull with Jud's name engraved below it. He never took off that belt."

I took a moment, another deep breath, and then I walked back to where she was standing. No chair stood at the desk now, so I perched on the edge. "Robin, did you ever wonder how I was able to move to New York when I turned eighteen? How I managed? You were only fourteen, but did you wonder?"

"I know it was hard. You used to write funny stories about the place you lived, but I could read between the lines."

"Even terrible living conditions in Manhattan cost a small fortune." I let that settle a moment. "I had a little money to help me get started."

"You told me Betty helped at first."

I guessed it had been as good a lie as any, although if she had considered it at length, she would have realized Betty had no interest in helping anybody, even herself.

"When I left, you moved to the group home," I said. "You had a lot on your mind."

"Betty didn't help you." It wasn't a question.

"She did give me a few dollars from the state's final check. But not even enough for the bus fare. I got that from Jud."

"*Jud* gave you money? Before he left town?"

"Not exactly." I sighed, long and slow, and then I was sorry because I had to take a deep breath to replace it and I couldn't stop coughing. "I stole it," I said, when I was breathing normally again.

She looked surprised but not shocked. "From Jud?"

"I started keeping books for the ranch just a few months after we moved here. The books were one of the many jobs he hated, and I took business classes from ninth grade on. Remember? Mrs. Davis insisted I learn some skills that would help me survive when the system cut me loose. She hoped I would go to college, but she wasn't optimistic I would get the aid I'd need. I was good in math, still am, so we settled on accounting and bookkeeping. At first that's how I survived in New York. I did the books for a little deli near my apartment, and along with a paycheck I got leftover coleslaw and potato salad."

I was rambling. Hedging. I made myself move on. "Jud was a blowhard, but not a very smart one. He didn't graduate from high school, and his reading skills were poor. People who claim to know everything are afraid to ask questions. I figured out pretty quickly that he couldn't make heads or tails out of his books. I could move money around, open accounts and move money into them without him becoming suspicious. As long as I only took a little at a time. A few bucks here, a few more there."

Robin looked fascinated, not distressed. "Wouldn't you need his signature to open an account?"

"I took over most of his jobs, and after six months or so I signed every check that came through this office and made out the deposit slips for him. It was easier, since I was doing all the paperwork anyway, and pretty soon I was able to forge his signature so well nobody ever suspected. The smaller checks went into a new account I set up in his name at a different bank from his usual. He never once noticed they were missing."

I opened drawers, as Robin had, for something to do while I confessed. Nothing remained inside. "Jud thought I was willing to do the office stuff because he took over some of the outside chores. But the real reason? I was building a nest egg. Eighteen was right around the corner. I knew you would only be fourteen by then, and I couldn't let you stay here on your own. So I saved money to get both of us out when the time came."

"You used to talk about running away together. I thought it was just talk."

"He owed us. Both of us. So did Betty. They were being paid to take care of us, but they used us like farm laborers. We were supposed to have a clothing allowance, spending money, but you know how that went."

"You did this until what, you turned eighteen?"

"Until the day he walked out. After that things fell apart fast, but luckily I saw they might, so I cashed out and got rid of the evidence. Betty sold off the livestock, and when those final payments came in she took over the books. I backed away, and my plans changed. We talked after Jud left, remember? I told you we could leave together, that you could come with me and nobody would spend much time or money looking for you."

Her expression softened. "I remember."

"Then a new caseworker came to see us. I don't even remember her name, but she was one of the better ones. She said she found you a good place, well funded and safe. When

I told her I couldn't trust her promises, she took us *both* to see Live Oaks. Do you remember? It was far from perfect—"

"But we both thought the school I would attend was one of the better ones in the area, and I could stay there until I graduated. She more or less promised that. I told you I wanted to give Live Oaks a try."

"You did."

"You weren't the only liar in this house, CeCe. I didn't want to live there. Not at all. But even then I knew better than to let you give up your life for me."

I drew mold spores into my lungs again and closed my eyes to keep them from filling with tears. "I took the money I stole, and I got on that bus to New York."

"The rest is history."

"History. Exactly."

We fell silent, and I spent the next moments thinking about history in general.

It's never possible to know everything that happened in the past, so we are forced to fill in the blanks, hopeful we're on the right track, hopeful we've thought out all the possibilities and chosen the most likely scenarios. But unless we lived through every part of it, none of us can ever know for certain what really went on years ago. Not just because people lie more than they tell the truth—at least some people—but because our guesses are often completely wrong.

Life rarely unfolds in neat patterns. We might believe, for instance, that one day a man gets fed up and walks out on his wife. After all, he leaves a note that tells the whole story, so why question any of it? The pieces fit. The man and his wife fight constantly. A woman he is suspected of having an affair with leaves town the same day he does. The note is in his handwriting.

Robin rested her hand on my shoulder. "All these years,

CeCe, did you think I would be shocked you took enough money to get to New York? Is that why you never told me? Nobody knows better than I do what you were up against. You're a survivor. We both are. And in the years since, how many millions have you given to people who need it?"

"So you think I've been absolved?"

"You. Not them."

"Maybe Betty's looking for absolution. Maybe that's why she sends you a Christmas card every year."

She shook her head, either in disbelief or dismay. "We need to get out of here and breathe some fresh air before we have to come back later with the crew. Will you be ready?"

"I will look stunned and astonished right on cue."

She raised her camera, surprising me, and light flashed.

I won't know until I see that photo which Cecilia Robin caught.

There are so many.

44

—

Cecilia

An owl is screeching in the distance. I can hear him outside my window, over the drone of crickets and bellowing of frogs from the banks of Cold Creek. I'm riveted with fear, not because an owl out for a hunt has awakened me, but because of a closer noise, the slightest squeak of a door, the shuffling of feet. I think about where I can hide, and I struggle to sit up. Sitting up should be simple, yet I'm frozen in place. I can't breathe because I can't even remember how. Somehow I fling myself upright and air rushes into my lungs. I open my mouth to scream.

Then I remember what will happen if I do.

When my eyelids fly apart light is filtering through the sliding windows of my camper. There's a full moon tonight and a cloudless sky littered with stars. An owl *is* screeching, which makes it harder for me to distinguish this night from the one I lived just moments ago. But I have this nightmare so often everything about it is familiar. No matter where I am, which of my homes, which hotel in which city, which seat I've fallen asleep in on my tour bus, the nightmare is the same.

The only difference tonight is that the scene was more

vivid, more real. Because the sounds and smells outside this camper are the sounds and smells of my adolescence.

The sheet that was covering me lands on the floor, and I swing my legs to the side and rest my head in my hands.

Dealing with Nightmares 101.

The doctor who worked with me in Australia taught me a technique called Imagery Rehearsal. When I refused to explore my nightmares in our sessions, she suggested I order them, least frightening to most, and write down as many details of the first as I could remember, then rewrite it, changing the ending into a positive one. If I dreamed of falling, I might dream about wings lifting me so I could soar peacefully overhead. If I dreamed of drowning, I could imagine a lifeboat arriving or a raft to climb on. When I was satisfied with what I'd come up with I was to rehearse the new ending, think about it at length before bedtime, then let it drift away as I fell asleep.

Unfortunately just picking up the pen is too traumatic. I never get past the first sentence.

I stood on wobbly legs and turned on the light. I've had better luck with other suggestions she gave me, all of which eventually help clear a nightmare from my mind. Turning on a light, fetching a drink of water, reading a book. Combined, an assortment of those, along with a long shower, usually chase away the remnants, and hours later I'm able to get back to sleep. But lack of sleep was the final straw that landed me in the psychiatric ward of that Australian hospital, and if this nightmare returns over and over while I'm here in Cold Creek, I might end up in another.

"Damned owl!"

I sat again. The owl was real, and so were the crickets. But since Cold Creek, which ran behind the Osburn house and most likely this campground, was now dry, the frogs had gone elsewhere or dried up, too. And after a while, as I silently wished he would find a mouse and choke on it, the owl flew away.

The nightmare was receding. I went into the bathroom and washed my face, since a shower is complicated in a camper and necessarily brief. There was a bathhouse not far away, but I didn't want to dress and walk across the grounds to an unfamiliar building, then strip and shower where anyone could walk in.

Anyone.

When someone tapped on my door I was sobbing. Since Mick rented the entire facility we were able to place our campers so far apart I hadn't worried about waking anyone when I turned on my light. My site was spacious and private, shaded by pines.

The tapper was probably Robin, who was several sites away. I wiped my eyes on the hem of my gown and went to the door. "Robin?"

A male voice answered. "Donny."

I didn't have to think. I opened the door, then I stepped aside to let him in.

He took one look at me, and drew me into his arms. "A bad one?"

I began to cry again. And this time it took forever to stop. He held me as I sobbed and kissed my hair. "You're okay. You're okay. It's not real."

"I wish to God…that were true."

We stood like that until I was finally calm. I drew away at last. "How did you know?"

"I was awake. I saw your light. I expected it. Going through the house, letting Mick film you there today. You were so brave, so controlled, but something had to give."

"I thought I was okay. Coming early, going through first.

That's what you didn't understand. I wanted to innoculate myself. And if I fell apart, I wanted to do it alone. I didn't want to fall apart on film. I don't want a reputation—" I couldn't go on.

"As something other than a ballbuster?" He tilted his head. "Why do you care?"

"I eat men alive. I'm the strongest woman out there. I've built an empire on that. Remember Australia and how hard you worked to keep my breakdown out of the press?"

"Cecilia, I kept it out of the press because it was your life and your business, not because I care about your reputation. I care…" He shook his head.

"I don't know who this new person is. The woman who's letting the past rule everything. It's not like I repressed any of the crap that happened to me, Donny. It's not like it's all coming back after I stuffed it in some part of my unconscious for decades and now it's seeping out. I have never forgotten a moment of my childhood or my years in foster care. Not one moment. So why is it trying to destroy me now?"

"Because you're doing your best to face and share it, even if you're struggling not to share every detail. You're trying to look it in the eye so it'll go away. You thought this would be easy?"

"No. No, of course not! But I thought I could do it. I thought I knew how. I thought if Robin was with me. If you…"

His eyes were sad. "Sweetheart, we can't protect you from the past."

"How about the future? You're going to leave me forever when the filming ends. Everybody I love leaves, except Robin, and I think I tried to chase her away, too, by throwing her mother in her face. What's wrong with me, Donny? I am never going to live like a normal person. I'm going to spend my whole life making sure nobody gets close."

He watched me, but he didn't reach for me again.

"I don't want you to go." I stretched out my arm and with my trembling hand touched his shoulder. Then, with effort, his cheek. "This is all so sleazy, so sad, and I don't want you to be part of it. I want to be someone else for you, but even knowing how selfish this is, I don't want you to go."

He covered my hand and held it in place a moment; then he kissed my fingers before he let my hand drop to my side. "The thing is, Cecilia? I know who you are. Not everything that turned you into that woman, but the woman herself. I know you. I know about the nightmares and the weeks when you get so little sleep you're dead on your feet, but you keep moving anyway. I know when you finally admit you're tired, you're actually exhausted, and when you say you want to stop touring for a while, that means you're about to break into a million pieces. I know you don't trust me or any man, and you only married Sage because he wouldn't make demands you couldn't meet."

"You should run screaming."

"Yeah."

My next words were the most difficult I've ever said. "But please…don't." I bit my lip. "Don't run." I touched his arm, wrapped my fingers around it to hold him there. "The nightmares? They're bad enough. But needing you?" I swallowed, and my throat felt swollen.

"It's a scary thing, isn't it? Easier to push me away before it gets scarier."

"You have no idea."

He stepped forward and cradled my face in his hands. "Of course I do. You're terrified of any kind of intimacy. Being alone is easy in comparison. But I'm not the monster in your nightmares. I'm just the guy who loves you, every battered inch. I'm just the guy who would like to give you what you haven't been able to take before."

"I'm going to destroy you."

He smiled a little. "I'm not going to let you. You've seen me in negotiations. Nobody gets the better of me."

"I am so much more important to you than anybody who's tried."

"If you know that, and if it matters? We're going to be okay."

I pushed the words out of my aching throat. "You are... so much more important...to me."

"I love you, Cecilia. I'm not sure when it happened. I knew it was the worst possible idea, but there it was. Right in front of both of us, and at first I was as blind to it as you're pretending to be now."

"I don't know if I can love anybody."

"You already do. You don't have to tell me. Eventually you'll figure it out."

"Please...you're not going to leave?"

"Tonight? Or forever?"

I moved closer, my breasts pressing against his chest. "Don't leave at all."

He combed his fingers through my hair; then he bent his head and kissed me. I felt like I was melting, as if every inch of me was giving up the struggle to keep my distance.

"We'll take this slowly." He kissed my cheek, my forehead, my earlobe. "You can say stop, and I will."

My heart was speeding out of control, but I backed away. "You should know why I won't be any good at this."

His face was grim. "You almost broke my heart today when you refused to let Mick film you in the bedroom that had been yours. Your bastard foster father. Don't you think

I know what drives you? I never had details, but I think I've always known."

My knees felt weak. "There's more, Donny. You need to know what you're getting into. You need to know *everything* that happened on that ranch. You think you know…"

"It only matters if you need to tell me. But there's nothing you can say tonight that will change the way I feel about you. And nothing you can do, or can't."

"I have to tell you. I…"

I wondered if I would ever run out of tears. They were streaming down my cheeks again, but he didn't back away. "I can't do this unless you know…" I finally got it out. "Unless you know everything."

He moved to the bed and tugged me along with him. He lay against my pillows and pulled me to lie half across him. My nightgown was twisted beneath me, but I didn't care. I hid my face against his shoulder.

"We have the rest of the night." He kissed my hair. "We have as long as it takes."

I had no choice but to start at the beginning.

45

—

Robin

Yesterday, after Cecilia and I went through the house and before I drove back to the campground, I called Kris.

"I need you," I said with no introduction. "When can you get here?"

He didn't sound surprised. "I decided not to wait until you asked. I've already talked to Elena. She'll stay with the kids until Lucie can get a flight. I'll be in late tomorrow morning. You'll be okay until then?"

"This is so much worse than I thought it would be."

And it is.

Fourteen is a funny age. We're not children, barely teenagers and certainly not adults. Facts and fantasy aren't far apart. At fourteen we don't have the experience or brain development to make decisions, or even to commit reality to memory. What's real and what's not? At fourteen we can hide from ourselves and not remember that we did.

But sometimes hiding *and* forgetting are impossible.

"I'm worried about you," I told Cecilia as I took photos of her after breakfast. We were in her camper, and Wendy was doing her makeup and hair. She had already painted her nails a soft coral, and Cecilia was waving them in the air to dry faster. "Doesn't Mick have enough footage already? Can't we pack up and get you out of here?"

She looked exhausted and drawn, but I had noticed at breakfast that she and Donny were nestled side by side, and at one point he leaned over and kissed her cheek. I wondered if that was the reason she was so pale, or maybe it was the reason she wasn't huddled in a corner banging her head against the wall.

She waved a little faster. "You know we're filming around the barn this afternoon."

"CeCe, it's a barn and a barnyard. I'm not sure why it matters."

She nodded to Wendy, thanked her and made it clear her assistant needed to leave. Wendy exited quickly and gratefully. The camper was air-conditioned, but with three of us crowded inside, breathing took energy.

"I know that's where you mostly worked with Jud," I said.

Cecilia was sorting through jewelry and didn't look at me. She chose simple pearl studs and leaned toward the mirror as she fastened them in her earlobes. "The vegetable garden wasn't far away."

I changed the subject. "Kris is coming this morning. He should be here anytime."

"I know. He called yesterday and we talked."

Suddenly the fact that Kris had already asked Elena to do child care made more sense. "You talked him into it?"

"Ask yourself if I could talk Kris into anything. Would he have called for my opinion unless he was already well on his way? He wanted to make plans, but he wanted to be doubly sure his timing was good. He was afraid you might wait too long to ask."

Now I was relieved I'd called him. "Why did you tell him to come?"

"I want both of us in the barn this afternoon talking about the past. Mick's in favor. It makes sense visually. The two of us talking on film about everything that happened instead of me doing a voice-over. You've been on camera already. But if you do this, I think Kris ought to be here." She faced me so she could read my expression. "I'll understand if you don't want to, Robin. It's up to you."

"Why talk to me on camera in the barn and not in the house yesterday?"

"We lived on a ranch. We were outside most of the time, or at least I was. Mick has some of the old snapshots you took of me on the ranch horses and feeding the hogs. You know the way he combines elements to make his point. He'll intersperse them with whatever he gets today. Some of the photos are of you. I took those."

"And you kept them all these years?"

"It's the only past we have."

"You wanted to keep *those* memories alive?"

She didn't answer directly. "Did *you*?"

"No." My heart was racing. "Will this film really help you put the past behind you? Or is it making things worse?"

"I honestly don't know. But I think it's too late to stop."

"What if I say no?"

"I'll have to do it without you."

"Do what?"

She hesitated, as if she was forming the best answer. "Today I want to make it absolutely clear how bad things were for both of us. And maybe that will change something somewhere for somebody. Maybe if people know how often children are at the mercy of the strangers who are paid to protect them, they'll make sure they have the best possible systems in place."

"How long do you think their outrage will last? Ten minutes after they see the documentary? Then they'll move on to the next good cause."

"The film will stay around. And you know what? I'll always be a reminder. As long as people still want to hear me sing, they'll remember at least some of the things I've said."

"And that's how you want your fans to think of you? As a poorly treated foster kid?"

"It's just one of the ways they'll think of me, but if it's the only way?" She turned up her palm as if to say "so what?"

"What does Donny say?"

Suddenly she looked younger and vulnerable. "A lot, as always. And for the record, I won't be replacing him anytime soon."

"I'm glad."

"Yeah, me, too."

"I have to think about this."

"You have a little time. This morning we're filming behind the house where Cold Creek used to flow. Mick wants some footage with me, but I don't see why you need to be there."

"I'm not sure I understand why he's filming a creek that isn't there. It started to dry up when we lived here."

She didn't answer directly. "A metaphor? Anyway, part of the problem is the way the creek was managed. Jud dammed it for a livestock pond at the edge of the ranch. The creek is low up to that point, but it trickles to a stop after that. Measures could be taken to get it flowing through this property again."

"Too bad nobody did that in time for filming."

"He may go farther west to see if he can get some shots of the creek the way it used to. But a creek with no water will make its own kind of statement."

Knowing Mick, I could guess he'd get both shots and put them together as a disembodied voice—most likely Cecilia's—narrates local history.

I left her to finish preparing for the morning.

I didn't want to go with Cecilia to the creek. A dry creek bed so overgrown with weeds it blends into the surrounding landscape is a poor subject for photographs, and I already had a million of my sister in more interesting places. I knew where I did want to go instead, and I headed there now.

Twenty-five minutes later Kris found me standing in what had once been Betty's vegetable garden. While sad little citrus-tree skeletons now took up much of it, I could still picture it the way it had been.

Kris didn't say anything. He came up behind me and put his arms around my waist. I'd heard him pull up, and I'd glanced behind me to watch him get out, but I hadn't gone to greet him because I was struggling not to cry.

"I can't imagine you here," he said, before I could get the words out. "It feels haunted. Every inch of it. And you lived in this place, what, two years?"

"Just about." I covered his hands, but I didn't turn. "Thank you for coming."

"Nobody could keep me away."

I held his arms tightly around me. "We grew some of everything in this plot. It used to be more than an acre, no trees, and Jud sold our surplus at a neighbor's vegetable stand. In Virginia winter's a time to rest. Here winter was prime time, and even though workers came in to help during high season, mostly it was Betty and me. Whatever was left burned up in the hottest part of summer, but by the end of August we were back out here, cultivating the soil, and planting beans and cantaloupe, squash and pumpkins. There was always something to plant or pick, weed or spray. Never ending."

"What surprises me is that you still like gardening."

"When I lived here I liked being out of the house, and I learned to like watching things grow. I got home before Cecilia did because my school let out earlier. I would come out here to work and wait for her bus, and I always had a reason. Something needed to be done, and in the evening I had to work in the kitchen, so nobody really questioned me working outside in the afternoons."

"They expected you to do all that?"

"If our caseworkers questioned them they probably claimed it was good for us to work hard. They were 'building character.' I'm sure they had an entire repertoire of excuses. Too many kids don't feel needed. We knew how important we were to the ranch, and we got so much from it. Fresh, delicious food, a warm, happy place to live. Foster parents who only had our best interests in mind." The tears came suddenly, despite everything I'd done to prevent them.

Kris turned me to rest against him, and I cried against his chest. "That's what they told the authorities?" His voice sounded strained, as if he was afraid to let it out.

"They looked okay on paper," I said, when I could speak again. "Jud was the quintessential good old boy. Polite, funny, able to talk his way into—" I took a deep breath "—or out of anything. The house was run-down but sparkling. Betty didn't say much, but she always agreed with whatever Jud said. United front and all. They never fussed about having to go to meetings or training, never complained about the kids they took on. They talked about adding on to the house so they could take more, but that was just talk. Because they knew—" another deep breath "—they were lucky. They knew Cecilia and I weren't going to complain about the way we were treated. Because if we were removed, we would almost surely never see each other again."

"You've never really talked much about this before."

"What was there to say?"

"Plenty, I think."

"I just wanted to forget it." I stepped back so I could see his face.

Kris reached out and gently brushed my tears away. "It's part of who you are."

I took his hand and turned. "I'll show you the garden."

We did a quick tour, even though I knew he didn't really care about where the string beans and tomatoes had been planted. But explaining what we had grown and where gave me time to recover. We stopped at what had been the boundary farthest from the house.

"We had compost bins over here." I pointed to the corner where the rusted remains of posts that had held the fencing were still visible above ground. "One of my jobs was to fork it from one bin to the other so it would decompose faster. I took out what was decomposed and spread it as I went. If I waited too long, the pile got so tall I couldn't reach the top. So I did that two or three times a week. Sometimes Cecilia would help when she got home. If she wasn't too busy."

"What did she do the rest of the time?"

"She shoveled manure and brought some for the compost piles when she could. She fed the animals, cleaned their pens, gathered the eggs, groomed the horses." I realized I was standing stock-still, gazing into space. "Jud called her his 'little gal pal' because she worked with him most of the time. He used to brag about teaching her to be the perfect rancher's wife."

"This wasn't just about hard work, was it? The reason you were both so unhappy here?"

"He was a drunk and a bully. He used to laugh when he made Cecilia do chores she hated. He liked to say he was toughening her up, that by the time she was eighteen, nothing would get to her. If she complained he told her he'd get me to do it instead."

And then Kris said one of the nicest things he's ever said about my sister. "So she probably stopped complaining."

"I was terrified of the big animals. Especially Jud's boar and the bull. They were meaner than God intended because Jud made them that way. He liked to shock them with the cattle prod, just for fun."

"He's dead now?"

I hesitated a heartbeat or two. "Why, are you going to find him and finish him off?"

"I can't wrap my head around how this happened."

"Sometimes children die in foster care. It's more common than you think. And sometimes children thrive and bloom and get the new start they need. That's more common than people think, too. It's not a perfect system, and it's certainly an underfunded one. We got caught in the undertow."

"I'm not sure why you're here. Why can't Mick Bollard make that point some other way? Why put you through this?"

"Cecilia thinks it's necessary."

"She's not always right, Robin. You know that?"

If he'd said that last with any heat, I would have reacted. But he said it gently, and I knew he was worried, not angry.

"No, she's not always right." I thought about the way she had manipulated our caseworker to bring us here in the first place. Had Ichabod known what we would be in for with the Osburns? After she made her threat, had this been his own form of revenge?

And would I trade having her in my life then and now for a better place to live all those years ago?

"We're here now," I said. "*You're* here now. I'll get through this."

"Will she?"

I didn't know. But the next hours would be the test.

46

Robin

When I went into labor with Nik, I remember wishing I could turn back the clock and forget the whole thing. But it was too late by then to redo the past nine months and the night of enthusiastic sex that eventually propelled me to a hospital delivery room.

And now, somehow, it was too late to tell Cecilia I didn't want to explore the working section of the ranch, that I had finished facing our past together.

The problem? I love her too much to ask her to face it alone.

"We can do this once," Cecilia told Mick. "Just once." She looked pale, with a sickly greenish undertone. Even Wendy's best efforts with mineral powders and foundation hadn't made much of a difference. Cecilia also looked vulnerable, more like the teenager she'd been and, at the same time, somehow more like the old woman she would become.

"You can stop us anytime," Mick reminded her.

Mick wasn't pale. He was alert and wary, fidgeting, as if he was anxious to say something, but he wasn't sure what. I could tell he suspected that whatever he got today might be important.

He turned to me. "You're still willing to be on camera?"

I had dressed for it, although I was only wearing jeans and a fuchsia shirt I've always loved. Wendy had done *my* hair and makeup, too, but with restraint. I still looked like me.

He waited for my nod. "Then I thought we might start with a long shot of the two of you walking toward the barn from the front of the house. There won't be sound, so you can chat about anything. Just remember whatever you say won't be in the film. No big revelations, okay?"

I had learned so much from being part of the crew. I knew so much more about master shots, both moving and locked-off, medium and close shots, and the use of a servo zoom lens to bring subjects closer without the use of dollies and track. Our new camera operator had been placed right in our path in the bed of a pickup, which gave her stability and a great angle. Mick would use this footage to establish the scene and prepare the viewer for what was to come.

Cecilia and I glanced at each other, nothing more, but he seemed to take that as confirmation. He explained that Jerry would be waiting at the once-sturdy fence that surrounded the former corral. When we got there, whatever we decided to recount would begin.

Now Mick was checking notes as he spoke, more, I thought, to look unconcerned than for information. "I'm hoping you'll start or at least move toward what brought you both here. Before you move on to what it was like with this family."

Cecilia scuffed her boot in the dirt, back and forth until a ditch had formed. "And then?"

"We'll film in the barn."

She gave a short nod.

"It's safe?" I hadn't yet been inside.

"Siding's missing—that's obvious—but the structure is

safe enough. It seems to have been repaired more often than the house."

"Of course. The *animals* were valuable." Cecilia inclined her head, and she and I started our walk. The distance wasn't short, but we walked in silence. Halfway to the house we turned, as we had been instructed, and waited until we were signaled to start back. A viewer would think we had just come down the front steps, but actually doing so wasn't necessary.

By now we were, as he'd promised, out of earshot. Cecilia shifted her weight from one foot to the other. "How many times did we make this walk to the barn together?" She tossed a long curl over her shoulder. Florida humidity was taking its toll on her hair.

It wasn't a question that needed an answer.

Mick still hadn't signaled. He appeared to be consulting with the camera operator. She was proving to be talented and easy to work with, and Jerry was now free to set up more complex scenes.

"How honest are you going to be?" I asked when the silence stretched too long.

"About how we ended up here?"

"About that, about how cruel Jud was, about his drinking, about his threats…"

"Does it seem like a long time ago, or does it seem like yesterday?"

"I thought I'd shoved it so far away it would never see the light of day. But right now? Yesterday."

Mick made a spiraling motion with his finger, then he pointed. We turned and walked back toward the house, stopping every few yards and glancing back to see if he was happy. He finally gave a quick salute, to show we had reached the sweet spot. We waited again.

Cecilia smoothed the hem of her shirt into place. "I've

asked myself so many times why I let you become the center of my world. Haven't you? You needed me, but why did I need you?"

"Because until you met me, your world didn't have a center."

"I guess I could have saved myself a lot of time and asked you first."

"Did you come to a different conclusion?"

"Not really. I couldn't save Maribeth, but I thought maybe, if I tried really hard, I could save you."

"How'd that work out?"

"I don't know. Maybe I caused more problems than I fixed."

"Don't say that again."

Mick motioned us toward the pickup, and we began to walk, talking as we did.

"Mick asked me to refer to Jud as my foster father, not to mention his or Betty's names. You, too?"

"Legal issues. In case they want to crawl out of the woodwork and sue us or him."

"Anybody who cares enough can find out their names."

"Wouldn't that be just like Jud to reappear if he thought there was money in it?" I kept my voice light, but my stomach clenched. I glanced at Cecilia.

She wasn't smiling. "After we finish filming today I don't think even Jud would be willing to come out of hiding."

My stomach could clench no further. I wanted to find Kris among the bystanders, but even more, I didn't want to make this walk again because I had screwed up the first one by looking for him.

We got a thumbs-up as that shot ended. As instructed we continued to the corral. Once, the expanse had been surrounded by a sturdy three-rail fence that was perfectly capable of keeping larger livestock in place. Now there was no animal who couldn't plow through it with a nudge. Jud might have been lazy and mean, but he had realized the value of fences. He had been a master at keeping animals and humans in captivity.

We waited until Jerry finished his setup and gave us the go-ahead before we began to recount our past. Cecilia began. "You were only twelve when our caseworker left us here. Do you remember much about that day?"

"I remember being frightened. The only good part was that you were with me."

"I'm not ashamed to admit I made threats to keep us in the same home, and somebody took me seriously and pulled the right strings so we could stay together. After that our caseworker backed off and we rarely saw him, or the two who followed. Supervision was so minimal it was laughable. But I wasn't about to let anybody separate us. You were the only family I had."

I was impressed at the way she'd spun that, as if making threats meant very little. In fact, under the circumstances, threats sounded admirable. Cecilia was a pro.

I added my part. "I was a lot older before I finally realized how unusual it was that we'd been kept together. By then you were out of care and we *were* separated. You were in New York, but you took the bus all the way to my group home whenever you could, just to be sure I was okay."

"I wanted to see for myself."

"And every single time you told me if I needed to leave, I had a place to go."

Cecilia flashed a sad smile. "You made a good choice by not taking me up on it. It wouldn't have been fun. I was living with three other girls in a one-room Manhattan walk-up with junkies for neighbors. On the plus side, our mice were hospitable."

"I was lucky to have a safety net. It's not something most foster kids can say."

"Big sister." She wasn't smiling now. "It was my job to protect you."

"You protected me *here*, too."

"Yeah, but you know, if anything had happened to you, I wouldn't have been able to live with myself. I was protecting me, too."

"And there was a lot to protect me from."

She was looking straight ahead now, because I had just given her the perfect opening to talk about the ranch. "This was an awful place. Two years of hell, starting with the day we walked through the door."

"Our foster father showed us to our rooms. I'm not sure mine had ever been painted. It was at the opposite end of the hallway from yours. There were so many strange noises, I don't think I slept for a week. I was glad when the weather changed and it was hot enough to use the air conditioner to drown out everything else."

Cecilia was staring into the corral as if horses still galloped there. "He warned us we had to stay in our own rooms at night, no matter what. Something about needing to know where we were in case of fire."

We had developed a rhythm. It was my turn. "I didn't have time to unpack. Our foster mother took me down to the kitchen and told me what I would be required to do every day."

"And our foster father took me out to the barn and introduced me to the livestock. I got to know them well."

Cecilia had clearly tired of standing here talking. She began to circle the barn, and I walked beside her. Mick didn't stop us, and Jerry followed. These shots wouldn't be smooth. If these moments made it into the final documentary, this section would look exactly like what it was, cinema vérité. No fancy camera work, just candid revelations and a stab at finding the truth.

I spoke, since she didn't. Jerry was close enough that his mic would catch us. "I'd done a little cooking in our last home. It was fun there. Not fun here. There was no end to it. We started cooking at five in the morning and finished washing dishes around nine at night. If I had the energy, I finally did my homework."

"And you worked in the vegetable garden when you got home from school and on Saturdays. For hours."

"There's nothing left of the garden now, but back then being outside was better than inside, because you were out here, too. And I knew my jobs were nothing compared to yours."

We rounded the barn and walked along the north side, where the hog pen had been adjacent to the long wall.

Cecilia took up the conversation. "I was older and bigger, so…" She almost said Jud's name. I could hear it on the tip of her tongue, but she caught herself. "…our foster father made me the farm helper. All those people who think I've lived a pampered celebrity life? Get over it. I shoveled more sh—" she caught herself "—manure than they'll ever see." She listed some of the other things she'd done. "I didn't hate the animals, but I learned pretty fast not to get attached. Because… our foster father picked up on that, and those were the first animals to be sold or eaten."

"Which says all anyone needs to know about why you're a vegan."

"I grew to hate going into the hog pens, the chicken coop.

I knew if he was around, he would watch and cull my favorites."

"You liked working with the horses."

"Only because the bigger animals were safer from him. And I could pretend that at the end of the day I would jump on one and ride away and never have to see this place again."

I was remembering more than I wanted to, and the knot in my stomach was now a boulder, the way it had been during our two long years here. "We weren't allowed to complain."

Cecilia stopped and shook her head. "He made sure we didn't. His favorite way was telling me that he'd be glad to call our caseworker and ask to have us moved."

I repeated what was probably already clear and would likely be cut. "And if they did move us, we knew we would be separated."

She turned to me. "There were times when things got so bad, that seemed like a small enough price to pay, Robin. Didn't you think so more than once? Didn't you want to leave no matter what happened or where we went? But then he came up with a new twist. I could leave anytime I wanted, since I was the troublemaker, but of course there wouldn't be any reason for you to go."

This was new information. "He told you that?"

"He said he and…his wife would make sure you stayed here without me, that he'd make sure everybody knew I was the problem, the bad influence, and once I was gone, you would thrive."

"You never told me."

"It was bad enough that *I* had to worry about it."

We were quiet long enough that Mick stopped Jerry from filming and ambled over to put his arms around us both.

"How are you doing?"

I could feel the tension in Cecilia's body. She shifted away from him. "I want this over, Mick. Let's move inside."

He was hesitant, which surprised me. "I'm not sure that's really necessary. You may have said all you need to. You were overworked, intimidated—"

"I *haven't* said all I need to." She moved out from under his arm. "Let's go in. But get Jerry in place first. I'm only going to do this once."

Without a doubt now, I knew what was coming, even if I didn't want to know, had never wanted to know for certain. At fourteen, when I left the Osburn ranch, I might have been too young to understand, too uneducated, too sheltered by my sister. But through the years, when I've thought back on our time here, I've wondered. And now I knew.

Tears filled my eyes, and I put my hand on Cecilia's arm. "Don't! You don't have to."

She didn't answer. This once, I was not the one for whom speech was difficult.

Mick waved Jerry inside, and Cecilia started into the barn. Mick looked worried but also energized, as if he knew we were about to film something that would assure his backers there would be no reason to worry about ratings. Cecilia was going to make sure of it.

I followed her in, because where else would I go? I didn't look for Kris or Donny, although I hoped Donny would stay nearby.

Cecilia was already standing in the middle of the wide expanse, taking deep breaths. Shards of light streamed through gaps in the siding, the way light had never penetrated when we lived here. In my mind's eye I could see it the way it once had been, alive with animals who'd only had Cecilia to really care for them. Left to Jud, their lives would have been even more miserable.

I went to stand beside her, not to be on film but because she needed me. Mick waved to get our attention, looking more worried. "We're ready. But again—"

Cecilia sliced her hand through the air to cut him off. "We're ready, too."

We waited a moment, and then she turned to me. Jerry was already filming.

I took the lead. "Until now there was so much I didn't know. Not for sure anyway."

She knew exactly what I meant. "You wondered." It wasn't a question.

"Only when I was older. Only when I started to put things together. I just couldn't figure out why you would have…" Tears were running down her cheeks now. "But now I get it."

"I did everything I could to keep you from finding out what Jud was doing to me." His name was no longer secret. She had said it. Mick would remove if needed, but she didn't care.

I saw her hesitate, as if the next part was locked inside her. I couldn't let her suffer. How could I make Cecilia expose herself and what had happened when now I knew the worst?

I said the words for her. "He raped you. Here?"

She walked to the edge of a pool of light, jerky stilted steps so unlike the way she moves onstage. She gestured to the wall just feet from where the indoor part of the hog pen had extended. Hay had always been stacked there for the hogs and the horses.

Then she turned, her eyes still shining with tears, but her voice was steady when she spoke. "In the hay, if you can believe the cliché. Whenever he could get me alone out here. But the first time he raped me was inside the house. Maybe a week, two after we came to live here? He had to figure his angle, and that took some time. He had to figure out how he was going to cover what he was doing if I tried to tell anybody. He had to wait for it to get hot enough that it made sense to turn on the air conditioners."

I was crying now. "Cecilia…"

"He could reach my bedroom through the bathroom. He waited until…his wife was asleep. Her days were exhausting, and she slept like the dead, or so he said. Nobody could hear him…or me."

I put my hand over my mouth, afraid I would vomit.

"I always fought back. He liked that. But he was strong, and he told me nobody was ever going to believe me, that at most I'd be moved from the ranch. And later, when he realized how close you and I were, he said if I was moved, he would make sure *you* stayed behind because one sister was as good as the other."

I covered the few yards between us and hugged her. She put her arms around me, and we held each other, trembling and crying, until Donny and Kris found their way into our embrace and the filming stopped.

47

—

Kris

Robin fell asleep well past midnight. I didn't expect her to stay that way all night, but I thought she might for a while. Me? I needed fresh air, and I needed to walk, even if I couldn't go very far before the campground lights faded away. Staying close was fine with me. I needed to be nearby in case Robin woke up before I expected her to. I didn't want her to be alone tonight, and walking circles on the dirt road between campsites was better than nothing.

I slipped into sweatpants and sneakers, and covered my T-shirt with a light jacket. Earlier a thunderstorm had moved through, and while the sky was now cloud-free, the temperature had dropped, so the air was almost cool.

Under different circumstances I might find camping in Cold Creek appealing, but tonight all I could think about was getting Robin away forever. Unfortunately that wasn't going to happen immediately. Something was brewing for the end of next week. Even Mick didn't know what. After filming ended today Cecilia had announced that much. Apparently she made the arrangements herself, but as yet she's refusing to reveal details.

Keeping secrets is still a way of life for Robin's sister.

The camper door opened with a screech and closed with a metallic click. Once outside, I waited for a few moments, but Robin didn't wake up.

The campground lights were muted, certainly not bright enough for jogging. There were too many ruts in the road, and those ruts were now puddles. Once Robin told me that as a girl, in her happy foster home, she and Cecilia captured tadpoles from puddles that stagnated in a nearby vacant lot, hoping to watch them turn into frogs. Tonight, for the first time, I see how precious those carefree moments of normal childhood were for my wife, and why she had been so devoted to staying in touch with the Davises, who had given them to her.

And to Cecilia.

The distance between a nine-year-old and a thirteen-year-old stretches for miles. That Cecilia had taken the child Robin under her wing, cherished and protected her, taught her how to play, dress, laugh, even speak freely? How fortunate for all of us. But for Robin, being loved at last by another human being who continued to remain in her life despite every obstacle, a sister who watched over her, advised her and later adored Robin's children the way she had adored her? That has made all the difference in her life.

Why had it taken me so long to see clearly that somehow these two sadly broken children had healed each other and, in the healing, given the world something infinitely precious? Two intelligent, talented women who might have been lost in a system that tries, but too often fails, to protect and nurture children who have no one else.

Now I was face-to-face with the truth. And there was no doubt in my mind why I hadn't wanted to acknowledge it. The woman I loved had come close to not surviving her childhood. Without her sister she might have shriveled in her shell, become the desiccated cocoon-bound caterpillar, not the butterfly. And Cecilia was the most important reason Robin had learned to fly.

I had never wanted anyone else to be as important to Robin as I was. Right from the beginning I had been jealous of Cecilia. And it didn't take a lot to recognize that she had also been jealous of me. We had been locked in competition, but there had never been a need for it. Robin has enough love for everyone in her life, love she saved through the years and shared when each of us appeared.

On my second lap I was still mulling this over when I saw someone on the road in front of me. At first I couldn't make out who was approaching, but when she moved under one of the scattered lights, I realized Cecilia, like me, was hoping that the air and some exercise would finally help her sleep.

In a moment we were close enough to search each other's faces. "Robin's okay?" She spoke softly so she wouldn't wake those closest to where we stood.

"She's sleeping. The way you and I should be."

"That particular *should* is going to take a while." She managed the slightest of smiles, although it looked foreign on her drawn and shadowed face. She looked the way anyone would expect her to, exhausted, drained of emotion, wary.

"Months?" I asked.

"If I'm lucky."

"Donny?"

"He finally passed out. If a back rub goes on for hours, even the best of masseuses will eventually fall asleep. Hal and Ivan are under orders to leave me alone."

I nodded to the picnic area beyond us. "Sit awhile?"

"With you?" She smiled again, a little wider. "Why should this night be any stranger than the day that led up to it?"

The picnic area was well away from the campers. We found

a table that was sheltered by a massive live oak and, despite the rain, dry enough. I sat on the tabletop while Cecilia sat on the bench just below. No light filtered through the leaf canopy, although occasionally leftover raindrops seeped through and splattered my shoulders and head. I think we were both glad we didn't have to read the other's expression.

She lifted her hand toward the treetop. "My almost–adoptive family had a tree the size of this one in their backyard. They weren't the kind of people who like trees, but they kept that one, because cutting it down would have cost too much. No storm ever passed without a reminder I shouldn't stand under it when there was lightning nearby. So, of course, I stood there anyway. Every time."

"Rebelling?"

"You know what? I don't think so. I think by then I decided lightning was a quick, easy way to disappear. Poof. Gone. Just like that. I was a kid. I probably thought it would be like an alternate take on the *The Wizard of Oz*, lightning zapping me from one world to another, instead of a tornado. And by then I figured I was already living with the Wicked Witch and her family, so why not take a chance?"

I thought about that. "How did you do it? Become the person you are? I know Robin helped, the way you helped her. But with everything that happened to you, how did you get where you are today?"

"Where I am isn't everything it appears to be. *Who* I am isn't, either."

"Listen, you're preaching to the choir. Remember me? I've never been your greatest fan."

"True enough, and back atcha." If there was venom there, it wasn't audible.

I leaned back on my elbows and let the raindrops bathe my face. "But whether I wholeheartedly admire every little thing I notice when I'm with you or not, I'm also aware you are one fantastic piece of work, the whole package. Beautiful, talented, thoughtful—when it suits you."

Her laugh was throaty and, I thought, genuine. "It actually suits me more than you give me credit for."

"I think that's true."

"You're admitting you may have misjudged me a time or two?"

"More than that."

"Then as your reward I'll teach you a lesson about why some people survive terrible things and go on to flourish, at least more or less. Somebody loved them. Somewhere along the way somebody cared enough to stretch out a hand and help them along."

"That's it?" I asked when she stopped.

"Not quite. If the survivor is blessed with strength and some modicum of insight, then he or she may find the courage to keep moving through the bad times. It's all about percentages. How much bad. How much caring. How much strength and insight, not to mention mental health. But now I know I come from strong people, miners who risked their lives every single day to make a better life for the families who counted on them. Plus the women who loved them and did whatever they could to help everyone survive. I was given a talent and the ambition to use it. And those horrible years convinced me there was nothing left to lose, so why not plunge in headfirst and take whatever chance presented itself?"

She was silent a long time before I spoke. "I am so sorry. About everything that happened at the ranch."

"Yeah, back at the ranch."

"You protected Robin. I don't know how I can find words to tell you how much I owe you for that."

"Well, I didn't do it for you, Kris."

I punched her lightly on the shoulder. "But I reaped the benefit. And our kids did, too."

"At the time I wasn't looking into the future. Not really. I just knew I couldn't cope if Jud hurt Robin, too. I would have done anything to keep that from happening. She was the only good thing in my life."

"Cecilia... I know you're the original self-made woman, but you're going to get some help with this, aren't you?"

"Now that it's out in the open? It's not like I've repressed anything that bastard did to me. I haven't forgotten one single violation. It's with me every minute of every day."

"So maybe now it's time to start forgetting. The right person might help you."

"Are you and Donny in cahoots?"

Everything would change the moment I opened my mouth, but it was too late now to let that stop me. "No, but maybe we should be. Because, you know, as hard as this is for me to admit, we *both* love you. And in the same way you did everything to protect Robin, we both want to protect and help you."

I heard her take a deep, shattered breath. "I don't know if I deserve anybody's love."

"There is no question you do."

"You *are* in cahoots."

I slipped down to the bench and put my arm around her. "You're too close to everything that happened here. Haven't you done what you need to in Cold Creek? Isn't it time to call this place quits forever?"

"No."

"More secrets?"

"Closure."

She was shivering. I stripped off my jacket and dropped it

over her shoulders. Then I pulled her closer. She came willingly. Forever after our relationship would be different, and both of us knew it.

"Then we have to stay, because you do need closure," I said.

"Robin does, too."

"Will this do it? Whatever you have planned?"

"It's the kind of grand gesture I like best." She looked up at me as if deciding whether to elaborate. In the end she did. "I won't need a lawyer, Kris, but it will be good to have one present when the grand gesture is revealed. Just in case. I'm glad you'll be with me and Robin."

"What are you planning?"

Her eyes glistened, and I wasn't sure the sheen was tears or excitement.

"I'm going to burn the place down," she said.

I was immediately appalled. "You can't do that."

"But I can, Kris. Because these days I own every square inch of the Osburn ranch."

48

—

Robin

Nobody burns down a house without months of preparation. Cecilia has been planning this moment since she and Mick began negotiations. Even before the accident and before I signed on to take photos. But knowing my sister, one way or the other she would have made sure I was here to see it.

Now we were on the sidelines watching the preparations for a training burn, but she had been busy all morning, greeting firefighters, discussing details with the training instructor, Randy, and his team, conferencing with Mick about where the film crew could stand and how close they were allowed to get. I had been busy taking photographs. This was our first chance to speak privately.

Ten days had passed since we filmed inside the barn. Kris and I had gone home the next day, and Cecilia and Donny had headed for New York.

I stayed in Virginia three days; then, with Nik in tow, I flew to California to take photos of Mick and his editors at work as they sorted through more archival footage and went over the hours of live film.

Nik had his chance to ask questions of everyone involved, but also to talk with some of Cecilia's people about their jobs.

He also got heavy-duty tutoring from Fiona on how to use *my* smartphone to make quality videos, as well as advice about a few add-ons to make that happen. I'm not sure which impressed him more, the sweet allure of making his own films or Fiona herself. I do know that the basic cell phone Kris bought him will be another technology relic after his next birthday.

Nik had been thrilled to accompany me, and we'd had the kinds of great conversations we might not have again during his adolescence.

Since then I'd only seen Cecilia for a few minutes on the day Nik and I left California. I know that she and Gizzie have spent the two days between then and now working on more music for the documentary. Mick says what he's heard so far is well beyond his highest expectations.

At the moment, clad in light sweaters and jeans, we are out of the fray. Beyond us Cold Creek's fire department and several departments from nearby townships have gathered for their preentry briefing. The Osburn house and barn will be cinders and smoke by evening, and in the process, more than a dozen of the firefighters will receive training to sharpen their skills.

"The paperwork was mind-boggling, but my business manager handled most of it," Cecilia said.

"You could have lit a match and walked away."

"I think they call that arson. And why not make something good come from this? To do it right we had multiple inspections. We had to find and remove asbestos, make sure the house was structurally sound."

"Structurally sound so they can burn it down?"

"They can't have trainees falling through rotting floors after a fire's been set. Between my people and theirs we had to disconnect utilities, check for things like fuel tanks, historical significance. They had to shore up the porch, nail plywood over windows so the burn will progress the way they want, chop holes in the attic roof to—"

"To match the ones Mother Nature provided?" I remembered our morning in the house together. "Is that what happened to the wallpaper and the flooring?"

"Wallpaper can catch fire and cause a flashover. Smoke from vinyl floors is polluting. You wouldn't believe the licenses and permits. My business manager threatened to quit about halfway through."

We were talking logistics, but I still wanted to know something more important. "Why, CeCe? Before all this talk of burning the place down, you bought the property. You've had it for a couple of years? Why?"

She took her time. I thought she was considering her answer, because maybe she didn't really know. "So many reasons," she said at last. "None of them sensible except that I paid a bargain price and with some work on the irrigation system, the land will be valuable someday."

"I'm sorry, but I'm sure you didn't buy it as an investment."

"An emotional investment, I guess. This time I want to be the one who decides what goes on here."

"And burning down the house and barn accomplishes that?"

"Some of it."

"You could have dismantled the buildings and hauled them away."

"Imagine what a load like that would do to a landfill?"

I listened as she rattled on, but I thought there was more to it than a concern for the environment. When she finished, I said so.

"You didn't want to imagine the house or barn in a landfill, rotting slowly and taking up space in your heart, did you? You wanted this whole episode finished. Purified by fire."

She turned to look at me. "You're right. I'm going to build a residential facility for girls on this land, and I don't want evil spirits haunting it. I have a team working on the concept. Vivian refuses to leave her position at CFF, but she's on board to help us find the best people to create a similar model here."

I hadn't suspected, but I wasn't exactly stunned. How better to make the ranch come alive? "And you thought of this when? You never said a word."

"I got the idea when we were filming. I can't adopt all the Hayleys in the world, but I can help some of them move on to a healthier adulthood. I'm living proof we never completely transcend our beginnings, but the more help we have, the better our chances."

I slung my arm over her shoulders. "I honestly thought after today we would be done with this place forever."

"We'll never be done with it, Robin. You know that."

Of course she was right.

The firefighters, mostly young, muscular and male, wearing identical black T-shirts emblazoned with the name of their company and yellow turnout pants held up with suspenders, were horsing around while they waited for the meeting to begin. One of them winked at Cecilia. I watched her wink back as one of the two women, who was sitting beside him, punched him in the arm.

"Admirers everywhere," I said.

"My plan will take years to get up and running. I thought burning down the house and barn was bad, but building something new will be a thousand times worse. I'm determined to get this right."

"That's going to be the end of the documentary, isn't it? You announcing this?"

"As the barn burns to the ground. Mick knows. He's beside himself with joy."

"Everyone seems to know about this but me."

"Just Mick, Vivian, a few experts in the field who are advising me."

"Donny?"

"Of course."

Cecilia was widening the circle of people she loved and trusted. In the long run an expanded circle would be good for both of us. I always worried about her isolation, if you can call having millions of fans who love you isolation. I felt responsible for my sister, as she felt responsible for me. Too responsible.

Both of us had sacrificed too much.

"I wanted to tell you in person," she said, "but I thought you needed a little time first to absorb everything we've gone through these last few months." She swept her hand in front of her. "Are we better off? Am I crazy to think I can bring laughter and love to this place after everything that happened here?"

I had been waiting for the right moment to tell her something myself, and now I had my opening.

"After I went home this last time I wrote Betty Osburn."

I had surprised her. She was speechless, then angry. "Why would you do that?"

"I wanted to tell her what Jud did to you. I wanted to know if it was old news or if she'd known all along."

"Why do you care?"

"Maybe I wanted to believe she was better than he was. I don't know why. Maybe I wanted to believe in spite of all her other faults she wouldn't have let him. If she knew."

"And you think you can believe *anything* she says?"

"The letter came back. Somebody scribbled 'deceased' on the envelope."

"So. She's dead."

"I made sure. I found her obituary on the internet. She died in January."

Cecilia isn't as hard-hearted as she lets on. She can get misty-eyed over puppies and sunsets, but she wasn't misty-eyed now. "Well, that's one less Christmas card to toss next year."

I didn't tell her I had never *tossed* Betty's cards. Instead I filed them in my cubbyhole of an office, where no one else would ever stumble on them. And I didn't tell her that after I learned Betty was dead, I finally went back, opened and read them all.

As it turns out, I hadn't needed to read more than one. Each had been identical. One word, followed by her name.

Remember.
Betty.

Kris was like a little boy, watching everything the firefighters did, even following from a respectful distance as they hauled in straw bales and wood palettes to start fires in each room. I was beginning to suspect my husband had a secret desire to give up the practice of law and start putting out a completely different type of fire.

He repeated what I already knew, but I loved his enthusiasm.

"They could burn down the whole place in less than an hour," he said, as if he would love to see that, "but there wouldn't be much training in it. So that's why they set the fires one at a time, room by room, put them out, bring in a new group, start all over. Each one presents a different set of problems. Not to mention stairwells, attics. At the end they set one more and let it catch for good. After that they'll burn down the barn." He pointed toward the house. "That backhoe over there is standing by to push the debris in on itself so they don't start any unintentional fires."

I couldn't wait for this day to end. The whole scene was a photographer's dream, but for me, being here was closer to a nightmare. I just wanted to finish and go back to Virginia.

The firefighters were donning their turnout jackets, reflective tape glistening in the sunlight. Some already had on helmets and masks, oxygen tanks strapped to their backs, boots and gloves. I could no longer tell the women from the men.

"We have to stay a hundred feet away," he said. "Cecilia can go a little closer if she wants. They have extra protective gear if she decides to."

"We'll see what Donny thinks about that." I saw the two of them off to one side talking, but the conversation didn't look like an argument. Donny was too smart to protest for long. They might be falling in love or already there, but Cecilia was still her own woman and always would be.

"Let's get lunch and find a place to watch," he said. "Before anything big happens."

I already had photos of the firefighters suiting up, of their work inside, their strategy and training meeting, of the interior diagrams perched on an easel with Randy pointing out where the exercise would begin. Betty's parlor had been chosen. Some part of me thought I should be sad, but Betty's dreams went up in smoke a long time ago.

"You get the lunches," I said. "I'll find a place where I can take some good shots if there are any to be had in the next half hour."

He left for the taco truck Cecilia had reserved. As a thank-you she wanted to feed everyone on the property, and the truck was the easiest way. I scouted for a good spot to sit and watch, but also to launch myself and my camera if the occasion called for it.

Kris returned with two boxed lunches and a tarp. He spread the tarp under the shadow cast by an evergreen, where we could see what was happening beyond us.

He opened the first box to show me three assorted tacos, guacamole salad and a luscious-looking brownie before handing it to me. "You and Cecilia looked like you were having an important conversation."

"I asked her why she bought the property." I hesitated. "Then I told her Betty Osburn is dead."

Kris looked up from his own box. "Your foster mother?"

"The woman who lived here." The word *mother* had never seemed appropriate.

"How did you find out?"

I took my time squeezing a packet of hot sauce on a bean and cheese taco. "After we moved to Meadow Branch she began sending me Christmas cards. I didn't open them."

"Do you think it was wise not to find out why she had gotten back in touch?"

"I didn't want to know." Since Kris always wants the facts, I could see that was hard for him to understand.

"How did she get our address?"

I shrugged, because I didn't have a clue. "The internet? A private investigator? It couldn't have been easy."

"Do you think she wanted to connect? To apologize in her own way?"

"Betty wasn't the kind of person who apologizes."

"Maybe she wanted to tell you she'd finally heard from or about her husband. If she did, wouldn't it be good for Cecilia to know where he is?"

Kris was still thinking like a lawyer. Nothing but more facts would make sense to him.

"If he was still alive Jud would be in his late seventies, but even back then he had life-threatening health issues. Cecilia will have to deal with his ghost, but not the flesh and blood man."

"It's always sounded odd to me that he just disappeared the way he did. Wasn't the ranch worth enough to hang on until his wife finally decided to divorce him? You said they fought all the time."

"He wasn't a good rancher. He let things go if they were too hard to keep up with. He spent whatever cash they took in on himself or his women. That's one of the things he and Betty used to fight about. The ranch was deeply in debt. Cecilia would know how deep, since she kept the books." I took a bite of taco and chewed awhile before I added, "But I'm guessing he waited until he thought nothing more was coming his way except trouble. Then he took off."

"So you woke up one morning, and he was gone?"

I made myself swallow, although it took effort. "He walked away late on a Saturday afternoon. He left a note saying he wasn't coming back and didn't care what Betty did with the ranch or herself. And that was that."

Kris was frowning. "He just drove off forever? Was there a fight first?"

I opened the water bottle that had come with my lunch and took a big swig, an unnecessarily big one because I was figuring out what to say.

When I couldn't drink any more I answered. "Not a fight I witnessed, no. In fact Betty and I were at Southern States buying fertilizer for the garden. There was a waitress at the diner—Lupita, I think her name was—somebody he flirted with whenever he went into town, although I guess *flirt* doesn't quite cover it. She was from somewhere in Latin America—I'm not sure where—but I do know Betty despised her. Betty used to say the guy who ran the diner paid Lupita under the table and she was probably here illegally. There were a lot of migrant workers in the area. She may have come to town with one of them, then split up."

"Why does she figure in?"

"Because she left town the same day Jud did. It seemed obvious they'd gone off together. In fact Jud's old farm truck was parked up by the main road. Betty found it there the next morning. It looked like he'd used it to get that far, then Lupita had picked him up in her own car and off they went."

"And nobody ever heard from either of them again?"

"Why would they?"

"Because he sounds like the kind of guy who wouldn't let go easily. Seems like he'd have wanted to be sure there was nothing coming his way after the sale."

"He probably figured by the time he hired an attorney—I hear they don't come cheap—" he smiled, and I managed to smile back "—and fought with Betty in court, not a thing would have been left. If there was anything to start with."

"And while this was all going on, you and Cecilia had to worry about your own futures. I don't know how either of you made it."

"I think we both know Cecilia would rather have worried about her future than about Jud."

Kris put his hand on my knee and waited for me to look him in the eye. He asked the question I had known he eventually would. "He never touched you?"

"He tried." I gathered myself to finish. "Once. Jud always scared me, so I tried to stay out of the house if he was in there alone. But that day I had to go in to get something. I didn't know he was there, but he was in the kitchen, already drinking hard, although it was only early afternoon, and when I came in he grabbed me. I pushed him away and before he could try again, Betty came inside and slammed the back door."

His expression darkened. "I wish he *were* alive."

"I was able to get away, Kris. I thought he was just drunk that day, but now I know it would have been a matter of time. Luckily he walked out not long after. Even though that changed everything for me, I was so glad to see him go."

"Does Cecilia know?"

"She doesn't need to. She did everything she could to protect me. And now she's going to extend her protection to other girls like us." As we ate our lunch I told him about Cecilia's plans for the ranch.

"Those are some good photos." The afternoon sun was sinking toward the horizon when Mick handed back my camera. I'd given him a peek at several shots of the burning house that I was especially pleased with. I was looking forward to moving them to my computer screen for better viewing.

We were standing well back from the barn, which was about to be consumed by fire. The house where I had spent two miserable years of my life was now a smoldering heap. Jerry was about fifty yards away filming the barn as the firefighters moved in and out, but I had gotten all the photos I needed for a few minutes. Now I wanted to simply stand and wait.

Mick had other ideas. "We haven't really talked about what Cecilia said in the barn that day."

"I'm glad Fifi wasn't there to hear it. But she'll see that segment on the film. If Cecilia decides to let you use it."

"She's courageous in so many ways. I feel honored I've had the chance to share all this with her. And with you."

"Thank you for taking a chance on me. And for helping me get back on my feet professionally."

"We'll work together again. Or maybe you'll turn into my greatest rival. You're still planning to explore making films?"

"I'm going to see where the winds take me, but at best I'll be good enough to stand in your shadow."

He laughed, kissed me on the cheek, then went to talk to Jerry, who in a few minutes would film my sister, the blaze as her background, telling the camera her plans to establish a residential facility here.

"He's half in love with you," Cecilia said.

I hadn't realized she had come up behind us. We threaded our arms around each other's waists and stared at the barn, which would soon be no more.

"I have the man I want," I said.

"Did Kris tell you that we established a truce?"

"He said you're on your way to being friends. Same thing?"

"We agreed to stop vying for your love and attention."

I hugged her closer. "How do you feel now that burning down the house is a fait accompli?"

"I can't say until the barn is gone, too."

It was going to happen fast, which was why Mick was getting ready for Cecilia's announcement. "Kris told me there weren't going to be many teaching moments here. They plan to set the fire and get out immediately. It's a big barn. It's going to be a big fire."

"It can't happen fast enough."

Shouts interrupted whatever else she'd intended, followed by three loud blasts from an air horn. I knew from watching the house go up in flames that this was the signal to be sure everyone inside had evacuated.

We watched someone count as people emerged, then check a list. From what I could tell at this distance, everyone seemed to be accounted for.

Donny came to join us, and Kris followed his lead. In a moment the four of us were standing together, woven together as a unit.

Smoke curled out of the spaces where siding had been stripped or torn away. We stood in silence for a few minutes until flames followed the smoke's path. They licked and curled around boards, darting back and forth, and rising higher as we watched.

Donny spoke at last. "'In each moment the fire rages, it will burn away a hundred veils. And carry you a thousand steps toward your goal.'"

"What's that from?" Cecilia asked.

"Rumi, thirteenth century. Retooled for this moment."

I could feel Cecilia pull away just far enough to rest her head on his shoulder. "Thank you."

The fire was catching now. We were standing a good distance away, but I could already feel the heat. Kris was right—the barn would catch quickly, and soon be a bad memory. I wondered how far in the distance the smoke or even the flames would be seen.

In a moment Mick would signal for Cecilia. He would film several takes of her announcement against the backdrop of the fire. She had given him the perfect ending, so I knew he had to be thrilled. I planned to take my own photos. My camera was ready to go, the strap slung over my shoulder.

Cecilia held out her hand, and we left Kris and Donny where they could stand and watch together. We walked a short distance before she turned again to watch the flames lick higher and smoke pour from every crack, spiraling toward the roof.

She was still gripping my hand when the barn seemed to explode and fire shot in all directions. I could feel a shudder go through her. "Donny wanted to put fireworks in the loft so they would go off when the fire reached them, but Randy said it wouldn't be dark enough to see much of anything, and he promised the barn going up in flames would be enough of a spectacle. He was right."

"Donny understands what this means to you."

"Donny understands everything." Before I could ask what she meant, she changed the subject. "You asked earlier why I wanted to burn the house and barn? Why I didn't just bring in a wrecking company and cart them both away?"

I remembered our earlier conversation. "The purifying effects of fire."

"Maybe the ranch will be purified. I hope so. But the truth? Fire is the only fitting goodbye for Judson Osburn. Because I know for a fact he's already in hell." She turned to meet my eyes, and she didn't blink. "I sent him there."

49

—

Cecilia

The stars igniting the night sky are so thick the heavens seem engulfed in flame, but for a while I'll probably see fire everywhere. Hours have passed since we returned to the campground for a goodbye barbecue. We had ribs and burgers for the meat eaters, and platters of grilled vegetables for the vegetarians. Afterward I tried to sleep, but images of the house and barn collapsing into embers filled my mind, and sleep wasn't going to come easily for a long, long time.

Sleeping would be difficult for another reason. Embossed over those images was Robin's face at the instant I told her that I had personally consigned Jud to the flames of hell.

So right now, instead of sleeping like I should be, I'm walking in circles, the way I did the night Kris and I met last week. With too many practice laps behind me, navigating the campground path in the dark is now mindless exercise. I know the location of every root and shrub.

Hal and Ivan didn't accompany us on this leg. Not until this morning when I showed up at the ranch did anyone local, other than the fire chief, know who the property belonged to. Then, between Donny, Kris and a host of hunky firefighters, I felt perfectly safe. I posed for selfies with everyone, and in return they all promised not to tell friends and family I'd been there until I was in the air tomorrow, heading back to California.

Robin and I didn't have even a moment to talk about what I said. Immediately afterward Mick signaled me to get into position to film my announcement. I was just as glad, because I had no intention of elaborating, which is probably why I timed it the way I did. If she quizzed me tomorrow I would tell her the truth. I was certain hell was where Jud had gone after everything he did to me.

I'm not going to burden her with the *whole* truth.

I'm not sure why I said as much as I did, except that watching the barn go up in flames, I had known, at last, that if any evidence of Jud's last day at the ranch had lingered, it was finally, irrevocably consigned to ashes. I'd felt freer than I had in a long time—from the law, if not from guilt.

I was passing Robin's camper on my second lap when I realized her rental car was missing. I stopped, wondering if I should knock. Someone inside was snoring intermittently, and since Robin rarely does, I knew Kris must be inside sleeping.

But unless someone had stolen their car, my sister was not.

I knew where she had probably gone, although why escaped me. Had she, like me, stared too long at the ceiling of her camper and thought about what we had done today? Had she decided she needed to go back to the ranch to assure herself that the barn and house really were gone, that the rubble, still glowing and billowing smoke, had now, hours later, been reduced to ashes?

Had she needed to go back to consider what I had said and how she should respond tomorrow?

Now I wanted to see those ashes, too. While it made no sense, I realized I had to see them before the debris cooled so it could be carted away to a landfill. Randy had assured me the department would let the fire burn as hot and long as necessary to reduce the barn to cinders. The day had been perfect for the training burn—cool, with no wind. Rain was expected in the morning, and if embers lingered, the rain would help put them to rest. Before that happened I wanted to see for myself how much remained.

A full moon and a cloudless sky would help. I would get the reassurance I needed, find my sister and make certain she was all right.

Wendy's camper, shared with Starla, was located at the outskirts of the campground, and when I'd walked by a few minutes ago, I had heard them talking. They were both hyped up, plus I was pretty sure they were sharing a bottle of wine or something stronger. Rather than try to silently back the rental car out of my parking space without waking Donny, I tapped on their door, and when Wendy answered, I explained what I needed. In a moment I had her keys and a promise that no, she wouldn't tell anybody I'd gone back to the ranch unless I was gone too long.

We settled on two hours. I was just as glad to have a little backup.

Ten minutes later I crossed the cattle guard. I was immediately struck by how barren the landscape seemed in the moonlight. No house hugged the horizon in front of me, and to the west, no barn. Trees remained, and in areas farther away from the building sites, thick underbrush stood ready to take over the land. But the history of generations of Betty's family had been wiped away.

When I bought the property, returning the land to wilderness was my only plan. I had hoped the ground would cleanse itself. Leave any piece of land alone long enough in Florida—a scenario that developers disapprove of—and subtropical vegetation will spring to life, followed quickly by the animals and reptiles who inhabit it. My new plan is so much better, but now, as I thought about it, I decided we should leave acres of green space to encourage native plants and wildlife. All living things should be allowed to flourish on this ranch. New beginnings.

The fire trucks and other heavy equipment had left even more ruts in the sandy soil, so I drove slowly. My headlights swept the road in front and a short distance to each side, but I didn't see Robin's car until I had nearly passed it. I braked and opened my door without bothering to pull over.

Outside the car I searched for Robin herself. She wasn't hard to spot. A flashlight glowed softly in the darkness thirty yards to my left. I saw her standing where she had spent so much time in our years here. At the back of Betty's garden.

I picked my way toward her, watching carefully so I didn't stumble. I had a flashlight, too. We'd each been given one to help us find our way to the bathhouse at night.

I was a few feet away before I spoke. By then I could see she had a shovel in her hand, a small one like seasoned campers use to dig drainage ditches around their tents.

I gestured to the ground where she'd been working. "Planning to take home some old compost?"

She didn't answer. She straightened and waited for me to say more.

"We used to dig for worms after it rained, remember? You'd have more luck tonight if the soil was wet."

She didn't smile. "I found what I came for."

I looked beyond her, to the hole she'd dug, but I couldn't see inside. "Am I wrong? Isn't that where the compost pile used to be?"

"CeCe, it's time to tell me what you remember about the day Jud disappeared."

I recalled the days when conversation had been painfully

difficult for her. I would sit on her bed at night, paging through simple books and cajoling her to read to me. I had believed she needed to hear and accept the sound of her own voice. Now I was almost sorry my efforts and those of others had worked so well.

"There's no statute of limitations on murder." I cleared my throat, and not because smoke still drifted from the direction of the barn and all the animal pens that had surrounded it.

"I know."

"You don't need to hear things you might be forced to repeat someday."

"I have to hear them."

Moonlight puddled on Robin's bare arms and cheeks, and as I considered, she swatted a mosquito. I wondered what other predators lurked in the darkness. From a distance on one of my walks I had seen a snake, possibly a rattler, but more likely a garter snake. There were armadillos, raccoons, coyotes and more. When we lived here we knew better than to wander outside at night.

"We don't have to do this," I said. "Jud disappeared. That's all anybody ever needs to know. As the locals say he up and left, and nobody cared. The story has stood all these years."

"It may stand forever, but not between us."

She wasn't going to back down, and I realized I really didn't want her to. We had talked about purification. Telling the truth about that day had to be a part of it. Robin had realized that before I did. Or maybe I'd realized it, too, and that was why I said what I did while the barn was burning to the ground.

Her words were a command. "Start at the beginning."

I closed my eyes. "The day Jud disappeared, we were working in the hog pen…"

The weather that May day had been scalding hot, and even

though the sun was on its way down, working outdoors was still miserable. Despite that, as soon as I got home from high school I changed into jeans and a long-sleeved shirt. When I was at the ranch I had learned not to dress appropriately for the weather. Jud celebrated shorts and halter tops as excuses to molest me. If I dressed in skimpy clothing, it was clear I was trying to seduce him. Women liked to pretend they didn't want sex, but they always gave clues.

Of course for Jud, everything I did was a clue. My only protection was staying away from him, and that wasn't always possible.

If nothing else, Jud was methodical. When he was able to pin me down he always used condoms. The one outcome he didn't want was a baby, because then what he had done to me would become public knowledge. And no matter how hard he tried to insist that I had seduced him, nobody would look favorably on a foster father impregnating a girl in his care.

I opened my eyes, because I didn't like the images I saw. "Jud's boar had knocked out several of the two-by-sixes at the bottom of his pen. I doubt you remember. Jud used cattle panels, cheaper than hog panels, but they weren't as low to the ground, so he nailed boards along the bottom."

"He used to torment that boar," Robin said. "All the animals. He was a sadist."

"That and more."

Jud had decided to remove all the rotting boards at the bottom and put in new ones so the next litter of piglets wouldn't escape. The hogs were always penned in the same wide area up against the barn, fenced off from each other with partitions. The boar's area was beside the newly weaned sows, to keep him interested. Jud loved to mate his animals, and the more violent the process, the better he liked it.

There was a smaller area inside the barn where the boar

could get out of the sun, and Jud had poked him with the cattle prod enough times to get him inside so he could pen him there with a makeshift gate. The gate was just another section of cattle fencing wired to a wooden post reinforced by a metal one and fastened with a rope looped over another reinforced post on the other side. He had done the same with the sows, herding them into their area. One of the metal posts had rusted, and he had replaced it earlier, tossing the old one in the pen before he moved the hogs.

Robin was waiting for me to continue. I picked up where I had left off.

"I'd removed the partitions in the outside pen and cleared everything out except the old straw. While I did that Jud sawed up new boards. The hogs were upset at being penned into smaller enclosures, more upset than usual. The boar kept throwing himself against the gate that separated him from us. He hated Jud, and Jud had been free with the prod to get him into the barn that day. But I think what upset the boar most was the way Jud had used the prod on the sows."

"He used that prod whenever he could find an excuse."

He had used it on me, too, the first time I tried to fight him off in the barn, and he had threatened to continue every time he came after me. That was more detail than I wanted Robin to know, but tears clogged my throat, and I took a few moments to recover.

"Afterward we were going to shovel out the old straw and put in new. I hauled bales to one corner to spread when we finished, and I'd already snipped the twine. I was hopeful Jud would be too tired and hot to try anything with me that day. Plus I had decided if he did, I would warn him I was going to report him. I was going to be free soon, anyway, finished forever with high school and foster care, and you and I had nothing to lose. Even if nobody believed me, they would still be forced to find you a different place to live once they cut me loose. The agency wouldn't risk the possibility I was telling the truth."

"Did…he… Did you tell him?"

"When we were almost finished he came up behind me as I was reaching for one of the new boards, and he grabbed my breasts. I could feel his erection, and I knew what was coming. I whirled and slapped him. He laughed because violence excited him. I backed away and almost tripped over the metal pole he'd discarded. I told him what I just told you. I told him if he left me alone, you and I would tell the caseworker you had to go somewhere else, but not why. But if he tried anything with me ever again…"

I took a deep breath and looked beyond her, because that was easier. "And that's when he told me that he knew I'd been embezzling money from the ranch, Robin. That the new bank had called about that account I'd opened, some technicality I had overlooked. In response he did some checking. The awful thing? He wasn't upset—he was delighted. Because suddenly he had something new to hold over my head other than you and me wanting to stay together. So he said if I reported him, he would pretend he had just discovered what I did and he would report me to the sheriff."

"Oh, CeCe…"

"That was nothing. Because next?" I took a deep breath. "Next he said if I just left quietly and left you right where you were, he wouldn't turn me in. I could give back the money, leave you here where he…could keep you happy, and take off. He said he was sure you wouldn't mind, since if you made a fuss he'd report the theft and they would go looking for me. But in the meantime he wanted me ready and willing…."

I realized Robin was crying. I stepped forward and wiped away her tears with my fingertips. "He came after me again.

I lost it. I picked up the pole and slammed it against his shoulder. The pole was heavy and unwieldy, but I hit him as hard as I could. He was stunned, probably mostly because I'd dared to fight back after he'd outlined what he thought was a foolproof plan.

"For a moment he didn't move. He reached up and felt his shoulder, and it must have really hurt, or maybe it was broken, because he made an awful sound and started toward me. By then I was in a rage, thinking about what he planned to do. The second time I swung at his head. He couldn't protect himself because he still had his hand clamped over his shoulder. He tried to duck, but I caught the side of his face. He fell to the ground and tried to roll away. I went after him and hit him once more. I was beyond furious. I wanted to kill him, to finally get back at him for everything he had done. He stopped trying to get away and just lay on the ground as still as a stone."

Robin didn't say anything, but what could she say?

I waited until I could speak again. My voice shook, but I pushed on. "When he didn't move for probably a minute, I stooped and felt for his pulse. I was shaking so hard, and my hands were so sweaty I thought I just wasn't feeling for it in the right place. I tried his wrist, his neck. And then I realized I must have killed him."

"Oh, Cece..."

I had to finish. "I didn't know what to do. I knew I had to find you, and we had to get out of there. Even if I left on my own, this whole thing would blow back on you, and I couldn't let that happen. I wasn't thinking clearly, but I had a dead man at my feet, in the middle of an empty hog pen. So somehow I managed to drag and roll his body to the corner where I'd piled the straw, found a tarp in the barn and covered him. Then I forked some of the fresh straw on top of the tarp. Jud was suddenly invisible, like he had never existed. There was blood on the ground where I'd hit him, but not much, not as much as I would have expected. I managed to turn over the old straw so the blood wasn't visible. It was the best I could do."

Robin was trembling. Even in the moonlight I could see that. "You went to look for *me*?"

"You and Betty were off somewhere in the good truck. You told me later you were at Southern States. But at that point I didn't know where you were or how much longer you would be gone. I just knew I had to do something. I was frantic. Then I remembered Jud had been in a black mood when I got home, because Lupita, his favorite waitress at the Blue Heron, was leaving town that day. He said the diner's owner had told him, and Jud was furious. That's probably why he was crueler than usual to the animals."

"So you forged a note from Jud that he was leaving town and left it for Betty to find. And you drove the farm pickup to the crossroads and left it there, like he had gone off with that waitress. You walked back?"

I was glad I hadn't had to recount that part. "For years I've wondered how I managed to come up with any kind of plan on the spur of the moment. But I was desperate, and I didn't see any choice. The trip back from the crossroads took almost an hour. And the whole time I had to slink through woods and disappear into heavy brush if I heard a car, so nobody would see me. The whole time I was just waiting for the sheriff to roar by on his way to the ranch. I was sure Betty would figure out the truth, find Jud's body under the straw, have me arrested.... I was sure nobody would believe me when I said he'd molested me. I'd already lied about the caseworker."

"What happened next?"

"I've never been sure. Like I said, at best I thought my plan would buy a little time. I would find you, and we would get out of there. Only by the time I got back Betty was ranting that Jud had deserted her for Lupita. Like some kind of sick miracle, she believed the whole story. Later I decided that whether my fabrication was fishy or not, Betty had realized she could finally be free, sell the ranch and get out of there, so she didn't want to look closely. I thought maybe I was going to get away with it. There was only one more thing I had to do."

"You had to uncover his body and bury him."

This part was almost the hardest to explain. "I couldn't get away earlier, and besides, I couldn't bury him in daylight. Betty was so worked up, and the animals had already been fed before we got them in their pens, so there were no emergency chores for me to do. I didn't leave the house until long after she went to bed."

Robin broke in. "I remember how upset she was. She kept screaming about what a mistake she'd made marrying Jud and how she'd given him everything. At one point she went outside to check on something. You offered to do it, but she told both of us to stay inside. It was her ranch now, and she was going to take care of things. She didn't want any interference."

Robin was probably right, although at the time I had been so horrified by it all, so unsure what I should do next, that I'd hardly heard her. All I remember was terror that Betty would find the body.

I took up the story. "When the house was finally quiet and Betty was in bed, I sneaked outside to bury him. It was all I could think of, Robin, and I was still trying to decide where to do it. But when I got to the barn, the boar was in the outside pen. Betty must have let him out when she went outside. It would have made sense, since the inside pen was so small. But by then the straw where I'd left Jud's body was strewn all over. And the body…"

It was still hard to fathom what I had found, or rather not found. There was no sign of the murder or the body. With no other explanation available, I was forced to face the truth. After Betty let him back in the pen the enraged boar had destroyed all evidence. It isn't unheard of for a boar to attack, and less likely—but again, not unheard of—for one to devour human flesh. In the years since that night I've seen morbid stories in the news and warnings to farmers to treat their boars with caution and hunters to beware of the game they stalk.

As hard as it was to believe, even the next morning when the sun came up, I couldn't find a trace. Jud Osburn had disappeared forever.

"His body was gone. The boar…" I shrugged because I couldn't say the words.

Robin reached into her pocket. She rested what she'd retrieved in her palm and held it out for me to see.

Jud's rodeo belt buckle, tarnished and filthy but still in one piece and unmistakably his, was just visible in the moonlight.

I said the only thing I could. "You *knew* what I did? All this time?"

She shook her head. "Not what *you* did, CeCe. Not until now."

I had no idea what she meant, but she held up her hand to silence me.

"It'll be hard enough to say this once. So let me. You've told me what you know about that afternoon. Here's what I know. Betty and I came home from Southern States, and she set me to work pulling bags out of the back of the pickup and wheeling them to the garden. Afterward we were going to go inside and start dinner. I was heading back to the garden with the second load when I heard Jud yelling."

My stomach did a free fall. Robin must have known what I was feeling, because she rested her hand on my arm for a moment to steady me. "No, you didn't kill him. He was alive when we got home."

"You heard him? You're sure?"

"He was screaming your name. I dropped the wheelbarrow and ran to find you. I was terrified he was going to come after you for whatever you'd done, and I wanted to warn you. I had never, never heard him sound so angry."

"But I… I was gone. I wasn't there when you and Betty got home, because I was driving the pickup to the crossroads to leave it by—"

"I realized I had to find out what was going on at the barn so the moment I found *you*, I could warn you. I got there and saw Betty…" She took a long breath. "Jud was staggering toward the fence. His head was bleeding, and he was holding it and stumbling. The boar was slamming his body against that gate he had rigged up, making such an awful racket it was hard to understand everything Jud was saying. He kept screaming that you would get yours when he got hold of you…. That this was your fault."

Now she clasped both hands in front of her, almost as if she was praying. "At the time it all seemed obvious. I thought the boar must have attacked when Jud was trying to get him in the pen. It wouldn't have been the first time. Maybe Jud accidentally dropped the prod, or maybe it just wasn't working. But for some reason he blamed you for his injury. Maybe you were supposed to help with the boar, but you didn't? I didn't know, but he kept saying it was your fault."

I started to interrupt, but Robin shook her head. "Then he said he was going to teach you a lesson you would never forget. And that's when Betty started screaming back. She said he had already taught you too much, and she wasn't going to stand by this time."

I felt that like a blow. Betty *had* known. How long before that afternoon had she guessed the truth? How long had she *allowed* her husband to molest me without saying a word? Had she been afraid of him, or had she been relieved that Jud was taking his pleasure and inflicting pain elsewhere?

Robin went on quickly, as if she had to get the story out before she thought better of it. "He shouted that when he found you, Betty was just going to shut up and let him deal with you, the way he always did. And that's when she picked up the cattle prod."

"Betty had the prod?"

"It was lying on the ground in a gap under the fence. She stooped and grabbed it, and when he got there she shocked him. Not a quick shock, like he used with the animals. She held it against his chest until he collapsed to the ground. I couldn't watch. I was screaming, and she told me to stop. Then, when he revived enough to try to get up again, she climbed over the fence, and she held it against his chest until he convulsed, and then his head rolled to one side and he didn't move again."

"She killed him?"

Robin was silent.

"Betty *killed* him because he threatened me?"

"I'm not sure that was the reason she went after him, CeCe. Maybe that, plus years of hating him and not being able to walk away because his name was on the deed. Fear of what he might do to us, or just as likely the price she would have to pay if you reported them. But I'm not a hundred percent sure she was the one who killed him."

"You think he got up after that and walked away? What

about this?" I lifted her hand, the belt buckle still riding on her palm.

Robin had tears in her eyes, although I had no idea why she was crying. "Betty and I stood there staring down at him. He wasn't moving. His eyes had rolled back in his head, his tongue was protruding. I didn't know what death looked like, but I was pretty sure that was it. I knew he had a heart condition, and the shocks had probably stopped it once and for all. But I remember thinking, *what if he isn't dead? What if he's just unconscious?*

"Betty finally climbed out of the pen, grabbed my shoulders and shook me so hard my teeth snapped together. Then she said if I ever told *anybody* what I had seen, she would testify that *you* murdered him. She claimed she knew things that would make her story believable, things that had happened that gave you a reason. Nobody would believe my version, because everybody knew I would lie to save you."

"Robin." I hugged her, and she hugged me back.

She finished without moving away. "I knew I had to do something to make her believe I would never, never tell what I'd seen. So I did the only thing I could. By that time the boar was beyond enraged. Animals pick up on human emotions. We both know it's true. He kept throwing himself against the gate, and I was in a panic. But I climbed into the pen and onto the gate, and unhooked the rope that was looped over one post while he threw himself against the gate and me. I rode the gate as he broke through and headed for Jud." She gave a little sob. "Then I leaped into the barn and took off for the creek."

I couldn't imagine this. Robin, who was terrified of the boar even when he wasn't angry, had risked her own safety, even her life, to let him into the pen.

"I don't know what happened after or to...the remains,"

she said. "All these years I thought Betty was the one who concocted that story about the waitress. I thought *she* was the one who drove the truck to the crossroads. It wasn't until you told me how well you learned to forge Jud's name that I even began to wonder if somehow you had been involved."

Robin hadn't suspected just how much I'd been involved, but Betty had known. Jud had probably screamed the truth before Robin got there. And when she found the forged note and learned the old truck was down by the crossroads, Betty had known that I believed I'd killed her husband.

She had let me go on believing it. And she had tried to make sure Robin would never tell anyone what she had seen.

We held each other, and I tried to imagine how things had gone so wrong. A man had died, and all these years Robin and I had carefully hidden the truth about our parts in his death from each other. As close as we were, neither of us had ever breathed a word of what we knew.

She finally moved away and finished her story. "I think Betty came outside when she told us to stay in, or maybe after we went to bed that night, and took care of…everything. But at the time I didn't know that, and the next morning before dawn I made myself go out to see. I was afraid someone would find him. I was afraid you would be blamed. That's when I found the buckle. It had been kicked under the fence, and I guess Betty must have missed it. Back then there were shreds of leather attached, but I guess they rotted away in the ground. The dirt under the compost heaps was soft, and I dug as deep as I could and buried the buckle. Then I flipped the compost from the other bin into the one that was here."

"And after all these years you knew exactly where to find it."

An indrawn breath ended on a sob. "Some things are hard to forget, but you know that. Better than anybody."

"All these years I thought I killed a man."

"Maybe *I* did. We'll never know. I'm not a doctor, and I can't say for sure Jud was dead when I opened that gate. That was part of the reason I had to do it. Betty needed to be sure I would stay silent. By involving myself, she had something to hold over me, something to keep me quiet forever in addition to her threats against you. Those Christmas cards? Her annual reminder."

"We were all responsible."

She made a noise low in her throat, but I shook my head. "Or maybe none of us were. We'll never know when his heart stopped, but I do know the real cause of death. Jud Osburn died because of all the things he was and did to every one of us."

Robin spoke again after a moment. "Betty's gone now. Should we tell the authorities what we know?"

"What do we *know* that we can tell them? And what can we tell them that will make a difference? It's not even a cold case. No crime was ever reported. As far as anybody else knows, one afternoon Jud left town with another woman, and that was that."

She turned away and scuffed dirt back into the hole until it was mostly filled in. Together we started toward our cars.

We stopped at hers, and she leaned against the door as if her legs didn't want to hold her. "This whole thing has colored so much of my life."

And Jud's death had come close to destroying me. Even now I wondered how the truth would change mine. I hadn't killed a man, but I had tried. And yes, swinging that post had been self-defense. But did that, and the fact that Jud had survived, at least for a while, absolve me?

I would consider that for years to come. For the first time since I'd fallen through time and space in Sydney, I thought

I might finally seek professional help. I could tell my story without fear. The woman who most likely killed Jud Osburn was dead. I would never have to confess to his murder. Not to a therapist, not to the police.

"Donny..." I realized that I would have to tell him what actually happened. "I told him what I thought I had done. He deserves to know the truth, and I want him to."

Robin looked up at the sky as if she were counting the stars smeared above us. "It's funny. You always said you were the liar and I was the one who couldn't tell a lie if my life depended on it. But I've been living with this one a long time, CeCe. Even Kris doesn't know what happened that day."

"You weren't given much of a choice. You were trying to protect me."

"And you were trying to protect *me*."

"Nobody else was willing, were they? At the mercy of strangers."

"What will we do with this?" She looked down at her hand and held out the buckle.

"You'll give it to me, and when I get back to California, Donny and I will take his sloop and sail as far out into the Pacific as he's willing. And then I'll toss it overboard. No matter how deep we bury it again, I don't want it here, haunting this ranch. I don't want anything that ever belonged to Jud Osburn to be part of this place."

She held it out to me. I took the buckle, but I couldn't make myself slip it in my pocket. Instead I set it on the hood of her car to retrieve when we finished talking. I would wrap it in something when I got back to the camper, and it would stay wrapped until it found a home on the ocean floor.

Robin's face was pale in the moonlight. "And now what? Will this come between us? Every time you look at me, will you see that terrible afternoon before you see anything else?"

"I'll see the woman who loved me enough to be sure I didn't go to jail for something I didn't do. We were sisters right from the beginning. We took care of each other. That's what real sisters do."

I leaned over and kissed her cheek. Then I took the buckle, walked around her car and got into my own. Tomorrow our paths would part again, mine to California, Robin's to Virginia. But I didn't think they would part for long.

When we were sisters, young and heartbroken, we had learned to watch out for each other.

We were still sisters.

Epilogue

Robin

One Year Later

Cecilia has never mentioned who chose the Tampa Theatre for the preview screening of *At the Mercy of Strangers*, but when Kris and I arrived in the limo that picked us up at our hotel, I immediately saw her hand in the decision. Like my sister, the theater itself is in-your-face spectacular. Nostalgia must also have played a part. Once upon a time the Davises brought us here to celebrate Cecilia's birthday.

All these years later I don't remember which birthday or what movie we saw, and until now, I hadn't even remembered the theater. But one look and the memories came back.

Before leaving the hotel I had done a little research. Even by the standards of the 1920s, when elaborate movie palaces were built all over the world, the Tampa Theatre is over-the-top. The architect—a "mad genius" by some accounts—specialized in something called "atmospheric design." While the exterior, with its blade sign and old-fashioned marquee, was designed to attract moviegoers, the inside, an elaborate Mediterranean courtyard with a ceiling of "stars," had encouraged them to come back.

And now *we* had come back, Cecilia and I. The Davises had brought us to this theater for a special celebration because our happiness had mattered. *We* had mattered. If they hadn't helped us through so many of our formative years, Cecilia and I would be very different people. I will always be grateful.

As our driver got out to open our door, Kris peered out the limo window. "All this place needs is a red carpet."

"The last time I was here I spilled popcorn in the lobby."

"No popcorn for you tonight."

I doubt popcorn will be on the menu. After the screening the lobby will be mobbed with more than a thousand supporters enjoying catered goodies and vintage wines. The audience paid a fortune for this first glimpse of Mick's latest masterpiece, which will have an official debut later in the month at Sundance. Cecilia says a number of celebrities are slated to be in the crowd. The fact that she and Gizzie will perform the theme song live onstage doubled the price of admission, and tickets still sold out immediately. All money raised will go toward increasing awareness of children's rights, a campaign that will run in tandem with the PBS airing in the spring.

We slid out, and our driver refused Kris's tip. "All taken care of," he told us. He shepherded us to the front door, where the audience was beginning to gather, and wished us a lovely night. A young man in a dark suit quickly checked a list and ushered us inside.

"Your sister is expecting you." He led us across the fabulously ornate lobby and finally down through the theater, where both of us tried not to gawk at gold walls adorned with elaborate statuary and gargoyles. I nearly tripped over my own feet during an extended preview of the sky mural on the ceiling.

Kris took my elbow to steady me. "Familiar?"

"I remember feeling like I'd been plunked down in the middle of a fairy tale."

"Cinderella."

"Most likely."

"This is so Cecilia."

"And so Talya. Wouldn't she have loved it?" I thought about my friend, as I still did so often. Talya had been thrilled with her new job managing a local theater, but now the thought of a life cut short wasn't followed by a stab of pain. Talya and all the memories of our years as friends were part of me and would be until the day I died. Channa and Michael were still in our lives, and for that I was grateful.

We picked our way backstage until our escort stopped at one of the dressing rooms and tapped on the door.

Hayley opened it and broke into a grin when she saw us. I glimpsed Roscoe, who was happily taking up a share of the only sofa, and he yapped a greeting before he closed his eyes and settled in for another nap.

"Aunt Robin's here. And Uncle Kris," Hayley called.

I hugged her, but I know the rules. Hayley still isn't a fan of prolonged embraces, so I made certain mine was brief, and Kris settled for a fist bump. Hayley's reasons are her own, but I can guess what they are. She's in therapy, one of the ground rules Cecilia laid down before proceeding with the adoption, and Cecilia says she's making progress. Calling me Aunt Robin is a sign, even though Cecilia is still only "Cecilia," not yet Mom. My sister takes that in stride. No therapist will ever understand Hayley better than she does, and Cecilia thinks Hayley might change what she calls her once everything is finally official in a month.

We stepped inside, and Hayley closed the door. Her dress was a deep turquoise with a beaded bodice, and her shoulder-length hair was drawn back from her face with a rhinestone headband. She looked adorable.

I was still slightly dizzy from the scenery. "Have you ever seen anything like this place?"

"I told Cecilia I want my room to look just like the lobby."

"What did she say?"

"Knock yourself out."

I laughed. I could hear Cecilia saying it. "Petra might be able to help, but I doubt you'll end up with anything quite this grand."

Cecilia came out of the bathroom, and Kris and I were smothered in hugs. Her perfume was subtle but probably as expensive as our mortgage payment. Her makeup was perfect, and so was her hair, which she wore in glamorous forties-style waves down her back, maybe as a salute to the venue. Both makeup and hair were exaggerated for the stage, and a contrast to her camp shirt, jeans and bare feet.

"You two look fabulous!"

Kris wears a tuxedo well, and he really did look fabulous. I had splurged on a silver lace sheath that I could also wear to Singer's formal in the spring. Even though Kris is now a professor at GW Law, he remains connected to the firm and will take on the occasional case. But the formal will be more fun this year because there won't be anybody there he has to impress.

Cecilia turned to Hayley. "Do you mind looking for Donny?" She hiked her thumb toward the door. The dressing room was small. Hayley looked happy to escape and did.

"She looks so good," I said after she was gone. Three months had passed since all of us had been together in Virginia for Thanksgiving. In that time Hayley had put on a little weight and grown at least an inch. She, like my children, was barreling down the road to adolescence.

"She likes living in Pacific Palisades. She likes her school."

Cecilia had found an ideal situation for her new daughter. The school had other children with famous parents, so Hayley didn't stand out. Class sizes were small, with a multitude of special services for children who needed them. Best of all, the administration was accustomed to children going on location with parents in the film industry. Assignments could be packed up at a moment's notice so students could work with tutors or nannies until they returned. Hayley didn't have a nanny, but she did have Wendy, who had a degree in education and supervised whenever Hayley traveled with Cecilia.

Cecilia said she'd already missed too much of Hayley's life and didn't intend to miss more. Their system might be a bit unorthodox, but it suited the two of them, since they were unorthodox, too.

Cecilia was still explaining. "Nothing's perfect, but I think she's happy. She won't say she is, but I can guess. She hasn't tried to sabotage the adoption in maybe three weeks."

I gave a low whistle. "A record."

"She's figured out we're in this for the long haul. She says she guesses she can stand me for another seven years. I tell her it's going to be a lot longer than that. I want her at the nursing home spooning out my gruel."

"And Donny?"

Like most people with red hair, Cecilia should blush easily. Except that Cecilia finds very little to blush about. Now her cheeks turned pink. I was fascinated.

Seconds elapsed, then she held up her left hand. "Notice anything?"

I took her hand and squinted, and at first, I didn't. Then I saw it.

The viper was gone, replaced by...

Cecilia solved the mystery. "A Celtic wedding band."

I looked up from the intricate but classy tattoo which cleverly camouflaged the old one. "Wedding band?"

She gave the slightest of shrugs. "I guess I'm not letting him get away. It's a prelude to the real thing. I couldn't wear a real wedding band over a snake."

Donny, also gorgeous in a tux, took that moment to appear. I hugged Cecilia first, hugged her hard, then him. "You're getting married? And nobody asked my permission?"

"May I marry your sister?"

"Are we invited?"

"All our family, and a few others. We're going to have the ceremony at a manor home in western Ireland. Early summer. We've prescheduled a couple of dates. But we're keeping the whole thing a secret."

I couldn't stop smiling. "Good luck with that."

Hayley leaned against Donny, and he slung his arm around her shoulders. She didn't move away, even more of a testament to her progress than anything her new mother had said.

She gazed up at him. "I'm selling your plans to the press."

Donny pulled her closer for just a moment. "Nice try. I'm going to adopt you anyway. I have to. You need a last name."

"You think I'm kidding."

"I think you'd better be."

She grinned before she moved away. "Fifi said I could watch them prepare the film for viewing. Is that okay?"

"It's wonderful you asked," Cecilia said. "A nice treat. And yes, go for it. But plan to be down front with Donny in half an hour."

Hayley signed something as she left. I was afraid to look, but Cecilia laughed.

Hayley's request was a reminder that we hadn't seen anybody else from the film backstage. "Everybody from the crew is here?"

"Jerry couldn't make it. But Starla's here, Mick, Fiona." She named others.

Donny and Kris were chatting by the door, and I moved closer to Cecilia for privacy. "Have you seen any of the clips?"

"Some. I had to give permission. It's okay. Mick's Mick. He handled the hard parts beautifully."

There had been so many hard parts. I would be glad when this night was over, but also sorry. Because nothing I'd done or would ever do again was more important than being involved in this project.

The film had changed my life. It had changed Cecilia's.

"Plans for New Beginnings Ranch?" I asked.

"Coming along on schedule, but as you can imagine, everything about it's complicated. While the film's being shown tonight a crew's going to set up the proposed model in the lobby for the audience to view afterward. I want them to be enthused when I hit them up for donations. Of course groundbreaking is still pretty far away. We have to get this right from every angle. I'm not going to make mistakes. Not with children's hearts and minds."

Organ music seeped in from the theater. The original Tampa Theatre Wurlitzer from 1926 had been rediscovered and refurbished after the theater itself was rescued and restored. The music meant people were coming inside now, and we didn't have much more time before the program began.

Cecilia looked happier than I've ever seen her. She's busy with her career, but she and Donny are exercising care. Her new album will come out in the spring as the film airs. She tabled her plan to record blues standards and instead she chose to record original material, some that she and Gizzie had written for the film, including the theme, and some she had written by herself after the filming ended.

I only heard bits and pieces at Thanksgiving, but the whole

album is a departure from her usual stomp through the male psyche, more introspective and nostalgic, with softer strings and woodwinds. There's one selection I've yet to hear. About Maribeth. Cecilia calls it "Yellow Curtains," and she performs it with nothing but a harp accompaniment. Cyclonic is wary, but Cecilia is not. She says it's time for her music to change now that *she* has. And Donny thinks the album is her best work ever.

As always, she was interested in me. I told her about my children, who were back at the hotel. Kris and I had decided not to bring Nik and Pet tonight. As a former foster child Hayley wouldn't be surprised at what she saw, and given the choice and a careful explanation, she had decided to be here. But Kris and I wanted a quiet living room and a remote control when we watched the film with our children. I expected to pause for multiple discussions along the way.

"And your new project?"

I gave her a quick synopsis. With *At the Mercy of Strangers* behind me, I had signed up for several local filmmaking classes, but before I could finish I'd been offered a gig doing photographs for a friend of Mick's. I'd agreed, but only if he also allowed me to be the assistant camera operator when one was needed. Since then I've taken several more offers, and right now I'm honing my skills with a director who's making a documentary about the Baltimore Orioles. I do know *something* completely new. I want to produce. I want to choose my own subjects and use my talents in new ways. Someday, I will, and Cecilia is cheering me on.

Somebody else tapped on the door, but that didn't stop my sister from asking a final question. "And you're still coming to Sanibel this weekend?"

"We're coming."

"You're still okay about this?"

My nod was tentative, but she understood why. Tomorrow morning Kris and the kids and I are heading to Everglades City to meet my mother and her husband, and the next day to Sanibel to be with Cecilia, Donny and Hayley for a few days.

Over the past year Alice and I have carefully, slowly, begun to weave a relationship. Even though she left her phone number that day at the restaurant, I never called her. Months later she found the courage to locate my number and call me. While neither of us is comfortable and may never be, I want my children to meet their grandmother.

If I'm honest, in my own way I want to get to know her a little, too. Some wounds never heal, but the right treatment can make them more comfortable. And perhaps, for both Alice and me, that will be enough.

Donny welcomed Mick into the suite, followed closely by Gizzie, who was wearing a tortoiseshell tux and a bright pink necktie. There were kisses and greetings all around. When Cecilia finally announced it was time to finish dressing, I gave her one final hug.

"This is Nik and Pet's first unsupervised evening together, so we have to get back to the hotel before too late tonight, but we'll see you in Sanibel."

"Joined at the hip, joined at the heart," she said, bumping her hip against mine where our tattoos would forever meet. "We're here tonight, Robin. Despite everything, just don't forget. We made it."

Everyone but Mick went to the front, where a row had been reserved for us. Donny claimed two seats, leaving an empty one for Cecilia between us. I chatted with others from the film crew and with Hayley, who joined Donny, until the organist, who had been playing film favorites, completed her concert and the organ was lowered from view.

The theater was now filled to capacity.

Kris took my hand and put it on his lap, wrapping his around it. "I'm so proud of you."

I blinked hard and squeezed. "I like hearing that. Just don't change your mind if I dissolve in a puddle of tears somewhere along the way."

"I'll be surprised if you don't."

The lights dimmed. As the stage crew wheeled an impressive grand piano into place, Mick came out to introduce the film. He's almost as good a speaker as he is a filmmaker. He talked about children, about the need to protect them, and how we haven't always done a good job and still don't. I listened as he carefully made the transition to Cecilia, about her courage in agreeing to be part of the production, and the revelations she had made on camera.

"Nobody can know what it's like to be at the mercy of strangers except somebody who *has* been. But Cecilia is anything but a victim. I hope you'll take these images home with you and tell your friends how important it is to protect children, and to make sure that the systems we have in place are operating the way they must."

Like any good showman, Mick knows when to stop. He said a little more about the making of the film, then he welcomed my sister and Gizzie to the stage.

Cecilia wore a long ice-blue dress, cut low in the front and nipped in at the waist. She looked like the star she is. The audience leaped to its feet, and the applause went on for a full minute until she held up her hands. As they settled again, she smiled at Gizzie, who was her only accompanist tonight.

Cecilia hadn't sung "At the Mercy of Strangers" for me, not in its finished form. She'd said she wanted me to hear it tonight with everyone else, but I think she knew it would be too hard to sing it when we were alone.

I was ready for her to begin, but she surprised me by stepping forward, mic to her lips. She waited until she found me in the audience, and then she said, "Robin, without a doubt, this one's for you."

Gizzie began to play. The melody was different from the snatches I'd heard, haunting, thoughtful and evocative. The introduction was extended. Cecilia looked composed, but our eyes held for a long a moment before she began.

"As memories fade, your touch, your face
I reach for you through time and space.
Did you look back or did you go
Without goodbye, without hello?
I'll never know.

At the mercy of strangers
We are borne on the winds of fate
At the mercy of strangers
We wait."

She had never sung with more feeling or depth. I was transfixed as the words and melody wove their spell. Cecilia and Gizzie had captured the spirit of the film and everything it meant.

Through the years Cecilia and I *had* shared memories that, blessedly, were fading at last, moments of abandonment and rejection, as well as moments of terror. But earlier in the dressing room my sister had been right.

We are no longer at the mercy of strangers. We no longer wait.

Together and apart, each of us is finally right where she belongs.

★ ★ ★ ★ ★

Acknowledgments

My thanks to the following: Galen McGee of Peak Definition in Asheville for carefully vetting my pages on photography. Shelly L. McGee, Esq. for doing the same for law firms and lawsuits. And *guardian ad litem* Jasmine Cresswell for sharing knowledge of the Florida foster-care system in a conversation over oyster po'boys. Of course any mistakes or missteps are mine.

Thanks also to my brainstorming group, Connie Laux, Serena Miller and Shelley Costa Bloomfield, whose suggestions and comments always make such a difference. Thanks to longtime editor Leslie Wainger who from the beginning was enthusiastic about this book as well as the title. Thanks, finally, to Michael McGee, who will brainstorm new ideas and critique old ones over wine on our lanai anytime I ask him to.

Two books in particular helped inform my understanding of the foster-care system. *To the End of June: The Intimate Life of American Foster Care* by Cris Beam. And *Another Place at the Table*, by Kathy Harrison. A series of lectures in 2014 at Chautauqua Institution by filmmakers Ken Burns and Geoffrey Ward ignited my enthusiasm for creating my own documentary within the pages of this novel.

WHEN WE WERE SISTERS

EMILIE RICHARDS

Reader's Guide

1. Robin is unhappy with the hours her husband, Kris, puts in at his law firm and his lack of involvement with their family. Did you feel she had a reason to be upset and to force him to spend more time with their children by leaving him in charge?

2. Cecilia seems to have everything—fame, money, beauty— yet her nightmares and panic attacks say differently. Did Cecilia's plan to attack her problems seem to fit the kind of woman she is?

3. Can facing and revealing old secrets begin a healing process? Was facing their mutual past the best way for Robin and Cecilia to move into the future? Have you had a similar experience in your own life?

4. Cecilia and Robin met in foster care. How many of the problems they encountered were due to the foster-care system and how many were due to the dysfunctional families they were born into?

5. The documentary *At the Mercy of Strangers* highlights both good and bad foster-parent programs and placements. Do you have firsthand knowledge of the foster-care system as either a former foster child, a parent, or an interested professional or citizen? What are your own thoughts about changes that might need to be made?

6. *At the Mercy of Strangers* shows the interworkings of a particularly good program in Tennessee with small group homes and caring house parents. What is the ideal foster-care model?

7. Hayley, a foster child whom Cecilia immediately connects with, does her best to be certain nobody will love her. She claims it's easier than waiting to be rejected. Do you know children and adults who operate on the same assumption? Will unqualified love solve her problems, or will she need more?

8. Kris's attitude toward his job slowly changes as he is forced to be home with his children. Robin's confidence in her abilities as a photographer grows as the documentary progresses. Can two professionals find ways to be involved, devoted parents despite work pressures? What are the most essential factors to achieving success?

9. Cecilia often avoids the truth and tells lies without guilt. Were you able to empathize with her reasons? Was she a sympathetic character?

10. Robin let both Kris and Cecilia steer the course of her life, but now she is making her own way. Was her part in the drama of her adolescence believable and sympathetic? Will both women recover and move on?

*International bestselling author Emelie Schepp
introduces us to the enigmatic, unforgettable
Jana Berzelius in this first novel of a chilling trilogy*

When a high-ranking head of the migration board is found
murdered in his living room, there is no shortage of
suspects, including his wife. But no one expects to find the
mysterious child-sized handprint in the childless home…

A few days later, the body of a pre-teen boy is found on a
nearby deserted shoreline, marked with initials that spark a
terrifying memory in lead prosecutor, Jana Berzelius,
uncovering a connection that shakes her to the core.

Now, to protect her own hidden past, she must find the
suspect behind these murders, before the police do.

⊕ HARLEQUIN® MIRA®

Bringing you the best voices in fiction

🐦 **@HQstories**
📘 **Facebook.com/HQStories**
📷 **Instagram.com/HQStories**
▶ **Youtube.com/HQStories**
🎵 **Spotify.com/HQmusic2016**

M462_MFL

You can erase the memory
But you cannot erase the crime

Jenny's wounds have healed.
An experimental treatment has removed the
memory of a horrific and degrading attack.
She is moving on with her life.

That was the plan. Except it's not working out.
Something has gone. The light in the eyes.
And she's getting worse.

It may be that the only way to uncover what's wrong is to
help Jenny recover her memory. But pulling at the threads
of her suppressed experience will unravel much more
than the truth about her attack.

And that could destroy as much as it heals.

#NotForgotten

One Place. Many Stories

M453_AINF

From the New York Times Bestselling author of *The Good Girl*

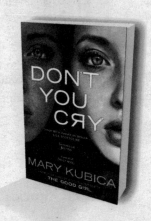

In downtown Chicago, a young woman named Esther Vaughan disappears from her apartment without a trace. A haunting letter addressed to My Dearest is found among her possessions, leaving her friend and roommate Quinn Collins to wonder where Esther is and whether or not she's the person Quinn thought she knew.

As Quinn searches for answers about Esther, so unfolds a twisted thrill ride that builds to a stunning conclusion and shows that no matter how fast and far we run, the past always catches up with us in the end.

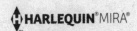

Bringing you the best voices in fiction
🐦 **@Mira_booksUK**

M449_DYC

HQ
One Place. Many Stories

The home of bold, innovative
and empowering publishing.

Follow us online

 @HQStories

 @HQStories

 HQStories

 HQ Stories

 HQMusic2016

HQ_SM